ACCLAIM FOR ANN
FOR TWICE

T0037416

"*For Twice in My Life* is a timeless, enchanting love story. Annette Christie's writing is easy to fall for, brimming with wit and gentle compassion. This book completely swept me away!"
—Rachel Lynn Solomon, bestselling author of *Weather Girl* and *See You Yesterday*

"Captured my heart from the very first page! Layla is my favorite kind of main character—flawed and messy but still completely charming and totally real. Christie's effortless banter is perfection, and she uses her sharp wit to make Layla's career, family, and relationship struggles so relatable. I wanted to pack up my real life and move into the world of this book so we could all be friends. This is a book I'll return to again and again!"
—Falon Ballard, author of *Lease on Love*

"Second chances take center stage in this cute contemporary... Christie does a good job fleshing out Layla's backstory so that readers will sympathize with her despite her deception. This is a charmer."
—*Publishers Weekly*

"Equal measures heartfelt and surprising, Christie's instantly compelling premise leads to an unforgettable novel of how our mistakes might lead to our meant-to-be's. Full of wit and warmth, *For Twice in my Life* is a moving, memorable love story."
—Emily Wibberley and Austin Siegemund-Broka, authors of *The Roughest Draft*

"A clever take on *While You Were Sleeping*...Christie deftly upends romantic comedy tropes. Her characters are complex and realistic, even in heightened situations. A unique love story that will keep readers guessing." —*Kirkus Reviews*

"A solid romantic novel in which you do root for Layla, and hope she gets her second chance. But then secrets are revealed, and just who has been lying to whom? Fans of the genre will enjoy this one." —*Red Carpet Crash*

"Annette Christie writes with an unmatched charm, wit, and sincerity, depicting Layla's struggles to decide between doing what she knows is right and doing what *feels* right with such genuine authenticity that it's impossible not to root for her…If there was ever a book I wish I could read twice for the first time, it's this one."
—Jenny L. Howe, author of *The Make-Up Test* and *On the Plus Side*

"Annette Christie is a thoughtful, talented, and clever writer who explores the messy realities of living in an imperfect world that nevertheless expects us to be perfect."
—Kate Clayborn, author of *Love Lettering*

"Annette Christie knows how to write an emotional, complicated love story. *For Twice in Your Life* beautifully depicts the ways you can lose yourself…and then find yourself again. I'll be thinking about this book long after I've turned the last page."
—Alicia Thompson, bestselling author of *Love in the Time of Serial Killers*

"A stunning and hilarious novel that captures the beautiful messiness of finding yourself and love along the way. Annette Christie will make you laugh one sentence then tug at your heartstrings the next with her incredible ability to tell a story.

This novel is for anyone who wished for a second-chance, but got something even better in the end." —Mazey Eddings, author of *A Brush with Love* and *Lizzie Blake's Best Mistake*

"Annette Christie approaches the page with utmost sincerity, heart, and humor, leaving readers enraptured and in love. *For Twice in My Life* is a stunning, heart-tugging look at true love, second chances, and the belief we place in ourselves. Christie consistently establishes herself as a cutting-edge voice in romance; a steadily rising star not to be missed!" —Courtney Kae, author of *In the Event of Love*

FOR TWICE IN MY LIFE

ANNETTE CHRISTIE

BACK BAY BOOKS

Little, Brown and Company

New York   Boston   London

ALSO BY ANNETTE CHRISTIE

The Rehearsals

Copyright © 2023 by Alloy Entertainment, LLC

Little, Brown and Company
Hachette Book Group
1290 Avenue of the Americas, New York, NY 10104
littlebrown.com

Originally published in hardcover by Little, Brown and Company, February 2023
First Back Bay trade paperback edition, October 2023

Back Bay Books is an imprint of Little, Brown and Company, a division of Hachette Book Group, Inc. The Back Bay Books name and logo are trademarks of Hachette Book Group, Inc.

The publisher is not responsible for websites (or their content) that are not owned by the publisher.

The Hachette Speakers Bureau provides a wide range of authors for speaking events. To find out more, go to hachettespeakersbureau.com or email hachettespeakers@hbgusa.com.

Little, Brown and Company books may be purchased in bulk for business, educational, or promotional use. For information, please contact your local bookseller or the Hachette Book Group Special Markets Department at special.markets@hbgusa.com.

ISBN 9780316451031 (hc) / 9780316451130 (pb) /
9780316561242 (Canadian paperback)
LCCN 2022941579

Printing 1, 2023

LSC-C

Printed in the United States of America

For my mom, who has always given me
a safe place to land
And for my dad, who reminds me that
"good things happen too"

FOR TWICE IN MY LIFE

CHAPTER ONE

THERE IS A perverse pleasure in being able to pinpoint exactly where you've gone wrong in life. To take a failed moment and place it on your memory's mantel, to be examined only in your darkest hours: On Sunday afternoons when the rain is coming down and you can't stop listening to Sinatra sing "In the Wee Small Hours of the Morning" or in the middle of the night when insomnia is your only friend and, frankly, he's a bit of a dick. Or, perhaps, when you are on the verge of making another grave mistake and you aren't sure you can stop yourself.

At least, that was Layla Rockford's experience. And right now, her apartment was one big reminder of everything she'd lost. Of *him*. She dreaded being there as potently as she craved its hidey-hole comforts. And yet that was where she was headed, if she ever made it off this stretch of crowded Seattle sidewalk, because these days, when work was over, there weren't a lot of other options. She couldn't bear being at a restaurant surrounded by couples. Or being at a bar surrounded by couples. Even Sunday dinner at her parents' house meant being surrounded by *couples*, which was why she'd opted out for the past two weeks.

She sped up, the wool pants she'd chosen that morning making her legs itch. In their original glory, they'd had a satin lining. She'd seen the remnants of the shimmery pink fabric when she bought them at her go-to vintage store in Belltown, and she'd vowed to replace the lining herself. It hadn't happened yet. She silently swore she'd tear the pants off and throw them in the back of her closet as soon as she made it home.

Layla dodged a teenage couple making out under the awning of a coffee shop, and her heart hiccupped.

Thinking about Ian was like pressing on a bruise. A dull, familiar pain washed over her.

She sidestepped a man in a suit traveling by on a Segway and turned to watch his ponytail flap behind him. Ian had been keeping track of their Segway Man sightings. If he were here, he would've looked at her, a twinkle in his eye, and mouthed, *Twelve.* She could picture it: his single, playful dimple flickering as he smiled, his blond hair ruffling in the coastal breeze. Layla would've reminded him that when they got to twenty, they'd agreed to go on a Seattle Segway tour themselves, and Ian, laughing, would've protested that he'd never agreed to those terms, and she'd have reached for his hand...

She didn't know why she was still counting. The number didn't matter anymore.

Layla finally arrived at her apartment building—fifteen stories of brick stacked up to the overcast sky. She sighed, used her key card to buzz through the main entrance, and rode the elevator (which made just a little too much noise for comfort but not quite enough for her to track down the super) up to the eighth floor, avoiding her own eyes in the elevator's mirror. She got off on her floor, unlocked the door of her studio apartment, and heaved an even greater sigh.

It was a space her best friend, Pearl Kaes, referred to as the Museum—or had back when Layla dusted and vacuumed regularly. And not just because it was clean but because everything in it was carefully curated and placed just so. Ian had helped Layla make sure of that.

To give the impression there was some separation between the bedroom area, the living-room area, and the kitchen, Layla put up lovely antique dividers Ian had gamely helped her carry home from a flea market—dividers that were currently closed and leaning against the far wall so Layla could watch TV from her bed more easily. Ian had also suggested hanging her large mirror with the art deco frame by the stub-wall galley kitchen to create the illusion of space where, quite frankly, there was none. It also caught the light from the lone kitchen window. It'd been a great idea.

These days, the mirror was covered in multicolored Post-It notes emblazoned with self-affirmations. And the Museum looked like it'd been looted—clothes were strewn over every piece of furniture; her mail had become a small mountain, overwhelming the entry table carefully placed by the door; the coffee table was currently host to a peanut butter jar with a spoon sticking out of it *and* a Nutella jar with a spoon sticking out of it (and a jar of raspberry jam, for which, regrettably, she'd had to move on to the forks).

First things first. Layla pulled the vinyl copy of Ella Fitzgerald's greatest hits out of its sleeve and was about to lower the record player's needle when her phone rang. Seeing Mom on the caller ID triggered a familiar wash of conflicting emotions. Layla swiveled the needle back to its resting place and put the call on speaker. She flung her purse and then herself, facedown, onto her bed and tried to shimmy out of the offending pants despite the awkward position.

"Hey," Layla said, turning her head to the side so her voice wouldn't be muffled by her rumpled sheets. She attempted to sound perkier than she felt.

"There's my girl!" No matter how often Layla spoke to her mom, Rena always greeted her as though they had just been reunited after some dramatic tragedy. It was one of the best things about Rena. But today her mom's enthusiasm sounded forced. Layla's familiar guilt complex engaged.

Layla's orange tabby cat, Deano Martini Rockford, emerged from the kitchen, hopped onto the bed, purring, and parked himself on her butt. Perfect. The pants stayed on. She'd adopted Deano after moving out of her parents' place (for the second time), because living alone had been surprisingly lonely, and when she'd seen him on the local shelter's website, he'd seemed surprisingly lonely too.

How could she have known that behind his big, soulful eyes lurked a manipulative misanthrope who demanded love on unpredictable terms?

"How was your day, Mom?" Layla finally managed. "You mentoring the next Jerry Lee Lewis?"

Rena was a part-time piano teacher, a saint of a woman who could listen to the atonal plunkings of children all day and still put her arm around their little shoulders and tell them they were coming along. She'd tried to teach Layla when she was little, but Layla didn't have the patience to practice. She preferred to tap-dance around the piano making up lyrics to the songs her mom played.

"I hope not," Rena said. "You know as well as I do that Jerry Lee Lewis was a pervert."

Layla let out a surprised laugh, a bit strangled by the constant tightness in her throat. Deano, irritated by this disruption, let out a disgruntled meow and hopped off Layla. Somehow he managed to sound like a lifelong smoker whenever he was displeased. He glared at her from his new place on the floor beside the bed.

"You okay, honey?" The concern in her mother's voice, so

familiar to her—and so upsetting *because* it was so familiar— sharpened the ache in Layla's chest.

With Deano off her back, Layla successfully shimmied out of her wool pants. Without getting off the bed, she grabbed a pair of nearby sweats with her toe, bent her knee, and flung them onto the bed where she could better reach them. Under Deano's disdainful eye, she slid them on.

"Mm-hmm," Layla replied, not trusting her mouth to open without letting an embarrassing sob escape. Desperate to change the subject, she said, "That guy came into the theater again."

"Which guy?" Was it her imagination or did Rena sound a bit distracted?

"The one who drinks at Mowery's every day—"

"But sometimes chooses the wrong door," Rena supplied. "Oh, dear. What did he walk into?"

Layla worked for Northwest End, a sleeper theater company in downtown Seattle. Northwest had been chugging along for ages with a small but loyal following, one killer review away from really breaking into Seattle's bustling art scene. Or one *bad* review away from shutting off the lights, although no one wanted to think about that. Layla's job title was technically office administrator, but most days she thought of herself as the human fire extinguisher. Usually the fires were figurative—except at last year's cast party, when an actor decided to show everyone how flammable powdered coffee creamer was. The answer? *Very.* Powdered coffee creamer was *very* flammable. Luckily, Layla was in charge of getting the theater's *actual* fire extinguishers checked every year and knew exactly where they were.

"We were striking a set," Layla said. "And as the fake walls were being carried out, the guy came in and started yelling, 'What the hell happened to the bar?'"

Rena chuckled softly. Appreciating that her mom really was her best—and, right now, only—audience, Layla sat up and continued. "It took me ten minutes to convince him to head next door."

"I'm sure he was relieved when he made it." There was a pause and muffled conversation. "Your dad wants me to ask you how Deano is."

"Same as always. Tell Dad Deano misses him." Layla's smile faltered, despite her unending appreciation of how obsessed her cat and her dad were with each other, as the effort of pretending to be okay wore her down.

As though Rena could hear it happen, she asked, "How are you *really?* You've missed the last two family dinners."

The words caught in the lump in her throat as Layla lied, "I'm sorry, there's just been so much going on."

The truth was, she just couldn't go. Not when that meant being squashed at a table with her four siblings and their four partners. Not when that meant fielding insensitive questions about why Ian had ended things (for the thousandth time, she didn't *know* why). And not when that meant letting her parents see how miserable she was, which would make them worry about her "unstable behavior" all over again. So Layla had opted out. She'd opted to stay home, drink something called Chardon-Yay! straight from the bottle, and hang out with her grumpy cat instead.

"Well, we miss you." Rena persisted: "Can I volunteer at Northwest End and ease things that way? Or maybe you need some help paying bills, just for now?"

Shame blazed Layla's cheeks. Financial trouble was a ghost that would forever haunt her. She picked at her flaking nail polish and mouthed, *Can you believe this?* to Deano. He could not.

But also. Thanks to the Sunday Chardon-Yay!, she had indeed done a *teensy* bit of online shopping.

"I'm fine," she insisted, kicking two boxes of recently purchased go-go boots and a hatbox containing a 1940s fascinator under her bed. "Work's fine, my finances are fine, it's all fine."

There was an uncomfortable pause.

"I should go feed Deano," Layla said at last, looking at her cat, who yowled in response. He barely knew his own name, but the darn creature was well acquainted with the words *food, feed,* and, more bafflingly, *frangipane* (this one thanks to *The Great British Bake Off*). If he didn't get some kibble within seconds of hearing any of those F-words, he had a fit.

"You'll be at Sunday dinner, right? You're not going to miss it three weeks in a row, are you?"

"I'll be there," Layla said, already flipping through the reasonable excuses she'd use once the time came.

Rena issued an audible sigh of relief. "I'm so glad. Have a good week, honey. We'll talk soon."

"Yep. You too." Layla summoned enough energy to return to the record player and start Ella's crooning, then meandered the short distance to the kitchen. She filled Deano's bowl and began opening cabinets at random, pretending to decide what to make herself for dinner but knowing full well she'd resort to one of the frozen pizzas with Paul Newman's face on the box—even on cardboard, the man knew he had beautiful Joanne. Smug in-love bastard.

Dodging Deano on the way to the fridge, she tripped over a teal-green velvet slingback he'd apparently pulled out of her closet.

And just like that, she tumbled into the memory of the night her life had gone from black-and-white to Technicolor.

Layla had first laid eyes on Ian Barnett while wearing that very shoe at Winston and Tux, a chic rooftop bar overlooking South Lake Union. After noticing Ian—tall, blond, handsome, smiling Ian—Pearl had dared Layla to pick him up without saying a single word. But Layla had only just moved back out of her parents' house in Bellevue, had only just upgraded her financial situation, going from the horrors of credit card debt to the quieter, creeping dread of *just* student-loan debt—and her heart still felt too bruised for something romantic. She was about to remind Pearl she wasn't looking for a boyfriend when two guys, dangerously close to the balcony's edge, started shoving each other, punctuating every push with monosyllables like "Bro," "S'up," and a high-pitched "You want this? A piece of this?"

"Maybe we should get out of here," Pearl suggested, shifting gears. She was bored by even the scent of toxic alpha conflict.

Layla wasn't interested in witnessing any barbarism either. But in that moment, her feet, which were encased in the 1960s teal-green velvet slingbacks she loved so much, were stuck to the spot. She couldn't look away from Pearl's tall stranger, who had unexpectedly stepped in to gently push the bros apart.

In the glow of the globe string lights scalloped overhead, she saw that his carefully parted hair was more of a sandy blond than a *blond* blond. She saw that his jaw was so sculpted it might've been formed in the palm of Zeus himself.

In addition to his Instagram good looks, she was struck by his demeanor—the way he took control, speaking with authority until the bros looked sufficiently chastened. When the handsome stranger finally turned away from them, his eyes met Layla's. Her debt, her worries, her fresh start—suddenly none of it mattered. Layla knew this was fate.

Pearl settled back into her seat. "Go get him," she whispered.

Layla dug around in her purse and found the pen she'd accidentally stolen the last time she'd been at the bank. As though in a trance, she grabbed a semi-soggy cardboard coaster off their table and scrawled, *Thanks for saving us from a bro fight—you're a hero*, followed by her phone number. She strode over to him, as sexy and smooth as she'd ever been in her entire twenty-six years of existence, and slipped the coaster into his hands with one gentle squeeze. Then she turned and walked away.

It felt as though the room had stilled, the rowdy crowd parting to let her return to her table with grace. Reaching Pearl, Layla released the breath she'd been holding and let her smile fall just enough so she could hiss, "Let's go before I pee my pants." Pearl had laughed, delighted and proud, and grabbed their purses.

Ian called the following day and asked her to go to Bite of Seattle, the summer food festival. If she'd been intrigued at the bar, she was fully smitten at the festival. It was overwhelmingly crowded, and he'd offered to hold her hand early on so they didn't lose each other. Her palm tingled when her skin met his. He was everything all her exes hadn't been: considerate, attentive, kind. She felt safe with him.

They'd had almost two precious years together. But two weeks ago, it all came screeching to a halt. They'd gone to a tiny Italian bistro to have Layla's favorite dinner: dessert. Layla should have known there was something wrong. Ian barely touched the tiramisu and only dabbed his spoon in the gelato. Normally he'd check his work e-mail whenever there was a lull in their conversation—he worked in finance, and his clients were relentless—but he didn't once look at his phone. He didn't seem to look at anything at all. *He's having an off night,* she remembered reasoning. *Who doesn't have off nights?*

But when she pulled up to his building and parked in one of the guest spots in the tree-shaded lot, he'd turned to her, grave. Instead of grinning and asking her to come up the way he always did, he simply said, "I love you, Layla. I've loved being with you." He rubbed his hands over his eyes and down over his late-night stubble. "But we've been trying for so long to make our schedules work and we still barely see each other. My hours are endless, and yours are erratic. Doesn't it feel like we're trying too hard? That it shouldn't be this hard?"

She was embarrassed to remember how her chin had trembled—at least a three on the Richter scale—when she replied, "You're breaking up with me because you don't see me enough? So now you don't want to see me at all? That doesn't make any sense."

He'd apologized, he'd agreed, but he hadn't changed his mind. He climbed out of her car, settled the seat belt carefully, and said so softly she could almost convince herself later she'd made it up: "What am I doing?" Then he shut the car door.

In the absolute quiet he left behind, she became breathless and speechless, and here she was, two weeks later, still both.

Layla picked up the green slingback. She considered throwing it out the window. She considered finding the other shoe, lovingly wrapping the pair in tissue, and donating them to a secondhand shop. She considered taking a photograph of it and posting it online as a beacon for the one who got away.

In the end, she carefully put it back in her closet.

CHAPTER TWO

CLIPBOARD IN HAND, Layla stepped over the extension cords blocking the door to Northwest End's dank basement. It was once again time to do inventory for concessions. Not her favorite task. Not that she had a lot of favorite tasks these days. Although she was employed by a crackerjack theater that had a reputation for taking risks with classics and for being experimental as well as relatable, work was...work. At least she got to hang out in a historic—if dilapidated—building with coworkers she loved. Still, she'd be keener to throw herself into her job if she could do something that was actually creative and not just a series of tedious, Sisyphean chores.

"I come in peace," she called, hoping to placate any ghosts lurking among the bottled sodas and king-size candy bars.

She flicked on the weak lights but knew she'd still have to use the flashlight on her phone to see the stuff at the back of the shelves. When she pulled the phone out, she saw Rena had texted: Lasagna or chicken for Sunday dinner? Reflexively, Layla winced, knowing the subtext: *You're still coming, right? You're not disappearing again?*

There was also a message on their family text chain, which

Rhiannon, Layla's oldest sibling, had named "Rockford Peaches." Layla kept that chain on mute since, with seven people, it could get rowdy. The indicator was currently at forty-two unread messages. Layla simply did not have the emotional reserves to click on it and catch up.

After a few deep breaths to collect herself, Layla returned to the banal task at hand: counting the snacks.

"Layla!" a voice hollered. "Are you down there?"

Layla could see a backlit figure at the top of the stairs: Manjit, the theater's artistic director. Since Layla reported to Charlene, the general manager, having Manjit look for her was unusual. Layla flicked off the lights and jogged back up the stairs.

"Hey, Manjit. What's up?" Layla forced a smile. Pretending to be cheerful with her boss, with her mother, with everyone she encountered during her day, was exhausting.

Manjit was dressed impeccably, as usual, in a perfect skirt suit with just the right creative bursts of color. Layla had to stop herself from smoothing down her own loud orange 1960s minidress with white daisies for pockets. She mentally debated whether she'd achieved the Carnaby Street glam look she'd been going for. Next to her boss, she felt a bit like a kid on her first day of kindergarten. Fashion was full of fine lines.

Manjit scooched herself and Layla out of the way just as a pack of crew members juggling tools streamed by. She pushed her dark wavy hair out of her face and grimaced at the sound of a piece of the set hitting the stage. "Some of the items for the silent auction have fallen through."

"For *tonight?*"

Manjit nodded grimly. "Charlene's already begging for favors from nearby hotels and spas. Any chance you and Pearl can go charm our friends down the street?"

Manjit didn't need to ask twice. Layla loved browsing the neighboring shops.

Pearl was waiting for her by the lobby doors holding Layla's red mod raincoat and her own sleek black one. Her thick dark hair, which she'd inherited from her stunning Chinese-Filipino mom, was tinted blue-black these days, and it spilled over her shoulders and honeydew-colored crop top. Pearl, too, put fashion above finance. That was part of the reason why they'd become instant friends when they met at the UW School of Drama ten years ago. Layla knew Pearl's fashion risks were not only an expression of who she was but also a way for her to stand out in her family, where her twin brothers soaked up most of the attention.

Layla knew how that felt.

"Ready to blow this Popsicle stand?" Pearl shook Layla's red coat at her.

"Goodbye, ghosts," Layla called. The comment was for Pearl's benefit, proof Layla could still be facetious and light, that she was okay.

The weather had turned ugly; a gale-force wind propelled Layla and Pearl forward as soon as they hit the pavement. Layla didn't even need to pull up her hood—the wind slapped it onto the back of her head. Rain hit her freckled skin from what felt like every direction.

"Are we sure there isn't a tornado warning?" Layla asked, wishing she could be at home in bed. She remembered snippets of last night's dream: She and Ian had been back at the rooftop bar and she'd asked him, "How's this going to end?" Instead of answering, he'd smiled, his sexy dimple on full display, and then leaned in to press his lips against hers...

Pearl yanked her sleeve. Layla hadn't even realized she'd stopped walking.

"Suck it up, buttercup," Pearl said. "This isn't a tornado, this is—"

"A Tuesday in Seattle?" Layla supplied.

Pearl gave her a puzzled look. "Pookie, it's Friday. Get your head in the game."

They made their way to the cozy wine market half a block down. Every store in Northwest's neighborhood was older, all of them cared for by their owners like longtime friends, maintained with fresh coats of colorful paint. Layla and Pearl asked the owner, Toni, for a wine donation; she stepped into the back to choose some bottles, and they settled in to browse as they waited for her to return.

Running her fingers along a shelf of rosé, Pearl surprised Layla: "Sometimes I'm so tired of dating, I wish I could just fall in love with one of my roommates and be done with it."

Pearl wasn't usually so cynical. "Which roommate would you choose, though?" Layla ticked people off on her fingers, trying to lighten the mood. "The guy who makes his own cheese and then doesn't clean the kitchen afterward? Or the one who keeps trying to convince you to call him King Snake?"

"Nickname guy thankfully moved out. He's subletting his room." Pearl dropped her hand and coyly turned to admire the whites. "Or rather, his curtained-off section of the loft."

There was something she wasn't saying. "Pearl," Layla pressed. "Who moved in?"

Pearl shrugged. "Just some sculptor named Devin who may or may not resemble Elliot Page."

"So, basically your type."

"One hundred percent my type," Pearl confirmed, whirling back with a grin. "You should come over and meet him. Someone needs to drink all my tequila and perform every Shakespeare monologue we can remember from college."

"I'll come by soon," Layla promised her, wanting to mean it. She loved the loft. In fact, she'd lived there for years, from her college days to...the days she'd rather not think about. The last time she'd been by, and, yes, gotten drunk and performed Viola's monologue from *Twelfth Night* (terribly, it was worth noting), was just before Ian broke up with her. She'd been so happy then, so tipsy and carefree. God, she missed being tipsy and carefree. These days she managed to achieve only half that equation.

"Please tell me that sad little look on your face isn't because of someone whose name rhymes with Schmian Shmarnett." Pearl narrowed her eyes.

"I…" But Layla had nowhere to go with that sentence. Because thoughts of him clung to her like a shadow. She missed the way he towered over her. How he always pulled her to his chest when he greeted her. She missed the way he laughed at her jokes, like when she admitted she thought flavored club soda tasted like millennial disappointment. She missed splitting appetizers at Purple Café and Wine Bar and how he'd work beside her while she watched Cary Grant movies and how it didn't matter that he wasn't watching her favorite films because she could feel the warmth of his body next to hers.

"I'm so sorry," Pearl said, frowning. "Breakups are the worst. The only way over them is through them. And that means excavating nine hundred layers of crap."

"Yeah," Layla agreed idly. She was achingly aware of how tiresome it was to be around someone who was perpetually moping, but she didn't know how to pull herself together.

"And I realize"—Pearl continued gently—"that excavating those nine hundred layers of crap also means revisiting the Randall of it all."

Layla felt like she'd been sucker-punched. She'd survived the haunted basement, her mom's guilt-inducing texts, and a tornado just for Pearl to bring her down here?

"I don't…" Luckily, Layla didn't have to finish her sentence because Toni had emerged from the back carrying a basket of older bottles.

After thanking Toni graciously, the two made their way back

outside. As they walked, a wicked smile slowly spread across Pearl's face. "Have you considered getting back on the horse? And by horse, I mean another human person. I know it's only been two weeks, but maybe it's time for a palate cleanser?"

Well. This was not the distraction Layla had been hoping for. But it wasn't fair to resent Pearl for not knowing what Layla needed. Hell, *Layla* didn't know what she needed.

Yes, she did. She needed *Ian*.

"Maybe," Layla eventually replied because she didn't want to argue. She was an easy crier to begin with; videos of toddler/dog friendships often reduced her to tears, as did most of her favorite songs and books. But the thought of even downloading a dating app gave her emotional whiplash. She'd spent the first week after the breakup scouring the internet for Ian as a way to be near him; inspecting his social media pages with the intensity of a forensic scientist, looking for signs he was dating someone (in which case she'd simply die) or that he was as miserable as she was (*Please, please, please*). By week two, even seeing his avatar sent her spiraling, so she'd stopped opening most of the apps on her phone altogether. She vehemently avoided even her own Instagram profile, where the carefully curated depictions of her once happy life were now unrecognizable. All this to say, dating apps were definitely off the table.

"Honestly, I don't think I'm ready to get on *anyone*," Layla finally admitted. "I'm a disaster of a person."

"You're not," Pearl said, voice softening. "You're just going through a really hard time right now."

Right now and before and always, Layla thought. Now that Randall's name had been conjured, he was manspreading in the middle of her thoughts. To her horror, she felt the telltale wobble of her chin. It was T minus mere seconds before she started crying outside this lovely wine market.

Layla felt Pearl's hand catch hers. "Pull yourself together, pookie. You're embarrassing me in front of our neighbors. And you know I don't embarrass easily."

Despite herself, Layla smiled. The wobble steadied.

The wind was dying as they approached their next business target, an art store about four blocks down from the wine market. Pearl was heading inside, holding the door open, when Layla's phone started buzzing. Figuring it was Manjit checking in, Layla waved Pearl on. But she nearly dropped her phone when she looked down.

The caller ID said Maybe: UW Medical Center.

"Hello?" she answered, her voice shaky, her mind racing.

"Is this Layla Rockford?"

"Yes." *Please let everyone I love be okay. Please let no one be sick or hurt or maimed.* "What's happened?"

"We have you listed as the emergency contact for Ian Barnett. Could you come to the hospital?"

CHAPTER THREE

IN COLLEGE, LAYLA had double-majored in theater and business, and if an acting professor in an improv class had told her, "You've just gotten a phone call saying the love of your life, whom you haven't seen in weeks, is in the hospital. Show me how you would feel. *Show me what that looks like*," Layla would've clutched her heart. She would've gone wide-eyed, chin trembling. She would have screamed to the heavens and tangled her fingers in her hair.

But Layla had never been a very good actor—hence the double major. And what she didn't know then was that when that call comes, you feel nothing. Right now, her body was hollow. Her veins had dried up.

Layla had vaguely registered that Pearl came back out of the art store to check on her, that she'd somehow communicated what was happening (what *was* happening? The hospital hadn't told her anything); that she had put one foot in front of the other and somehow ended up in her car, hands trembling, soaking wet from a torrential downpour that had erupted at some point.

Pearl had returned to work after making Layla promise to call, and Layla started driving. Her head was empty; her head was too full. Her brain was definitely not functioning the way it was supposed to when you were operating a motor vehicle.

If you don't focus, you could end up in the hospital too, a tiny voice of reason said just as a car swerved around her and its driver laid on the horn. That jolted the fog from her thoughts. The tiny voice was right. Ian was in the hospital, and he needed her. She didn't know if he was sick or hurt or dying or dead...

She banished the worst-case scenarios that flooded through her mind the only way she could: by thinking of Ian.

The truth was, Ian had snuck up on her at a time when she hadn't felt worthy of anything good. Sure, she'd been the one to approach him at Winston and Tux. Sure, she'd been immediately attracted to him. But Layla was attracted to a lot of people. Attraction was *fun*. Attraction was easy. Everything else about Ian—*that* was what had surprised her. Because Ian was a caretaker, something Layla hadn't known she wanted in a partner until she experienced it. She couldn't believe that she was lucky enough to be loved by someone so thoughtful.

The first time Ian met Layla's parents, known music lovers, he'd gifted them tickets to the symphony. Layla's dad had been a college DJ, and her parents' eclectic taste ran more toward rock, disco, folk, and a bit of new wave, but they'd still loved the experience, excitedly texted them both pictures from their front-row seats. When Ian finally saw their record collection in Bellevue and realized what they actually liked, he called dibs on four tickets for an outdoor Heart concert that were floating around his office (courtesy of a client), and they all went on a double date. Bill put his arm around Ian as they raised their lit cell phones during "Alone"; Ian cheered Rena on as she sang every single word to "Crazy on You." Layla had never envisioned herself going on a double date with her parents, but after an evening of singing, laughing, and dancing, her body practically hurt from the joy of it all.

But Ian's thoughtfulness didn't end there. When his mom and stepdad retired from teaching, he'd gifted them a Mediterranean cruise. He presented the tickets to them at their retirement party. It was the first time Layla had met them, and her eyes had teared up along with Jeannie's and Craig's when they opened the envelope and realized what Ian had done. It almost made up for the fact that Ian's younger brother, Matt, hadn't been able to make it—the story was his car had broken down somewhere in New York State, but Ian didn't seem convinced.

Layla and Ian's first argument had been over Ian wanting her to join him on a weekend trip to La Jolla and Layla not feeling comfortable enough to ask for the time off work. A sweet argument at its core—they were both upset because they wanted more of each other. Ian had apologized with flowers and a rhyming poem that had been so bad, she'd laughed until her eyes prickled with tears. That poem and a single dried rose from the bouquet still lived in a keepsake box under her bed.

When she weighed his flimsy "We don't see each other enough" reason for the breakup against so many wonderful memories, the scales tipped heavily in one direction.

But she hadn't heard from him since he'd ended things. Why was he asking for her now? The only explanation was that the hospital had called the emergency contact Ian had given them the previous time he was there. She'd driven him in to get stitches after he'd cut his hand on the fence at the batting cages, and when he paused while filling out the medical forms to ask, "Will you be my emergency contact?" Layla had nearly swooned.

She'd never expected to be called.

She'd never expected their relationship to end.

She'd never expected she'd have to wonder what kind of shape he was in if he couldn't ask them to call someone else.

By the time Layla pulled her hatchback into the hospital

parking lot, she was ready to vomit or pass out or both. Her desperation to see him alive overrode her nerves.

Layla turned off the car, silencing the Dinah Washington album that she hadn't even realized had been playing. The sound of the rain outside seemed magnified. She got out of the car and marched toward...she didn't know what. All she knew was that if Ian needed her, she'd be there for him.

The person at the front desk gave her directions to the emergency department, but every hall looked the same, so it took Layla several tries to find it, her worries multiplying with every passing second. She finally found someone at a reception desk who pointed to an area of curtained-off cubicles about fifteen feet away. Layla watched as a nurse came out of one and pulled the curtain shut behind her.

Layla did an awkward half jog over to her. "Is Ian Barnett in there? The hospital called me and told me to come."

The nurse was a short, attractive Black woman whose name tag read AUTUMN. She asked for Layla's ID and then gave her a tight smile. "Layla. Ian's been asking for you."

Layla's mind squeezed the meaning from those five words: He could still talk. He'd *been asking for her,* which sounded like it'd happened more than once. "Is he okay?" Layla barely got the syllables out.

"He's okay," Autumn replied. "Pretty banged up, though. You should see his helmet."

"His helmet?"

"Cracked right down the middle," Autumn told her. Before Layla could ask her why Ian had been wearing a helmet and if any part of *him* was cracked down the middle, Autumn pulled back the curtain.

"Your girlfriend's here," she said, leading Layla in. "Myrtle, the volunteer in the gift shop, will be disappointed. She just tried to trick me into giving her your phone number." Autumn raised her eyebrows in amusement. "She wants you to know she's ninety years young and has plenty of moves left."

Your girlfriend's here. Not *ex-girlfriend.* Layla flushed with embarrassment and bewilderment.

And then she saw him for the first time in weeks. Two weeks, to be exact.

Lying there, Ian didn't look like the guy who broke up bar fights. He didn't look like the guy who wrapped his arms around you when you were cold—and Layla was always cold. This Ian looked *frail.* He was wearing one of those ugly pilled gowns, and Layla could see his forearms and elbows were bruised and he had a cut on his cheek.

Layla's heart catapulted into her throat; the room was so quiet, she could hear her dress dripping rain onto the hospital floor. But then she registered the way his face lit up when he saw her.

"*Layla.*" The small quaver in his voice nearly broke her.

She wanted to check every inch of him for more bruises; she wanted to melt into a puddle. She wanted to wrap her arms around him but also demand to know why the hell he'd asked her to come here. More than anything, she wanted to cry with glorious relief because he was alert, in one piece, and talking to her. And then her gaze fell on the helmet sitting on the table next to Ian. It looked like someone had taken a baseball bat to it. What would've happened if Ian hadn't been wearing it?

"Come here," Ian said, his voice raspy, his arms outstretched. Although Layla wanted to throw herself against him, she was hyperaware of how broken he was. And how much more broken he could have been. She was also aware that it was very odd that he was holding his arms out for her.

Perhaps his accident was making him sentimental? She'd be a monster to deny him comfort after whatever had happened today.

She crossed the room slowly and tucked her hand in his. "Are you okay?"

He let out a shaky breath and nodded. "Yeah. I'm okay. Just...I don't know. Still processing? Glad the car wasn't going any faster than it was?"

"You were hit by a car?"

"And lived to tell the tale." The corners of his eyes crinkled, but there was distress behind them.

"This man has not stopped talking about you since he got here," Autumn said, gathering up medical paraphernalia on the other side of the room.

Layla opened her mouth but found she had too many questions to choose just one. Autumn must've interpreted that as concern over what Ian had been saying because she followed up quickly with "All good, of course. He kept referring to a girl who was named after a song and who looked like she'd stepped out of a time machine. I'm happy to see that's all accurate and not confusion from the concussion."

"Concussion?" Layla looked from Autumn back to Ian.

"He's got a devil of a headache right now, but he'll be okay. The doctor will come in and explain all this to you, but he'll just need to be careful for the next few days. Make sure he gets rest, stays hydrated—and avoids screens." Autumn gave Ian a very pointed stare, followed by "I know how you finance guys get."

Layla felt defensive on Ian's behalf. Yes, his phone was basically another appendage, but he was good at his job.

"You know that's a moot point." Ian leaned back and squeezed his eyes shut. "The only thing more banged up than my helmet is my phone."

He wordlessly pointed to the nightstand, and sure enough, behind his cracked helmet was his totally shattered phone. It was a miracle he was okay, Layla realized. She wanted to drop to her knees and thank every potential higher power there was.

"Be that as it may, you'll need to keep a close eye on him," Autumn said comfortingly to Layla. "But he should be all right."

Keep a close eye on him.

"I…" Why hadn't Ian called his parents, or even his brother? None of them lived in Seattle, so she supposed they wouldn't have been much help. Still, why hadn't he called a friend? Or his hot neighbor? The way that woman hung around, Layla knew she would have injured *herself* to be beside this hospital bed. As much as Layla wanted to take care of Ian, she knew that spending time with him would only prolong her own pain. She still loved him. *So much.* And the tenderness he was showing her was only going to make it harder when he took it away again.

Sensing her distress, Ian asked, "Is work busy? Are you doing a show this weekend? I'm sorry, my brain's fuzzy and I can't remember. I'd check the shared calendar you made us, but…" He gestured feebly toward his broken phone.

Realization splashed over Layla like a bucket of ice water.

Ian had been in an accident. His head was *fuzzy.* He was vulnerable and confused and acting as though they were still together. Did he…had he forgotten he'd dumped her?

"So what do you say? Are you okay looking after your boyfriend this weekend?" Autumn asked.

"No," Layla whispered, meaning *No, he's not my boyfriend.* Was it possible his concussion had reset his brain, like when a computer crashes and then reboots? Was their breakup an unsaved document lost in Ian's head? Layla felt a fierce regret for not having paid attention in biology. That couldn't be happening. But what else made sense?

And what was she supposed to do? Say *I'd love to take care of him, Nurse Autumn, but it feels inappropriate, not to mention kind of masochistic?*

But when she realized Ian and Autumn had misinterpreted her

response, she quickly recovered. "I mean no problem. Of course I'll look after him." She gathered the courage to meet Ian's gaze. Softly, she repeated, "Ian, of course I'll look after you."

"Are you sure?" he asked with concern. But was it because he knew this was a wildly inappropriate request or because he thought they were still together and he hated feeling vulnerable around her?

"Of course I'm sure. All that matters right now is your recovery." And she meant it.

"Good. I'll get the doctor," Autumn said.

After Autumn left, Ian sat up as much as he could. "Your hands are shaking," he pointed out. "And you're soaking wet. You must be freezing. You want to come under my covers?"

As he pulled back his thin, scratchy hospital blanket and patted the mattress, Layla couldn't deny it: *He has no idea we broke up.* Layla tried to smile through the tears blurring her vision. "I don't want to hurt you."

He looked down at his bruised arms. "You can't possibly do more damage than that car."

"*Ian.*" The tears spilled over as she let out a nervous laugh. "Please don't joke when I'm this worried about you."

He patted the mattress again and she sighed and sat down as carefully as she could. There wasn't much room. She could feel his body heat and it was a beautiful kind of torture.

"I know you say you're okay, but I'm looking at your helmet and your phone and..." She went to touch his cheek just below the cut but stopped herself.

Ian smiled and folded her hand in his before she could pull it away. He pressed it gently to his face. "Hey. I'm feeling better now. Really. Especially with you here. Going through this alone was..."

He closed his eyes, and she carefully splayed her fingers across his cheek. Every sweet emotion she'd felt for him, all the ones she'd been trying to smother, rose like a wave and crashed through her. *But for how long?* her brain reminded her. *How long before he remembers?* In the wave's wake, guilt and worry settled in. Was this really what Ian needed right now? For her to deceive him?

"Anyway, thanks for coming," Ian said quietly, bringing her attention back to him. "This day has been…"

"Terrifying?" Layla supplied, fresh tears rolling down her cheeks. "Heart-wrenching? Overwhelmingly horrific? Butt-clenching?"

Ian exhaled a laugh. "Yeah. All of those things."

Layla was afraid to move, to speak, to do anything that might shatter whatever was happening between them. The familiar worry line between Ian's eyebrows appeared. "I'm sorry I scared you," he said.

"Please don't apologize when you're the one who nearly died."

"I didn't nearly die. I was wearing my helmet," he said, his eyes locked on hers.

"Your helmet *definitely* died," she said, barely above a whisper.

He gave her a wobbly smile she felt her own mouth match.

Autumn pulled back the curtain and came in, followed by a woman in a white coat.

"This is Ian's girlfriend, Layla," Autumn told the woman. The words sent a shock through Layla every time she heard them. The second woman smiled. She had pale skin and short, bleached-blond hair. Despite the fact that she looked like a woodland sprite, her presence commanded respect. "I'm Dr. Amanda Carroll."

"Before you ask if she's related to Coach Pete," Ian said, perking up a little, "let me save you the disappointment. Dr. Carroll doesn't watch sports and has barely even heard of the Seahawks."

"That's too bad. We love Pete." Layla played along, still dizzy from the intimate moment they'd just shared. She understood approximately forty percent of football on a good day, but Ian's enthusiasm was addictive. As were all those delightful Sunday-afternoon snacks.

"Do you know who was a real disappointment last season?" Autumn chimed in. She walked over to Ian and launched into a football-related diatribe full of names Layla only vaguely recognized. She seized the opportunity to speak with Dr. Carroll semiprivately.

"Thanks for everything," she said to her, backing away from Ian's bed. "He seems okay, all things considered."

"Your boyfriend is really lucky. It could've been a lot worse," the doctor told Layla gravely, flipping through a chart. "But everything looks good. He's had a scare and is a bit banged up, and he'll probably have a headache for a day or two. As I'm sure Autumn told you, we'd like someone to keep an eye on him, just in case."

"I can definitely keep an eye on him. But...um...he seems to have forgotten something. Something kind of important?" Layla picked at the nail polish on her little finger nervously. "Maybe it's because of his concussion?"

"That would be atypical for a case this mild." Dr. Carroll cocked her head, intrigued. "How much has he forgotten?"

"It's more like one specific memory?" Layla's voice was rising. She wanted reassurance Ian was fine. She also very much wanted to know when he'd suddenly remember he didn't want to be with her anymore.

"Hmm." Dr. Carroll considered this. "Everyone copes differently with trauma. If this memory was particularly stressful, I suppose it's not impossible he's subconsciously suppressing it so his body can relax and heal." She looked over the notes on her clipboard, then back at Layla. "More likely, he's just a little shaken up. As his headache and confusion clear, he should be back to normal."

Back to normal.

Layla didn't want to go back to normal. She didn't want to go back to missing the way he was looking at her now from across the room. She gave him a little wave and he waved back. "I'll make sure he rests," she said finally.

Dr. Carroll gave Layla a reassuring smile. "Like I said, early confusion is common with concussions. The brain is a remarkable and mysterious organ. You'll see."

Unsure of what else to do, Layla thanked Dr. Carroll again. When the doctor left, she turned her attention to the stack of paperwork Autumn had placed in her hands. Ian went into the bathroom to change out of the hospital gown, and when he returned, they both dutifully listened to Autumn's instructions about rest, hydration, and limiting Ian's exposure to screens, after which they walked out of the hospital holding hands.

Holding hands.

Outside, Layla shivered in her damp dress.

"Do you need my jacket too?" Ian asked, automatically shrugging it off. "It's a little..."

They looked at the jacket in his hand, torn and dusty from the accident. He paused for a split second before tossing it into a nearby garbage can.

"Are you ready to talk about what happened?" she asked gently.

He closed his eyes briefly. She stopped him from stepping off the curb into the parking lot and guided him to a bench.

"I still can't believe it. I was biking to work—you know, because of the benefits exercise can have on stress." They sat down and he shook his head. "But you already knew that, right? My head feels like a puzzle right now. None of the pieces are really fitting together. And some are missing."

"Of course I knew," she lied, hating herself a little bit for it.

"I think I was worrying about something at work, and it was so cold and windy—"

"It was a pretty miserable morning to be biking." That, Layla didn't have to lie about.

"It was," he agreed. And then, brightening: "Actually, I remember I was thinking about you. There I was, trying to pedal my stress away in a hurricane, and I thought about how you told me that work angst was best battled with television and snacks."

"I maintain that eating two-bite brownies and watching a marathon of *The Carol Burnett Show* can cure anything," Layla confirmed, her pulse racing. *I was thinking about you*, he'd said. Why? Had he been missing her too?

"It did sound a lot better than what I was doing. Anyway, I was just around the corner from my condo when a car clipped my bike tire and sent me flying. Into a pole, I think?" He paled a little, remembering, and Layla put a hand on his shoulder. "I'm just glad I was wearing a helmet."

"Ian, that's awful." A wave of tenderness overcame her.

He bit the inside of his cheek, then put on a brave face. "Which way to your car?"

They stood up and she began leading the way. "How did you get to the hospital?"

"My neighbor was walking by and saw the whole thing. I thought I was okay when I got up, but a headache came on and then I felt sort of sick. She'd had a concussion before and offered to bring me in."

Layla gave his hand another squeeze, hoping the neighbor he was referring to wasn't the hot one who bore a striking resemblance to Margot Robbie.

"And the damn car never even stopped," he said bitterly. "Like where they had to go was so much more important than my life."

"A hit-and-run? What an evil bastard."

At her car, Layla unlocked both doors and they climbed in; Ian moved the passenger seat all the way back to accommodate his long legs. They'd always joked about the physics of fitting her economy-size boyfriend into her fun-size car.

Her stomach dropped. Guilt and paranoia suddenly clawed at her chest. "When you say some pieces are missing, do you mean from the accident or..."

He froze. "I'm not hiding it very well, am I? I thought if I just relaxed, it would all come back."

"What would come back?" Layla was afraid to breathe, afraid to think too hard lest her brainwaves somehow hopped over into his head. At this point she didn't know what was possible.

"The last thing that's clear for me is...the baseball game we went to with my parents."

Layla nodded quickly. The baseball game? "Four or five weeks ago?"

"Everything from the last month is kind of a blur," he admitted. "I have flashes of memory, some images and some feelings, but I can't remember anything specific. I've been trying. I can't even remember how many Segway Man sightings we're at."

"That must be so scary," she whispered, willing herself to keep it together, knowing if she could've wiped the past two weeks from her own memory, she would have *Eternal Sunshine of the Spotless Mind*-ed herself in a heartbeat. "And, for what it's worth, we're at twelve."

"Eight more to go," he said. The effort behind his levity was obvious. "Anyway, I feel better now you're with me. But I *am* a little concerned about going back to work. If I'm not with it by Monday, people could lose money. Lots and lots of money."

It was a valid concern. But she was still hanging on the words *I feel better now you're with me.* She wanted to put whipped cream on those words and savor them. She recovered by saying, "Are you hungry? Should we stop for food? Or should I just take you home?"

Ian raised a hand to cover his eyes and leaned his head back against the seat. "Do you mind if we just go home? The nausea's returning. It's so bright out."

Even though the wind and rain had gone, it was still overcast. Layla figured the concussion was making his eyes sensitive. She turned off the radio and they drove in silence, a silence that started out uncomfortable, at least on Layla's end. As they worked their way through downtown Seattle, stopping and starting with the early evening traffic, it became something else. A familiar, companionable quiet.

"We're here," she whispered at last, pulling into Ian's lot. She left the car running.

Slowly, Ian pulled his hand away from his eyes and blinked a few times.

She realized too late where she'd stopped. In front of Ian's modern, high-rise condo with its greeny-blue glass exterior, yes, but in the very parking spot where he'd ended things.

Two weeks ago, they'd sat in this car in this exact place as her world had fallen apart.

"You're coming up, right?" Ian asked, looking at her expectantly.

Every neuron Layla had lit up and tried to say *Yes*.

This was the way their two-weeks-ago car ride should've ended. But it would be unhinged to continue with this charade—unethical, even. She couldn't do it.

Could she?

The words she could have sworn she'd heard him say the night of the breakup—*What am I doing?*—thrummed in her head, in her heart. He'd made a mistake. He'd regretted it, maybe immediately. And now some part of his brain was repressing that memory and giving them a second chance.

She turned the car off, still unsure what to do. Because going into his condo wasn't merely escorting Ian home.

However, if it wasn't his brain repressing things, did that

mean this was something bigger? The universe intervening, telling Layla and Ian they belonged together? Wouldn't it be even more unhinged to ignore such a blatant sign?

She thought about the connection she'd felt with him, physically, emotionally, in the hospital. The way he'd looked at her. And she knew it in her bones: *He needs me just as much as I need him.*

At the very least, she'd promised Autumn and Dr. Carroll that she'd look after him. She'd promised *Ian* she would.

"Layla?" Ian said, interrupting her internal debate. "Please come up. You're still damp and you look like you're freezing. I can't stand to see you this cold."

She opened her mouth and responded before her brain could protest any more: "Of course. Let's go up."

CHAPTER FOUR

IAN'S CONDO WAS modern and clean, if a little sterile. Layla had mentally redecorated it a thousand times, anticipating the day he'd ask her to move in.

She put her purse on the side table and hung her coat in the front closet just as she'd always done. Then she carefully guided Ian, who was still squinting, over to the couch.

Well. Now what? She knew what she *wanted* to do (pull his head into her lap and comb her fingers through his silky hair), but she was tap-dancing in an ethical and emotional gray area and didn't know what the protocol for this kind of thing was.

"I should call my parents," Ian said, temporarily saving her from her mental spiral. "Why don't you go grab something of mine to change into?"

Layla nodded stiffly. *Crap.* Did Ian's parents know about the breakup? He adored them, but he often got so wrapped up in work that he went weeks without calling. And when he did call, it was usually because Layla had reminded him to. So was it possible he'd never gotten around to telling them? Could the universe really be so on her side? She sent a little prayer up to her icons, the now-departed writers and performers of her favorite movies, who, she liked to believe, appreciated her devotion. *Dear Billy Wilder, Humphrey Bogart, Debbie Reynolds, and the rest of you: Please don't let Jeannie and Craig know about the breakup. Please let me have just a few more moments—or, preferably, countless more moments—with Ian.*

"Do you want to use my phone?" she asked him in her most normal-sounding voice.

Ian blinked. "Right. Of course."

Layla handed it over and then took deep breaths, trying not to freak out as she casually wandered into her ex's bedroom to rummage through his clothes. After a few seconds, she heard his voice in the living room.

"Hey, Mom, it's me...because I'm not calling from my phone...I'll tell you why, but before I go into it, please pay attention to this part: *I'm okay.*"

Ian's bedroom looked unchanged. It had been only two weeks; still, there were, blessedly, no new pieces of women's lingerie on top of his laundry bin. His bed was firmly made with sheets that hadn't been recently tousled. All good signs.

Layla took a faded Marshawn Lynch Seahawks T-shirt from his top drawer. She slipped off her damp dress, padded into the en suite bathroom, and laid it over the tub to dry. As she pulled the soft, threadbare shirt over her head, further mussing her hair, which had already been flattened and then frizzed by the rain, she caught bits of Ian's conversation with his mom.

"My helmet cracked—no, Mom, my head's fine *because* I was wearing my helmet. It's just a mild concuss—it's *mild*, Mom. Do you want to call the doctor yourself?" A chuckle from Ian, the kind that rumbled in his chest. "I'm sure you'd love to talk to Dr. Carroll, but I was joking...nope, no relation to Pete, unfortunately."

Layla went back to Ian's dresser and took her time working through his neglected "cozy pants" drawer. He was a dress-pants-or-jeans kind of guy, but every Christmas his mom and stepdad would buy him a pair of sweatpants as a gentle reminder for him to slow down, relax a little. She plucked a pair from the back and slipped them on, then cuffed the bottoms and rolled the waist to get them to fit, since Ian was nearly a whole foot taller than she was.

"Just a bit of a headache…yeah…yep…I'm taking Monday off, I promise," Ian was saying, sounding just this side of exasperated. *A day off?* That was new.

She couldn't stall any longer; the living room—and whatever Jeannie actually knew—was waiting.

Layla slowly walked back out. She took in Ian's familiar blue eyes, the dimple that appeared briefly whenever he was amused. But also the bruises on his strong forearms, the cut on his beautiful cheek, his beat-up dress shirt and slacks that would definitely need to be thrown out. Normally, Ian would never have sat down on his unblemished gray couch in dirty clothing. Gingerly, she took a seat next to him, steeling herself. He inched closer to her, close enough that she could hear Jeannie say, "Can you hold on? Craig just walked in. He's been coaching the volleyball team. He needs to hear this."

Ian's parents lived on Orcas Island, which wasn't all that far, but getting there involved a ferry ride, so Layla had never seen Ian's childhood home. Still, she could picture his mom, with her soft salt-and-pepper curls and bright eyes, clutching the phone.

"Ian? You still there? I'm going to put you on speaker— Craig! Get in here!"

"I'm here, Mom." Ian raised his eyebrows at Layla and they shared a smile. An intimate smile that said, *This is so typical Jeannie, but isn't she the best?*

Jeannie *was* the best, funny and kind and probably the most welcoming person Layla had ever met. Layla hadn't let herself think about Ian's parents for the past two weeks. With genuine warmth, Layla noticed that Jeannie gasped *again* when Ian told his story a second time, and Ian's stepfather let out an unexpected curse. She could finally admit it: she'd missed them. Because when someone broke up with you, their family usually broke up with you too.

She hadn't spent a ton of time with Ian's parents, but every few months they'd come into the city and Layla would join them for dinner or a Mariners game or a waterfront walk. They were like Ian's drawer of cozy pants—and the polar opposite of the Rockford Peaches chaos—comfortable and easy. Time spent with them slowed in the best way possible.

But just as Layla relaxed, the dreaded topic was brought up by Ian's stepdad. "Are you by yourself? Should we come out there?"

"No, no, don't come. I'll visit soon."

Jeannie chimed in. "We can call your brother—someone should be there."

"Mom, I'm fine. Definitely don't bother Matty with this. Anyway." Ian squeezed Layla's knee. "Layla's here."

Her whole body went rigid as she waited excruciating seconds for Jeannie to respond.

And then…"Well, that's a relief. Say hi to her from us, and tell her to make sure you don't work too hard."

Ian turned to her. "My mom and Craig say hi and want you to keep me in check."

"I'm on it," she replied loudly enough for them to hear while her heart thundered in her chest. Sitting still was no longer an option, not with her whole body buzzing. She got up and headed to the kitchen, ostensibly to start on her caretaking duties. Opening the fridge door, she realized her hands were actually shaking. The reality of what was happening truly sank in.

Unbelievable. *Unbelievable.* Call it fate, call it luck, but somehow Ian hadn't told his parents about their breakup. Maybe because he'd regretted it immediately? Maybe because he'd been planning on getting back together with her all along?

She couldn't get carried away. Telling herself to knock it off, she heated up a barely eaten tub of pad thai; she had it plated by the time he hung up with his parents. He joined her at the dining table, shoulders slumped sheepishly.

"Don't be surprised if my mom shows up in the middle of the night and hands you articles she's printed out about head injuries," he said, sitting down. "Thanks for figuring out dinner. I still feel pretty out of it."

"I love your mom," Layla said. "I'll take her company and her printouts any time of day."

His responding smile was interrupted as he winced at the overhead light.

"Hang on." Layla hit the switch and found the package of LED candles they'd used for Valentine's Day. Ian had been slammed at work and Layla offered to make plans, but unfortunately, she waited too long, and all the restaurants had been fully booked. So she'd bought them Amy's frozen meals and these candles, made a playlist of her favorite romantic songs, and turned Ian's condo into their very own exclusive spot. The night ended with them slow-dancing to "Night and Day." She might never have been happier.

Layla flicked the LED candles on and put them in the middle of the table. In the soft glow, Ian's eyes caught hers and she immediately grinned, her heart blossoming at the sight of him, a sight she still couldn't get used to.

"Autumn told me people often feel worse on the second day, so I'm going to apologize in advance if I'm not very fun tomorrow."

"You don't have to apologize," Layla assured him, mentally repeating: *Tomorrow.*

After they ate, chatting about soft topics like work and Deano, she did the dishes while he changed.

I should go, she thought, starting the dishwasher. *If Ian needs me, I can come back in the morning.* Layla had grabbed her vintage black-and-white chevron purse and was digging out her keys when Ian walked into the kitchen wearing low-slung sweatpants. And no shirt.

She nearly darted to the sink to splash cold water on her face.

"Wait—you're leaving?" he asked.

"I…" Unsure how to respond, unsure how to stop staring at the half-naked Adonis in front of her, she stammered, "I—I didn't want to disturb you."

"You've always stayed at my condo on the weekends." Ian stepped closer. "I thought the doctor asked you to keep an eye on me. Do you not want to?"

She pulled her gaze up, away from the familiar torso she'd held so many times. Past his broad shoulders, his neck, and his chin, which she'd often kissed when her tiptoes didn't give her enough height to reach his lips. Her eyes landed on his, where she caught a disarming flicker of insecurity. She remembered, in a rush, what it felt like to really kiss him.

"Of course I want to," she said, her voice quiet.

"Hey." He took another step toward her. "You look so sad. What's going on? I know I'm not my usual perky self—"

Layla cracked a smile, which he reciprocated.

"But I promise I'm okay. Or at least, I will be."

Afraid to speak, Layla nodded, desperate to feel the skin of his chest against her cheek, to have his arms reach out and pull the shirt she was wearing over her head…

Just then he wavered and leaned forward, bracing himself against the counter. Without thinking, she closed the distance between them.

"Ian, you need to lie down," she insisted, her hands on his

back, steadying him. His skin was so warm and smooth underneath her palms, she experienced a dizzying concoction of lust and concern. "I know you love to be the one to take care of people, but right now it's my turn."

There was a beat. Heavy and light, easy and yet so difficult.

"I want you to take care of me," he said, his voice low. Chills ran up and down her arms. She nodded in response. "I know it's far too early to go to bed, but I'm kind of dizzy," he said, running his hands along the goose bumps on her arms.

Whatever he wanted from her, he could have it. Early bedtime? Love? All the cash in her wallet? Anything.

He bit his lower lip. "Is it okay if we go lie down? I want you close."

She let him wrap his arms around her, succumbing to his embrace, her legs feeling weaker by the second as she asked, "Do you want to be the big spoon or the little spoon?"

"You know I always want to be the little spoon," Ian replied into her hair.

And that's how Layla ended up back in Ian's bed, holding the man she thought she'd never hold again.

CHAPTER FIVE

THE SUN WAS streaming softly through Ian's bedroom window. Layla could feel the warmth on her face. She wanted to capture every tiny sensation: the sound of Ian breathing, the rise and fall of his chest, the way the light grazed the floor and pooled on the dark blue comforter. Most of all, she wanted to bottle the overwhelming contentment in her chest so she would never lose it.

How many people got a second chance at love? And here she was, in Ian's bed. A shiver of delight rolled through her as she remembered the night. Layla had been drifting in and out of a restless sleep, and at some point, Ian woke up too. She'd heard his breathing change, and when she turned toward him, he was facing her, his nose, cheekbone, and jawline illuminated by the full moon.

"Hi," he'd whispered.

"Hi," she'd whispered back.

"I miss you."

At first, the confession had terrified her. Were his memories returning? Tentatively, she responded, "You don't have to miss me. I'm right here."

"But you're not close enough." A lopsided grin. "I thought I was your little spoon."

"You're the tallest little spoon I've ever seen," she mock grumbled, and she scooched closer and tucked herself against him as tightly as possible.

"Don't leave me again," he said sternly.

"I won't. I promise." And then they'd both fallen asleep, connected from chest to back, all the way down to where her feet grazed his calves.

Now, in the morning light, they were close but no longer touching. She took a moment to admire his back, the creamy color of his neck where it met his sandy-blond hair. He was ticklish in that spot, she knew, and she had to stop her fingers from reaching out and waking him so she could see the way he looked at her.

She glanced around Ian's room, smiling to herself about how everything had its place. He even had two hampers to keep his clothes separate to ensure maximum efficiency on laundry day. In fact, he actually had *laundry day* marked on his calendar app, which she loved to tease him about ("Are you up for seeing a movie at the revival house tonight or is it laundry day?"). At least, it had been on his calendar app—before his phone was smashed.

Ian was endearingly organized and stable, so unlike the last man she'd loved.

In her early-morning fog, her defenses weren't sharp enough yet, and, without warning, her mind slipped back to that other apartment, the one in LA.

To the cardboard box she and Randall'd half-heartedly used as a laundry basket after they'd broken their real laundry basket by using it as a stool to change the dingy light bulbs in their dingy apartment. It had never mattered, though, since most of their clothes ended up torn off each other and tossed on the floor.

Her body felt a shadow of that perpetual LA fatigue caused

by shift work and the unrelenting tension with Randall—the
overdue bills that piled higher and higher, her parents' names
flashing on her phone as they called and called, begging her to
tell them where she was...

Layla squeezed her eyes shut and when she opened them
again, she was back in Ian's apartment. Safe. Everything in its
place, including the jumbled pieces of her past, which belonged
where she kept them, locked deeply away.

Wanting to let Ian continue resting, Layla rolled out of bed,
grabbed her now-dry dress off Ian's bathtub, and tiptoed to the
guest bathroom down the hall. She brushed her teeth using a
new toothbrush she found under the bathroom sink, ignoring
the twinge of pain she felt when she imagined him throwing out
her old one.

As Layla dressed, she hummed the classic "For Once in My
Life," and then, with a smile only for herself, sang quietly: "For
twice in my life." She made her way into the hall and quickly
checked her phone, nestled in her purse.

There were two new texts. One was from Pearl. Pookie! Why
haven't you checked in? I told Manjit and Charlene you had a
personal emergency, which got you out of the silent auction, but
please text/call/holler and tell me if everything's okay. Layla sent
her a quick message to assure her everything was better than
okay and she'd fill her in later.

The second text was from Rhiannon and had been sent at the
unholy hour of six a.m. I get that you're going through something,
but Mom's stressed, and I think it's because she's worried about
you. I'm pulling rank and telling you you'd better show up for dinner
tomorrow.

Sure, in their family, the kids could turn on one another, but
they all knew to protect their mom at all costs. Rena was the
family adhesive, after all, and heaven knew the Rockford Peaches
needed someone to keep their ragtag group together.

But Rhiannon's self-righteousness made Layla's jaw clench. She considered sending her a text telling her to shove it, but despite her youngest-sibling bristles, Layla knew she couldn't leave her mom hanging. Not when Rhiannon was right and Rena was clearly so worried. Layla shifted her weight and deliberated. If she went to Sunday dinner, she'd have to talk about Ian. Out loud. Layla didn't have a clue what she'd say. But if she came up with an excuse now and didn't go, she'd *still* be the main topic of conversation. *Where's Layla? Why hasn't she been here in three weeks? Did she run away again? When's she going to get her life together?*

The road to peace, albeit a temporary one, was procrastination, so Layla put her phone away. A moment later, she was relieved to hear Ian stirring in the bedroom down the hall, and her breathing quickened. She'd held on to her fantasy for these few wonderful moments, but what if he woke up and remembered everything? Or what if he was in worse shape than yesterday?

"Layla?" he called out groggily.

"Hey." Layla kept her voice soft and low as she approached his room cautiously. "How are you feeling?"

"Not too bad, considering," he said, sitting up, and he seemed to mean it. Despite the lines between his eyebrows indicating he still had a headache, his face was full of adoration.

"Okay, tough guy. Tell me how you're *really* feeling," she mock demanded to cover up how she was flushing under his gaze. "I know you're not one to complain, but you've earned the right."

"That's my reward for getting hit by a car?" Ian's dimple flashed, but he was squinting. Layla simultaneously swooned and worried. "I get to complain guilt-free?"

"That's your reward," she confirmed, inching toward him. "I want to hear it all."

"My head hurts, but I'm definitely less exhausted." Ian sat up a little more, wincing a little as he did so. "Since you're on strict orders to keep me alive today, do you want to get…"

She could see him totally blank. She finished her journey to the bed and gently laid him back down, making sure his pillow was fluffed beneath his head. "Why don't you stay here and I'll go get us some brunch."

"*Brunch.*" Ian's smile was embarrassed. "That's the word."

Layla made a mental note to google everything about concussions on her way to get food. Honestly, she wouldn't have minded some of Jeannie's printouts.

"Didn't Autumn say the second day was the worst?" She brushed back the hair that had flopped onto his forehead. His eyes closed briefly in response. When he was in a suit, Ian looked like a bona fide movie star, with a jawline that could make him the next Batman. But she liked him best like this: cozy, low-key, human. When his eyes didn't open for several seconds, she added, "I think you need to take it easy today."

He nodded, clearly still tired. Layla tiptoed back out of his room.

Luckily, Layla knew that when Ian said *brunch*, he really meant only one place: Eggs Benny and the Jets. As she walked the familiar route to the restaurant, she took in the bright, clear morning and the blooming cherry blossom trees lining the street, remembering last year, when she'd insisted on taking his photo in front of them. They'd been so beautiful, just like now. His Facebook profile still featured a shot from college, and she'd made him upload the new pic instantly. Each time she'd peeked again during their breakup, she'd ached to see he still used that photo.

Now she took a picture of the blossoms and posted her first photo to Instagram in weeks, captioning it with lyrics from the Cole Porter classic "I Love Paris." Except, with all due respect to Mr. Porter, she changed the line to "I love *Seattle* in the springtime."

A puff of wind ruffled her minidress and shook blossoms off the tree. She felt a few fall into her hair. She wondered if Ian's unchanged photo had been a sign that he'd never really let her go. In the photo, he wasn't looking at the camera but at something slightly to the left. He'd been staring directly at Layla and smiling so big, she thought it would take an entire afternoon to kiss him from one end of his mouth to the other.

By the time she made it back to his condo with the food, Ian was out of bed and had taken a shower, though he was wearing his sunglasses inside. They ate their breakfast sandwiches, fruit, and hash browns on his bed, where he could rest more comfortably. Layla felt a little thrill at that; Ian never let them eat in bed. He used to say she ate chips like Cookie Monster ate cookies, crumbs flying haphazardly. She would open a bag right in front of him with mischief in her eyes, and he'd chase her around the condo with his dust buster while she yelped and jumped on the furniture, much to his good-natured chagrin.

"So, I have kind of an out-of-left-field idea," Ian said after a while, sipping on his coffee. "And I don't think it's just the concussion."

Layla braced herself. *This is it. Here's the other shoe.*

"I want to ask Matty to come out here. Permanently."

"*Matt?*" Layla's knowledge of Matt was limited. She knew Ian's younger brother was a nomad who had done some writing but hadn't held a steady job in years. She also knew, based on the fact that she'd never met him or witnessed so much as a text exchange between them, they weren't close. "What made you think of him?"

"You." Ian looked at her proudly.

"What do you mean, *me?*" Layla was starting to worry that Ian wasn't the only one forgetting things. She nibbled on her fruit skewer, waiting for him to go on.

"You know I've always admired how close you are with your

family. How, no matter what, you all make the effort to show up for Sunday dinner. How you check in with your parents regardless of how busy you are. How you and your siblings talk all the time."

"Rockford Peaches?" Layla managed carefully, trying not to think about Rhiannon's text.

"Exactly." Ian gave a sheepish shrug. "I want that too. So I want to ask Matt if he'll take a break from couch-surfing and live with me for a bit."

"Wow" was all Layla could think to say. Because she couldn't tell Ian how precarious her relationships with her family members truly were. Couldn't show him the unread family text chain that she didn't participate in because she didn't know the shorthand her siblings seemed to share, all of them now partners and parents. *Yeah, school drop-off is totally like the Battle of Helm's Deep,* she imagined herself responding, not knowing what either term really meant. *Now, can someone come pour a can of cold water over my head because I drank too much last night and I have to get ready for the admin job I might secretly hate?*

Nor could she tell him that what he perceived as her closeness with her siblings was actually superficial—the reason she checked in with her family so often was to assure them that she wasn't about to disappear again. She couldn't tell Ian that she felt like the love of her family was conditional and she had to work like hell to deserve it.

Because if Ian knew about any of that, it might change the way he was looking at her.

"*Wow* what? Is this a terrible idea or a great idea?" Ian asked.

"I think it's a fantastic idea," she said, getting her act together. She added, "I'm excited to finally meet him."

They ate quietly for a moment, Ian's brows furrowing. "Can I admit something?"

She swallowed, her heart racing at the word *admit*. "Of course."

"I feel like…I mean, I'm wondering if…" Ian bit the inside of his cheek in consternation. Suddenly his face changed. He looked as though he'd been about to say something that had just occurred to him but then changed his mind.

"What are you wondering, Ian?" Layla prompted, bracing herself for whatever was to follow.

"I think the accident—I think it may have been…a sign." He risked a glance at her.

Of all the things she had expected, this was the last. Signs? *Ian?* The man was all logic. Rationality. She wished on stars; she threw coins in fountains. He'd give her his spare change, but Ian never made wishes himself. He believed in hard work and doing what was right. He'd always teased Layla over her devotion to finding guidance from the universe—she looked everywhere from the Astro Poets' Twitter account to the buskers singing outside Pike Place Market.

In her defense, one time a busker had sung "You Can't Always Get What You Want" directly to her, and when she walked into her favorite gelato place, they were out of bacio. And Mercury was *definitely* retrograde the night Ian had ended things.

But the most undeniable sign was right in front of her, and it had come when the hospital called her because her ex was asking for her.

She tilted her head. "What do you mean?"

"I mean…" He raked his fingers through his hair. "I feel like I've been failing everyone in my life for the past couple of years."

"Ian—*what?*" Layla was stunned. "For as long as I've known you, I've watched you take care of every person in your life."

He opened his mouth, then something behind his eyes changed again.

"You're the best person I know," she assured him, needing him to believe her. If Ian was a failure, she was a human Blockbuster card. "You're not failing. At *anything*."

She watched him rub his eyes, something she knew he did only when he was stressed, before responding. "I don't see my parents as often as I should—I haven't been out to the island in eons—and...you..."

"What about me?" Layla's hands suddenly felt cold.

"It's the same thing with you and me. We haven't seen each other enough. We *don't* see each other enough. Because I let work get in the way."

"You have a demanding job," Layla said, her kneejerk response, but then she paused. How long had she secretly wanted to hear him say that? Could he *mean* it? Shoot, she should've googled *concussions* after all, but she'd been distracted by the cherry blossoms. In any case, there were two people in their relationship. So she added, "My job's demanding too, just in different ways."

"Yeah. But I think the universe is telling me it's time to back off a little. To reprioritize. Do you think that's stupid?" he asked, so honestly that her heart nearly shattered.

"No, of course I don't think that's stupid. You know I'm all about paying attention when the universe starts flicking your ear," she said, believing this now more than ever. "I think this perspective change is really beautiful. And I think good things can come from it."

"I'm promising myself I'll make the most important people in my life my top priority. That means you," he said, taking her hand. "And my parents, of course. And I want to repair things with Matt."

He'd never mentioned that things with Matt were *broken*. "What do you mean? Haven't you just grown apart?"

He winced again, and she felt guilty for pushing him too hard. But he clearly had more on his mind. "We had a falling-out years ago. I'm embarrassed to say how many years. And things had been rocky for a while before that. But at the hospital, before you came, I kept thinking about when Matt and I were young. When it was just the two of us. How can I have let that bond go? He's my brother, you know; he should be in my life. And if he's having a hard time, well, maybe I can help him."

"I bet he'll be thrilled to hear from you." She kissed his hand and released it. "But if you're going to call and invite Matt to live with you, you'll need something very important."

Ian squinted for a moment before the realization dawned on him. "Ah, yes. My phone was laid to rest yesterday."

"Your phone hath perished and is now in phone heaven with all the flip phones."

"And car phones."

"Don't forget rotaries."

"You and your love of rotary phones." Ian clucked his tongue and sighed. "Let's go get one now. I could use some fresh air."

"You sure?" she asked, dubious. Even though the store was only three or four blocks away, she didn't know if he was up to it.

"I'm sure." Ian sat up straight. "New day, new me. Now let's go get a new phone."

Ian walked slower than he normally did and wasn't as chatty, but the fresh air did seem to invigorate him. Layla vacillated between worry and the unexpected thrill of being back in his neighborhood, holding his hand as they passed their coffee place, the CVS, and the music store, where he'd patiently waited time and time again, answering work e-mails on his phone, as she flipped through secondhand vinyl. They passed the small greenspace where two adorable older gentlemen played chess every afternoon. Layla always cheered for the one in the fedora and open-collared shirt, while Ian cheered for his opponent with neatly combed hair and a tie.

"Get that queen, you deserve her," Layla encouraged Fedora today.

"Nah, you've got it in the bag," Ian told his favorite.

"Nice to see you two kids again," Fedora called after them. It was an innocent comment, but Layla's stomach still flipped. She checked Ian out in her periphery. He didn't react.

Purchasing a new phone was quick, but since his original phone, including the SIM card, was toast, Layla figured he'd lost all his contacts and pictures.

"Your memories," Layla said dramatically, clutching his arm.

"Layla," Ian said with a chuckle, "I backed my phone up. It's fine. Everything's on my hard drive at home."

"You can back your phone up on a hard drive?" Some people—particularly Ian—seemed to have instruction manuals on how to live a responsible life. She'd clearly played hooky the day they were handed out.

"Oh, Layla," Ian said, pulling her in for a hug. She let his arms surround her, resting her cheek on his chest. Hopefully he'd never look at that hard drive again. She wondered if it contained any evidence of their breakup.

He seemed to be looking for reasons to touch her just as much as she was. A sexy, gentle game of tag reminiscent of when they'd first gotten together. There'd always been some excuse, like an imaginary eyelash on her cheek or a crumb on his shirt—right over his chiseled abs. She always needed to be *very thorough* in wiping it off.

"Layla?" a voice behind them called as Ian was paying for his new phone. "I thought that looked like you."

Curse my distinctive style, she thought, trying to flatten her red raincoat, but it was too little, too late. Ian released her and she spun around to see Bernadette, a woman who had lived at the loft with her and Pearl briefly after graduation. She'd moved out when she'd scored a gig as Daisy Duck on a Disney cruise.

Ian shook Bernadette's hand and they introduced themselves. Layla beamed internally as she watched her old roommate give Ian the once-over, clearly impressed with his hotness (it was pretty impressive).

"It's nice to meet you," he said, and Layla could have sworn she heard Bernadette reply, "I'll say," under her breath.

"How are you?" Layla asked tightly. As fun as it was to show off Ian, Bernadette was a friend from Layla's early twenties, a wilder time in her life that Ian was not acquainted with. And that wasn't relevant to who she was now. Who *they* were now.

Bernadette's topknot bounced as she made a *so-so* hand gesture. "Auditioning for everything, getting nothing." She gave Ian another up-and-down. "This guy wouldn't know what I'm talking about. I'll bet he can get whatever he wants."

"I'm in finance, not acting," Ian said, clearly amused.

"Figures." Bernadette turned to Layla. "What about you? What are you up to?"

What was the fastest way to wrap this up? "I'm working at No—"

Before Layla could finish, Bernadette squealed, "Oh my God, I just remembered the last time I saw you. It was my goodbye party! Weren't you all over one of Pearl's twin brothers?"

Her instinct was to grab Ian by the hand and yell, *Let's get away from this pathological lunatic!* Instead, she avoided his eyes, laughed, and said quickly, "Whoa, are you sure that was me?" Mentally correcting: *It was both of Pearl's brothers, actually.* It was time to get Ian far, far away.

But before Layla could make an excuse and bolt, Bernadette lobbed one more grenade. She wagged her finger between Layla and Ian. "So, this must be new. That's exciting."

"What do you mean?" Layla asked, sweat beading at her chest and back.

"I ran into Pearl's roommate the other day—you know, the

guy who makes cheese? I swear he said you were single and he was hoping to make a move."

There was the largest, ugliest cavern of a pause. Actually, Layla wanted to fling herself *into* a cavern. And then Ian put his arm around her and squeezed. "You're going to have to tell the cheese guy that Layla's very much taken."

Layla nearly wept with relief. When she finally found her voice again, it came out just a little too loudly. "Anyway, we should get going. This poor guy got into an accident yesterday."

"Oh no," Bernadette cooed, looking ready to nurse Ian back to health herself.

That job's spoken for, sister, Layla thought, ready to throttle her. She finally got up the courage to look at Ian, whose face was unreadable. "Should we head back?"

"Sure," he agreed. "Nice to meet you, Bernadette."

"Yeah, you too. Let's catch up some time, Layla. Call me," she said, then cheekily added, "Either of you."

Layla prayed Ian wouldn't have any follow-up questions about Pearl's brother, partially because that night existed only as a vague drunken memory. And she couldn't even begin to think about the rest.

"She seemed…" Ian began once they were safely outside the store.

"Like a piece of work? Trust me, she is." Desperate to change the subject, she asked, "Are you going to text Matt as soon as you get home?"

"Yeah." He ducked as they walked under a cherry blossom tree with branches too low for his tall frame. They were moving even slower than they had on their meandering walk there. Layla had to admit, she was enjoying the lazy pace with him.

Ian took her hand, and she leaned her head against his arm briefly, taking in his sturdiness and the scent of his laundry detergent. "I have something else I want to run by you too."

Excitement brewed in her belly. "I'm listening."

"I've been thinking about the last thing I clearly remember. You know, the Mariners game?"

"Ah, yes," Layla said. "That's still it, huh?" *But for how long?* She worried her bottom lip. *He's happy. I'm happy. The universe is into this and I'm pretty sure the universe knows best.*

"Unfortunately, yeah. But didn't my parents invite us back to the island then?"

Layla's face lit up at the memory. Ian had splurged for good seats since Jeannie was such a big baseball fan. Like Layla, Craig was more interested in the stadium food. While Jeannie and Ian theorized about future trades and contracts, Layla and Craig had ranked hot-dog toppings (mustard the clear winner) and *cheers*-ed their oversize Diet Cokes. "They *did*, you're right," she said as if she hadn't mentally packed for the trip and then cried over its disappearance for the past two weeks.

It'd happened during the seventh-inning stretch. After Layla belted "Take Me Out to the Ball Game" with Jeannie and Craig, definitely embarrassing Ian, Jeannie had swatted him on the shoulder. "When are you going to bring Layla home?"

"Oh, I'd love to come," she gushed. "I've never been to the island." And Craig said, "It's settled. You two are officially invited and you're officially coming."

"Sooner rather than later," Jeannie added.

Layla had been slowly accepting that day would never come, but now Ian was saying, "Let's go visit my parents in Eastsound next weekend."

"I would love that," Layla said as they approached Ian's building again. "I'm one hundred percent in for a trip to Orcas Island."

"Good," Ian said. He held the door open for her.

Layla truly couldn't believe her luck. Not only were they back together, they were actually making progress in their relationship—*already*. The universe clearly knew what it was doing.

She headed inside, noting the look of fatigue on his face, the way his eyes were squinting. She would talk him into a nap once they got upstairs. Even if it meant she had to spoon him. *Especially* if it meant she had to spoon him.

CHAPTER SIX

"I'M SORRY, WHAT?" Pearl was gliding her rolling chair toward Layla by taking tiny little steps while seated. Layla was doing the same; they looked as if they were two tiptoeing, seated ballerinas.

It was Saturday night, and they were at Northwest End to help with the ticket booth and concessions for a traveling show. Since it was a performance night, they could dress as formally and outrageously as they wanted. Layla was in a 1950s swing dress, and Pearl was wearing a jumpsuit with a V so deep, Layla hoped she had plenty of double-sided tape, because she looked fantastic in it, and she would hate to see her best friend arrested for indecent exposure. Although the mug shot would be fire.

The business office where they both had desks was just off the lobby and otherwise empty, allowing them to speak freely. Sure, they could've snuck in to watch the show, but there were important things to catch up on.

"Ian doesn't remember that we broke up," Layla repeated, flushing again with the wonderful improbability of it all, making a little spin in her chair.

Pearl wasn't spinning. "So you're taking advantage of a man who has recently suffered a brain injury to live out a fantasy?"

"Pearl! *No*, that's not what I'm doing," Layla insisted, wondering if that was exactly what she was doing. She hurried to tell Pearl the same things she'd been telling herself for the past twenty-four hours. "When I picked him up from the hospital, the nurse was adamant about someone looking after him. And he was so relieved to see me. He *needed* me. He'd been asking for me all day! What was I supposed to do?"

Pearl tapped her chin with her index finger and pretended to think. "I don't know, maybe say, 'Hey, Ian, I will absolutely help you out. But just so you know, we broke up two weeks ago.'"

"I didn't want to alarm him," Layla protested. She stood up; the crinoline beneath her satin polka-dot dress swished as she poured more cheap wine into their red Solo cups. "Once we were together, though, it was like we *hadn't* broken up. He keeps talking about how this accident was a sign from the universe—"

"I'm sorry, *Ian* said that?" Pearl accepted her refill, considering this. "Well, what the hell do I know? I live with a billion roommates and all our bedroom walls are made of ugly bedsheets. Live and let live, baby."

Pearl's loft had no walls except around the bathroom, so they'd always improvised. Layla had loved her days of living in the loft with the paisley cotton non-walls, but now? She wouldn't trade her real ones.

From the theater, a pan flute began playing and the audience erupted in laughter. Layla vaguely regretted not watching the show. When was the last time she'd snuck in just to enjoy the evening? But she had big questions to ask.

"Pearl...is this a bad idea? Am I a bad person?" She knew what answer she wanted Pearl to give her, but she also trusted Pearl to tell her the truth. After all, she knew Layla better than most people. Even better than Layla's siblings, who were currently placing bets in the family text chain about whether she'd show up for Sunday dinner.

"I know it's only been one day," she continued, "but when we're together, it's like we're finally getting it right. I've never felt so comfortable with him, and he has this new perspective on what he wants out of life."

"And what does Ian want?" Pearl asked.

"*Me.* He wants *me.*" Layla bit her lip. She imagined herself waking up next to Ian every morning—a vision that was becoming closer and closer to reality. If she could just get her conscience, aka her best friend, on board. "You should see him, Pearl. He's still Ian, but Ian with a grander purpose. He wants to slow things down with work—"

"I adore the guy," Pearl said, cutting Layla off. "But I've witnessed him e-mailing under a table of pizzas on a Saturday night."

"I *know.*" Layla's defenses were rising, and she tried to keep her cool. She needed Pearl to understand—and then confirm—that things were different now. "This isn't just lip service. This is *action.* He wants us to go visit his parents on Orcas and he invited his brother to live with him. *In twenty-four hours.* I'm telling you, the universe is talking and we're both listening. Maybe we really are meant to be."

Pearl put her cup on the floor and righted it when it nearly toppled. She took Layla's face in her hands, squished her cheeks, and said gravely, "Then you hang on to him and thank the fucking universe he's back in your life. But pookie? I watched you crumble after one breakup with Ian Barnett. I pray there's no encore performance."

CHAPTER SEVEN

THE ROCKFORD FAMILY Sunday dinner was a mercurial beast, both the best and worst night of Layla's week. Or at least it was when she actually attended it.

Already, the Rockford Peaches text chain had nineteen new messages, and it was only ten a.m. They ranged from Do people still eat potato salad or is pasta salad in vogue (from her mom) to Is Layla showing up today? She's ghosting family dinner as often as she's ghosting this group chat (courtesy of Cecelia), followed by Jude's Did she run away with another guy with bad credit and a shower phobia? after which Layla's dad had chimed in with a lecture on being sensitive and a reminder that Layla had recently been dumped (*Thanks, Dad*). Even Rhiannon had added Too soon, Jude, but it wasn't like anyone could erase the offending text, so there it sat.

It had been two years since she'd run off with Randall—who actually *did* shower, but only when he was experiencing writer's block ("I need a shower epiphany," he'd mumble). But the thing about bad credit? That was true. A condition she'd learned was highly transmissible.

Thankfully, that was in the past. *This* week, her life was back on track and she could face them all again. It was only on her drive over that Layla realized her mother had been conspicuously silent after Jude's tasteless crack. That it had been only her dad and Rhiannon defending her.

Now, lurking for a final moment of peace in her car before she crossed the threshold into familial chaos, Layla bit her nail and took a quick peek at the matte satin tea-length dress she was bidding for on eBay. It had a killer V-neck *and* V-back. It would be perfect for the next time Ian invited her to one of his classy work functions. The kind that took place in an upscale restaurant, a live band playing romantic music while she coaxed him to hold her close and sway on the dance floor.

As hard as Layla was trying to honor the universe's current gift, there was a small, petty part of her that still had something to prove to her siblings, and that part was in full force today. As she finally got out of her car and headed toward the house, she remembered the T-shirt they'd given her for her twenty-second birthday. It said I HEART DIRTY BOYS WITH NO MONEY.

Well, wouldn't they be surprised to hear that the one good guy she'd chosen (sort of) had come crawling back, that she wasn't continuing to be the family screw-up. For two years, Layla's carefully curated Instagram account had showcased her as an adult with her shit together (for example, Here I am buying fresh produce from the farmers' market—*that I will inevitably forget about because I keep snacking on cheddar and sour cream Baked Lay's instead of crudités.* And Here I am looking studious at my administrative job—I'm even wearing glasses! *No, they're not prescription, but don't they make me look responsible?*). Today she was actually living that life instead of pretending to live it.

She put in another bid for the V-neck dress and stared at the front door. Layla had invited Ian to come today, but he'd wanted to try and do some work at home since he wasn't going into the office on Monday.

There was a part of her that was relieved he'd said no, since her family was unpredictable. She'd sent a text to the family chain two hours ago: Ian and I are back together. We don't like talking about the breakup, so please don't bring it up. But telling her siblings not to bring something up was like putting them in a room with a mysterious big red button and a sign beside it saying DO NOT TOUCH. Although what else could she do? It was a real damned-if-she-said-something, damned-if-she-didn't situation.

She unbuckled her seat belt, got out of the car, and steeled herself with a deep breath. For the most part, Layla really did love going to Bellevue, to the home she'd lived in since she was a kid and that had been passed down from her grandparents. Her grandfather had built the house with his own hands (Layla was adept at building sandwiches with her own hands but not much else). Inheriting the house was the main reason her parents had been able to afford to stay in the desirable city near Seattle, filled with natural beauty and new tech money.

The house sat on a rather large lot, giving Layla's nieces and nephews plenty of room to play. The kids were already out today, and Layla immediately joined them. They never judged her for not having a wedding ring or a "normal" job, only for her inability to do a cartwheel.

"*No*," said Izzie, aka Izzie-Bear (because at six, she was both cute and ferocious), stomping her foot. "You aren't keeping your legs straight."

"You gotta keep your legs straight," Desmond, also six, agreed solemnly.

In the middle of Layla's next attempt, which all nine of her nieces and nephews had gathered to watch, the back door opened, and Layla's mom hollered, "Come on in for dinner."

It broke Layla's concentration and she landed on her tailbone as eight miniature bodies took off running.

"You'll get it next time." Desmond placed his little hand on her back.

"Thanks, Des. I will certainly try." Layla brushed the grass off her pedal pushers and followed the kids inside. Her parents had set up two small card tables in the living room for the under-twenty-five crowd, and Layla eyed them longingly. The big kitchen table was for the adults.

Present were Layla's sister Rhiannon, her wife, Kit, and their three kids; Layla's sister Cecelia, her husband, Luis, and *their* three kids; Layla's brother Jude, his long-term partner, Rachelle, and their two kids; and Layla's brother Bobby and his toddler. Carmella, Bobby's wife, who traveled a lot for work, was the only one missing. Layla couldn't help but envy her a tiny bit.

Layla scanned the kitchen table as everyone gathered around choosing seats, wondering where to place herself. Her hesitancy made the decision for her, and she wound up between Rhiannon and Bobby.

The meal started out with much back-and-forth between the tables as her siblings sorted out what their kids were eating (the answer: mostly pretzel buns and grape juice). Once they were settled and had full plates, Bill took a fork to his glass to get everyone's attention. He and Rena exchanged a twinkly look and sang the hook to "Tell Me Something Good." They started every dinner off this way, a tradition that evoked both groans and cheers. Though if Layla were being honest, Rena seemed a little off today. Distant. And was it her imagination or had she avoided looking her way? Or, Layla thought, maybe Rhiannon's scolding text had just gotten to her—surely two missed dinners couldn't bother her mom *that* much?

Layla pushed down the guilt and rolled her eyes along with her siblings. It was a long-standing tradition that the meal started with everyone relating something good that had happened the previous week. She half listened to Cecelia talking about an upcoming vacation (it was really more of an educational retreat, which was typical Cece) and Jude talking about Little League games that had been won (Jude was the coach; Layla wasn't sure he realized he wasn't in the majors). After Rhiannon told everyone that her oldest daughter, Cassie, had tested into the gifted program, Layla was up. Usually, she had to scrape the bottom of the barrel for good news. This week felt different, but where to begin?

"Well," she began, stalling, "I..."

Her phone chimed and she whipped it out, grateful for the distraction.

"No phones at the table," her dad chided as though they were still teenagers. But Layla barely heard him because the message was from Ian. I'm outside. Is it too late to join you?

Without explanation, she bolted up from her chair and ran to the door, swerving around Bobby's toddler, who had escaped the living room and was crawling toward their table, pretending to be a dog. She opened the door, and her whole body lit up when she saw Ian standing there, looking sheepish.

"What's the point of a near-death experience if you don't actually change your ways?"

She threw her arms around him, and he hugged her back. "Thank you for coming," she said, her voice muffled in his chest.

"I promised I was making changes and I meant it," he whispered. "Besides, I've missed everyone."

"How are you feeling?" She pulled back, scanning his expression for any sign of pain.

"Layla." He chuckled and tucked a lock of her hair behind her ear. "You can stop worrying about me. I'm good."

Layla pulled him inside, both thrilled he was there and terrified her siblings were going to blow this somehow. She snaked Ian around the toys and tables in the living room, and her heart warmed at all the yelled hellos from the squirming half of her family. The exception was Desmond, who, instead of hello, yelled, "I saw a bunny this morning, Ian Barnett!"

The vibe in the kitchen was very different. Her parents' taste was eclectic, and the various antique vases on display and the whimsical wallpaper adorned with hummingbirds and lemons reflected that. But it wasn't disorganized, and she'd never been ashamed to have Ian come home with her. On the contrary, she liked sharing her world with him. And her world liked him right back. As soon as Bill spotted Ian, he enthusiastically got up and procured another chair. "Ian, hello! Welcome," he said, squeezing the chair in next to Layla's seat.

"My something good just arrived," Layla sang, and Bill beamed at her. Rena smiled too, Layla was pretty sure, although her mother was busy filling up a plate for Ian, so Layla couldn't see her face clearly.

"Now can we talk about 'something nauseating'?" Bobby quipped. Layla elbowed him in the ribs.

"Welcome back, Ian," Cecelia said. "I guess we scared you off for a while."

"We didn't scare him off," Jude said. "Layla did."

Ian sent Layla a puzzled look that she pretended not to notice. She gave Jude the finger as their parents were settling back in.

"Very mature, you nerd-bomber," Jude said wryly.

"You're both middle-aged children." Rhiannon brushed her asymmetrical aubergine hair out of her eyes.

"Layla couldn't scare me off if she tried," Ian said gamely, accepting the circulating bowl of pasta salad. Layla loved that he never backed down from her overbearing siblings. She ignored the puzzled expressions around the room, her heart racing. How was she going to get through this dinner without someone exposing their breakup?

"Oh yeah?" Cecelia asked, taking his question as a challenge. Before Layla could loudly change the subject, Cece continued, "Did you know about the fan letter Layla wrote to Shaggy from *Scooby-Doo*, offering to let him sleep on our couch if he was ever in Bellevue?"

Layla laughed along with Ian, relieved the story had nothing to do with their relationship. She'd forgotten about that. One of the best things about hanging out with her family was their shared history, that they saw the full picture of her.

"Did Layla tell you about the time she got so drunk in high school, she streaked through the marching band's practice?" Jude asked. Rachelle glowered at him disapprovingly. Ian raised his eyebrows in surprise.

This time Layla didn't laugh, and she hadn't forgotten about that. One of the *worst* things about hanging out with her family was their shared history, that they saw the full picture of her— including parts she would prefer Ian didn't see. As for the members of the marching band? Well, there wasn't much she could do at this point about all the parts of Layla *they'd* seen.

"Did Layla tell you—" Bobby began, but Layla managed to send him a look so intimidating, it shut him up. Normally, it was best not to resist Bobby's teasing—even as an adult, he thrived on getting a reaction out of her—but Layla would be damned if Bobby's big mouth was going to interfere with the buzz of having Ian beside her again.

"Why don't we stop talking about Layla and get back to everybody's something good?" Rhiannon said gallantly. "Mom, you haven't gone yet."

"Oh." Rena seemed caught off guard, as though her mind had been a million miles away.

"What's going on with you?" Layla asked, shoving aside another shiver of guilt. "Any piano concerts coming up?"

"No, we're done for the year. Actually, I was thinking of

starting a new project. Since you kids have all been out of here for a while," Rena said.

"With the exception of Lay—" An entire table of dirty looks cut Bobby off. Layla thought of the previous Sunday evening, which she'd spent in her peaceful apartment with only Deano to contend with, not an entire table of Rockfords. Shame heated her cheeks and she hoped, *prayed*, this wouldn't scare Ian away. Again.

"Anyway," Rena continued, blatantly ignoring Bobby's interruption, "I think it's time for me to do a little redecorating. Mix things up, you know? Maybe turn one of your old bedrooms into a dedicated music room or a proper playroom for the grandkids."

"We're reclaiming our house," Bill added good-naturedly. He rubbed at the stubble on his cheeks (he'd never been good at shaving, always leaving patches) and the cleft in his chin. "That means you rascals need to take all your old stuff with you. We've been getting after you for years, but today it happens."

"There's too much clutter," Rena agreed.

"Are you sorry you came yet?" Layla said to Ian out of the side of her mouth. "Seems like we're actually here to work."

"Not sorry for a second. No such thing as a free meal." He took her hand under the table and gave it a squeeze.

Once plates were cleared, Bill heavily supervising the grandchildren as they tidied up, Rena called Layla and her siblings into the study.

"Is everything okay, Mom?" Cecelia asked gently, placing a hand on Rena's arm. Cece's mind often went to worst-case scenarios, a trait that was magnified by her career in social work. "What's inspired all this?"

"Everything's fine, don't be silly." Rena patted her hair. Layla noticed that she'd recently stopped dyeing it, and her natural silver-gray was finally coming through. She'd also gotten a pixie cut, revealing bone structure that let her pull it off. "I've just wanted to redecorate for a while. And I have all this stuff from when you were growing up. Art projects, report cards, diaries." Rena indicated a pile of boxes in the corner. "Can you go through them, pick out what you want to keep and what I can recycle? I'm going to go get started on dessert." As she turned to leave, she kindly nudged Ian's shoulder. "Ian, you don't have to get dragged into this. Why don't you come play Monopoly with the kids?"

"Is that okay with you?" Ian looked over at Layla earnestly.

There were minefields in each scenario. If she told him to go, a kid might let something slip, like ask why he hadn't come to Izzie-Bear's school play. If she kept him close, he'd be in the same room as her siblings.

Oh yeah. That second scenario was *much* worse.

"Go. Save yourself," she blurted, pushing him out of the study and praying the kids stuck to board-game capitalism.

Ever the oldest child, Rhiannon gave Jude and Bobby a push over to the boxes. She carefully removed her array of silver bangles, as if she was about to get her hands dirty. Cece, who always followed Rhiannon's lead, passed the top boxes back to the brothers and grabbed one to go through on her own. Layla waited for them to clear out of the corner, busying herself with finding some good going-through-old-boxes music.

There was a record player against the wall and a shelf of albums that her father had arranged according to decade. She flicked through the crooners, her preference, and tried to find something they could all enjoy. Sixties folk rock, seventies rock, eighties new wave... maybe she could get out of sorting through dusty boxes if she just played DJ.

"Stop everything, you guys need to see this," Cece suddenly exclaimed. Rhiannon, Jude, and Bobby leaned toward the eight-by-ten photograph in her hand. Not wanting to be left out, Layla scrambled over.

"Is this from Halloween or something?" Jude asked, barking a laugh.

It was Rena, only much younger, with long blond wavy hair. She was wearing a top with a plunging neckline and spaghetti straps. From the waist down, she seemed to be draped in various flowy shawls.

"You think Mom went as Stevie Nicks one year?" Rhiannon snatched the photograph from Cece to take a closer look.

"There's a microphone stand and a band in the back," Layla chimed in. "That'd be a pretty elaborate costume."

"Yeah. Hey, look at that gomer on the drum set and the one holding the bass." Bobby chuckled at their feathered hair. Both men were staring intently at the camera, clearly desperate to be seen as moody sexpots.

"Lead guitarist is hot," Rhiannon said, tapping the lanky brunette in bell-bottoms.

"These women are definitely smoke-shows," Layla agreed. "*Mom!* Can you come here? We just learned about your double life!"

Within seconds, a somewhat alarmed Rena appeared in the doorway. "What double life?"

Bill's head popped up behind her. "Double life?"

Rhiannon flipped the photo around and Layla watched Rena's pale, freckled skin flush an unexpected strawberry. Her father, however, appeared delighted.

"They found your old band photo," Bill exclaimed.

Even though they were looking at the evidence, this confirmation was still shocking. In all the photo albums, the anecdotes, the history Layla'd learned about her mother, she had never heard about a band.

"Please tell me your stage name was Rena Glamour," Bobby said.

"Were you guys as incestuous as Fleetwood Mac?" Jude

asked. "Because the lead guitarist is clearly the only good option. Where did you find these other dweebs?"

"I know you said you and Dad were set up by mutual friends," Cecelia said thoughtfully. "But was that a lie? Was Dad your groupie?"

Layla laughed, glad for once not to be on the receiving end of the room's attention. "Did he throw his underwear on the stage?"

"Do you still take requests?" Rhiannon asked. "I'm pretty sure, apart from 'Tell Me Something Good,' the only thing I've heard you sing in years is 'Itsy Bitsy Spider.'"

Rena had yet to respond. Layla thought her eyes looked a little unfocused.

"I don't know why you're all so surprised," Bill finally said. "All five of you are named after songs."

"Yeah, but we assumed that was because of you." Layla pointed at her father. "You're the one with the vinyl collection that would make any hipster weep with envy."

"Did either of these douche-canoes weep with envy when you got together with Dad?" Jude asked. "Seriously, what were their deals?"

On closer inspection of the photo, Layla saw that both men were wearing fringed vests without shirts underneath. She made a mental note to look for something fringed later. The douche-canoes hadn't pulled the vests off, but Layla damn well could.

"Who cares about those guys." Cecelia grabbed the picture. "Can we all just agree what a goddess Mom is? I mean, look at her!"

"Iconic," Layla agreed. And it was true. Her mom was positively luminous as the lead singer of...Layla squinted at the writing on the drum. "Heaven Under the El?"

"We got our name from that poem by Allen Ginsberg. And

two of the members were from Chicago." She raised her eyebrows at Jude. "The *douche-canoes*."

"How old were you?" Layla asked.

"Oh God, that would have been—what?" Rena exhaled and glanced at Bill. "Right after college?"

Every new piece of information begged more questions and a little more teasing. Finally, Rena waved them all off and took the picture in her hands. A million emotions passed across her face. "First of all, that record collection is mostly mine, you should know. Your dad just likes to play DJ. Second, our band did sound a little like Fleetwood Mac, but I didn't date any of the other members. Although I did kiss Juliette once."

"Is that the lead guitarist?" Rhiannon squealed, leaning forward to high-five Rena, who allowed a little grin as she obliged.

"Third, we played our last show when I was pregnant with *you*, kid." Rena directed this to Rhiannon. "The late nights and equipment lugging just got too hard."

"Do you miss it?" The question left Layla's lips before she could think it through. She watched her mother's eyes get a little misty for the briefest moment, but then Rena shook her head. "Being your mom was way better. I don't regret a thing."

But as Rena gave the photograph back to them, Layla wondered if that was true.

CHAPTER EIGHT

"DO YOU THINK he'll want to write by the window or by the closet? Is the window distracting?"

Layla had never seen Ian so insecure. In fact, she wasn't sure she'd ever seen Ian insecure *period*. He'd kept his promise about not going into the office today, but he'd sounded so antsy when Layla called to check on him that she'd ducked out of work early and dreamed up this desk project to keep him occupied.

They had somehow managed to fit the small desk, a flea-market find of Layla's years ago that she'd always intended to refinish, into the back of Ian's Audi (thankfully, the seats folded down). Getting it *out* of the car had been a comedy of errors that made Layla laugh so hard, she fell into a bush. Ian helped her out of the bush and lovingly and painstakingly removed every tiny leaf from her mini-bouffant without so much as disturbing the wide hairband holding her do in place.

They were now camped out on Ian's deck sanding down the desk. Finally restoring it and giving it new glory felt good. Layla hoped Ian's brother would appreciate all the effort Ian was putting in. She held up the paint swatches they'd looked at that morning. They were leaving the top its natural oak, but she wondered if the blue-gray they'd chosen for the drawers was too boring. She eyed the emerald-green swatch.

Unwittingly, she flashed back to that LA apartment again. To the dull, stained walls, to the way they'd rummaged for used furniture so Randall would have somewhere to put his laptop. At first, it had been exciting, an *experience*. They'd eaten their meals sitting on musty pillows on the floor and told each other it was romantic, *bohemian*, instead of just the beginning of lower back pain. But then things had changed. She could still feel the thud of Randall slamming the bedroom door shut, somehow always angry, when she went for long walks in their neighborhood, never feeling at home. She was once chased by an unwell woman carrying a twenty-four-pack of Bud who accused Layla of taking up too much of the sidewalk.

"Layla?" Ian's voice brought her back to the present. To his sunny deck with its matching furniture. To the desk they were sanding and painting together. "What do you think? Where should it go?"

"I don't know about Matt, but I think I'd prefer a desk by the window. Staring at a blank wall feels too on-the-nose for a writer."

Randall staring, his face stony, scary in its intensity. Layla swatted the image away. She didn't want Randall to color her impressions of Matt just because they were both writers. *Allegedly.* In reality, Layla was dubious. As far as she knew, Matt had spent the past several years doing anything but writing. His list of odd jobs was long. A farmhand, Ian thought, and maybe a pet-store clerk? And she knew how being a writer had worked out for Randall. Regardless, she was determined to keep an open mind because reconnecting with Matt was important to Ian, and Ian was important to her.

"What do *you* think?" she asked, pushing herself completely away from LA and back to Ian's condo. "You know Matt. What would he prefer?"

Ian paused, the square of sandpaper slipping from his tired fingers, as he contemplated something. "Sometimes I wonder if I really *do* know Matt."

"Tell me about him. About what you do know." Layla picked the sandpaper up and handed it to Ian. It would be easier for him to talk freely if she kept him busy, loosened him up with a little labor. She selected her own new square and they sanded together. Eventually he spoke.

"Matty has a hard time staying in one place. You think he's fine because he's sitting down, quiet and still. So still. And then, without warning, he'll leap up and just take off."

Layla watched Ian give a half smile at the thought. She and Matt might get along after all. Someone whose inner life burbled and banged around until he physically had to react...she could understand that.

"He's coming here from New Mexico?" Layla asked, crawling on her hands and knees to the other side, noticing Ian watching her ass. She gave him a wink. "Busted."

"I could watch you crawl around this desk all day," he said, and her heart fluttered. And then he added, "No, New Mexico was months ago. Matt's coming from California. I think he was working with animals, but I'm not sure. My mom talks to him, then she tells Craig, and then Craig sends me these text updates. Usually *as* my mom talks to Matty. So I'm getting everything thirdhand."

"Wait." Layla stopped sanding to laugh. "Craig basically live-tweets Jeannie and Matt's phone conversations for you? Maybe you'll get more out of Matt if you talk to him directly."

"Technically Craig live-*texts* me, but yes." He began to say something else and stopped.

"Ian?" She put down the sandpaper. "What's up?"

"I've called Matt myself a couple of times." He nodded as though trying to convince himself of something. "It's...the conversations are pretty monosyllabic on his side right now, but it's a start. And *you* have dust on your freckles." Ian moved from the squatting position to sit back more comfortably on the old sheet they'd put down to protect his outdoor rug. Inside, Dean Martin was singing "I've Got My Love to Keep Me Warm." It was widely considered to be a holiday song, but Layla was almost always cold, so she thought of it as a year-round tune. And it wasn't like Ian was going to put on music himself. He always told her he didn't care what they listened to.

"Some would say I have a dusting of freckles," Layla shot back cheekily, lowering herself down beside him. Her clogs only reached to his midcalf when she stretched her legs out.

"What you have," Ian said, leaning in and using his thumb to brush her cheek, "is dust on your dusting of freckles."

Layla felt a tingle of excitement, almost long forgotten. But she knew Ian was supposed to be taking it easy and she wasn't sure how that applied here. She couldn't exactly text Dr. Carroll and ask, *When is it okay to jump my boyfriend's bones again?* She'd googled *How long should you wait after a concussion to have sex* but had gone down a rabbit hole of conflicting advice. Her plan had been to wait until Ian was well enough to make a move on *her*. But. There he was. Leaning back on his hands, hair shining in the sunlight. Lips parted ever so slightly. Wearing those torn jeans and a T-shirt the color of a blue jay, the cotton stretching across his chest and biceps in the most alluring...

Maybe sex was off the table (*Is it? Damn it, Google, make up your mind!*), but kissing had to be okay, right? She leaned in and brushed her nose softly against his before their lips slowly met. The heat between them ratcheted up. He brought a hand up to cup the back of her head. She grasped the edge of his T-shirt, her nails grazing the muscle beneath. Ian shivered in response, kissing her harder, faster. Her corduroy skirt was riding up under his hands and she was almost ready to tear off her short-sleeved sweater and give the neighbors a show when Ian's phone buzzed.

"Do you want to…" she managed to ask without her lips leaving his for long.

"Ignore it," Ian said, pulling her onto his lap so she was straddling him.

The sun was hot on the backs of her arms; Ian was hot beneath her. Layla felt deliciously alive with frisky need. But the buzzing continued. Incessantly.

"Your phone's cockblocking me," Layla said. She was about to plunge her fingers into his hair but remembered his injuries. She paused, and so did he, and the heat between them cooled one molecule at a time.

"Why did you stop touching me?" he asked, so sweet and confused she wanted to kiss him all over again.

"I'm worried about hurting you," she admitted.

He nodded, then flipped his phone over to look at the screen. She registered the frustration that flashed in his eyes before he rearranged his face into a more serene expression. "It's work…stuff."

"Ah." Layla un-straddled Ian and plonked down on the sheet again. She knew that he wanted to put up work/life boundaries and that his job was likely to resist. "It's okay if you need to deal with something, Ian."

"Yeah." His eyes fluttered closed briefly. When he opened them again, they were smoldering. "Just so we're clear, if I could, I'd toss this phone off the balcony and pick up where we left off."

Her stomach dipped as heat shot through her again. She managed to nod as he went inside to take the call. She heard the sliding door of the condo next door open and then close. She peered around the concrete pillar that divided the two decks and caught a glimpse of Ian's gorgeous neighbor, the one who looked like Margot Robbie. For once, Layla was unbothered. She sat back. Who cared anymore? She didn't. Not after Ian had kissed her like that; not when his gaze alone could make her weak in the knees.

But at the thought of small talk, especially with someone who might have noticed she'd been a bit...absent lately, Layla too scurried inside. Ian was just ending his call.

"Hey," he said, setting his phone on the table and sitting down.

"Hey." She adjusted her skirt and smoothed down her hair, wondering if they could silence his phone and bring the mood back in here.

"I had a really good time out there," he said with a wink, gesturing to the balcony.

"Me too." Her heart sped up and she stepped toward him.

"But I also think it's okay if we move slowly again," he said, stopping her in her tracks. Her mind froze. As it thawed, she recalled how long they'd waited to sleep together when they'd first started dating. At the time, she'd still been reeling from Randall—not that Ian knew *that*—but still, he'd seemed to sense her hesitation and respectfully let her take the lead.

"Again?" she inquired, trying to sound innocent. She wished she *were* innocent.

"Yeah, since the accident," he clarified. "It shook us both up."

She exhaled a relieved metric ton of air. And a little disappointment. And, although she refused to acknowledge it, a smidge of guilt too. But if time was what Ian needed, he could have every second in the world. Their relationship had so many more layers than just their physical chemistry. She crossed over to him, and he stood up to take her into his arms. She planted a kiss on his sandy cheek.

"Okay, let's take things slow," she said, stepping out of his embrace and slowly tracing the neckline of her top with her fingertips. She put on her sex-kitten voice. "But when we're ready to speed up? Mmm, you'd better look out, sailor."

Ian laughed. "Noted."

"Now let's get back to that desk. I think it's ready for paint." She sashayed away, giving her hips an extra pop, knowing that he was watching.

"How are things going with the ex-new-boyfriend?" Pearl asked over her shoulder as she poured coffee into their favorite work mugs at the office's kitchen counter. It was Wednesday, but Pearl's mug said MONDAYS, AMIRITE? with a picture of a cat that looked just enough like Garfield to make its point but not enough to warrant a cease-and-desist. Layla's was a floral number with swirly script that said OKAYEST EMPLOYEE. They'd both come from the kitschy shop across the street, which Layla admittedly loved. For her and Ian's first Christmas together, Layla had had the shop make a mug for Ian that said PART-TIME HERO, FULL-TIME DREAMBOAT in honor of the bar fight he'd broken up the night they met.

"Things with Ian are *perfect*," Layla said, staring dreamily into her OKAYEST EMPLOYEE mug of okayest coffee. "I feel like I'm Deborah Kerr, and Cary Grant and I have finally reunited."

"I understood, like, thirty percent of that statement, but if you're happy, baby, I'm happy. Now let's go figure out what this all-hands-on-deck meeting is about."

Layla's (new) white go-go boots clomped on the old wood flooring as they made their way to the foyer, where three long folding tables were set up in a U-shape. It was the format Manjit and Charlene always used for the first read-through of a new show, which all employees were invited to listen in on. But as far as Layla knew, the next show wasn't scheduled for another month or so.

She and Pearl took a seat near one end, as the middle table was unofficially reserved for higher-ranking employees. While the exact hierarchy wasn't stated, Layla and Pearl knew where they belonged, and it wasn't with the heads of the departments.

The tables filled up with Northwest End employees. Manjit and Charlene, seated dead center, both looked as though they'd been up all night. Even on the most stressful days, they were always well put together, so their rumpled clothes and possible bedheads were shocking.

"Thank you for coming so quickly," Charlene began. She took off her glasses and rubbed her eyes. "Manjit? Do you want to fill everyone in?"

Manjit pursed her lips and steepled her fingers under her chin. "There was an emergency meeting called by the board of directors last night in regard to Aaron Masfield, the emerging playwright for our next production."

The room went silent.

"Apparently, he's been accused of plagiarism." Manjit folded her arms, then put her hands on the table, nervous energy radiating from her. "His last play, the one that was produced at the university and that got him so much press and attention, they're saying he stole it from an undergrad."

"An undergrad Aaron then had kicked out of the school under false pretenses, likely to cover up his plagiarism," Charlene said.

There was a collective groan as the news sank in. If they moved ahead with Aaron's play amid a scandal, it could damage the theater's reputation. But if they didn't have a show featuring an emerging playwright, something this year's funding was dependent on, their ability to secure future grants would be at risk.

Layla and Pearl exchanged worried looks. For an irresponsible split second, Layla wished this *would* lead to layoffs. What would she do next? But then she thought about her credit card bills and reminded herself she loved being so close to (usually) amazing shows.

"When I called this all-hands-on-deck meeting, I meant it," Manjit said. "We have just shy of seven weeks to pull a new show together. If any of you have suggestions for playwrights, I'm open to them."

"But," Charlene added, "we have certain guidelines based on our grant applications for the year. We made promises to the organizations that fund us, and if we break those promises, best-case scenario, they cut back our funding; worst-case, they cut it altogether."

There were murmurs and then a few suggestions, most of them involving remounting popular shows they'd done in the past.

Manjit sighed, running her hands through her thick, dark hair. "According to our grant, the show needs to feature an emerging playwright who *hasn't* had work produced professionally yet. Remounting an old show wouldn't qualify."

Layla's phone buzzed and she checked the message. It was from Ian, saying he'd swing by at 5:30 so they could meet Matt for dinner. Nervous energy burbled inside her. Up to this point, she'd been worrying about giving Matt a fair, non-Randall-influenced shake, but it occurred to her now that it was just as important for Matt to like *her*.

"I don't want to scare anyone," Charlene said, her words snapping Layla back to attention. "But if we don't find a new playwright soon, we could be in some trouble."

"Do I need to start updating my résumé?" a voice called from the back, attempting to break the tension. A few people chuckled, but when Layla saw the expressions on Manjit's and Charlene's faces, she bit her bottom lip. Having worked on the grants, she knew how much money was at stake, and one slipup could destroy Northwest's future.

"Is anyone here writing in their spare time?" Manjit asked,

her nose wrinkling in a way that indicated this was not her first choice. "Or maybe you know someone who has a brilliant script collecting dust in their drawer?"

When no one spoke up, Charlene took over. "You have my full permission to spend time this afternoon scrolling through social media and checking in with old friends." Charlene looked down and noticed her shirt was misbuttoned but only patted it absentmindedly.

Layla had never seen her bosses so desperate. But she knew she didn't have any gems hiding in her Instagram or Twitter followers, where the numbers were few. Besides, apart from some family members, the Venn diagram of Layla's followers and Pearl's was a perfect circle, and Layla had deleted her original accounts. The ones she used now were only a couple of years old and designed to distance herself from her past. Mostly the people she'd dated.

Her early twenties had been wasted on Petey B., a cute guy who made his living busking, doing death-defying stunts in front of crowds at Pike Place Market. His biceps were almost as big as her head, but he had a sweet disposition. Whenever her family teased her about dating a "street gymnast," she'd get defensive and say, "He's a performance artist!" Which was, coincidentally, the same thing Petey B. had said sanctimoniously to Layla when he'd dumped her after she graduated from college, claiming that they were on divergent paths in life. The truth was, he had a direction (ridiculous though it seemed), and she had none.

She'd wasted the next portion of her dating life on a soulful singer-songwriter named Garrison. Their love had been of the mad, can't-keep-our-hands-off-each-other variety, but a year into their relationship, Garrison got his big break: opening for a Canadian musician named Hawksley Workman who was just starting to get some radio play in the Pacific Northwest. Layla discovered Garrison was cheating on her by following the tour photos and videos posted online. She'd been humiliated. It was worse than the breakup with Petey B., whom she had developed a sense of humor about by that time. To make matters worse, Garrison had ruined her ability to listen to Hawksley Workman.

And then there was Randall.

In her mid-twenties, she'd vowed not to date any more performers of any kind. So Randall, a passionate and adorably grumpy screenwriter, had seemed perfect. He'd been sexy in a young–Marlon Brando way, usually wearing a uniform of beat-up jeans and a fitted white T-shirt. And he was practical—he'd just gotten his degree in screenwriting and planned to move to LA to kick-start his career. Within months, she'd been addicted to Randall like the most potent and beckoning of drugs. When they ran away together, both of their disapproving families in the dark about it, Layla remembered thinking: *If we're doing this for love, how wrong can it be?*

As it turned out, *so* wrong.

"All right, everyone," Charlene bellowed, shaking Layla from her reverie. "Get to your social media pages, get back to work, let's figure this out."

"Yikes. That was unexpected," Pearl whispered as they pushed back their chairs.

Layla nodded and made her way to her desk, thoughts of Randall, of how easily she could screw up her life again, twisting her insides. Instead of scrolling through social media like the rest of her coworkers, Layla allowed herself to fall back on a little dissociative stress-shopping, scouring ModCloth and Etsy because, really, could one have too many vintage jeweled hair clips when humidity season was nigh? And there was that little serotonin bump she got when she clicked *Add to cart* and the bigger bump she got from clicking *Check out*.

By the time Ian arrived to pick her up at the end of the day, she was feeling a little better. Several ideas were being kicked around, and the office was filled with a unifying determination. Ian waved to her through the glass door of the lobby before opening it up, looking happy to see her.

She waved back and decided to take a page from his book: Focus on the future and let this new chapter really mean something. Now was not the time to dwell on the past. Not on the likelihood that those hair clips were overpriced, and definitely not on old boyfriends.

CHAPTER NINE

"HI, HANDSOME," SHE said, standing on her tiptoes to kiss him.

"Hello there. Boy, do you look good in a miniskirt," Ian said when she gently pulled away.

"You like?" Layla did a little twirl and tried to ignore the images of him pulling it—and the go-go boots—right off her. Especially since, as of today, Matt would be living in Ian's condo. Having him there would definitely help them commit to taking things slowly.

She grabbed Ian's hand and they wandered out to his car.

"What do you want to listen to? Yacht rock?" she asked as he turned the key in the ignition. Once they'd gone to a restaurant at a marina and a nearby boat had blasted Steely Dan through their entire meal.

"Empty threats," he chided. "We both know you're going to put it on the Sinatra channel."

"Damn straight," she said and pushed the preset button she was thrilled to see was still reserved for her favorite channel. "Call Me Irresponsible" came through the speakers, which she immediately took personally. She wanted to tell Bobby Darin to mind his own business.

She was about to turn down the music when Judy Garland started singing "Come Rain or Come Shine." *Much better.*

"I realized as I was on my way to pick you up," Ian said, "that I've never been to one of the shows at your theater. That feels weird. Is that weird?"

"It's not that weird, considering our work schedules," Layla said, inwardly flinching at how close this was to what he'd said to her when they broke up. "Anyway, there may not be a show to see. We found out the playwright who's supposed to work with us is a skeeze and so we're firing him. Manjit and Charlene are freaking out."

"What's the plan?" Ian, ever the fixer, asked. "Do they have a replacement show or will they just cancel the whole thing?"

Layla shrugged. "We're looking for a new writer."

"You could ask Matty," Ian offered, though even he looked dubious at the suggestion. Plenty of people claimed to be writers, but someone who was focused enough to put something coherent and moving together in a short time was another thing altogether. Everything Layla knew about Matt indicated he wasn't a go-getter who carted around a drawer of polished scripts.

"Maybe." Layla shifted, turning toward Ian. "Enough theater drama. Talk to me about the wild world of finance."

Ian grinned at her and spent the rest of the drive recounting the meetings he'd had over the past two days about hedge funds and shareholders. Evidently, he was feeling well enough to keep up at work, despite taking Monday off. She found herself making polite listening noises and just basking in the moment, the simple act of telling Ian about her day and then having him do the same. Her mind floated to her favorite fantasy, in which they lived together, catching up each evening, lazily making crepes each Sunday morning, laughing as Layla—wearing those heeled slippers with fuzzy pink-feathered toes—put a dollop of cream on Ian's nose, which he would bat off, and one thing would lead to another and...

"Hey," he said at a stop sign as they waited for the post-work pedestrians to cross. "Where'd you go just now? Am I boring you?"

"No, *no*," she insisted, making a mental note to google those sexy-heeled-slipper things. And then, honestly: "I'm just having a really nice time with you already and we haven't even gotten to the dinner part yet."

His eyes crinkled as he smiled. "You're such a wackadoodle," he said lovingly.

"What? I really like being in the car with you, listening to music—"

"Half listening to me tell boring work stories?"

"You, my egregiously tall, unbearably good-looking man, could *never* be boring," she assured him.

"Well, if you think I'm interesting, just wait until you meet my baby brother." Ian's dimple appeared, but his smile wavered.

It clicked. Ian was chattering about work because he was nervous. She thought back to his indecisiveness about where to put the desk for Matt, about how seriously he was taking this step with his long-lost brother. Her heart melted a little for him and she promised herself to make sure tonight went well no matter what.

Ian pulled his car into the parking lot of their favorite hole-in-the-wall sushi place and raised his eyebrows. "You ready? I feel like I should warn you about Matt somehow, but I don't even know what to say."

"I think it's great he came out here so quickly. And, hey, if you love him, I'll love him," Layla assured Ian.

"I'm pretty sure he came out here so quickly because my mom wanted him to check up on me." Ian rolled his eyes, though not without affection for his overprotective mother.

They got out of the car and walked to the entrance, but there,

Layla stopped cold, because next door, in a little shop with rows and rows of sheet music, a little shop with a sign offering piano, guitar, drum, and trumpet lessons for all ages, was someone who looked very much like Rena Rockford.

"Hang on," she said to Ian. "You go ahead so you aren't late—I just have to check something."

"Everything okay?" Ian asked, his brow furrowing.

"Yeah, I just...speaking of moms, I think I see mine." It wasn't totally surprising that Rena was in a music shop in the city, but it was a little strange that she hadn't texted or called Layla to tell her she'd be around.

"Huh. Well, say hi to Rena for me," Ian said, and he disappeared into the restaurant.

Layla opened the door to the music shop; it had a bell at the top that gave a little jingle. She expected her mom to turn and see her, but Rena Rockford seemed to be having a very heated conversation with the good-looking silver-haired Indian man behind the counter. Neither one of them acknowledged her presence.

"I don't know what to tell you," the man was saying. "Of course I've thought about it."

"And?" The voice coming from Layla's mother was unfamiliar. Rena sounded tremulous. She smoothed down her already smooth silvery hair, jangling her chandelier earrings. She shifted her weight in her light brown cowboy boots, the handkerchief hem of her patchwork dress swaying as she did. The last time Layla had seen her mother this dressed up was...never.

The vibe was odd. Layla felt like she was barging in on something, and before she could let her brain muse on just what she was barging in on, her mouth opened and let out a far too loud *"Hi."*

The man and Rena whipped their heads toward Layla like members of a synchronized swimming team.

"Hi, can I help you?" the man said. He was in his mid- to late sixties but was wearing a burgundy hoodie with a threadbare T-shirt underneath. She couldn't see his feet behind the counter, but she'd bet money that he had on either Vans or Converse sneakers.

"Layla!" Rena exclaimed, sounding surprised and not in a good way. "Did I tell you my favorite Bellevue music store just closed? Now I have to trek all the way here for sheet music."

"Or you could order it online," Layla pointed out, not missing the way the man behind the counter narrowed his eyes at Rena's explanation. There was no way the tension between them was about sheet music.

"I like to see it all in person, you know that," Rena trilled as though she and Layla had often discussed this. "What are you up to?"

"Just having dinner with Ian and his brother next door." Layla shifted her weight, an echo of her mother's action. The go-go boots might look fantastic, but boy, after a few hours…

"Well, I won't keep you." Rena looked back at the man. "Or you, for that matter." She gave Layla a hug that lasted just a few seconds too long and left.

Her mother had never brushed her off like that. Layla considered texting her siblings—or maybe just Rhiannon—to relay the bizarre exchange. For once, she had dirt her siblings didn't. For once, the Rockford Peach being shady wasn't Layla. But the story would travel through the other four Rockford kids like the gossip it was, and Layla knew firsthand what it was like to be the subject of family chatter. She'd never do that to her mom. Not when there was probably a very reasonable explanation for why her mother looked like someone showing off her fabulous mall makeover. *Probably.*

As the bell jingled, Layla turned to the man behind the counter. But he was disappearing into a back room.

CHAPTER TEN

WITH SUCH AN important dinner ahead, Layla tried to put the odd exchange with her mother out of her mind. She scanned the restaurant and saw Ian turn to her and beam, his dimple clear even from a distance. Following the track of his smile, she weaved her way through the bustle of customers and servers.

As she approached the booth, she realized that Matt was both what she'd expected and *not* what she'd expected at all. His hair was so dark, it might've been black, though she'd need to see it in natural light to be sure. It was wavy and pushed away from his face, which was sporting some scruff. Ian was always clean-shaven—something she appreciated because of his swoony jawline. But Matt's almost-beard suited what she knew about him. He was wearing a T-shirt that had seen better days. When she looked closer, she saw the vague remnants of what she believed to be the cast of the *Golden Girls*. And he seemed to be scrutinizing her right back, unbothered by her once-over. When their eyes connected, she felt a hammering in her chest. There was something intrinsically familiar about him.

Randall. No. She wouldn't think that.

"Matty, this is Layla, the woman I've told you so much about." Ian stood up to let her slide in beside him.

"Hi, Matt." Layla gave a little wave as she shimmied between the bench and the table and took her seat. "It's nice to meet you."

"Yeah, you too." Matt didn't sound even remotely sincere.

It was then that she clocked the tension between the two brothers. It was worse than what she'd just experienced in the music store. Ian was still smiling, but it was tight, like he was willing himself to be cheerful. Matt was completely closed off. He wouldn't meet Ian's eyes and barely looked at Layla, although he raised his eyebrows ever so slightly at her go-go boots. Screw him. Her boots were *fantastic*.

"How's your mom?" Ian asked, glancing at the pad of paper listing the restaurant's offerings that served as the menu.

"Um..." Layla tried to answer that question as honestly as possible. "Okay, I think?"

He nodded and picked up one of the little pencils provided, looking at Matt and Layla expectantly. "Should we get one order of everything?"

"I should've predicted you'd say that. Some things never change," Matt said dryly. "Except for, apparently, what does. Layla, how are *you* doing with this new Carpe Diem Ian?"

Layla's skin prickled. "I think Ian's doing great." She put a hand on his shoulder proudly. "And I can't believe you missed the opportunity to call him Carpe D-*Ian*. I mean, it's right there."

Matt stared at her for a beat, but he didn't smile or acknowledge her joke. Was he trying to make her feel stupid? *That* joke was on him; Layla was more than capable of making herself feel stupid on the regular. Like, for example, now, because her fantastic boot had somehow gotten stuck on the wrong side of the table leg, leading to her current discreet efforts to gracefully jerk it free.

"One of everything it is." Ian ticked boxes off on the menu and handed it to the server as she passed.

Layla's boot came loose and she relaxed. At least until she remembered Ian's words: *I feel like I should warn you about Matt somehow, but I don't even know what to say.* Now she was seeing the real wedge between them. She decided to try and break the ice. "So, Matt, I hear you were in California before this?"

He nodded and took a drink of water. "Among other places. Ian's been bugging me to give Seattle another go and I'm between jobs, so I thought why not."

"What jobs are you between?" The question came out a little sharper than she'd intended. Layla told herself she was just making conversation. But the way Matt'd immediately dunked on Ian's new zest for life had put her on the offensive.

"Matty here has done a little bit of everything," Ian said. "Surf instructor, mushroom farmer, and weren't you working at a pet shelter or something?"

"I was training guide dogs." Matt's eyes were striking, the color of dark chocolate, and they flicked from Ian to Layla.

Uncomfortable under his scrutiny, unable to tell what he was thinking, she squirmed in her seat. She tried to cross her legs under the table, but the action nearly hooked her boot behind the table leg again. "That sounds like a dream job."

"It was."

"Why'd you quit?"

"Bold of you to assume I wasn't fired." Matt's dark chocolate eyes moved to the beer menu.

Did you get fired for being a curmudgeon? Layla wanted to ask.

The edamame, tempura vegetables, and array of rolls arrived and they all dug in. Layla recalled that, even when she was feeling alienated from her siblings, nostalgia for their childhood tended to bridge the gap. Perhaps that was the way to make this dinner less uncomfortable? "What were you two like as kids?"

she asked. "I haven't heard the stories yet. Did you get into trouble?"

The brothers' eyes met for perhaps the first time since she'd sat down.

"We-ell…Matt did like to practice all the tricks we did at the community pool on the waterbed in my mom's room," Ian offered.

"Your mom had a waterbed?" Layla nearly choked on her sashimi.

"She did until Matt did a belly flop on it while holding a skewer he was pretending was a sword."

"Oh *no!*" Layla laughed. She noted Matt had lightened up just a smidge.

"Ian kept yelling, 'We've sprung a leak,'" he added, fiddling with his chopsticks, "until our mom came in with a patch."

"And Matty took off running," Ian said.

"Who stays at the scene of a crime?"

"You tried to hide behind the couch in the living room and you were still holding the skewer," Ian pointed out, chuckling. "Anyway, Mom fixed the waterbed and sold it the next day. She said we weren't responsible enough to have it in the house."

"I hope you stopped running around with a skewer in your hands after that," Layla said to Matt.

He shrugged and drained half the beer the server had placed in front of him only moments earlier. Just when she thought he was warming up, he'd turned ice cold again. *Living with him must be exhausting*, she thought and gave Ian's leg an affectionate squeeze under the table.

There was a small lull in the conversation. It wasn't uncomfortable—or at least it didn't seem like either of the Barnett brothers felt awkward any longer. Layla got the impression that they were accustomed to being quiet around each other. But when things got too quiet, Layla's thoughts got loud. She started thinking about her reconnection with Ian, about how it had led to meeting the missing piece from his family. *Meeting and deceiving*, Layla's conscience reminded her, but she tried her best to ignore it.

"What were *you* like as a kid?" Matt suddenly asked Layla, catching her off guard.

"What do you mean?"

"Were you a responsible rule-follower? Were you a rebel?"

Layla pretended to think about it. Ian didn't know much about the rebellious side of her apart from what her siblings had said in his company. All he knew about her time in LA was that she'd had trouble with her roommate and had hated the traffic, so she'd moved back to her parents' place for a bit while she figured out her next steps. She'd tried to tell him more for a while but hadn't known where to start.

"I definitely had my rebellious period," she said carefully, "though it was probably a bid for attention. I grew up with four siblings."

"Were they protective of you?"

Layla paused, reflecting. She didn't usually think of her siblings that way. "Well, if anyone outside our family tried to mess with me, they were. But they definitely teased me a lot," she said. "In their defense, I was a quirky kid."

Matt casually leaned back. "Quirky how?"

"Um..." His sudden interest was muddling her thoughts. Ian, too, looked curious. Layla licked her lips and debated which embarrassing story to tell. "My oldest sister, Rhiannon, was really into comics. I used to steal her X-Men issues. She hated it, but I couldn't stop staring lovingly at this character named Gambit."

"Ah, the Cajun with exploding cards," Matt confirmed. "I get it."

"You had a crush on a comic-book character?" Ian asked

Layla. His eyes crinkled at the corners. "I thought you only fell for guys in black-and-white movies."

"What can I say? I contain multitudes." Layla thought back to the days when she would lie on her stomach reading, kicking her feet back and forth, daydreaming. "Finally, Rhiannon got so mad at me she hid her comics. After they were gone, I tried to find something else I loved. My other sister, Cecelia, was the academic, but I wasn't into chasing grades. She had that covered. Jude, one of my brothers, was the family athlete, while I still can't do so much as a cartwheel, as my nieces and nephews inform me. My other brother, Bobby, was student council president basically every single year and now he's really involved in local politics, but I was always too overtly weird for the politics scene."

When Ian's phone rang, she became aware of how long she'd been talking about herself. She was self-conscious until she realized Matt was still listening.

"What was your thing? Did you find it?" Matt prompted as Ian looked at the caller ID and said, "Sorry. I'll be right back."

"No worries," Layla said, trying not to look longingly after him as he slipped out of the booth.

Matt took a sip of his beer. "You haven't answered my question."

"What question?"

"Did you find out what your thing was?"

Layla nodded slowly. "I started going through a bunch of my grandparents' old stuff. They'd passed away by that point and we were living in their house. I found records—Shirley Bassey, Dinah Washington, Mel Tormé, Sinatra. I'd play them in the study, and it was like..." Her mind drifted back to the rainy afternoon when she'd first uncovered all their music. The sultry voices, the sense of romance. The tongue-in-cheek humor of the lyrics. She'd learn later that some of those singers were problematic—affiliated with the Mob, serial cheaters, hardly role models. But if she took the songs for what they were, she could fall through them forever. "I'd always felt like I was living in the wrong time," Layla finally said. "Like I was the odd one out. And suddenly I found where I fit. I started really getting into the history, the pop culture, and then the vintage stuff."

"Hence your whole look," Matt said. It wasn't approving or judging, simply a statement of fact.

"Right."

"It probably helped you stand out among all your siblings."

The comment wasn't offensive, and she was self-aware enough to know that it was a contributing factor, but for some reason, it irked Layla all the same. "My mom was really great about it all, actually."

"Oh yeah?"

She thought of Rena. Not the version who had just bolted from her in the music shop or the one she'd been trying so hard not to let down again but the Rena who'd been the star of Layla's childhood. "Yeah. Some days she'd let me skip school so I could stay home and watch classic movies with her. We'd drink tea and eat popcorn and talk about the fashion, the dialogue, the glamour. Which Hepburn I was more like, Katharine or Audrey."

"You're clearly a Katharine." Matt was giving her a strange look, as though he was trying to figure her out.

But she didn't want to be figured out. And of *course* she was a Katharine.

"For a long time, my mom was my best friend." She unfolded and refolded her napkin. "I mean, she deserves the title. She introduced me to *Singin' in the Rain*."

Matt didn't respond, so she assumed she'd finally bored him. And then he moved ever so slightly, and she could see that he wasn't bored, he was thinking quite intently. She sat up, ready for whatever he was about to say.

"Your idea of romance is, I don't know, Julie London singing 'You'd Be So Nice to Come Home To,' and yet you've been dating a guy for a year and a half who eats most of his meals on a conference-room table," Matt said flatly.

As impressed as Layla was that Matt knew one of her favorite songs, the implication that she and Ian didn't fit together was more than a sore spot. It was a sore region. "That *guy* is your brother, and he has a lot going for him."

"Oh, that's undeniable," Matt agreed. "And you're the office manager of a theater?"

"Office administrator." She set her jaw at the condescension in his tone. If he was judgmental of Ian's life, he was definitely going to mock her for making a living by ordering pens from a catalog. *Whatever*. It was fine. She was accustomed to the variety of reactions people had to her job. Everything from the dismissive *That must be so fun* to *But is this really sustainable?* (the latter from her brothers and sisters).

"Do you like it?" Matt asked, one eyebrow lifting practically in slow motion. The action infuriated her and not just because she hadn't mentally prepared for his interest.

"I love it," she shot back a little too aggressively. She checked her tone and tried again. "Well, I don't *love* it, but it's in a creative field and still allows me to afford..."

"Things?" Matt unhelpfully supplied.

"I was going to say it allows me to afford the luxury of working in the arts."

Matt put his hands up as if to say *I surrender*. "Hey, no need to get defensive. Who doesn't love things? Things are great."

She reminded herself for the tenth time she was talking to Ian's brother. And if he was grilling her, maybe it was because, even though the two men weren't close, he was still protective.

"I'm sorry," Layla eventually said. "I'm the youngest of a whole pack of kids. I'm used to being cornered, and my back goes up like a cat."

"I get it." And it actually sounded like he did. "If you love what you do, who cares what anyone else thinks?"

His response was so unexpectedly nice, she felt a dose of encouragement. Maybe he was just the type of person you had to wear down a little before he stopped being prickly.

"I understand you're a writer—" she began.

"I don't think you understand anything about me," Matt said so abruptly, she felt as though she'd been slapped. Before she could recover, Ian appeared and sat down beside her.

"Sorry—again, it couldn't wait. So?" Ian said. "What did I miss?"

"Nothing really," Matt said with a shrug.

Nothing? Maybe Matt wasn't just prickly—maybe he was a bit of an asshole.

Oblivious to the tension, Ian grinned at them both. "Okay, good. Who's up for dessert?"

Feeling the warmth of Ian's arm against hers, Layla forced herself to breathe a little more easily. Never mind Rena's strange behavior, the impending work crisis, and Matt's whip-lash-inducing personality. All that mattered right now, in this moment, was that she and Ian were back together.

But.

Layla's heart was still pounding from the mental and emotional gymnastics Matt'd put her through. She reminded herself that his arrival had nothing to do with her own second chance with Ian.

She was on the right track. Everything would be fine.

CHAPTER ELEVEN

THE WEEKEND CROWD was out in full force at the ferry docks. Seattleites lined up in their cars, desperate to get away to the slower pace of the San Juan Islands. At least, Layla was. People wandered around on foot too, stretching their legs and getting last-minute snacks from the nearby shop. Ian and Layla were parked in the middle of it all, waiting for the ship that would take them to Orcas Island to arrive.

The fact that they'd been sitting in the car for at least ten minutes and Ian hadn't so much as glanced at his phone had not gone unnoticed by Layla. He really was much more present these days. Layla was so excited to finally be doing this trip, to see Jeannie and Craig again, that she stared out the window and willed the cars ahead—and the ship pulling in—to move faster.

"Hey," Ian said, interrupting her thoughts. "What are you smiling at?"

"I'm just happy," she answered truthfully. "And looking forward to seeing your parents again. And where you grew up. You know, so I can get a sense of your origin story."

"I broke up one fight," Ian said with a good-natured eye roll. "Hardly superhero material."

A family walked past them, a couple with two small children, a boy who was solemnly holding the leash of a Boston terrier and a girl who was seemingly trying to convince the dog to run away with her.

"I wonder which one of those kids you'd have been," Layla teased. She imagined Ian, even as a child, being the most responsible person in the room. In any room. "I'm totally going to convince Jeannie to bust out the photo albums."

"I don't know," Ian hedged. "You may not be emotionally prepared for just how adorable young Ian was." He reached over and took her hand. "You know, seeing someone's childhood home is a pretty big step. You sure you're ready for this?"

Layla let out her most dramatic scoff. "You've not only seen my childhood home, you've listened to my bratty siblings tell humiliating stories about me. I am *more* than ready for this."

"Well, I can tell you right now, you won't find any love letters to Scooby-Doo in my room," Ian replied.

"First of all, it was a *fan* letter, and it was to *Shaggy*, who is a human, not Scooby-Doo, who is a dog."

"They're both cartoons..." Ian said, deliberately trailing off.

Layla turned her body so she could more easily swoon over his gorgeous face. "Now, tell me: Is your room still the same as when you lived there or did Jeannie turn it into a gift-wrapping station?"

"Jeannie always forgets to buy wrapping paper, so she usually wraps gifts using Craig's T-shirts. All of which now have little sticky marks from the tape." Ian cringed a little.

"I love your parents so much," Layla said, beaming at the anecdote but also at how she and Ian were both the odd people out in their families.

"My parents love you too." Ian leaned in and kissed her. Gently at first, then with more energy, more insistence. Layla's insides lit up. God, she'd missed this. How something so small, like a tone of voice reserved just for her or a small touch or a kiss, could make her body feel like it was made of starlight. If there weren't so many people around, she would've stopped kissing him long enough to push the recline button on the driver's seat. But this kiss was enough. For now.

The car behind them honked, scaring them both, which made them laugh again. The line had apparently started moving while they were kissing. Ian put his Audi in gear and drove onto the ferry. After they parked, they followed the rest of the crowd up the metal stairs and onto the deck. The azure sky was striped with lazy clouds, and the wind was picking up, ever present when you were on the water. They made their way to the bow, holding hands, and let their hair be blown into tangled tornados as they clung to each other and excitedly pointed to a pod of porpoises off the side of the ship. Layla pulled out her phone and videoed a clip she subsequently posted on Instagram. Even with the wind and the ferry's engine, Ian's laugh was recogniz-able in the background, as was the way he said, "Layla, isn't this incredible?" It was a moment she wanted to capture (and one she was happy to post for her siblings and ex-boyfriends to see, should they look).

Layla realized just how liberating getting away from the city and onto the ocean she so often took for granted was. She hadn't known how much she'd needed this break, this time away with Ian, until now. It'd always been her intention to save up enough money to travel after college. Get on an international flight, drop into an unfamiliar country, and have an adventure. But seven years later, on top of her school debt, she somehow kept accruing credit card debt, and that plane ticket had yet to materialize.

For now, exploring her own corner of Washington would have to scratch that itch.

"I want to do this more often," she yelled into the wind.

"Do what more often?" he yelled back.

"Explore all this. With you. I spend all my time in the city; I forget this is so close." She waved her arms to the vistas around them.

"I'm glad you feel that way, because I want us to travel more too." He grinned, moving closer to speak into her ear. "Remember that trip to Vancouver?"

Beaming, she flashed him the ring on her hand. The one she'd tucked away during their breakup because it had made her too sad but had dug back out. She'd bought it on Granville Island when they'd gone there for a weekend early on in their relationship. Designed by a local artist, it was somehow formed with shells and sea glass. Ian took her hand and kissed it.

When the ferry docked, Ian wanted to give Layla a tour of the island.

"I always forget how good I feel here," he said, rolling down the car windows and letting the fresh air flow in. "I get so fixated on my schedule in the city, the ten-mile radius I exist in, that I forget what it feels like to break free."

Layla reached over and tousled his hair. Pre-accident Ian would've smiled at her, then immediately finger-combed it back into place. New Ian, to her delight, grinned and let the wind whip his golden locks around even more.

From the dock in the cute little community of Orcas Village, they drove north. Ian told her stories about growing up on the island, about kayaking on the weekends and working as a busboy for the Barnacle, a local restaurant, after school. While driving past a camp nestled in the trees, he mentioned that he and Matt had been counselors there several summers in a row, and she begged him to take the exit.

"You can't see it," Ian told her. "The campground's been converted to an affordable glamping destination."

"Oh no! Your childhood!" Layla exclaimed, but Ian chuckled and kept driving.

"It's fine by me. I like to see progress on the island. The stuff I care about is what's permanent. The ocean views, all the trees and how...I don't know. I guess how it *feels* to be here."

"I get it," Layla said. And she did. She loved Seattle. It was eclectic and busy and fun. It had plenty of beauty of its own, but the island was something else altogether. Rustic but also fresh, with a palette of greens and blues and grays she wished she could just *wear.*

They drove several more miles, and Ian stopped the car at Rosario so they could walk around the beautiful resort. Inhaling, Layla took in the smells of pine and surf. Being here, ensconced among overgrown ferns and ivies, baptized by a light mist, made her feel reborn. And being here with *Ian* made her feel like someone with a serious future, one filled with romance, family, and stability. Everything she'd wanted since she and Ian first held hands at Bite of Seattle.

Layla paused their stroll when she spotted a pair of identical houses across the horseshoe-shaped cove. They were white with gray roofs, each with steps leading up to a lovely wide porch overlooking the ocean. The two were mirror images of each other. "What's with those twin houses?"

"The guy who founded this area of the island, Robert Moran, built them for his two brothers."

"Did he lack imagination?" It was like looking at a spot-the-difference page in an activity book.

"There was a rivalry between them. Or maybe between their wives? I can't totally remember. But Moran figured if the houses were exactly the same, neither brother could be jealous."

"Well, that's one way to keep up with the Joneses."

"This is the same guy who put a player organ in his own mansion, which is now the resort and restaurant over there"—Ian pointed to the left of the matching houses—"and pretended he could play. He'd put on 'concerts' for his unsuspecting guests."

"Hold up—he mimed playing songs just to impress people?" Layla laughed. "What a nut."

"I hear he was pretty convincing."

"Fake it till you make it," Layla quipped, shoving down a tinge of self-awareness.

"Or fake it forever," Ian said. "I don't think the guy ever learned to play. Anyway, he's not a complete nutter. He came to Seattle from New York with nothing and ended up with a mansion on Orcas Island. So he did something right."

"Ah," Layla said, understanding. "He sounds like your kind of guy."

Ian shrugged. "I don't know if he was a good person or not, but I can definitely respect that kind of ambition and that drive to look after his family, even if he took it to extremes."

"If someone gave me a free house here, I wouldn't complain about *anything*," Layla said, taking his hand. In truth, she wasn't sure she'd ever be able to afford a house of any kind. Whenever she started thinking about mortgages, she blacked out a little. But maybe some of Ian's innate adultness would rub off on her? She made a mental note to ask him (again) about setting up a 401(k), but then sighed. Who was she kidding? She couldn't see how she'd ever make enough money to justify a nest egg. She might as well spend it on vintage purses. At least that way she could take it with her, so to speak.

They turned away from the matching houses and walked up toward the resort. Ian pointed to the restaurant, which had wraparound windows overlooking Rosario's sleepy marina. "Growing up, they did this seafood buffet once a week. It was the height of luxury for us. We actually only came a couple of times. One of those was when my mom and Craig told Matt and me they wanted to get married."

Layla imagined little Ian, probably in a collared shirt, maybe even a little bow tie, serious and sweet. "How did you feel when they told you?"

Ian took her hand. "Matt and I used to sneak into each other's rooms at night to talk. We'd snack on packages of raw ramen and wonder if Mom was okay, if she was happy."

"You two did that?" Layla's heart squeezed as she looked up into his eyes. "I don't know how many kids would be so emotionally intelligent, to think about what their single mom was going through."

When he tried to shrug off the compliment, she took his other hand, needing him to know that she saw him. "I mean it, Ian. You're an incredibly thoughtful person. I guess you always have been."

That compliment landed and he closed his eyes briefly before leaning down to kiss her forehead. "She was a great mom. The *best* mom. But after she divorced our biological father, we worried about her. Worried she was lonely. Waterbed shenanigans aside, we tried not to be too much trouble. And she tried to make sure we didn't miss out on anything, which wasn't always easy, because money was tight."

"Miss out on things like what?" It was unusual for Ian to open up this much. She wanted to keep him talking.

He considered her question. "When I wanted to invite every kid in my grade to my birthday party, she figured out how to do it practically for free. She set up this elaborate treasure hunt in the forest by our house, and our neighbor baked a cake that looked like a chest of gold coins. None of the kids even noticed they weren't getting a bunch of candy and going to the movies or renting a whole whale-watching boat like they did at other parties. When it came to Christmas, she'd take Matty and me to the grocery store and let us pick out whatever sugary cereal we wanted—we're talking the kind of stuff she'd never normally let us eat—and she'd put a bow on it for us to have on Christmas morning. We got so excited. We never, ever wanted to make my mom feel like she wasn't doing enough."

"I want to hug those little guys."

"We were pretty happy," Ian said softly. "Besides, those little guys had each other."

Layla slipped her arm through Ian's. "And then Craig came along?"

"Craig came along." Ian visibly relaxed. "And it was like our mom was still our mom, only lighter. Sunnier. It felt like she had more attention and love to give to us, more energy for her students. It's funny...when you're with the right person, even if there's a lot going on, you can find the capacity to give more, you know?" He turned to her, his blue eyes warm and inviting. She knew he wasn't just talking about his mom and Craig.

"I know." Layla touched his cheek. The feeling overwhelming her was confusing. Love, certainly, for this precious man who was opening up to her. But it was interwoven with something else. *Guilt.*

Everything good that was coming from this second chance was painted with the same brush as the lie that had started it all. And now she was about to spend the weekend with his family, whom she was essentially lying to as well.

She turned back to the resort, the marina, and decided to refocus on what made it all worth it: Ian. "This place is so idyllic. What made you decide to leave and become a big shot in Seattle?"

He put his arm around her, seemingly having missed her darker moment, and gave her a squeeze. "I'd always planned on going to college in Seattle. We didn't get to the city very often, but when we did, I got so excited about the energy, the pace. I remember seeing the way people walked, and they all seemed so...purposeful. I wanted to move like that."

Ian grew quiet as seagulls cawed around the shoreline. The

tide was coming in and Layla watched as a small rock beach slowly disappeared into the sea.

"My freshman and sophomore years at UW," Ian suddenly continued, his voice faraway, "I was still trying to find my footing. It was weird, being away from my family. Matt seemed to..." He scratched his neck, seemed to consider something, then shook his head. "Having me gone didn't seem to be good for Matt, I guess. Even though he had my mom and Craig, something changed during those two years."

"It makes sense," Layla replied gently. "You two had been relying on each other for so long."

"Yeah, and Matty had always walked the line between screwing up and keeping it together, you know?"

I know that line like I know every Shirley Bassey song ever recorded, Layla thought. Out loud, she asked, "You were the one keeping him out of trouble?"

Ian walked a few steps toward the shore. His chest rose and fell, and he nodded. "It seemed that way. I always felt guilty for leaving."

Layla let him take his time. She watched a boat glide into the dock as gracefully as a ballerina, waiting for the pieces of this puzzle to fall into place and finally reveal its form.

"Anyway, the winter before Matt graduated high school—he barely scraped by—he talked me into doing a polar-bear plunge with him at Cascade Lake, telling me he'd heard from some people that it was amazing and offered clarity and some other woo-woo bullshit."

"The polar-bear plunge, like you run into the lake when it's just above freezing?"

"Yeah." Ian's face hardened at the memory. "It was the first time we'd really hung out, the two of us, since I'd gone away. At that point, I already felt like a bit of a 'big shot.'" He softened a touch. "I was so condescending to him."

"I think that's pretty typical for college students," Layla offered. "I remember feeling like I was on top of the world when I was finally on my own."

"Yeah," Ian agreed, then wrinkled his nose. "But I doubt you had the same know-it-all tendencies I did. I'd come home and I'd get a little critical when the house was cluttered. I loved being on my own, but back at my parents' place it felt like someone was always just right... *there*, you know?"

"Ian," Layla said kindly. "I grew up in a bungalow with six other people. Trust me when I say I get it. And I think you're being too hard on yourself."

"I was an ass," Ian told her. "I can still be that way at my worst. Trying to control things and getting upset when I can't."

The tide engulfed the rest of the beach as she spoke. "You're not controlling people, you're trying to *look after* the people you care about. I love that about you. Now, finish telling me about the polar plunge because I'm really enjoying imagining you jumping into a lake in a pair of thin cotton briefs. And take your time telling me how tiny they were. And how tight."

He gave her a somber look, but his dimple let her know he was enjoying her teasing. And then his eyes grew stormy. He took her hand and led her to a bench overlooking the marina. On it was a plaque dedicated to someone's BELOVED ERIS DODDRIDGE.

Ian sat beside her, his body tense, and Layla felt unsettled. "What happened with the polar-bear plunge, Ian?"

"It was dark, there were a few dozen people there, and someone had a horn. When it went off, there was a lot of splashing and screaming. I just went for it and ran. But Matt stayed on the beach."

Smart guy, Layla thought. But there was something about Ian's tone that warned her against levity, and she waited for him to keep going.

"I came out of the water like, 'What the hell, man, I thought we were doing this together?'" Ian shook his head again, sucked air through his teeth. "And Matt said, 'Yeah, I changed my mind.' And then he told me he'd been trying to track down Dennis."

"Dennis?"

"Our bio dad. Matt said that after graduation, he'd decided to 'eschew college.' Who says shit like that? And it was so he could chase this guy, the one person who'd abandoned us. Matt admitted that he'd never even sent in his college applications, which meant he'd lied to Mom. He'd lied to all of us." Ian's head dropped, his eyes on the ground. Then he stood and began to pace until he was behind the bench, his hands resting just above Eris's plaque. "I was only home for winter break, I was trying to do this crazy thing that *he'd* suggested, and he had the balls to tell me all that. It was like a slap in the face to me, my mom, Craig. Like we weren't all enough for him. He didn't even know where Dennis was; he was just going off addresses from the sporadic birthday cards Dennis'd sent us over the years. It made me so angry. I'd been feeling guilty about being in Seattle, knowing he was struggling in school without me there to remind him to do his homework, get after him for cutting class. When he stood on that beach while I was soaking wet and freezing and told me that he was chasing Dennis, that he needed to know the whole story before he could figure out what came next in his life? He wasn't the best friend I'd had as a kid. He was a different person."

"Oh, Ian—"

"So that's when I decided that I would find a way to make enough money to take care of my mom and Craig forever, even without him. Matt could be selfish, but I didn't need to be."

Suddenly Ian's tendencies toward grand gestures—the symphony tickets, the tickets to Heart, the cruise—made much more sense.

There was so much to excavate here; Layla had a million

follow-up questions. But first, she rose and wrapped her arms around Ian's waist. For a second, he stiffened. In that hesitation, she took the shame that was building inside of her, that she couldn't—*wouldn't*—open up the same way to him, wouldn't tell him about Randall, wouldn't tell him about the breakup...she took that tower of shame and she kicked it over. Because clearly, having her back in his life was good for Ian. There was a *reason* they were back together. All the other stuff could wait.

The spring day was turning colder, but between them was an infinite supply of warmth. *We're making each other whole*, she told herself. But she was still dying to know the end of the story. Before she could ask, *Did Matt find Dennis?* Ian released her.

"Should we keep going on the tour?" he asked.

No need to rush. There was time for her questions, time for his answers. They had all the time in the world now. And so she looked up at his handsome face, seeing anew his determination and his strength, and replied, "Definitely."

CHAPTER TWELVE

THE BARNETT FAMILY home was nestled in an overgrown forest where slivers of an ocean view and neighboring houses could be glimpsed between trunks and deep green branches. Ian's Audi had barely inched up the driveway when the front door flew open and Jeannie and Craig Barnett burst out and ran down the porch stairs. Craig insisted on helping them with their suitcases, despite the fact they'd packed only small overnight bags, while Jeannie pulled everyone into a group hug that took Layla's breath away.

"Ian, how's your head? That cut on your cheek—is that healing okay?" Jeannie scrutinized as much of Ian as he'd allow. His bruises had faded into a yellowish color, only days away from disappearing, and his cut looked much better. For the sake of Jeannie's obviously tender heart, Layla was glad she hadn't seen her son sooner.

"Okay, Mom, that's enough poking and prodding. I'm okay," Ian said, but he paused to kiss the top of her head while Layla got a better look at the piece of Ian's life she'd been curious about for over a year.

Ian's childhood home was a charming older bungalow in

Eastsound, situated among million-dollar infills that were clearly vacation homes. Even amid the McMansions masquerading as cabins, she liked his place the best. It had the most character, with its teal wood siding and brick chimney. Lining the porch was a bed of wildflowers and a blackberry bush that Layla imagined little Ian collecting fruit from for breakfast.

Jeannie and Craig led them inside. The interior of the home was as welcoming as the people who lived there. It was painted in deep burgundies and creams, the finishings were all warm woods, and the furniture and rugs were well loved. Knickknacks adorned endless bookshelves; gifts from past students with messages like *Come back and visit, Mr. and Mrs. Barnett!* decorated the walls.

"When you show Layla around, check out your pillows," Craig said with a wink.

"Craig put chocolates on them as a welcome token—that's what they did on that cruise Ian sent us on." Jeannie was beaming.

"You start putting chocolates on my pillow and you're never going to get rid of me," Layla threatened as Ian took her by the hand and led her away from his parents, who were clearly embarrassing him.

Technically the house was a bungalow, but the attic had been converted into a bedroom. Ian's room was toward the back of the house and featured a small window offering a view of the backyard, which was, much to Layla's utter delight, a pretty enchanting forest. The room had a dark blue feature wall and was as tidy as she'd suspected it would be. His old double bed was made up with plain sheets, and, sure enough, on each pillow, there was a little Hershey's Kiss. Layla snagged them both, popped one in her mouth, and offered the other to Ian. He unwrapped it and put that chocolate in her mouth as well. Chipmunk cheeks of chocolate aside, Layla went more than a little weak in the knees as his fingers grazed her lips.

"So this is where the magic happens, huh?" she said, taking a look around.

"Sadly, no," Ian replied. "I had one girlfriend in high school and the only magic we did in here was study enough to ace our SATs."

"*Sure.*" Layla openly snooped around his very unsnoopable room. His desk was tidy, accented by organizers for paper and pens. Against the wall was a bookshelf lined with worn Hardy Boys paperbacks and old textbooks.

She couldn't help but juxtapose it all to her own childhood bedroom—one she'd shared with her sisters. Rhiannon had gotten her own bed, but Layla and Cece shared a bunk bed, and Layla had been on the bottom. As the youngest, Layla hadn't been given the right to do much decorating and had to store most of her belongings under her bed. To this day, it was where she kept precious things. She dropped to the floor and looked under Ian's bed.

"Can I help you?" he asked, still standing.

"Yeah." She lifted the comforter to get a better look. "Where's all the good stuff?"

"Probably in my condo in the city."

"Nope." She stood up and dusted off her pants. "I've snooped there too."

"Well, then, let's try Matt's room," he teased. "Maybe *it's* more titillating."

He led her up to the attic, which was indeed full Matt territory. It was even smaller but featured fabulous vaulted ceilings. The quilt on the bed didn't really match the pillowcases, and the slanted walls were covered in posters from obscure bands and movies. There was a desk by the window—*Not the wall*, Layla noted a touch smugly—on top of which were sketch pads and a bobblehead of Bob Ross. In the corner lay a bongo drum and a ukulele.

"Is this better?" Ian asked. "More good stuff in here?"

Layla shrugged. "The Bob Ross bobblehead is pretty cute. But I was hoping for juicier reveals. Embarrassing photos, potential blackmail material, you know, *good stuff.*"

"You're such a nut."

"It's one of your favorite things about me," Layla said. To her delight, he conceded the point before returning downstairs and unpacking his bag (he always put all his clothes into a hotel's dresser, even if he was there for only one night). She wandered back to the living room, where a bay window offered a view of the surrounding forest and a peek at the ocean. Her phone buzzed with a notification that turned out to be a very rude update on her screen-time average. Layla did not appreciate her phone tracking just how many hours she'd spent shopping. Her home screen unlocked with facial recognition and she saw there were thirty-nine unread messages. Likely all from the Rockford Peaches, which she intended to ignore, but she checked them all the same. At the top was one from Rhiannon that said, Judging by the ferry video on IG, I'm guessing Layla won't be at Sunday dinner?

Shit. She'd forgotten to tell her parents. *Yep! Spending the weekend with Ian and his family! See you next week!!* She hoped the extra exclamation point softened the blow. It was so frustrating that, even years after Layla's so-called disappearance, her family felt the need to track her like an endangered animal. She'd need to strategically post some *Look at how stable and responsible I am* photos this weekend to ease their paranoid minds.

"We are just so thrilled to finally see you again," Jeannie gushed, joining Layla at the window.

She pocketed her phone. "I'm so happy to be here."

Jeannie put her arm around Layla and gave her a squeeze. "And you always look so cute. I swear someone should sign me up for that lovely *Queer Eye* show. Put some oomph back into my wardrobe."

Layla blushed. Even Matt knew she was a Katharine, but she'd channeled Audrey when she'd gotten dressed that morning, opting for a soft cream sleeveless turtleneck sweater paired with her favorite plaid pedal pushers and little ballet flats. Was the scarf she'd tied around her neck too much? Who cared. But Jeannie deserved to feel good about herself too, so she replied honestly, "I think your style suits you. That chunky necklace is top drawer."

Ian approached them just as Jeannie was waving off Layla's compliment. Jeannie turned to him. "Isn't Layla such a sweetheart?"

"Don't let her fool you. I played charades at her best friend's loft and when Layla lost, she nearly flipped a table," Ian said cheekily.

"I did *not*." Layla blushed. "I *leaned* on the edge of the table, a *teensy* bit frustrated, and I didn't realize one of the legs was broken!"

"Don't hold back here, Layla. Competitive streaks are encouraged in the Barnett house." Jeannie looked thoughtful for a moment. "Gosh, when was the last time we saw you two? Was it the Mariners game?"

"It was," Craig said, joining them at the window. "Layla made me chug my entire soda when the camera caught me for the jumbotron."

"The heartburn was worth the cheering, right?" Layla teased.

"Why did it take you so long to bring her out here?" Jeannie admonished Ian. "We miss *both* of you."

"I know, I know," Ian said sheepishly. "Life kept getting in the way. I'm making amends, I promise."

"Good. I notice you haven't even pulled out your phone once. That thing is usually glued to your hand." Jeannie tossed that last part to Layla, who nodded in agreement. Jeannie turned her attention back to her older son, who patted his pocket self-consciously. "It's about time you stop letting things get in the way. When you fall in love, that person becomes part of the family. Right, Craig?"

"Well, we're happy to have you here now. And we're especially happy to see Ian in one piece," Craig said. He had the face of a mall Santa, all apple cheeks and twinkly eyes. But after he glanced out the window, his demeanor changed. He started fidgeting, folding and refolding a blanket on the couch, making more room for people to sit. "It looks like Matt's back from the store."

His reorientation made sense to Layla now that she knew snippets of his history, of the way Matt had chased after his biological dad. She felt a fresh stirring of anger. How could Matt not appreciate this gentle man?

And then Matt appeared in the front doorway, wearing a worn plaid jacket over a black hoodie, his hair and beard glistening from the light rain. He was carrying cloth shopping bags, the leafy green stems of carrots and what appeared to be a wine bottle sticking out the top.

"I don't know if Mom actually needed this stuff or if she was just trying to get rid of me," he said by way of hello. Craig wasn't the only one whose vibe had shifted. Ian had visibly tensed. Oblivious or determined, Jeannie bustled toward him.

"I'm never trying to get rid of you." She patted his cheek affectionately. "Sometimes you're just so restless. I gave you something to focus on. And, hey, I got wine out of the deal!"

It was an interesting observation. From what Layla had seen of Matt thus far, he had a tendency to become unsettlingly still, not restless. But she remembered Ian saying something similar.

To his credit, Matt leaned in to kiss his mom's temple. "I'm not one of your students, Mom. You don't need to give me tasks."

But judging by the tension between Matt and Ian, who hadn't even looked at each other yet, some intervention was needed.

"While the barbecue's heating up, why don't you all have a seat in the living room?" Craig finally said. "I'll get us some drinks." He took the grocery bags from Matt and retreated to the galley kitchen.

Matt leaned back against the closed door, as if not ready to come in the living room completely yet.

"Remind me," Craig yelled to Layla from the corner. "You don't have any allergies, right? From what I remember, you're up for eating just about anything."

"That's right," Layla replied. "And never forget that I can eat you under the table."

"You'd just made me chug an entire soda. *Of course* I couldn't finish those nachos," Craig insisted.

Layla sat down on the couch next to Ian. It was overstuffed, with a faded floral pattern, and sucked her right in like a lover. "Oh. Wow. This couch should be illegal."

Matt raised an eyebrow, his eyes fixed on her, and took a seat in the chair near the window.

Jeannie's laugh tinkled as she leaned against its arm. "I swear, sometimes I'll sit down to knit, and I won't get up for hours."

"I could move into this couch," Layla agreed. "Speaking of moving in, you must be happy to have your boys together again."

"Can you believe it?" Jeannie accepted a glass of wine from Craig, who was circling the room with a tray like a pro. She leaned forward, glass in hand, and gushed, "It's been so long since Ian and Matty have been in the same state, never mind the same home."

Craig returned the tray to the kitchen and took his place on the love seat next to Jeannie.

"I kept hoping my next roommate would be a lot cuter." Ian caught Layla's eye and she felt herself flush. Was he really thinking about them moving in together so soon? Although, she reminded herself, in Ian's eyes they hadn't been together for a week; they'd been together for a year and a half.

Ian added jovially, "But Matt and I are making it work."

"It's been one week." Matt shrugged. "And you were the one who begged me to come back to Seattle, remember?"

"I was joking, Matt." Ian looked regretful. "I'm glad you're back."

Layla peered at Matt with interest, waiting for him to reciprocate the sentiment. But he was now luxuriating in the La-Z-Boy like he didn't owe anybody anything. She knew why Ian had invited Matt to move in, but she still didn't have a handle on why Matt had said yes.

Jeannie patted Craig's leg. "Let's go get started on that barbecuing. Kids, can you get the side dishes prepared? We'll need a salad, and someone should check on those potatoes."

Layla bit back a smile at being referred to as *kids*. It was the same way at her house. No matter how close her siblings got to middle age, they were always treated like teenagers. Well, *Layla* was. By her entire family. At least here, she was on a level playing field with Ian and Matt.

"Don't forget the bread," Craig said to Matt with a wink.

Layla followed Ian and Matt into the kitchen, which was a little tight for three people—especially since two were broad-shouldered—but she managed to squeeze between them to gain access to the cutting board. While she prepared a salad and Ian checked on the roasted potatoes, Matt took out a loaf of bread and began slicing and placing it in a basket lined with an embroidered cloth. Matt and Ian weren't speaking, so she decided to take the initiative.

"That looks homemade," Layla remarked.

"The bread or the cloth?" Matt asked, eyes fixed on the task at hand.

"Both."

"I can't take credit for the embroidery, that's all Mom," he said, sparing her a single glance, "but I did make the bread earlier today."

His tone was clipped. It was as if her very presence annoyed him, even though she had no idea what she'd done to set him off. She was playing nice, which was more than surly James Dean deserved.

"Matt's always been a great baker," Ian said kindly as he retrieved some seasonings from the cupboard.

"The last time I tried to bake, I sifted flour onto my cat, and he still hasn't forgiven me."

"Deano's a tough room," Ian confirmed, and then to Matt: "You should meet Layla's enormous ginger cat. He's more intimidating than my boss and he likes only two people: Layla and her dad."

Matt made a noncommittal noise. *Icy bastard.*

"Anyway, the bread looks delicious," Layla said brightly, trying again to defuse the tension. "Mind if I take a picture?"

"You do seem like you're into appearances," Matt mumbled as soon as Ian's back was turned.

She couldn't decide whether that was a dig at her fashion or the fact that she was dating Ian. She was annoyed on both counts. She loved Ian for his goodness and generosity. She loved her vintage clothes because they made her feel more like herself. And as if Matt could talk—he clearly wore his I-don't-care-about-clothes clothes like armor.

Still, she was trying to help Ian, so she said, "Why don't you *both* get in the picture?"

"Our first roommate photo," Ian teased, putting an arm around his brother and smiling brightly. Matt placed his hands on either side of the breadbasket. He wasn't scowling, but he definitely wasn't smiling either. Layla snapped the picture and immediately posted it on Instagram: *Eat your heart out*, GBBO.

By the time everything made it to the table, Jeannie and Craig were coming back into the house with a tray of perfectly grilled chicken skewers. They all settled in, and between bites, they chatted about Layla's job and made Ian tell the story of his bike accident once again. Matt was mostly silent, and Layla kept finding herself observing him, trying to decide if he was being sulky or if this was just who he was. She was getting the impression that Matt chose to speak only when he really had something to say. She couldn't relate. Growing up in a house with four older siblings, she was always fighting to get a word in. Talking was one of her superpowers.

Ian was like her. The two of them had never run out of things to say to each other—not in the months they were dating before, and not now that they were back together. She pictured them growing old in their own little house in a quirky neighborhood in Seattle, hosting dinners with their friends, talking late into the night.

"Shall we bush for dishes?" Craig asked, scraping his fork over his plate a final time and breaking into her reverie.

"Bush for dishes?"

"It's a game we play to determine who does the washing up," Ian explained.

"You okay with a little gambling?" Jeannie's eyes were twinkling. Layla couldn't say no to that expression.

"Absolutely."

But Ian tilted his head. "Are you sure you're all ready to see Layla's competitive side?"

Craig pretended to check the sturdiness of the table. "Seems like we should be okay."

"Clearly I missed something," Matt said to himself.

"Mock my intensity all you want, Barnetts," Layla said. "I come from a family of seven, plus partners and offspring. Winning *anything* is a big deal when you've got that much competition."

While Matt eyed her curiously and Craig retrieved a jar of coins, Ian and Jeannie took turns explaining the game. The gist was this: Each person got three coins. Everyone was to keep their hands under the table and out of sight. At the beginning of each round, players could put zero, one, two, or three coins in one hand, bring that hand up, and rest it on the table, closed. Each person took a guess at how many total coins there were. The winner of each round was out and whoever was left at the end had to clean up.

They did a practice round, which Jeannie won, then started for real. Jeannie won again, followed by Craig.

"I'm happy to come in second place to this firecracker," he said sweetly. Jeannie swatted his shoulder, but Layla could see she was pleased.

It was down to Layla and the brothers, both growing increasingly intense—Layla saw right through Matt's exaggeratedly casual posture to the way his knuckles were turning white against the table.

This is really about psychology, Layla thought as their three sets of hands rummaged underneath the table, then came up.

"You can go first, dear," Jeannie said to Layla.

Layla eyed Ian's closed fist. Maybe she was overthinking, but instinctively she knew he'd put three coins in there. It was an all-in move with just a smidge of humility. Perfectly Ian. She herself had one coin, bringing the total to four. She turned her attention to Matt. One look and she guessed he didn't have any coins in his hand. It was a brat move. A bit cheeky. And there was something in his expression, the way he was looking at her, that told her she was right.

"Four," Layla said confidently.

Ian guessed six, Matt guessed five, and they all opened their palms. Sure enough, there were three coins in Ian's open hand and Matt's was empty.

"I won," Layla shrieked, pumping her fist in the air. Craig, Jeannie, and Ian laughed at her excitement.

"Our table survives another day! Join the winners' circle, Layla," Craig said, beckoning.

The boys put their hands under the table, waited a moment, then brought them up.

"Three," Matt said, his fist so tight Layla could see the tendons in his hand.

Ian paused. He paused for so long, Layla nearly clawed their fists open herself. She was apparently *very* invested. Ian leaned in ever so slightly, then his shoulders dropped. She could see the fun, competitive pull seep out of him. Layla could read his mind: He was trying to repair his relationship with his brother, not fight him—not even in a low-stakes game.

Finally, Ian spoke. "It'll go faster if we do the dishes together."

"It'll go faster if you make your bet," Matt lobbed back, and she nearly chucked the leftover bread at his head. "Or are you afraid of losing?" Matt added.

"I'm not afraid of anything," Ian replied, his tone neutral but his shoulders squaring. "I just don't want you to be stuck at the sink all night while the rest of us relax."

Three, Matt mouthed.

"Fine." Ian shrugged. "Four."

They opened their fists. Each of their palms contained one coin. They'd both lost.

It served Matt right.

"Why don't you two do the dishes together, like Ian suggested." Jeannie pointed at her sons. "But none of this 'Who can wash or dry the dishes faster' nonsense. I've lost more wineglasses that way."

"I'll help too," Layla offered.

"No, no, that goes against the rules." Craig topped up her wineglass and handed it back to her.

"I guess I'll supervise, then," she said.

"That's more like it." Craig raised his glass to hers and headed to the living room, where Jeannie was setting up a game of Scrabble.

It was suddenly so quiet in the Barnett home Layla could hear the seagulls fighting for a late dinner at the nearby beach. Matt was washing the dishes, Ian drying and putting them away. Layla wandered to the fridge, where a photo was held on by a little heart magnet. In the picture were two little boys in too-short dress pants sporting matching bow ties. Behind them was a beaming couple Layla recognized as a younger Jeannie and Craig.

"What is this adorable photo?" she asked Matt, who was at the sink beside the fridge.

"*That*," Matt said, "is one of the only photos from my mom and Craig's wedding day. Mom dug it out because their twentieth anniversary is coming up and she's feeling nostalgic. Anyway, it's the only good photo of the four of us that day."

"What are you saying about me?" Jeannie called from the living room.

"I'm saying you could beat Craig at Scrabble drunk and with both arms tied behind your back," Matt told her.

Ian finished stacking clean plates in the cupboard and came over to look. "That's it? The only good family photo we've got from that day?"

"I don't know if you remember, Ian, but it was a pretty quiet day. Didn't a stranger take that?" Matt's tone was too even. There was clearly a story behind that lone photo.

"Right," Ian said, his face falling. He pushed up the sleeves of his gray sweater and folded his arms. "I guess I wasn't thinking about the minimalist guest list."

Layla turned to face Ian, who was so close, she had to tip her head back to see him. "Okay. What am I missing?"

"Mom was self-conscious about making a big deal, since it was her second wedding and her first husband had been a source of town gossip. Nothing cruel, but still..."

Layla nodded, understanding better than Ian would ever know.

"Basically, it was a quickie ceremony, and that photograph"—he tapped on the fridge—"features the only invited guests."

Layla pushed down dark memories threatening to surface. Of her own guest list of two. Of the day she wished she could cut out of her past with scissors and feed to the seagulls outside. She took a sip of wine that was more of a gulp and called on every acting class she'd ever taken when she said, "That's too bad. I'm sure there were a lot of people who were happy for them and wanted to be there."

"Probably the whole island," Matt agreed with an endearing smirk. "Mom was the most popular teacher at her school. Craig was a close second."

"They're both pretty lovable." The alcohol was already doing its job, banishing bad memories, and a bolt of inspiration hit Layla, a way to bring a little joy to Jeannie and Craig. And possibly to give the Barnett brothers something other than their harried past to focus on. "Their anniversary is coming up, right? What about throwing them a surprise party?"

"Layla, you beautiful genius." Ian's eyes widened with excitement. Layla tried to see Matt's face but he was still at the sink with his back turned. "Better yet, for years they've talked about having a big celebration and renewing their vows. How about that? We can finally give them the wedding they deserve."

That was definitely *not* what Layla had suggested and she tried not to flinch at the words *vow* and *wedding*, shoving her memories beneath the surface. She took another big gulp from her glass and nodded with feigned enthusiasm.

Ian misinterpreted her hesitation. "Or is work overwhelming right now because of that flailing show?"

"What flailing show?" Matt asked, finally turning around.

"It's fine, don't worry about it," Layla said to Matt, inadvertently being as short with him as he'd been with her as she tried to keep herself intact. She turned back to Ian. "No, that's not really my problem to solve, I can definitely help plan this...event for your parents."

"Anyone want to know what I think?" Matt asked, irked.

"It's the perfect idea, Matty, even you have to agree," Ian said. Then, softer, "And it'd be great if you helped too."

Matt seemed to deflate just a little. "I don't know that Mom would want all the attention, but I think she deserves it."

As Layla began to envision what a vow renewal would look like, her chest squeezed and she struggled to catch a proper breath. She wriggled her toes in her ballet flats, trying to keep herself grounded in her body. *Damn it.* Why didn't she make enough to afford a therapist? Why couldn't she leave her past in the fucking past? Why couldn't she just be *normal* in this moment?

"What do you say?" Ian asked, eyes full of hope as he tucked stray strands of hair behind her ear. "Want to help me plan a wedding?"

"Of course I do." Her voice cracked at the end, but Ian had turned around to flip the pages on his parents' kitchen calendar, already looking at dates.

She took a deep breath, and several more *sips* of wine, reminding herself things were better now. Different. One deep breath turned into several, and she finally felt her shoulders relaxing.

The kitchen was so small, she knew Matt had heard her labored inhales, her pushed-out exhales. She watched him absorb the sound. He stayed like that, still and thoughtful, for another moment before turning the faucet on and rinsing a few dishes that were already clean.

CHAPTER THIRTEEN

SATURDAY ON ORCAS Island was utter perfection. Layla and Ian spent the morning hiking, followed by a visit to a café in what looked like a log cabin. There they were served coffee and the best cinnamon rolls Layla had ever tasted by a bubbly woman who showed them pictures of her adorable goldendoodle. Afterward, they went back to the house and curled up for a delicious nap. Because instead of stealing every spare second to check up on work, now Ian *napped*.

On the docket for that evening was dinner with the rest of the Barnetts followed by more Scrabble, but as Layla headed downstairs to see what she could do to help, she heard a text come in. She pulled out her phone. It was Pearl, an all-caps message followed by a series of nonsense emojis. Layla clicked it open:

WHY DIDN'T YOU TELL ME IAN'S BROTHER IS FAMOUS

I HAVE SEEN EVERY EP OF COMMON PEOPLE AT LEAST FIVE TIMES.

YOU SHOULD ASK HIM TO WRITE THE SHOW FOR NW.

Hold on. Matt was famous? Like, *famous*-famous? So famous that Pearl recognized him from one photo on Instagram? This was definitely worth looking into. She had just opened Google when she spotted him in the dining room, holding place mats. *Might as well get the story from the source.* She jumped in to help him set the table, grabbing cutlery from the drawer. Matt barely paused to look at her.

"So, what have you been up to today?" she casually asked. Maybe engaging Matt was like approaching Deano; she would move slowly at first to let him get her scent before offering him a treat. Or, in this case, acknowledging his celebrity status.

Matt put down a place mat and a cloth napkin, which Layla immediately topped with a knife and fork. Instead of answering her question, he eyed her handiwork and said, "Well, you're efficient."

Perhaps she *was* following a little too closely. She was just excited to have something real to talk to him about and time to do it, since Ian was still singing in the shower. She didn't recognize the tune (bless his heart), but eventually she figured out he was singing "Free Bird," by Lynyrd Skynyrd, and she got the impression he was going to be a while.

"I'm efficient because I waitressed briefly after college and then again in LA," she explained, then caught herself. The words had popped out without passing through her regular filter. She *never* talked about LA.

Matt put another place mat down and she reached out, waiting for him to put the napkin on top. But he didn't. "I didn't know you lived there."

"I didn't know you were famous," she replied. "Now we've both learned something new. Some might say we're bonding."

His eyes flashed. "I'm not *famous*," he said at last and put down the rest of the place mats and napkins at record speed. Layla trotted behind him, unwilling to be shaken off. This wasn't how this was supposed to go. Who didn't like flattery?

"That's not what my friend Pearl said. She saw your picture on Insta—"

He stopped short. She nearly bumped into the back of him. His voice came out low and slowly. "And *why* would a picture of me be on Insta?"

Why was he being so weird? Well. He wasn't the only one who knew how to be indignant. She crossed her arms and narrowed her eyes. "I posted the one I took last night. But if it bothers you, I can take it d—"

"It bothers me," he said. And he grabbed his coat and walked out the front door.

He must've texted his mom, because when they sat down to dinner half an hour later and Ian asked, "Where's Matty?" Jeannie grew very focused on serving everyone equal portions of homemade mac and cheese and said in a thin voice, "He had some things to take care of back in the city."

Ian looked disappointed, but then rallied. "Maybe he had a job interview or something?"

But Layla knew the truth. She'd scared him off. The confusing shame of it could have flambéed the pasta in front of her.

They didn't see him again the rest of the weekend.

Despite Matt's conspicuous absence, the trip remained lovely. She and Ian chatted about the things they wanted to do that summer: food and pride festivals, concerts, trips to the San Juan Islands. Ian was eager to see the year ahead as an opportunity, even if he currently seemed a little down.

"I'm sorry Matt left early," Layla said on Sunday morning. She was seated on Ian's bed, watching him repack the clothes he'd put in his old dresser.

Ian closed the last drawer and tucked the extra socks he always brought into one of the zipper compartments. "It's not your fault."

Yes, it is, she thought. Out loud she said, "What was the deal with that TV show he worked for, anyway?"

"*Common People?*" Ian asked, closing his bag. He paused. "It was a show based on his blog entries. From when he drove around the U.S. looking for Dennis and finding himself or whatever."

Layla nodded, but she didn't quite get it. Would it be weird to watch the show now? She couldn't decide.

They brought their luggage to the front entrance and gave Jeannie and Craig goodbye hugs. As Craig loaded their bags into the car—he insisted—Jeannie made them promise they'd be back soon.

"You seem so much happier lately," Jeannie said, cupping Ian's face in her hands. "Don't forget about what's working here. Don't lose this."

Layla had to turn away to collect herself. What Jeannie didn't know, what none of them knew, was that it was precisely what Ian *had* forgotten that was making him so happy. Love and guilt collided within her as she found herself rationalizing—again—her choice to keep the breakup from Ian.

As they drove to the ferry, she looked out the window at the endless trees and blackberry bushes.

"You're quiet," Ian said softly.

"Sunday scaries." Because the truth was too complicated.

"But you love your job," he said.

Not really. She loved theater; she loved watching sets and costumes and people come together to create magic. She did *not* love hassling people to volunteer because the theater couldn't afford to pay them. She did *not* love getting yelled at by the shop foreman for buying the wrong ink for the printer. She did *not* love counting candy bars in the musty basement.

Ian misinterpreted her expression and continued, "I get it. Sundays are hard for me too."

There were no porpoises alongside the ferry that day. This time, the wind was biting instead of refreshing, so she and Ian went inside and sipped tea. They made a game of trying to guess the jobs and lives of their fellow passengers, which cheered Layla up a bit.

Ian had a four a.m. call with London the next day, and Deano had already been left alone for his two-night maximum (a third night without Layla's company meant he'd take revenge on the fabric headboard of her bed). So, alone that night in her cramped studio apartment, Layla got tipsy on Chardon-Yay! and impulse-bought a chartreuse hand muff that wasn't even cute. Deano, curled up on her lap, shedding fur as if in the middle of an elaborate costume change, lifted his head, took one look at the screen, and meowed his smoker's cough of a meow. Even *he* knew the hand muff was a waste of money. Layla put her laptop aside, lifted half-asleep Deano (who actually liked to be carried like a baby when he was tired), brought him over to her bed, and turned on the TV. On a whim, she searched for *Common People*, pulled up the first episode, and watched. And then she watched the second. And the third.

She barely slept that night.

In the morning, Layla awoke to the buzzing of the TV, which she'd forgotten to turn off. She'd also forgotten to wash her face, and her mouth felt like someone had stuffed a dirty sock in it. Thinking through the day ahead, she remembered Northwest's crisis and groaned. She reached for Deano, who stretched out his little kitty legs and kindly put a paw on her hand as she scratched under his neck.

If the theater couldn't find a playwright, she'd lose her job.

If she lost her job, she wouldn't be able to afford her rent.

If she got kicked out of her apartment, she couldn't move in with Ian because Matt had just arrived. And because that was still a bridge too far—wasn't it?

But if she couldn't move in with Ian, there was a chance she'd have to admit defeat and move in with her parents.

Again.

Think positive, she reprimanded herself. And then she thought back to Pearl's text. And Ian's original suggestion about hiring Matt. And the expression on Ian's face when he understood Matt had left Orcas Island early.

If those weren't signs from the universe, what was? It was time to do something gutsy. But it would be for the good of the theater and her nonreckless future self.

She took extra care in picking an outfit, selecting a cheerful geometric-print A-line dress. She washed her thick hair and took the time to painstakingly blow-dry it with a round brush. She added an extra layer of mascara to make her eyes pop. Every detail was a piece of armor, preparation for the plan forming in her head.

Layla arrived at Northwest End well before she was supposed to and long before she usually did, but Manjit had still beat her there. Well, no time like the present, she supposed.

Layla rapped softly on Manjit's open door. "Good morning."

"What can I do for you?" Manjit's skipping the pleasantries wasn't a good sign. Nor was her harried appearance or the way she flipped her phone over quickly so the screen was facedown.

Layla's words spilled out like water from a tipped jug. "I haven't talked to him yet, but my boyfriend's brother is famous— well, semi-famous—and he's a writer, and I was wondering if you wanted me to talk to him? About the show?"

Manjit looked confused. Down the hall someone coughed. "How. Famous." Even though it was a question, it sounded like two complete sentences.

Still lurking in the doorway, Layla chewed on her bottom lip before answering, unsure whether her response was going to be impressive or get her laughed out of the office. "His name is Matt Barnett, and he was involved with a TV show. *Common People*?"

Manjit flipped her phone back over and started typing, presumably googling everything Layla had just said. After a moment, she looked back up. Her gaze had sharpened. "I'll be honest. We've considered our other options. We can put a call out for emerging playwrights and have an in-box full of shiny new plays. But going through a slush pile takes time, which we don't have. Besides, there will be questions about why we replaced Aaron Masfield. The only way through all this, as far as I can see, is to have an exciting new playwright." She pushed her chair back from her desk with sudden energy. "One of the writers from *Common People*? That's exciting. That's a headline."

"That's a headline," Layla repeated, trying to process this. She hadn't expected Manjit to jump on board so quickly.

But for the first time in days, Manjit looked enthusiastic. "Layla, this is really good work. And now I am *begging* you to get us Matt Barnett. Ask him, bribe him, blackmail him—no, don't blackmail him...unless you think it'll help? Just get him to say yes." Manjit's frantic energy was buzzing across the room, infecting Layla.

"Wow, okay." Layla nodded vigorously. "I'll talk to him. I'm glad I could help." And before she could screw it up, she turned and left, completely terrified by her own boldness.

And by what Matt might say. Especially since the last time she'd spoken with him, he'd stopped saying anything at all.

Layla spent the rest of the morning trying to get all her regular responsibilities off her plate, but she was so anxious about talking to Matt, she struggled to focus. In the afternoon, Pearl came by her desk. She was wearing a blouse with shoulder pads that would've been ridiculous on a lesser person, but Pearl looked hella chic.

"Did you have a good lunch with your mom?" Pearl had made popcorn at the concession stand and was throwing one piece at a time into the air and trying to catch it in her mouth.

"What are you talking about? I ate my lunch here." Layla was fiddling with her phone, working on a text asking Ian for his brother's number. Before she could overthink it, she hit Send.

"Weird. I saw your mom down the street a second ago," Pearl said. She caught a piece of popcorn tidily between her teeth. She made a very confused Layla put down her phone in order to high-five, then asked, "She wasn't here to say hi?"

"Are you sure it was my mom?" Layla picked up her phone again to ensure she hadn't missed a call or text. Pearl rolled her eyes; she had known Layla's parents almost as long as she'd known Layla. She'd even joined the Rockford family for Thanksgiving last year when her own family was out of town.

"Was she by herself?" Layla asked, wondering why her mother would be so close and not attempt to see her. *Again*. Was she upset about Layla missing another Sunday dinner?

"She was talking to some silver-haired fox just outside the bubble-tea shop. Why?"

Layla flashed back to the music store. "What did he look like? Did she see you? What was she wearing? Tell me everything."

"Whoa. Talk about interrogation." Pearl put down the popcorn and perched on the edge of Layla's desk. She ticked off the details on her fingers. "Your mom looked hot. Like Jamie Lee Curtis circa *Freaky Friday*. The dude she was with had darkish skin and was dressed like he was on his way to the half-pipe at a skate-fest. Despite that, they seemed happy. They were laughing. Who is he?" Pearl paused. "Actually, I'm not sure if you want to hear this part, but she was touching his arm. A lot."

If Layla's worst suspicions were true, she would... she didn't know what. She'd figure it out when it happened. "I'm calling her."

She waited as her mother's phone rang, convincing herself this was all innocent. It wasn't a crime to run errands in a new part of town. By the time she heard her mom say hello, she felt ridiculous. She was being ridiculous. "Hi, Mom," she said cheerfully.

"Hi, Layla."

Was it her imagination or did Rena sound disappointed? She was *never* disappointed to hear from Layla. "Am I catching you at a bad time?" Layla tried to keep her voice light. Unaccusatory.

"You know"—her mom clucked her tongue—"I'm just between piano students right now. And—oh, it looks like George and Charlotte are here."

George and Charlotte were best friends who'd decided to take up the piano in their seventies. They were delightful, and her mother was a dirty rotten liar. There's no way Rena would've made it back to Bellevue by now. Never mind that Layla could hear downtown traffic in the background.

"I'll call you later, hon," Rena said in a rush. "Love you." And then she hung up.

Hung up.

Just then, Ian texted her Matt's number, saying he hoped this was about the show.

One crisis at a time.

CHAPTER FOURTEEN

AS LAYLA WALKED home from work that day, her mind swam with theories about her mom. One theory, actually. And it was that she was taking her doting, kindhearted husband for granted to throw herself at a man-child. Layla thought about how she'd felt when she learned Garrison was cheating on her, and she multiplied that by the number of years her parents had been together, the number of times they'd sung "Tell Me Something Good," the number of hugs they'd exchanged, and the number of kids they'd had. And that number was...well, figurative, really, but no matter how high it was, how could Rena do this? Never mind the fact that Rena had been the one who'd come for Layla when Layla couldn't take LA anymore. Who, after hours of silence in the car ride back to Bellevue, had said, "You are not alone in this world, Layla. But that means you have to do better. For all of us."

Weaving through the post-work crowd—and the idiots who had their umbrellas out in a light sun-shower—Layla felt ill. She wanted to slow down her thoughts, stop them altogether. After taking the weekend off, Ian wasn't sure how late he'd be, so Layla figured she was on her own. She popped into the bodega a block away from her apartment to buy her usual: ten little multicolored canisters of M&M Minis, a "party size" bag of Doritos, and a bottle of Chardon-Yay! These flavors absolutely did not mix, and they would absolutely give her rancid breath, but it didn't matter. Maybe once she had a good buzz going, she'd have the guts to finally text Matt. *One* good thing could come out of this shit-tastic day.

And then every one of her thoughts shut down as she rounded the corner. Because there, leaning against the wall beside her building's entrance, was Matt himself. She hadn't even texted him yet. Or opened one canister of her M&M's.

If this was another sign from the universe, she was in no mood.

Her full tote bag weighed shamefully on her shoulder; her instinct was to grab Matt by the collar of his faded Bob Dylan T-shirt (he probably thought liking Bob Dylan was a whole personality) and say, *Don't you know I currently lack the bandwidth to deal with you? Wait for my text—and for me to deal with my blood sugar.*

Her second instinct, a seemingly more mature one, was to greet him in a friendly yet restrained manner and suss out what he was doing there.

"Hey, Matt. What's up?" The sun was suddenly out in full force, and she was glad her cat's-eye sunglasses prevented him from seeing the wariness of her stare.

"Ian called me an hour ago and said you wanted to talk? He gave me your address."

"Of course he did," she said, simultaneously grateful and a little irritated that Ian was nudging her along when she wasn't at her best.

"Oh, and I found this at my parents' house. I assume it's yours." Matt reached into the pocket of his beat-up bomber jacket and revealed the shell-and-sea-glass ring she and Ian had bought in Vancouver. Layla remembered wearing it on the ferry over. She hadn't even realized it was missing.

"Thanks." Knowing she needed to butter him up, she blurted out, "Sorry if I offended you."

"Offended me when?" He was so tricky to read, she couldn't figure out if he was being deliberately obtuse. He stood there at ease and out of place all at once. She wondered if this was how Matt always moved through the world. Was he someone who made small talk in the grocery line? Or did he only shop at night when he could flicker in and out like a ghost? He probably exclusively used the self-checkout, Layla decided, even when he had too many items.

"Back at your parents' house. When I brought up that you're famous."

"I'm *not* famous," he corrected her.

Pulling out her eyelashes one at a time would have been less painful than this. She shifted her tote bag to her other shoulder. "Right. Got it."

That clearly wasn't the way in, then. She tried a different tack. "Ian's excited to have you around again."

"Yeah, we'll see how long that excitement lasts." He stared at Layla. Layla stared back. "What did you want to talk to me about?"

"Right." She looked around. There was a so-called greenspace down the street, but it was really just a patch of grass the size of a Smart car, better for scoring heroin than having a business discussion. She thought about inviting him up, but that seemed weird. Too intimate somehow.

"Layla? Is this a bad time? Should I just go?" Matt raised his eyebrows and pushed off from the brick wall just as three women rode by on bicycles, forcing Layla to step closer to him to get out of their way. One rider, an attractive younger woman, put on her brakes so abruptly, her tires left skid marks on the sidewalk. She yelled at her friends to stop. They all whispered to one another and then stared at Matt.

"Do you know what's happening?" Layla asked him, confused. He shrugged but seemed to have some idea. One of the women shouted, "Hey, Matt! I wanna sleep with common people like you!"

Matt grudgingly replied, "I'll see what I can do."

The cyclists squealed, burst out laughing, and finally rode off. The suggestive lines sounded familiar. The syncopation of them.

"Do you know them?" Layla asked curiously.

"Nope."

The beat of the lines clicked in her head, and she recognized the lyrics of a nineties song by Pulp, the one at the start of Matt's show. But she feigned ignorance because he didn't need to know she'd been watching it. "You just have a habit of reciting suggestive Brit-pop lyrics to strangers?"

"It was the theme song to the TV show I worked on," Matt said with a sigh, the act of explaining seeming to take a lot out of him.

"Ohhhh. So you're *really* not famous, then."

He crossed his arms. "Fine. I think the show is on Hulu or something. It has a bit of a cult following."

Now that he'd admitted it, she had him cornered. What if she could talk him into this? It would be good not only for Northwest but for Layla—could she use this coup as leverage to actually work on the show? Do something other than beg for volunteers and count candy bars? "Hey, Matt, you wanna come upstairs? I really do have a business idea I'd like to run by you."

He eyed her cautiously. *Say yes, you scoundrel,* she challenged him with her eyes. His voice was equally wary when he said, "Sure."

CHAPTER FIFTEEN

THE ELEVATOR SEEMED even noisier than usual. Jerkier. The smell of old takeout more potent. Matt leaned back against the wall, and Layla suddenly felt too keen, too close, so she took a step back and leaned against her own wall. He saw her do it, but when she raised her brows, daring him to make fun of her, he averted his gaze, looking down at an unidentifiable stain on the floor. Suddenly, Layla couldn't look away from the stain either (was it marinara sauce? Blood? Both?). She silently willed the elevator to reach her floor faster. And then she thought about what was waiting for them at the end of the ride: her apartment.

"You aren't allergic to cats, are you?" she asked as the doors creaked open.

"Nope. I love cats."

"Is that why you were fired from your job as a guide-dog trainer?" she asked wryly, pulling out her keys and leading him down the hall. "And you may not love *my* cat. He already has it in for Ian, so he might put a hit on you too."

Matt let out a puff of air as though he were *almost* amused. "Who said I was fired?"

She furrowed her brow, pushed the door open, and let Deano, who was sitting on top of her bed like it was his royal throne, finish his gruff bark of a hello before replying, "You did. That night we met at the sushi restaurant."

"I didn't say I was fired, I said it was bold of you to assume I *wasn't* fired," Matt reminded her as he looked around her apartment. His gaze settled on the black-and-white prints of the Rat Pack, one of her favorite thrift-shop finds. She was particularly fond of the one that featured Sammy Davis Jr. laughing uproariously between Dean Martin and Frank Sinatra. Whenever she was frustrated, she tried to channel that energy. Matt nodded appreciatively before moving his attention to the turntable on her credenza and her collection of vinyl albums underneath, many of which she'd bought from the shop by Ian's condo.

Deano hopped off the bed and sniffed Matt's shoes, miraculously allowing him to lean down and give him a scratch behind the ears. Then the traitor actually started purring. *Don't let your guard down, he's not to be trusted,* she telepathically told her cat. Deano must've received the message, because he trotted off and flopped onto the floor a few feet away, his orange fur splashing out like spilled paint.

"Ah, okay. So do you ever actually say what you mean?" Layla asked. Her irritation was growing, and she momentarily forgot she was supposed to be buttering him up.

"Maybe I always do, but no one's really listening," he tossed back.

A sound came out of her that was somewhere between a snort and a scoff. It wasn't pretty, and if anyone other than Matt had heard it, she might have been embarrassed.

"What," Matt said flatly. When she didn't respond, he asked again, softer, "What?"

"This whole 'no one understands me except my ironic T-shirts' act is a little clichéd, don't you think?"

"My shirts aren't ironic. And is it any more clichéd than your manic-pixie-dream-girl shtick?"

Layla let out the tiniest of gasps and watched him register that the blow had landed. He immediately looked away, probably to hide his smirk.

"Let's talk about this job." She crossed her arms, telegraphing that this wasn't a social visit and she wasn't going to prolong it.

"Okay, sure." He skirted around Deano's dignity-free body and plopped down on her couch like he owned the place. "I assume it's about your 'flailing show.' Aren't you going to ask me if I want something to drink first? Some water? Tea? Coffee?"

"Nope." She jutted her chin at him. "But by all means, make yourself comfortable."

He moved the slightest bit forward like he was going to get up, seemed to think better of it, and relaxed back again. She couldn't really blame him. The couch was old. Second- or third-hand. It was also the prettiest soft mint green, a velvety fabric, and more comfortable than her bed.

"I could move into this couch," he said, echoing her line from the weekend.

Was he serious or was he mocking her? Deano got up, meowed, and set up camp next to his food bowl, his stare withering. Layla sighed and followed him.

"Your cat's subtle," Matt remarked.

"At least he says what he means," she mumbled, filling Deano's bowl with kibble.

"Are you mad at me?" Matt asked, and he had the nerve to sound surprised. Maybe his life as a semi-famous loafer made him think he was entitled to free beverages?

Layla was bending over to pick up bits of kibble that had flown out of Deano's bowl, realizing too late she was giving Matt a full view of her ass. She resented being asked such a loaded question when she was in this position. She stood back up and spun around, unsure how to answer. And then she decided not to.

"Have you ever written a play and/or had it produced at a professional theater company?"

"No." Matt regarded her. "And no."

She walked over and took a seat on the opposite end of the couch. He backed away a little, even though she was at least three feet from him. "You actually wrote for that *Common People* show, right? Your credit with them is legit?"

"Sort of." He closed his eyes as though this conversation were taking all his strength. "I wrote a blog, and season one of *Common People* was based on that blog. I was in the writers' room. So, yeah, I got a writing credit."

Best to get straight to the point. "Yes, this is about the show. We've had a, um, setback, as you heard, and we need an emerging playwright to do an original production with us. With your cult following but lack of theater experience, you're perfect. You'll save our publicity and possibly draw a bit of a crowd."

Now she had his attention. He sat up, ramrod straight. "Hold it. Are you *telling* me I'm writing a show for you or *asking?*"

"Tomato, potato, as long as you do it."

"It's tomato, to-mah-toe."

"Not to a manic pixie dream girl." Layla gave him a steely gaze. He couldn't turn her down. She didn't have a backup plan. And, honestly, wasn't this good for him too? "What kind of show would you want to work on? Maybe tell me about *Common People.*" *And let's pretend it wasn't on this very TV screen last night.*

Matt sighed. "Think of it like that series based on the Modern Love column but for working millennials. Fictionalized storylines that come from real experiences."

Her own Modern Love stories would probably be deemed too unbelievable for the column. "Do you get recognized often? When you're just out and about, like today?"

His eyebrow went up a fraction at the term *out and about*. He sounded guarded when he said, "The show cut between me reading my blog entries and the fictionalized reenactments. I don't know why they wanted me on-screen at all."

"Did you ever watch it?" she asked, frustrated he couldn't see what fans could see—what *she'd* already seen in those episodes, the brilliant way Matt's narration skewered and celebrated being in your twenties.

"No. Who wants to watch themselves on-screen?"

A small pink container of eye cream suddenly flew across the room. Layla and Matt turned to see Deano sitting on the desk she also used as a vanity batting items off one at a time.

"He do that often?" Matt asked, clearly fascinated.

"Yes," Layla replied, irritated at her cat, at Matt, at the way this whole conversation was going. "Deano would probably *love* to watch himself on-screen."

"I bet he's a really talented actor. I bet he's like the Pedro Pascal of cats."

She hid her unexpected amusement by marching over to the desk and lifting Deano up just as he was about to send her eyeshadow palette flying. *Matt's just trying to change the subject.* "I'm just thinking out loud here, but maybe you'd understand the appeal of the show if you *did* watch it. Especially now, with a fresh perspective."

She'd said something wrong. He shook his head and got up at the same time she was sitting back down with Deano. In the confusion, the cat immediately hopped off her lap and meandered back to the desk.

"Sorry you're in a bind, but I'm not the person to help you," Matt said.

"Why not?" She'd meant to challenge him kindly. Plead with him. Instead, those two words were a clear accusation.

"Because I don't know anything about theater, I'm not actually a writer, and you can barely stand to be in the same room as me. Even your cat is upset I'm here."

He hadn't yelled, but the force of his response nearly knocked her over.

"*I* can't stand to be in the same room as *you?* You're the one who took off last weekend just because I tried to help you set the table." She stood up too, desperation rising. She hadn't expected him to turn her down. This was a genuine opportunity! "Look, I know about theater; I can help you if you want. And you *are* a writer, otherwise *Common People* wouldn't have optioned your blog."

Nothing. No response. Matt didn't even blink.

She tilted her chin up. "Quite frankly, Deano's being nicer to you than he is to most people. When he's upset, believe me, *you'll know.*"

Matt raised one eyebrow, daring her to go on. The jerk was going to make her say it. *Fine.* "And I *can* stand to be in the same room as you." She raised an eyebrow back. "I'm doing it right now."

Matt looked unconvinced. How could she tell him that it wasn't that she didn't like *him*, it was that he reminded her of the worst time in her life? God, Matt had even come to Seattle by way of California. Also, she *didn't* really like Matt. He was smug, aloof, judgmental. Hurtful. No wonder Ian'd had so little to do with him for years. "Please, Matt?" Layla dug deep to where her dignity ended and desperation began.

Matt opened his mouth to respond just as her apartment buzzer rang. Most buildings had their security wired to tenants' cell phones, but hers was still old-school. She walked over to the intercom, giving Deano a dirty look as he batted her hairbrush to the floor.

"Hello?" she said, holding the button down, all her impatience infused in those two syllables.

When she released the button, she heard Ian say, "Surprise! I'm here with Thai food."

Her anger and anxiety loosened at the sound of his voice. He'd said he was working late tonight. "Come on up!" she said with relief.

When she returned her focus to Matt, he was staring at the ceiling. *At least he's still here.* She kept her mouth shut and waited for him to speak.

The silence stretched out like a rubber band until it eventually snapped.

"You've got company coming. I should go." Matt attempted to move to her front door, but she was blocking his escape route.

"It's not 'company,' it's Ian," she told him, fiddling with the ring Matt had returned.

"Then I should *really* go. I already see that guy enough at home."

It was over. There was no way Matt was going to agree to this. She'd lose her chance to prove she was more than a trained monkey at Northwest End. The monkey would probably even be better at begging for volunteers—who could say no to a trained monkey?

"I really thought this could be a cool opportunity for you," she said. She surprised even herself by how much she meant it.

Matt's stubborn eyes were locked on hers.

"What did I miss? What could've been a cool opportunity? Are you two talking about that show?" Ian had somehow opened the door without Layla noticing and now he was behind her. "By the way, I saw your super in the elevator and I think I finally convinced him to get that thing fixed."

Layla broke her staring contest with Matt and turned her attention to her boyfriend. He was still in his suit, his tie loosened just enough to undo his top button. If she hadn't been so agitated, Layla would've been tempted to nibble on his neck.

"That elevator's been on its last legs forever," she said, grateful. He kissed her cheek. Immediately, all the built-up tension from the day oozed out of her. "I kept meaning to bug him about it."

"No need, it's done." Ian held up a Juree's bag. "And I got your favorite."

"Perfect," she said, taking the bag from him. "I was just talking to Matt about the playwriting job at Northwest End. How was work?"

"Whoa, whoa, whoa." Ian followed her the two steps into the kitchen. As she unpacked the containers of pad thai and curries, he looked over at Matt. "Layla's offering you a writing job and you're turning it down, Matty?"

"It's not right for me." Matt was heading for the open door. "Have a good night, you two."

"Get back in here." Ian turned to Layla. "Is it okay if he stays? I'd love to have dinner with my two favorite people."

"There's no way I'm one of your favorite people," Matt said.

"You could be if—" Ian stopped himself. Took a breath. "I'd really love it if you stayed."

Layla didn't know how to coerce Matt into taking the gig, but she wasn't going to stand in the way of *Ian* coercing him. "We've got more than enough food, Matt."

Before Matt could say no again, she took out three plates and set them on the coffee table. At the last minute, she took the PART-TIME HERO, FULL-TIME DREAMBOAT mug out of the junk drawer, washed it, and put it on the table too.

"You told me yesterday that you didn't want to take a job just to have a job," Ian pointed out to Matt. "You wanted to try something new, do something interesting. And I *know* you still feel compelled to write. I've heard you clacking on the keyboard after I go to bed. Why wouldn't you try this?"

"It's not right for me," Matt insisted in a clipped voice. "And why do you want me to get a job so badly? So I can pay you rent or move out?"

"I told you I don't care about rent. Layla's going out on a limb for you." Out of the corner of her eye, Layla saw Ian put a hand on Matt's shoulder. Matt tensed. Matt was a few inches shorter than him, so Ian literally looked down at him, which probably didn't help the situation. "Can't you appreciate that?"

Layla was dying to see Matt's reaction. She straightened up to get a better view. Matt's eyes flicked to hers. "It sounds more like *she's* asking *me* to go out on a limb for *her.*"

The accuracy stung. Her cheeks got hot. She bustled back to the kitchen for napkins, wondering how she'd even begin to explain her swing-and-a-miss to Manjit. But when she returned, something had changed.

"Fine. I'll do it," Matt said softly. "It's going to be a disaster, but I'll do it."

What had Ian said? He was patting Matt on the back, and Layla's heart simultaneously sank and soared.

"Thank you, thank you," she said as Ian released his brother, who did not seem thrilled. "I know this is the right decision. It's practically fate."

Matt wouldn't look at her.

"Hey," she said, trying to lighten the mood. "You can consider this dinner your first payment."

Ian gave her a smile, but Matt shook his head. She tried again, awkwardly. "I mean, we'll also pay you in actual dollars, and, who knows, you might even enjoy yourself."

"I'll bet you'll love working with Layla," Ian said supportively. Matt grunted in response and reluctantly followed Ian to the couch.

Matt eyed the mug. "What's that?"

Ian threw his head back and laughed, just as he had when she'd given it to him.

"The night we met, I saw Ian break up a bar fight," Layla explained.

"Makes sense." Matt started poking through the containers of food. "Ian's a real hero type."

Layla had to agree. After all, by talking Matt into doing the show, he'd just saved her again.

But maybe the unholy union Layla and Matt were entering would help give the brothers a little more common ground too.

CHAPTER SIXTEEN

THE FIRST ROMANTIC interest Layla had ever brought to Sunday dinner was her high-school boyfriend Wally. He'd been so very pretty and so very dim. Their relationship lasted three months, which, in her teen years, had seemed epic. When she brought him home, sure he'd play well to her family, Jude and Bobby lured him into a conversation about the stock market that even *they* didn't understand just to see if he'd pretend to comprehend their nonsense (which, sadly, he had), and to this day, Rhiannon and Cecelia still referred to him as Layla's High-School Himbo.

For all their boisterous fun and wit, her family could be *ruthless*. Every time she brought a new love interest home, he was treated politely, then later given a nickname and mocked.

She'd learned Randall's nickname by mistake, and in some ways, it had been the worst of all. While eavesdropping on her mom talking to the rest of her siblings, she realized they only ever called him That Guy. As in, "Can you believe That Guy?" and "I'm so glad we don't have to deal with That Guy anymore."

When she'd brought Ian home for the first time, her family

had politely interrogated him over barbecue, laughed along with him during a raucous postdinner game of charades, and made him promise to join them again soon. The next day, she'd checked the family text chain, waiting for their verdict. Waiting for Ian's nickname.

Instead, they'd given him their ringing endorsement.

By that point she knew she was falling in love with him, but the way he fit in with her family made her tumble the rest of the way.

Having him back in her life, back beside her for Sunday dinners, felt so right. Especially after such a momentous week. When Layla walked into Manjit's office on Tuesday and told her the good news about Matt, Manjit had whooped and exclaimed, "You pull this off, Layla, and you can have any job in this theater! Except mine."

"And mine," Charlene yelled from the office next door.

In the moment, impulsive Layla took over, drop-kicking the filter between her brain and her mouth and saying, "How about codirector on this baby?"

Looking back, she regretted referring to a show as *this baby* (what was she, a Hollywood agent from the 1940s?), but Manjit had winked at her and replied, "You got it," which eased the embarrassment somewhat.

By Friday, after a week of meetings, her new title felt real. By Sunday, she couldn't wait to tell her family about her first nonlateral career move in years. Having Ian by her side was the cherry on top. She took his hand when he offered it and they walked up the steps to her parents' house together.

Rhiannon's wife, Kit, was the first to greet them. She was in the front entrance trying to talk Izzie out of turning the backyard into a martial arts ring. "You don't want to accidentally hurt someone, do you, Izzie-Bear?"

Izzie considered this for a very long time.

"Hey, Iz," Ian said, squatting to her level. "Maybe you and I can have an arm-wrestling match instead?"

Izzie brightened immediately and pulled Ian to the living-room floor. Layla's heart felt like a cherry blossom tree, bursting with color.

After Izzie beat Ian in a thrilling match, she demanded to arm-wrestle Layla next. Then she wanted Layla and Ian (the two losers) to arm-wrestle each other. Lying on their stomachs, face to face, Layla and Ian put on their best competitive grimaces.

"Trash-talk!" Desmond, who'd joined the growing crowd around them, commanded.

"I'm gonna end you," Layla obliged in her best professional-wrestler growl.

"I'm gonna pin your arm so fast, you'll think you're arm-wrestling a cheetah," Ian growled back.

"You're gonna think my arm's an all-powerful windmill and that a hurricane's blowing in." Layla squinted at him while her nieces and nephews cheered.

Izzie cupped their clasped hands with her tiny fingers, raised the whole bundle, and yelled, "Go! Go! Go!"

Ian was stronger than Layla, but he knew the importance of drama and pretended to struggle. The room was clearly on his side. "You can't let the bad guy win!" someone squealed.

"Hey!" Layla kept her grip locked but turned her head slightly. "Why am I the bad guy?"

"Ian promised to sneak us more dessert," Desmond stage-whispered.

"*What?*" Layla was laughing too hard to push back, and Ian claimed victory. The kids erupted in cheers. Ian slow-mo-jogged through them, high-fiving and fist-bumping all the little hands.

She loved him so much in that moment, her stomach hurt.

Layla's dad called them to their respective tables, where there were platters of sloppy joes (both beef and vegetarian), home-made french fries, and trays of fruit. With Ian beside her, for the first time in months, Layla didn't feel awkward, like the odd person out. She filled her own plate and helped the kids spear chunks of watermelon and strawberries.

At least, she didn't feel awkward until she saw her mom. With the chaos at work followed by devoted evenings with Ian, Layla had decided to ignore the cognitive dissonance of believing that the only reasonable explanation for her mom's recent behavior was that she was having an affair *and* that her mom was absolutely not capable of having an affair.

Rena usually shone during Sunday dinners, a pack animal who was happiest surrounded by the people she loved most. But tonight, she was distant. Layla caught her staring into space, noting how people had to say her name multiple times before she returned to planet Rockford.

But when it came time for Bill and Rena to sing, "Tell Me Something Good," Rena sang a new harmony, garnering applause from the whole table. Layla clapped along with everyone else and willed herself to stop worrying.

"Let's let Layla go first this week," Rena said, as if intuiting her good news. Or maybe out of guilt for lying on the phone earlier this week.

"I was just put in charge of a big project at Northwest End," Layla said, fiddling with her napkin in her lap, pushing her Rena worries as far down as they would go—and perhaps exaggerating the truth a tad. She wasn't exactly in charge, but she was in co-charge, which was close enough.

"Are you directing something?" Kit asked.

"That would be incredible," Rachelle, Jude's partner, gushed. "We'll come see it!"

"She doesn't do that kind of stuff," Jude said to Rachelle.

"I do now," Layla insisted. "In fact, I'm working directly with

a playwright to develop our next show—which I will be directing." Well, codirecting, but screw Jude. She wasn't going to give
him any ammo.

"And the playwright happens to be my brother," Ian added.

"Nepotism in the entertainment industry. That's unheard of,"
Bobby joked.

"Says the politician," Rhiannon said, rolling her eyes. "We're
proud of you, Lay. We can't wait to see it."

"Absolutely," Bill said, raising his glass.

"Ian's brother worked on a TV show a while back," Layla
explained. Normally she found the hot seat scorching; this was
the first time in ages she'd enjoyed the spotlight. "He's a great
get. Though Ian had to help me talk him into it."

"He can be a little stubborn." Ian tilted his head toward Layla.
"But he's really talented. I can't wait to see what he and Layla
come up with."

Neither can I, she thought. Even though Matt had agreed to
take the job only a few days ago, Manjit and Charlene were
already talking marketing strategies. All week Layla had been
staying late so they could chat. They had already settled on
a loose concept, a project that involved improv and audience
participation, which would limit the need for elaborate set and
costume designs and build on Matt's established reputation.

Coming up with a brand-new concept and pulling it off in less
than a month was a risk, and for the past couple of years, Layla
had studiously avoided anything risky. But being dropped into
the deep end of the theater was waking up a part of her that had
been unconscious for too long. Beyond being excited to prove
herself, she was excited about the potential of the actual show.

Providing Matt cooperated.

All week, he'd been difficult to pin down. She'd texted him
repeatedly about potential meeting times. His responses were
vague: Sometime next week should work, and Maybe an afternoon?

Frustration growing, she'd tried ambushing him at Ian's, but every time she dropped by, he disappeared. In the past week, she'd bumped into the hot neighbor more than she had Matt. It seemed like she was always milling about in the lobby or hallway. Layla was beginning to wonder if she wasn't the only one who was trying to pin down Ian's brother.

"Why wouldn't Ian's brother be interested in the job?" Cecelia prodded.

"Um..." The truth was, Layla wasn't sure why Matt had been so reticent. "I think he just needed to know more about it. Right now, the details are a little loose."

"The details of the job you're offering him are loose. Theater majors lack focus. Imagine," Bobby said. His wife, Carmella, smacked him on the shoulder. "What? It's a well-known fact people in the arts can be a little—"

"Layla's basically working two full-time jobs right now." Ian's tone was friendly, though the message was clear: *No cheap shots at Layla.* She squeezed his knee gratefully under the table.

But Cecelia wouldn't let her question drop. "I guess I still don't understand why Ian's brother—"

"Matt," Ian supplied.

"Right, why *Matt* wouldn't want the job. Is the pay bad?"

Rhiannon, who was seated beside Cecelia, elbowed her. "Let it go, Cece. Matt probably just feels awkward because of what happened between Layla and Ian."

The blood drained from Layla's face. Her hand, holding a french fry, stopped in midair.

Ian cocked his head. "What do you mean, what happened between us?"

The family exchanged looks as Layla's wheels spun. Inspiration struck quickly—*Thank God*—and she said, "It's not awkward that I'm dating the playwright's brother. That kind of stuff happens all the time. The theater world is small. No one will care." She gave Ian what she hoped was a carefree smile for good measure. Enough people nodded in agreement to embolden her further. "Who's next? Rhiannon? Jude? What's good in your lives right now?"

After being in a confined space with multiple Rockfords, Layla luxuriated in the peace of Ian's car. Traffic was light, the sun had set, and Ian had turned on a sexy, bluesy playlist she'd made for him for their one-year anniversary.

He hummed along to the music, and she alternated staring at his profile, illuminated by the moon, and watching buildings and trees flash by behind him. The soundtrack took her right back to their celebration. "Remember the hotel we stayed at for our anniversary?"

"In Portland?" He smiled. "Yeah. I wanted to sightsee, but you spent nearly the entire weekend in the bathtub."

"You've seen my shower-bath combo. The water pressure is permanently set to drizzle, and I have yet to find a plug the right size for my drain. If I want a bath, I have to shove a washcloth down there and hope for the best. Having a giant tub was a *gift*."

"Speaking of anniversaries, I was thinking we should have my parents' party at that restaurant I showed you, in Rosario?" Ian glanced at her, then returned his attention to the road.

Layla thought back to the picturesque marina view. "That's perfect. Especially knowing that's where they told you and your brother about their engagement."

"I think so too."

The music swelled and they drove for a bit in silence, listening. "Do you hate your apartment that much?" Ian eventually asked.

Layla considered his question. She'd loved it once. The way it'd offered her independence from her parents and from the chaos of living in the loft with Pearl. She'd loved adopting Deano and setting up her record player; she felt like the studio, despite or maybe because of the fact that it was small, was a safe harbor. "No. I just mean I don't want to live there forever."

"Don't want to settle down and raise kids there?" Ian's voice was teasing.

"Deano's not great at sharing the space," she said, not ready to even joke about kids.

"Speaking of your cat, is he mad at me?"

Layla burst out laughing. "You sound so concerned!"

"I am!" Ian's tone was comically sincere, and she laughed harder. "He used to love me. Okay, maybe *love* is a strong word, but he definitely tolerated me. Lately he's been..."

"Cold? Distant?" Layla patted his arm. "Do you want to ask him to go to couples counseling?"

"Sort of." Ian faux pouted. "Last night while we were watching that movie, I tried to pet him and I swear he gave me a dirty look."

"Maybe his problem wasn't with you so much as a movie about football."

"Layla. *Any Given Sunday* is about so much more than football."

"Even so, Deano really prefers classic cinema with strong romantic plots. Besides, all his looks are dirty looks," Layla pointed out. She leaned in gravely. "The magic between you and my cat isn't gone, just dimmed. Maybe you need to try a little harder with him. Bring him a treat now and again. Make him feel special."

She expected Ian to keep laughing. Instead, he grew serious and said, "Winning over your cat's probably easier than winning over my brother."

"Are things tense with Matt?" Of course she knew they

were, but she decided to protect him by pretending it wasn't so obvious.

Ian shook his head. "Sorry. We've talked about Matt enough tonight."

"I'm not sorry. Ian, if you want to talk about it—" But he clearly wasn't ready to, even if she was ready to listen.

A song came on that she loved, and she watched him adjust the volume. She hummed along to Keely Smith singing "What Is This Thing Called Love?" And then Ian's storminess subsided and he gave her a side grin.

"Matt stuff aside, I have to say, lately, I'm feeling like the best version of myself, you know? And things are really good between us." He adjusted his grip on the steering wheel, offering her another quick glance before returning his attention to the road. "I mean, they have been in the past, but since the accident they seem—"

"Yeah," Layla agreed, buoyed by the confirmation that he felt it too. The better things were with them, the further she felt from their breakup. And her teeny, tiny omission about it. "In *Love Island* they'd say we're really vibing."

That got a chuckle out of Ian. "I can't believe you watch that trash."

"It's Pearl's fault. She got me hooked against my better judgment. Besides, you eat cotton candy at baseball games and I like to watch the television equivalent," Layla said with a shrug. "Who are we to deny ourselves life's simplest pleasures?"

"That's what I've been thinking," Ian said cryptically, but he didn't say any more.

CHAPTER SEVENTEEN

LUNCH MEETINGS BETWEEN Layla and her bosses were becoming a regular occurrence. Manjit would talk Layla through the process of producing and directing a show—something Layla had only done years ago in college, on a much smaller scale. Charlene and Layla talked through the budget; Charlene gave Layla pointers on how to collaborate with designers and technicians and began to plan the rollout ahead. Layla had never been happier at work. She was galvanized by her new responsibilities and knowledge, but she had to remind herself to cover up her simultaneous panic. She'd made a lot of promises.

That Matt was ready to come in and sign a contract, for example.

Or that he had some killer ideas prepared.

Layla's last several texts to Matt had gone unanswered. One night she caught him at Ian's apartment, but within minutes he grabbed his plaid jacket and left.

"Where's he off to?" Layla asked Ian, frustrated.

Ian shrugged, frowning. "We don't talk much. Maybe I was naive or too rash when I invited him out here. It's been..."

"What?" Layla prodded. "You can talk to me about this. I want you to."

"I don't know. It's been harder to connect with him than I thought. And I think he feels like a third wheel when you come over."

"Maybe he'd be more tolerable if he had a girlfriend," Layla said offhandedly. She remembered Ian mentioning that Matt had been a serial monogamist in his twenties. Layla could relate.

"He has been asking about our relationship. Maybe he *is* lonely."

Layla's heart palpitated, but before she could clarify what exactly Matt had been asking, Ian continued. "It's got to be hard for him coming out here with no job, not really knowing anyone."

"Isn't that what he always does? And besides, he *has* a job, he just doesn't show up for it," she couldn't resist pointing out.

"He doesn't? Do you want me to—"

"No, no, leave the work stuff to me." Ian was busy enough with his own career. She didn't need to burden him with her work baggage too. And part of her really did want to do this herself. "So maybe that's the trick. Do you know anyone we could set Matt up with? Someone at work?"

Ian wrinkled his nose adorably. "I'm not sure Matt would go for the corporate type, you know? All his ex-girlfriends have been—what's that term you use for someone who dresses like a hippie but fashionably?"

"Boho chic?" Layla offered with a laugh.

"Exactly."

Once dinner was over, Layla got up to leave. As much as she wanted to stay, her meetings with Manjit and Charlene had been cutting into her administrative duties, and she didn't want them to think she couldn't handle both. "I should head out. I need to be at the theater early to catch up on some things."

"Yeah, I should go to bed too." Ian walked her to the door and was about to kiss her when there was a rapping on the other side.

"Knock, knock," a voice trilled.

Layla opened the door and came face to face with Ian's hot neighbor who was holding what appeared to be a tray of baked goods. Layla's basest instinct was to tell her to skedaddle, even though she had a feeling Ian wasn't the Barnett brother Margot was after...

Which was *perfect*, actually.

"Hi." Ian opened the door fully and let her in. "You remember Layla."

"Long time no see," Margot Robbie said even though she and Layla had passed each other in the hall only yesterday. Her eyes were impossibly big, her lithe limbs impossibly long. What was her real name again? Giselle? Gazelle?

"Hey...you," Layla managed, proprietarily slipping her arm through Ian's. "Whatever you're holding smells delicious."

"Lemon poppyseed scones." She dipped her head, tucked a lock of her perfectly sleek blond bob behind one ear humbly. "I'm addicted to baking."

"You're a baker, huh?" This was perfect indeed. "You should meet Ian's brother, Matt. He makes the *best* sourdough."

"I thought a new guy had moved in," she said, blushing. Yep. Layla had her number, all right. And thanks to those scones, now she also had breakfast for tomorrow.

Ian told Margot Robbie (whose name was Jojo, it turned out) that the four of them should set up a dinner. Jojo seemed *very* keen. At least Matt couldn't avoid her then, Layla thought.

Manjit must have sensed Layla's initial confidence was wavering. The next afternoon, she shut the door of her office and gestured for Layla to take a seat.

"I know you have a theater degree," Manjit said, sitting down at her desk. "I know you've directed, produced, and acted in shows."

"Not for years, though. Not since college, and those were totally amateur." God, she was an idiot. She might as well have said, *I'm a walking screw-up, don't trust me with small children or large productions! Oh no—too late on that second one!*

"You're not invisible, Layla." Manjit gestured to Layla's outfit, which today was a tangerine swing dress with a cherry print. "Clearly. And you're spending every day doing a job that, quite frankly, anyone can do. Is this all you want? Don't you want more responsibility? Don't you want a creative challenge?"

"Yes." The word came out in a rush of breath. Layla didn't realize she'd been clenching her fists until she felt the sharp pain of her fingernails against her palms. She remembered the improv troupe she'd ill-advisedly joined in high school. She remembered throwing together wild shows in college. She remembered experimenting with words and costumes and lights, collaborating with other people who were curious and sharply funny and whip-smart. Yes, the shows were amateur productions, but they were also entertaining as hell.

She remembered what it was like before she'd made all those big mistakes she couldn't undo, before the dark days of Randall.

"Get Matt in here to sign the contract. Once he signs, Charlene can send you yours and we can officially start paying you a fee for codirecting."

Layla said nothing. She'd *tried* to get Matt in here. She'd texted him over and over again, and nothing. Part of her wanted to release the reins and go back to her regular responsibilities. Sure, being office administrator was dull, but at least it was predictable.

But deep down in her gut, Layla knew she wanted this.

Across from her, Manjit was waiting for a response.

"I'm on it," Layla said and got up to leave before she could chicken out. She returned to her desk and resorted to the unthinkable—instead of sending him another text, she called his cell. Ian was at work, so presumably Matt would be hanging out at the condo doing…whatever Matt did.

It rang.

And rang.

And rang some more.

Each tone turned up the dial of Layla's frustration. She swiveled her chair to make sure no one was within earshot. She waited for the beep, and then, praying he actually listened to his voice mails, she hissed into her phone, "Hey, Matt, remember that time you committed to this show? I do. And I just wanted to point out that if you bail, not only will my job be on the line, but you might take down a whole theater company. We aren't corporate Scrooge McDuck tycoons, my friend. We exist year to—"

"Hey."

Layla spun around to see Matt making his way to her desk from the lobby. She hung up the phone and pocketed it. Stunned and a little embarrassed, she blurted out, "What are you doing here?"

"You texted me. Said I needed to come in and sign a contract?" He stood there, infuriatingly casual, one hand in his pocket, the other scratching absentmindedly at his dark beard. She noticed for the first time it had flecks of red in it. Not that the color of his beard was noteworthy. In that moment, she hated him, and yet she had never been so glad to see someone in her life.

"I texted you *nine times*. For a *week*." Keeping the disdain out of her voice took a great deal of energy. But she couldn't scare him off, not when he was finally right where she wanted him to be. She leaned back in her chair, wincing slightly as it creaked. "What made you finally decide to meander in?"

As if on cue, a scruffy man wandered in behind Matt.

"This isn't the bar, sir," Layla said loudly, barely breaking eye contact with Matt.

"What happened to Mowery's?" the man exclaimed.

With a sigh, Layla stood up and strode to the front door. "The bar told me it wants to meet you next door."

The man shuffled back out.

"That happen often?" Matt asked.

"At least once a week." As if this day could get any more embarrassing. "So?" she pushed, gathering her professionalism back around her. "We know why Day-Drunk Sammy wandered in here, but I'm still waiting to hear why you did."

"Because I've been told it's my job." He had the indecency to look amused. Suddenly, she wished he hadn't shown up. That she was working with anyone else.

Pearl walked into the lobby with a couple of other people from the back office, their lively conversation echoing off the tile floors.

"There is *no way* you met Patrick Stewart when you were in New York—"

"How many bald Irishmen say, 'Engage,' when they get in a taxi?"

"Excuse you, Sir Patrick Stewart isn't Irish, you moron."

The conversation got rowdier as more people joined in. Pearl waved to Layla, then deliberately changed her course so she could pass behind Matt and mouth, *Is that him?*

Layla gave a subtle nod.

He's hotter than he is on TV, Pearl mouthed.

Very helpful, Pearl, she mouthed back.

When she turned her attention back to Matt, he was no longer exuding cool detachment. His face was blanched, eyes darting from loud person to loud person.

"Are you okay?" she asked him.

He didn't look at her. His hands came out of his pockets; he crossed his arms, then immediately put his hands back in his pockets. "Can we…"

She thought back to yesterday's lunch meeting with Manjit. She'd warned Layla about working with difficult artists. As most people knew, the theater world had more than its share of egos. However, it also had plenty of artists plagued by insecurity. The number-one tip Manjit had offered, regardless of who you were struggling to connect with, was to say yes as often as possible. If the person made a request that was easy to accommodate, say yes, even if it didn't seem logical or reasonable. Bank those yeses so that when it was time to say no, you'd already established a nice cushion.

Since she finally had Matt in her sightline, she needed to keep him there. And right now, he was not at ease. She didn't know whether he wasn't a crowd person in general or if it was the vibe that was throwing him off. Regardless, if she wanted him to stick around, she needed to fix this.

"Let's go talk in here." Layla got up from her desk, grabbed a notebook and pen, and led Matt into the theater, feeling only a small pang that he was the first Barnett brother to enter the space.

The theater was blessedly empty, cool, and quiet. She always felt a little magic in there—and not just from the ghosts. It featured a proscenium stage that had been around for decades and the theater's original velvet curtains. The seats were upholstered with a variety of jewel-toned fabrics. It was reminiscent of London's West End theaters, which Layla had always dreamed of visiting.

She chose seats toward the back because they were shrouded in darkness and also offered a good view of the illuminated stage. Matt sat wordlessly beside her. Channeling Manjit and Charlene, Layla took a deep breath, let the ambience settle around them, then spoke.

"Sorry, let's try this again. I've been texting you for days. I just want to understand what made you finally decide to come."

"I'm still not convinced I'm the right person for this gig."

They both stared straight ahead as his words sank in. This time Ian wasn't here to pressure Matt, so she kept things simple. "Why not?" She wasn't asking just to keep him talking; she was genuinely curious. She vacillated between thinking he had an enormous ego and thinking he had no ego at all. She couldn't pin him down.

The sound of him exhaling seemed to fill the entire space.

"I'm not a trained writer. I have zero experience with all this." In a harder voice, he added, "If you asked me as a favor to Ian, I don't want it."

Oh. As it turned out, he was the no-ego guy. "It's not a favor to Ian," she told him. "It's a favor to *me* and, quite frankly, you. Besides, this position is for an *emerging* playwright, not an established one. You're perfect. Everyone's thrilled. So get on board already."

"'Get on board already'? Is this how you treat all the talent?" he asked dryly.

"It's how I treat *you.*"

The ensuing silence took years off Layla's life.

"*Fine,*" Matt eventually said. He crossed his arms. "I do have an idea—"

Layla moved to the literal edge of her seat and turned to face him. "That's fantastic!"

"Slow your roll there, Shirley MacLaine. My idea might be terrible, and I don't even really understand what you're asking of me."

"I sent you links to our previous shows," she pointed out, secretly thrilled at being referred to as the one female member of the Rat Pack.

"Yeah, but I didn't really understand how they pertained to me."

"I'll take any idea, even if it's terrible," she answered, trying to keep the Deano-like growl out of her tone. Terrible ideas she could work with. She just couldn't work with nothing.

"You know how I got picked up for *Common People* based on my blog entries?" Matt began. "I was thinking last night, when I couldn't sleep, about the early blog craze; Open Diary, LiveJournal, sites like that, when people would post their most personal thoughts anonymously on the internet, assuming they'd never be found. Or if they were, they'd be found by strangers. Then I was thinking about diaries in general and how social media is often about presenting ourselves at our best, but diaries and those old blogs, those are about exploring our real feelings. Working through shit, you know?"

Layla nodded again, surprisingly captivated.

"What if we ask the actors to share old diary or blog entries? Then I could adapt them, and we could have the cast perform each one as its own scene."

For Layla's tenth birthday, a friend had given her one of those little diaries with a gold lock and key, but Bobby and Jude quickly found it and performed dramatic readings. The experience pretty much killed any desire Layla had had to keep her thoughts anywhere but in her head. But what Matt was saying made a certain kind of sense.

"You don't seem convinced," Matt said. Worried she was going to scare him off when she'd only just gotten him here, she tried to protest, but he stopped her. "Don't lie to me, Layla, just tell me what you think of the idea. Honestly. No bullshit."

"Honestly?" she said. "I get the voyeuristic appeal, but I'm not sure how many people would want to participate. Air their dirty laundry, so to speak."

A slam somewhere offstage made them both jump.

"What was that?"

Layla shrugged. "One of our theater ghosts."

"There's no such thing as ghosts."

"Don't tell *them* that. They've got big egos and short fuses."

Matt grew silent and Layla wished they could turn on the lights. Turn on one of the hot, megawatt spotlights and shine it directly on Matt. It might help her get a better read on him.

"Not to get all clichéd and *On the Road,* but I've done a fair amount of traveling over the years," he eventually said. "At first I stayed in hostels, where I met people who offered to let me crash on their couches or camp out in their backyards."

As a woman, that sounded hella risky, but a small part of Layla was dying to live a life like that.

Nope. Noooope. That was Past Layla. LA Layla. Current Layla thought of Future Layla and would not succumb to irresponsible fantasies. She cleared her throat. "And? What did you discover as you made friends across America?"

Matt ignored her sarcasm, his eyes fixed on hers. "Everyone wants to tell their story. To be heard. Because when they do, more often than not, they find out that whoever's listening can relate."

Layla let his words sink in, wondering what it would be like for someone to know the darkest parts of her. His idea was taking root in her, but she knew she needed to play it cool. "Okay. I can definitely get on board with that. I told you Manjit requested we include an improv section to ease the burden on the actors memorizing this show...what if we also ask audience members to write down something from *their* lives, and then the actors perform that too?"

"I like that," Matt said thoughtfully, his posture changing. *A sign of excitement?* Layla thought. "We could discover some interesting things about how people tell stories about themselves, you know?"

"I think so too." Her words came out in a rush.

"I just worry it might feel disjointed," Matt added. "Or... forced?"

Layla sat up straighter and the synapses in her brain kept firing; to her delight, Matt sat up a little more too.

"We could ask the audience for specific types of memories. Ones that fell into certain categories," Layla suggested.

Matt's eyes lit up. "Like regrets, family conflict—"

"First kisses," Layla added. "Broken hearts."

"Unrequited love?"

"Exactly." Layla furiously jotted down ideas in her notebook.

"I'll think about which ones we should pursue." Matt nodded. "So, what's the next step? Casting? Production design? What do I do now?"

"I mean, we'll need to run this by my boss for approval first. But yeah. Casting will need to happen quickly in order to pull this all together in time—especially since the script depends on the specific performers," Layla said, thinking quickly. "Once Manjit's on board, I can post on some of the websites we use. We could have people come in to audition within the next few days."

"And I get final say on the cast?"

At first Layla assumed he was joking. *Really?*

"Layla. You yourself just said the script depends on the performers, and I'm in charge of the script. Yes, *really*."

"You're more than welcome to sit in on the auditions," she said the teensiest bit snappily, "but technically, those decisions will fall to Manjit and me. She's the theater's artistic director, and she and I are directing this show together."

"You mean directing this show together *with me*." Even in the shadows, she could see Matt's shoulders go up. "I mean, it's my idea, right? So I should have the final say in who I'm writing for, who I'm working with."

"It's a collaboration, Matt." Layla reminded herself of Manjit's rule: Say yes as often as possible. "Manjit and I would love to have your input, though ultimately, we'll get the final say."

"*You* get the final say over me?" His brows lowered into

awnings for his inky eyes; his voice hardened. "Why? What's your job description again?"

"My job description is I'm the codirector and the person who got you this gig," she shot back. "What else do you want? A silk robe? Backup dancers? A dressing room with only green M&M's?"

His face reddened and she felt her own cheeks burn. *Shit.* She shouldn't have snapped. Just then, Manjit and Charlene burst through the theater doors.

"Pearl told us we'd find you in here," Manjit said in her stage-ready voice. "Matt Barnett, it's so nice to meet you."

There was a round of official introductions that Layla did her best to be polite about, then Charlene produced Matt's contract and a pen as if out of thin air.

Matt took the pen, held it between his fingers, and paused. "Before I sign, can we talk about how much say I get in the production?"

"He's joking," Layla said, which everyone ignored.

"What do you mean?" Manjit seemed genuinely inquisitive.

"I mean, as far as casting goes and production design?" Matt clarified. "I want to make sure my name's associated with something I can be proud of, and if I don't know all the details—"

"He's new to the theater world," Layla reminded everyone. He'd already made her look bad by dodging her calls for this long. The absolute least he could do was muzzle the prima donna attitude and try to make a decent first impression. "Obviously Northwest has its own reputation to up—"

"I just mean that if I'm not involved in the major decisions, there could be surprises, you know?" Matt was completely bulldozing her. She burned with embarrassment. She was almost ready to tear up his contract herself.

"I explained to Matt already that you get the final say, Manjit," Layla said tightly. "I'm sorry that he—"

"Yeah, Layla doesn't seem to want to give me too long of a leash." Matt had the gall to flash her a winning smile.

"We'll make sure this is a production *everyone's* proud to be associated with," Manjit, the picture of professionalism, assured Matt. "Now, why don't you tell us more about what you envision?"

Layla smiled politely through Matt's pitch, which he delivered with annoying aplomb, and continued smiling at the accolades that poured from her bosses. But then Matt said, "It'll be a show about the choices we make. About the messiness of being human. I really want to explore the ways we reframe our histories. The truths, the lies. Are these lies actively hurting us or the people we're close to? I'd want the actors to explore that sort of thing."

Manjit was excitedly taking notes, clearly thinking of their copy.

Layla was self-aware enough to know that she was a teensy bit paranoid when it came to the topic of honesty. Keeping up the concussion-induced charade with Ian was making them both happy, but it would not necessarily be sanctioned by Chidi Anagonye or an actual nonfictional professor of ethics and moral philosophy.

However.

Hearing this new detail of Matt's vision put Layla on alert. High alert.

She barely registered the moment of victory when Matt finally put the pen to the paper and signed.

CHAPTER EIGHTEEN

TYPICALLY, LAYLA COMPLETED a work-induced stress cycle by going home, crying it out, and trying again, but she refused—*refused*—to give Matt any tears. He probably grew stronger from the tears of women he'd scorned, and she wasn't going to indulge that power. Even if he didn't see it happen, she was sure, somehow, *he'd know.*

Is Matt around tonight? she texted Ian.

Ian texted back, Funny you should ask; he has a date with Jojo. So...no. :)

If Matt wanted to go out with a groupie, that was on him, Layla thought, then remembered that setting Matt up was sort of her idea to begin with. This was a *good* thing.

She texted: Can I come over?

I'm on my way home now. Race you there?

For all of the questions that she was pretending didn't plague her in the middle of the night—like *Did Ian really break up with me because we didn't see each other enough?* And *Is not admitting to Ian that we broke up securing me a first-class ticket to hell?*—everything still felt wonderfully different this time around. Layla's spirits lifted. She thought back to what her dad had said after she'd finally left Randall: *Don't forget, Layla. Good things can happen too.*

This was her mantra as she tried to salvage her day.

Her apartment was within walking distance of work, but Ian's condo was not. She stopped by her place to freshen up and feed Deano, then drove over. The hug Ian greeted her with at the door was worth the effort. His chest was warm and the soft gray henley he'd changed into smelled of detergent. His strong arms reached around her, catching her in the crook of his elbows, his hands holding her tightly. The burning in her chest eased. Her lungs filled with air.

"Are you okay?"

Layla had already decided on the drive over not to give him specifics. She didn't want to put Ian in an uncomfortable position by complaining about his brother. Not when she knew he was already frustrated at his own relationship with Matt. Besides, she didn't need to talk about her frustrations. What she needed was to soak up some of that good Ian energy.

She tilted her head back to better see his handsome face. "I'm okay. Work was stupid."

"Work is for jerks," he said, quoting Layla from the earliest days of their relationship, back when they were both falling in shiny new love with each other and wanted to spend the whole day in his bed, legs entangled. He led her into the kitchen.

"Canned tomato soup and grilled cheese?" She grinned for the first time all day. Without prompting, he was making one of her favorite comfort meals.

"Nothing's too good for my gal." He rolled his sleeves up a little higher.

"Hubba-hubba," she said directly to his forearms, which made him chuckle in amusement.

She hopped up onto the kitchen counter and sat there while he finished preparing their meal.

"Should I make a salad or something?" he asked, picking up the spatula to press down on the sandwiches already sizzling in the pan.

"Vegetables are for jerks," she replied, and he laughed. Coming here had been the right decision. This was the key to life, she thought. Not avoiding all the bad stuff, but having someone to ease the pain just by being near. "What about you? How are you?"

He threw the spatula in the air and caught it by the handle. "I'm finally feeling like I'm one hundred percent. The headaches have stopped altogether; my focus is better."

"That's good." She hopped off the counter to find them something to drink. She opened the fridge and tossed behind her, "If it'd been me on that bike, I'd still be having nightmares."

She instinctively felt him go still. When she turned around, he was standing there, body tense, eyes downcast. "Ian?"

"I'm okay." It was clear he wasn't.

She turned off the burner, moved the pan, and wrapped her arms around him. "What's up?"

He paused before sinking into her hug. "I can't even bring myself to get back on my bike," he said, his voice barely above a whisper.

"Of course you can't." She squeezed him with just enough pressure. "What you went through was traumatic—physically, emotionally." It was weird to see him so rattled. "I mean, did the cops ever find the driver?"

Ian sighed into her hair. "No. And it's not even about the driver. It's just..." He pulled back to look at her. "I don't *want* to avoid things in my life. I want to face all this and be done with it."

That, at least, was classic Ian. "You'll get there," Layla promised him. "But it doesn't have to be today or tomorrow. Take your time."

He leaned down and gave her the softest of kisses. They broke from each other only when the door opened. Matt was home early. She instantly hated Jojo for not being a good enough date. And then she refocused her resentment on Matt, who was surely the real problem. Jojo was probably an angel.

"I thought you had a date tonight," Ian said to Matt without even saying hello. Were things between the brothers worse than Layla had suspected?

"I did. It's over," Matt said, without offering any other insights. "I thought you had that client dinner tonight."

"*Shit.*" Ian was instantly stricken with panic. He rubbed at his eyes with his hands and then looked around the kitchen. "Layla, I'm so sorry."

"It's okay," she insisted, pushing her disappointment down as low as it could go. It wasn't like Ian to be forgetful. Clearly he wasn't at one hundred percent quite yet.

A voice in her head asked: *What happens when he is one hundred percent? Will he remember?*

"Stay here, eat with Matt, and I'll call you tomorrow," Ian bellowed as he beelined for his room. She could hear his closet doors opening and closing.

Out of the corner of her eye, she saw Matt lean against the counter and cross his arms. She could feel his focus zeroing in on her. Willingly spend more time with Matt? That was a hard pass. "I'll just head out. Matt can eat all this," she called back to Ian.

Ian popped his head out of his room, hands furiously buttoning up his shirt. "Layla. Come on. I made you your favorite. You're not going to eat it?"

She pushed down a frustrated growl and smiled. "You're right. Of course I'll eat it. Thank you."

Ian ran his fingers through his blond hair, putting it back in place, and gave her a quick kiss goodbye before leaving. The sound of the door shutting behind him seemed to echo through the whole condo.

Layla got out plates and bowls, served herself, and left the rest for Matt to eat, should he so choose. In her peripheral vision, she saw him reach for a plate and bowl. She heard the rest of the soup stream in, heard the scrape of the spatula as he picked up the sandwich. Heard him cut it. She sat down at the small, four-person table in the kitchen. "You know, you could at least throw Ian a bone every once in a while. He's really trying with you." The words came out of her mouth before she could stop them.

Matt sat across from her. "Ian's only going to be satisfied if I become an Ian clone."

"That's not true," she said, not actually knowing if it wasn't.

In response, Matt shrugged and dug into his dinner.

She scrutinized his dark wavy hair, which had been washed and styled just enough to look like maybe it *hadn't* been styled. She took in what she figured was his date outfit—a black T-shirt and jeans. *How inspired.* She would've been far more impressed if he'd worn the *Golden Girls* shirt she'd seen him in the first time they'd met.

"You're not going to eat in your room?" she asked.

"Who eats soup in the bedroom?" he mumbled. He was about to taste it, seemed to think better of it, and clanged his spoon down on his plate. "I can't do anything right today, can I?"

The nerve—the absolute *nerve* of this guy. But. She was an adult. She was a professional, and she was shadowing one of the most gifted and respected artistic directors in the city, so there was no way she was going to let Matt ruin things. This was *her* moment.

With a serene smile plastered on her face, she said, "I thought we made a lot of headway with the show today. I was a *little* frustrated with the way things were handled in regards to your production demands. And the way you undermined me in front of my bosses. But I don't want that to affect our relationship at work nor our shared interest. Which is Ian."

"Why are you doing that with your lips? And did you just use the word *nor* in a sentence?" Matt leaned back in his chair, folding his arms across his chest.

What. A. *Brat*. He *liked* to push her buttons. To get her goat. Well, she wouldn't let him. Her buttons were off-limits. Her goat was *hers*.

"I'm smiling at you," she said through gritted teeth, "to be polite."

"I got your message, by the way. The one you left on my phone."

"And?"

"I particularly liked the part where you compared yourself to Scrooge McDuck."

So much for playing nice. She wanted to ball up her napkin and chuck it at his smug face. "I wasn't comparing myself to Scrooge, I was saying we *weren't* a bunch of Scrooge McDu—"

"That still sounds like a comparison."

She was going to flip the table, with her beloved grilled cheese and tomato soup, both of which were getting cold, right over. To avoid the instinct, she shot to her feet. "Why do you have to be such an ass?"

Her volume had crescendoed so quickly that Matt actually flinched.

I made him flinch. There was a bit of pleasure in that. The *tiniest* of pleasures. Just enough pleasure to fill a thimble.

She wanted a pint glass of that pleasure.

"Well." Matt uncrossed his arms, leaned in, and took a bite of sandwich. "Now we're getting somewhere."

"What are you talking about?" Layla suddenly felt stupid. She was still standing and they were evidently playing some game she didn't know the rules of.

"Please," Matt said, chewing like a caveman. "You can be polite and pretend you have everything together for everyone else, but don't insult me with that act when it's just us."

"*Fine*. You want me to stop being polite?" She plopped back down in her chair. "You were a dick at work today. You made demands that aren't yours to make, and after I told you no, you brought them up with my bosses anyway."

"Your bosses liked the ideas I came up with—"

"*We* came up with."

"And they seem to like me. They were open to giving me some say—"

"Were they? Or are they humoring the talent?" She made sure to add an extra layer of sarcasm to *the talent*.

Matt nodded, seeming to consider what she'd said. "But your boss—the director one, Manjit? She's technically in charge of the show, right? You're working as her assistant."

"Right," Layla agreed slowly.

"So it's smarter for me to ask her questions instead of you. Because you can say no, but her no is the one with all the power."

"That's not the point," Layla insisted. "And frankly, that's really rude."

"The point is I'm a dick?" Matt raised his eyebrows so high, they nearly reached his hairline. "Yeah, Ian should've warned you I don't play well with others."

Like a child, Layla cupped her hands around her mouth and went, "Boooooo."

Matt actually let a laugh escape. "Are you booing me?"

"Yeah, I'm booing you." If Matt wanted real, she'd give him real. "That is the douchiest thing I've ever heard anyone say. And I went to school with theater dorks *and* business narcissists."

That elicited a bark of a laugh from Matt. Layla hid her brief pleasure at the sound by scowling. She was about to get *extra* real with him. She started with the question that scared her the least. "Why are you even here? Why did you agree to move in with Ian?"

He froze. She'd caught him off guard. *Fabulous.*

"Maybe I'm sticking around to spend more time with *you*," he said, then he slowly, deliberately took the loudest of slurps of his soup.

She took her own loud slurp of soup. "Uh-huh."

He shrugged. "I was between gigs and needed a place to get my bearings."

She put down her spoon and narrowed her eyes. "Don't make me boo you again. I thought we were being real with each other."

He sighed. It seemed to last a century. "Fine. I was surprised by the invitation. Curious, even. I wanted to see what would happen if I said yes."

"Bullshit," Layla shot back. "You two used to be close. I think you miss him."

"That's quite the theory."

It was, but Layla noticed he didn't contradict it. She let that topic drop and gathered the courage to ask her next question. "Why did you say all that stuff about rewriting history and being honest with ourselves when you were talking to my bosses? We hadn't discussed that."

"Now, *that* is an interesting story," Matt said, and he stuffed the rest of his grilled cheese into his mouth.

Whatever she and Matt were about to get into, instincts told Layla that she needed to prepare herself. And that she didn't want to be completely sober when they did.

CHAPTER NINETEEN

LAYLA'S LATE-TEEN YEARS and much of her twenties had been punctuated by wild alcohol-fueled fun. She wasn't—*couldn't be*—that person anymore. But she knew she could still tap into that side of herself, if needed. And this moment felt as necessary as any yet.

"Hold that thought," she said, standing up. She started rummaging through Ian's cupboards.

"What are you looking for?"

"Truth serum." As soon as the words were out of her mouth, she regretted them.

She found the expensive bottle of scotch she'd bought Ian for his birthday in a cupboard next to the fridge. That was too special to sully, so she pushed it to the side. Matt's arm reached around her to get a better look at the bottle behind it.

"Blueberry vodka?" he asked with disgust.

"We used it to make cocktails." If she sounded defensive, it was because she was. She and Ian had taken a bartending class for fun last fall. It'd been Layla's idea, a way to break from their routines and carve out time together. More accurately, they had signed up for a bartending class, but they'd made it to only a couple of lessons because their schedules kept getting in the way. At the last class they'd attended, they learned to make some sort of blueberry-lemon thing. She didn't remember what it was called or how to make it, just that it'd been delicious.

"Well, it's either this monstrosity," Matt said wryly, "the bottle of scotch, or the pinot noir one of the neighbors brought over when they heard about Ian's accident."

"One of your neighbors brought alcohol to a concussion victim?"

"The world is not populated with geniuses." Matt palmed the flavored vodka while Layla located a couple of shot glasses. She was relieved Matt wasn't resisting. Clearly he wanted the buffer of alcohol to deal with her too.

"Was it Margot Robbie?" Layla pressed, wanting the perfect specimen of a hot neighbor to have at least one glaring flaw.

"Margot..." Matt's brow furrowed in confusion.

Damn it. What is her name again? "You know, the blonde. The one who looks like a sexy praying mantis."

Matt made a cough-choke sound and then swallowed. "Do you mean *Jojo?* Funny you should mention her. I went on a date with her tonight."

"Yet here you are. Interesting. So," Layla went on, because she was a terrible person, "she's a gorgeous nongenius?"

Unfortunately, Matt's glower made it clear he was done with the topic.

"Before we pickle ourselves, we should probably clean up," Layla said, quickly changing the subject and surveying the dirty dishes. Ian kept things tidy—exceptionally tidy—and she didn't want him coming home to a mess.

"Did you consult Ian's chore chart or something?"

"You strike me as someone who could use a chart or two in his life," Layla said, but instead of getting indignant, Matt smirked.

"Likewise."

Impulsively, she chucked a wet dishcloth at him; he caught it, but only after it soaked the front of his shirt. He gave her an *Of course you know this means war* look, which she ignored. She began clearing the table.

Together they cleaned the dinner dishes, wiped down the kitchen table, and carried the vodka and glasses into the living room. They moved like an Olympic team pursuing the same objective: the gold medal in desperate drinking.

As soon as they sat down—taking chairs on opposite ends of the coffee table—Layla stopped feeling so comfortable. Matt could say anything here.

"So what's this story you have to tell me?" she asked.

Instead of answering, he said, "I was thinking about *The Diary Project*."

"Is that what you're calling the show?"

"You like it?" Matt's face displayed a small bit of pleasure when Layla nodded. He continued. "If we want the cast members to use stories from their diaries, a moment in their lives that went off the rails, that's an intimate request. For this show to work, we're going to have to establish trust with the whole ensemble from the jump."

"O-kay…" She drew out the word, completely in the dark but relieved that whatever he was talking about had nothing to do with her.

"That trust needs to start with you and me."

Whoops. There went her relief. "Why?"

"We're the foundation of this damn show, Layla. You and me. *That's* why we need to establish trust. And because you roped me into this. And because we can't seem to communicate without biting each other's heads off."

She couldn't stop herself from being glib: "Does that mean you'll actually tell me your 'interesting story'?" She used air quotes like a brat.

He rubbed his eyes with his palms. The act was so reminiscent of what Ian did when he was stressed out, she inhaled sharply. In all her frustrations with Matt, she often forgot that he and Ian were *brothers*. They'd been best friends as kids, even if they'd grown apart. Layla *had* to make more of an effort. Not just for the good of the show but for the good of *Ian*.

"Go on," she said more softly.

Instead of responding, Matt filled the two shot glasses and set one directly in front of Layla.

"What I'm about to tell you…I don't talk about this—with *anyone*." He gave her a meaningful look, then stared at the shot glass.

She sat up. Matt was obviously a guy who kept his secrets in his pocket, and there was a thrill to being there when he reached a hand inside, pulled it out, and opened his fist; she surprised even herself when she said, "You spill your story, and I'll spill mine."

Whatever Matt was about to tell her, she could easily top, even without going into what happened with Randall, which she wouldn't bring up here. Not when she hadn't even told Ian.

Matt raised his head. "I think we're going to need to drink this aromatherapy vodka first."

They raised their shot glasses in a toast.

"To team bonding," Layla said.

"To the mistakes of our past," Matt countered.

As she brought the glass to her lips, she thought of the instant blueberry-muffin mix she and her siblings used to bake. She tipped the shot back into her mouth. Her nose wrinkled. This had definitely tasted better in the cocktail. Looked like Matt was no fan either.

"This is terrible," he said, puckering his lips slightly.

"Yep," Layla agreed.

"Another?"

"Yep."

They repeated the ritual, set the glasses down (Layla careful to ensure coasters were in full use), and stared at each other.

"Duck, duck, *goose.*" She pointed to Matt.

"All right, all right, I'll quit stalling." He leaned back, hands clasped behind his head, arms forming triangles on either side of his ears. The sleeves of his black T-shirt rode up on his surprisingly taut biceps. "We were never really religious, but I always liked the idea of confession, you know?"

"Who likes the idea of confession?" Layla had stories that would perm a priest's hair.

"Oh, come on. This idea that if you just voice the regrettable things you've done, suddenly you're pardoned for all your idiotic sins? Sign me up."

"Quit trying to distract me and spill." At this point, she was dying to hear what he had to say, and his preamble was making her twitchy.

"I fucked up the *Common People* thing."

It wasn't at all what she'd expected, and he'd said it so matter-of-factly.

"How?" She was proceeding with caution. Keeping things simple so he wouldn't shut down. She surreptitiously picked at her nail polish. Had she made a mistake in hiring him? Could the show be in danger?

Matt's relaxed body language shifted. His forearms fell to his knees; his center of gravity moved forward. "I didn't get it at the time, what they were doing. The way they wanted to highlight the struggles and victories of people our age trying to find a career—but also to find purpose. I hated—*hated*—doing those talking-head things. I just wanted to be a faceless member of the writers' room."

Layla didn't move, didn't know what to think. Her stillness seemed to encourage him.

"My frustrations...I didn't hide them well. I got this reputation for being difficult to work with." He risked a glance in
her direction, likely expecting her to make a smart-ass remark.
It took willpower, but she kept her mouth shut.

"Do you know how I learned they hadn't renewed my contract for season two? I showed up to work and they turned me
away at the security gate. Suddenly, I had to move out of the
apartment I was living in because my season-one paycheck had
been pre-success and minuscule. I'd been telling my roommates
I'd pay them back with season two. But there was no paycheck. I
borrowed money from Ian—which I eventually paid back, even
if he doesn't usually tell that part—and then...I just started
running. State to state, job to job."

Layla was speechless. His walking away from her when she'd
accused him of being famous, the way he'd corrected her, insist-
ing, "I'm not"—it all made sense. He wasn't being cavalier or
difficult. He'd been embarrassed.

That she could relate to. That and growing up with a sibling
(or four) who seemed to waltz gracefully into adulthood while
she stumbled her way across the ballroom. She thought back to
Ian's story about the polar-bear plunge.

"And at that point," she offered, her empathy slowly growing,
"things were already tense between you and Ian, so borrowing
money from him must have been extra-tough."

She watched Matt take the smallest but sharpest of inhales.
And suddenly she was asking him about chasing his dad. About
Dennis. Had he found him?

"What did Ian tell you about all that?" It was clear he was
trying to be casual, but she was starting to see through him now,
the hurt in his deep brown eyes, the way his arms were flexed,
bracing for an attack.

"Not much," she replied truthfully. "What do *you* want to tell
me about that?"

He held her gaze. "My biological dad, I didn't have any real memories of him. The ones I had, I wondered if I'd actually cobbled together from TV shows or something. Did we actually play catch in the front yard or was that some *Wonder Years* rerun? Ian, of course, had these really solidified ideas about Dennis, and they were all toxic. He told me that he remembered Dennis being casually cruel with our mom. That she'd cry. That he was barely home when he lived with us, and when he *was* home, he ignored us. Ian wanted nothing to do with him."

"But you didn't have those memories?"

"No. I didn't. And so Dennis was this big question mark." Matt rubbed at his arms as though cold. She wondered if he was remembering the polar-bear plunge he hadn't taken at Cascade Lake.

"Question marks can still be dirtbags," Layla said.

"Dads can be real dirtbags too," Matt said.

"You found him, then? Dennis?" This was news.

Matt nodded. "Actually, he wasn't a dirtbag. I mean, not in an obvious way."

"What was he?" Layla was sitting forward, still.

"He was…" Matt threw up his hands. "Nothing. That was the worst part. If he'd been a sweet misguided guy who deserved a second chance, that would've been something. If he'd been a clear villain, an asshole who yelled at me and told me to get out of his life, *that* would've been something. I'd spent so long driving and searching and building all these narratives in my mind about him, but when I finally met him…"

"He was nothing," Layla finished for him.

"He was nothing," Matt repeated. "Just some nothing guy who was living in a basement apartment in New Jersey and tending bar at some dive down the street. A nothing guy who didn't want to pay child support, who could have a relationship with me or not—no skin off his nose either way. And I had spent *years* chasing him. I'd spent years chasing...human vapor."

"*Matt.*"

"Most anticlimactic ending ever, right?" His tone was sardonic, his eyes pools of melancholy. Of shame.

"I think it takes real fucking guts to find out the truth," Layla said. And, oh God, she meant it.

"Oh yeah?" He raised his eyebrows. "Tell me about Layla's search for truth."

"I'm going to need more aromatherapy vodka," she whispered, feeling herself sway a little, not knowing what she would say. Besides Pearl, she hadn't leveled with anyone in years.

Wordlessly, Matt poured them each another shot. Even though it had been her idea, Layla hesitated. She knew she was at a tipping point; she knew the choice she *should* make. She should be responsible and stop drinking immediately.

But she also knew she could do her job tomorrow hungover. She could talk Pearl into getting sugary coffees and buttery pastries and get through one little workday. It wouldn't be the first time, after all.

So they raised their glasses to each other, gulped the liquor down, and slammed them back onto the table. For a split second, so tiny it made an atom look like a planet, Layla was tempted to tell him about the Dark Days. About sneaking in a drink or two just to slow her racing mind when a debt collector called. About the loudest quiet drive back to Bellevue with her mom. But she couldn't; Ian couldn't ever find out.

"I think my mom might be having an affair," she said bluntly, her edges growing fuzzy from alcohol.

"Interesting," Matt said flatly.

Her temper flared at his unexpected opaqueness. "What? Why is that *interesting*, Matt? I'm opening up to you. I haven't even told Ian that."

"Well, *that* is interesting," Matt said. "Because that's not all Ian doesn't know, is it?"

The lightness she'd felt from the blueberry vodka abandoned her. She could barely lift her eyes. "What do you mean?"

"When did Ian tell you he invited me to move in with him?" To his credit, Matt didn't seem to be taking any pleasure in this. If anything, his expression was pained.

Layla shrugged noncommittally, the act of moving her shoulders up and down taking great effort. "After the accident, when we got his new phone."

"Yeah, that's true. Do you know when we'd last spoken? Before that?"

Everything inside of her was freezing over. "When?"

"After he broke up with you."

Internally she expelled a high scream of panic, one that would've made dogs bark and glass shatter. Externally she released a very small "Oh."

"When he invited me to go out to dinner with you two, I figured you'd gotten back together. It took me a while to work out what exactly was going on. I asked him a couple of times if you'd had any rough patches and he claimed you've been going strong since day one."

They *had* been going strong, Layla wanted to say. Since day one of his accident. But something had happened before then. She knew it, and she still didn't understand. She wished she could shake some answers out of Matt. But given where she was at—and where he was at—she didn't trust herself to dive in.

She was sure Matt could hear how loudly her heart was pounding. "Are you going to tell him?" She'd always known there was a possibility that Ian's memory might come back or that someone might blow her cover. She'd always known. *And yet.*

"Are *you?*" Matt shot back. "I know he and I have our own

rough patches, but you don't expect me to do nothing, do you? This is my brother's *life*—and yours, by the way."

"I can't tell him," she insisted, a bit desperately. "Not yet, anyway."

"Why can't you?"

Because he might remember why he dumped me to begin with, or he'll be so disgusted with me for lying, he'll end things all over again. Because I'm not sure he loves me enough yet, but if I have more time, he will. I know he will. The universe says so.

Out loud, she threw a Hail Mary. "We're planning that vow renewal for your parents."

Matt threw his head back against the couch. "Oh yeah. The *party*. Now, *that's* a solid reason to keep lying."

"Matt, *please*."

His eyes softened, just enough to embolden her. *Shit*. She needed a better reason, something to buy her more time with Ian. *Think*, Layla silently urged herself, wishing she were more sober. Or maybe more drunk? Whatever it would take to get her brain to come up with the magic answer that would stop Matt from blowing everything to smithereens.

"You don't really want to ruin this surprise for your parents, do you?" she pleaded, stalling. Her motivations weren't wholly selfish, her drunk brain reminded her. She *loved* his parents. She reminded him of this too. "You know Jeannie and Craig deserve this wedding do-over. They're some of the best people I know. *Anyone* knows. They are good, bighearted people..."

Drunk Layla was rambling, so she searched for details, anything that might sway him. "Ian even wants to hold it at that Rosario restaurant where they told you—"

"They were getting married." Matt, whose head was still resting on the back of the couch, covered his eyes with his arm. "Yeah, that's the perfect spot."

"Right?" She moved closer to him on the couch, empowered

by this minuscule victory. "Imagine how happy they're going to be. Now imagine how sad they'd be if you told Ian the truth and Ian broke up with me. The party would be a sullen affair."

"I don't know if this is the vodka talking or you." He lifted his arm and gave her a wry look. "Do you actually believe what you're saying? Do you really think the success of my parents' anniversary depends on whether or not you're dating my brother?"

"No," Layla admitted, slumping, defeated. "I'm expecting you to keep your mouth shut because your brother's happy."

She'd unintentionally said the right thing. The world seemed to stop around them as he considered her words. An idea came to her that was both gutsy and stupid but just might work; her favorite combination when it came to alcohol-soaked ideas. At the very least, it could buy her time to solidify her relationship with Ian enough to withstand the fallout from the truth.

"What if I promise you I *will* tell him? After the party," Layla ventured. "We could have this one, uncomplicated thing, this vow renewal for your parents, which they so deserve, and *then* deal with my little lie."

He raised his eyebrows at her again, as if to say, *Little?*

"When you think about it, telling Ian now could also complicate things for *The Diary Project*," she added, her mind finally gaining traction. She knew Matt had become emotionally invested in the show whether he admitted it or not. "So here's what I propose: We get through the show, we throw your parents a vivacious celebration, and then I sit Ian down and tell him everything."

Matt sat back up. Stared her down.

She counted the seconds, waiting for him to respond. *One . . . two . . . three . . . fo—*

"Vivacious celebration?" he said. But he wasn't saying no.

"Think of the anniversary-party-slash-wedding-part-two as

being like Carol Burnett—it'll be lively, charming, lovable, and it'll give everyone new life."

He paused. Bitterly, he said, "You are epically weird. How did you and straitlaced Ian get together again?"

"Matt, I'm begging you." He couldn't take this relationship encore away from her. Not the anniversary party for Jeannie and Craig, not the show, and not Ian, the love of her reckless, embarrassing life.

They held a final long gaze until eventually, blessedly, he relented. "Fine. But if you don't tell him after the party—"

"I get it. You will." She stood up, suddenly woozy from all the blueberry nonsense. "I should go."

If she stayed, she might topple this fragile tower she'd just built, so she grabbed her stuff. She went to the door and opened it. She said a small "Good night, Matt," and closed the door behind her before he could reply. Before he could change his mind.

Outside, she took a deep breath, leaning against Ian's door, trying to slow the spin of vodka, guilt, and shame swirling in her head. Trying to quell the wave of disappointment Matt's ultimatum had unleashed. The party was in four weeks. *Four weeks.* That might be all she had left. And even that would feel like a stroke of luck. How had she gotten herself here?

Driving home in her condition wasn't an option, so she walked to a nearby café that was open late. And there, in a sticky vinyl booth, she sipped coffee, wondering if she could trust Matt to hold up his end of the deal.

CHAPTER TWENTY

KNOWING SHE HAD a deadline inspired Layla to re-double her efforts with Ian. If she had to tell him, she'd tell him—but she wanted to know their relationship was secure enough first. She didn't know *how* she'd know they were ready, but things were going well thus far. In the four weeks she had before the anniversary party, Layla swore she'd devote as much time and energy to Ian as she could. Unfortunately, he was slammed at work, as was she, so redoubling her efforts mostly consisted of texts and late-night phone calls. Still, although it was a struggle, it was worth it, because there was a scenario in which her confession *didn't* ruin everything, and she fantasized about it nearly every night, picturing his confusion, followed by his understanding of *why* she'd done it, and eventually his realization that, ultimately, the lie had brought them closer.

But there were *two* Barnett brothers to contend with.

The first time she saw Matt after he'd started the countdown-to-telling-Ian clock was at auditions for *The Diary Project*, which Manjit had invited him to. Layla was making coffee when he arrived, and by the time she walked into the theater, they were settled in the gem-colored seats and she had to choose between sitting next to Matt, who was closest to her, and walking all the way across the aisle to sit by Manjit.

Manjit was on the phone, turned away from them both. Matt looked at her expectantly. Seeing him in person again, Layla felt naked. This wasn't like Pearl knowing the truth; Pearl loved her. Matt's knowledge was a violation of her privacy.

She stood there, frozen, and he sighed as though he were truly disappointed in her, which, fair enough.

"You're seriously not going to sit down?" he asked, low enough that it wouldn't disrupt Manjit's phone call.

"I'm going to sit down," she said and gauged his reaction as she made a move for the seat next to his. How could she get through the next several hours after what they'd been through the other night?

"By all means, take your time." Matt started scrawling in his notebook, but she bet he was writing nonsense. "Because I hear we have all the time in the world to mount this show."

She flumped herself into the seat and hissed, "I don't want this to be awkward between us."

"Well." Matt raised his eyebrow at her. "Mission accomplished."

Before she could respond, Manjit ended her call and the auditions began.

Each actor performed a monologue and then shared an important story from his or her own life. The process was surprisingly moving—poignant at times, hilarious at others. One performer related the story of coming to the United States as a refugee; one talked about her miscarriage; another told about the worst date he'd ever been on. One guy even talked about the time he'd accidentally kissed his girlfriend's mom. With tongue.

Matt had been concerned about getting the final say in casting, but in the end his opinions aligned nearly perfectly with

Layla's and Manjit's. They decided to choose eight actors who hadn't had a lot of recent work, people with stories to tell and a hunger to prove themselves.

Even more amazing? As the day went on, Layla felt less and less uncomfortable around him. He was one person she didn't have to put on a show for, uphold this charade in front of, and somehow that put her at ease. In fact, being her worst self around him was kind of liberating. Life continued to be a mystery.

The first day of rehearsal, however, Matt showed up late, looking even more disheveled than usual. He skulked into the theater, dropped his beat-up bag a little too violently into a seat, and grunted when Layla said hello. A few of the actors exchanged looks. Manjit politely ignored him while she sidebarred with the stage manager.

Don't waste this opportunity, Layla told both herself and Matt. She decided to intervene.

"Do you need a minute?" Layla asked him quietly while Manjit talked the cast through the rehearsal process.

She saw him slump, clearly embarrassed. "No. I'm good. Sorry."

"An apology. Wow," she said, but not unkindly. "What's the occasion?"

"Layla." There was a lot of baggage in the way he said her name, but he didn't unpack it and neither did she.

"We're a team, right? We have a little more trust now? Wasn't that the point of subjecting ourselves to the blueberry vodka?" she ventured. He nodded, looking half annoyed. "Then I'm asking you to let go of the past, and let's just have some fun today."

"You sound like a camp counselor."

"You would know," she replied.

"Oh, so there *are* some things that you and Ian actually talk about."

"Booo," she said, cupping her hands around her mouth. "Low-hanging fruit."

"Booo," Matt echoed, almost fondly. "Even your defense mechanisms are weird." Layla bit back her grin, wondering if they would've been friends under different circumstances.

But when Manjit asked Matt to get up and talk about the show, Layla's nerves kicked in. He was still a loose cannon. Yet as soon as he stood up and ran his fingers through his beard, she saw him transform into someone who was exactly where he should be. Her mind flashed back to *Common People*, where Matt's quiet moodiness had translated into intriguing contemplation and an on-screen charisma. "The thing I hate most in life is being vulnerable, and right now I'm feeling pretty fucking vulnerable," he said. Layla could feel everyone in the room warm to him, herself included. *Damn him.*

"This show, this *Diary Project*, is about a lot of things. Being vulnerable is definitely one of them. But it's also about how every person in here, every human who's going to walk in through those doors—" He pointed and then paused, seemingly considering something, then shook it off and continued. "We're all one big Venn diagram of shared experiences. Your auditions were really... captivating. They were funny and raw and upsetting. That's why you're here. I want to capture all that in this show."

He's good, Layla thought, growing more excited herself.

The rehearsal passed by in a blur. Layla popped in as often as she could without completely slacking off as office administrator. She took some photos in case Pearl wanted to use them on the theater's social media pages, then decided to post one on her personal account too. Let the masses—okay, more like her two-hundred-and-something followers—witness her career glow-up.

As the day was winding down, she caught Matt as he was packing up.

"So?" she asked, knowing he wouldn't be able to deny having fun.

"So?" he replied innocently, infuriatingly.

"Are you going to thank me now or later?" She crossed her arms over her chest and gave him her most endearing smile.

"I loved it," he admitted, and her heart soared.

"I *knew* it." She uncrossed her arms. "Truthfully? So did I."

"I knew it," he replied. And then he tapped the pen he was holding on his Moleskine notebook. "Just...I need one thing."

"Anything." She could see the performers chatting excitedly, could feel Manjit's relief. If Matt wanted a bowl full of nothing but green M&M's, she'd pick them out of the bags herself.

Matt's eyes traveled around the room as he nodded. "This isn't the right space. I think we need a change in venue."

Layla's jaw unhinged. Any warmth she'd been feeling evaporated. "You want to change the venue. Four weeks before opening night. From this theater, which we happen to own."

"Yeah," he said, either not picking up on her tone or choosing to ignore it. "Maybe an outdoor space? This place just feels so impersonal."

"No. Not possible."

He looked taken aback. "You aren't even going to consider it? Even for a second?"

"I'm telling you, Matt," Layla said, enunciating every word, "it's not possible. Not in this time frame."

Before the conversation could continue, Charlene entered and Manjit approached Matt and Layla. *Not again.*

"I hear rehearsal went well today," Charlene said.

"It did," Manjit said, answering Charlene but addressing Matt. "You've taken a pretty dire situation for us and turned it into an opportunity. Well done."

"Well, thanks for taking a chance on me." Matt paused. Layla swore to herself that if he brought up moving the show, she'd tackle him to the ground.

And of course he did: "I wonder if we should look at alternative venues? I just think this show would be better served in a less obvious space."

That. Bastard.

"What did you have in mind, Matt?" Manjit's tone was unreadable.

"You know when shows are performed in, like, a house, for example? So you can go room to room to see different scenes?"

"Interesting," Charlene said.

"Definitely," Manjit agreed.

Shut your talking hole, Layla wanted to spit at him.

Encouraged, Matt said, "I was thinking maybe somewhere like that on Orcas Island."

Was this a way to compete with Ian? *You're throwing a party for our parents on Orcas Island? Well, I'm doing a whole production there!*

But this was going too far. She needed to show her bosses—and Matt—that she still had control over the talent. "People aren't going to want to take a ferry to see a show," she pointed out.

"That's a fair point, but staging the show somewhere unexpected might work to our advantage—maybe even get us a little extra publicity," Manjit said to Layla's total and irritated surprise.

Charlene touched her arm. "Layla, why don't you look into possible venues on the island. Bringing a production over would be helpful for tourism. Maybe we can get a deal?"

"But…"

Manjit and Charlene murmured to each other briefly, then Manjit said, "If we use a different venue, we can rent out our theater at the same time."

"Oh, okay. That all . . . sounds good," Layla said, all her previous excitement draining out through her peep-toe kitten heels.

Her bosses gushed about the show for a few more moments and then made their exit, leaving Layla alone with Matt. She couldn't figure out what to do—yell at him for being absurd, yell at him for undermining her, laugh in his face for his demands, or fire him and hope she could miraculously find a replacement.

Truth be told, she wanted to choose all four scenarios. Unfortunately, she didn't have the authority for that last one.

"You're mad at me," he said flatly.

"I'm not mad," she replied, her words so crisp they could've been deep-fried.

"Just disappointed?" The smug look on his face deserved to be wiped off.

"I'm not *mad*," she repeated. "I'm *furious*. You've just created a . . . a . . . *buttload* more work for me—and don't you *dare* make any smart-ass remarks about my use of the word *buttload*."

Matt opened his mouth and then closed it.

"Thanks for ruining what had been a perfectly wonderful day, Matt. This has been enlightening. Now I know what I'm in for. No task too small to become a problem, right?"

Before he could reply, she stalked off. Or at least she tried to. Somehow, the double doors were locked.

"Looks like your huffy exit has been thwarted," Matt called after her.

She ignored him, spinning around to look up at the window of the tech booth. She couldn't see anyone up there. She marched past Matt and onto the stage and peered around the curtains. No one was back there either.

"Do you think it was the ghosts?" Matt asked when she re-appeared center stage. "Do you think this means they're actually on my side?'

"Maybe they're holding us hostage because they're pissed

you're abandoning them." She hopped off the stage, although not terribly gracefully, since she was wearing a skirt. She stomped up the aisle and tried the doors again. They wouldn't budge.

Matt took a seat and leaned as far back as the velvety purple chair allowed. "This feels like a fire hazard. Is there someone in charge of that sort of thing here? Maybe an administrator?"

There were doors that led to the techs' offices, but they grew surly when people invaded their space. There were also doors behind the stage, but they led to a sketchy alleyway Layla tried to avoid. She growled, gave up, and flopped down on the seat next to him. Her inflated sense of self-righteousness was losing air. She pulled out her phone to call Pearl. Maybe she was still in the office.

"You might consider apologizing to the ghosts," Matt suggested. "Tell them you're finally relinquishing control to the theater gods."

She turned to him. "You're talking to *me* about being a control freak."

"I just want this show to be good." His eyes went soft. Annoyingly, it made her soften a bit too.

"So do I," she replied finally.

"I'm glad to hear it." Matt stood up. "Let's remember that we're on the same team."

"Fucking camp counselor," Layla muttered, watching as he walked to the exit and removed the little wooden door stoppers that had somehow gotten wedged underneath. With an ease that made her want to chuck her purse at him, he threw the doors open.

Layla gathered her dignity and her things and rose slowly. "Thank you," she said breezily as she walked past him and out the door, unsure how she could trust someone who held the power to ruin her relationship *and* her show.

CHAPTER TWENTY-ONE

THE FIRST WEEK of rehearsals, Layla managed to check in and shadow Manjit without interacting with Matt any more than necessary. But for reasons unknown, he was undeterred. One morning he brought her a coffee and a Nutella croissant, for which she politely thanked him. Another day he showed up at her desk and held a page of writing under her nose.

"Tell me what you think," he said. "I'm worried this one sounds too jaded."

She deigned to look at it. Matt had adapted a scene she recognized, one of the actors' stories about hitchhiking hundreds of miles to declare love to a long-distance friend. "You? Too jaded?" she said sarcastically, taking the sheet. He shrugged and walked away. A sliver of regret slid into her. Was she being too hard on him?

It's because he reminds you of Randall. But she knew by now Matt wasn't like Randall. Not really. Randall had been self-obsessed and cruel. For all Matt's faults, he had a good heart.

No, the real issue was that Layla was scared. Her most precious secret was in his hands, and he was unpredictable. And related by blood to said secret.

But Matt wasn't just *Matt*, he was also Matt Barnett, playwright of the show she was codirecting.

She read the scene carefully and decided the jaded tone was countered by enough humor to balance the scales. She wrote a couple of notes in the margin, then sauntered into the theater while the actors were on break. She found Matt in the back row.

"They won't bite, you know," she told him, taking a seat.

"Probably not," he agreed and gave her a sidelong glance. "I'm not sure I could say the same about you."

"I do get a little nippy." She passed him the paper. "This is really good. So good I'm afraid you might just have a career as a playwright."

He nodded.

"I mean it, Matt. You're really talented." And then, before she could put her foot in it, she got up and left.

The weekend finally arrived and with it a long-overdue getaway to Orcas Island with Ian. Their goal was to plan the vow renewal, but for Layla, the trip was also a chance for them to catch up on everything they'd missed in each other's lives. And for her to search for another sign from the universe that she was going in the right direction.

"I keep trying to slow down," Ian said after an epic yawn. The ferry docked, and he started the car. "But I'm beginning to worry that slowing down in this job just isn't possible." He'd been telling Layla how much caffeine he needed to deal with all his early-morning international conference calls.

"Do you want me to drive?" Layla asked as they exited the ferry.

"I'm okay," Ian assured her, his tired eyes creasing as he smiled. "You can entertain me to keep me alert. Tell me more about the show."

"It's pretty incredible," she said, wanting to gush about it while simultaneously worrying that gushing about it might jinx the whole thing. "The schedule's intense, but I'm loving it. Every day we have these thrilling mini-breakthroughs." Layla thought about the changes Matt had made to the monologue for Topher, who'd accidentally kissed his girlfriend's mom, and how at the end of it, the entire cast and crew erupted in such wild laughter, they'd had to pause rehearsal for a solid ten minutes.

"And Matty's doing okay?" Ian looked embarrassed. "I keep asking him for details, but he's cagey."

"He's doing great, Ian. Really," Layla assured him, reveling in the way Ian's blond hair was a little messy today.

"Does Matt talk to you much? Outside of rehearsal?"

She stopped reveling in his hair and started searching for signs of suspicion. "What do you mean? Why?" Layla tried to sound casual even though her brain was signaling *Red alert*.

"I don't know." Ian propped his left elbow on the car window, steering with his right hand. "I just feel like the longer he lives with me, the less I know my own brother. I was wondering if you had any insight? Anything that might help me get through to him?"

She mentally thanked her golden age of Hollywood gods that this had nothing to do with her. That they were still okay and he still needed her. Layla reached out and gently tidied the hair above Ian's ear with her fingertips as she thought back to blueberry vodka night. A few weeks ago, she would've heard Ian's complaint and assumed Matt was being selfish. Now she knew better. He was withdrawing from Ian because he was still ashamed about what had happened with *Common People*.

"He seems to be settling into Seattle," Layla offered, trying to figure out how to help Ian reach Matt without Matt knowing she was pulling the strings. "Maybe just give him some time to feel like he's got his own life here? When he's on firmer footing, he might be more willing to let his guard down with you."

Her mind wandered to the things she'd learned about Matt through his work. He could be poetic without being precious, sardonic without coming across as cynical. His script was sincere but, surprisingly, didn't take itself too seriously, and it was filled with pithy observations about the stages of life in which everything and nothing felt possible.

"So, go on. You were telling me about work and then I made it about me." Ian gave her an apologetic look as he pulled up to a four-way stop.

"Well, everything really is going smoothly. Except—" she paused, wishing she didn't have to bring things back to Matt again. "Matt has asked we change the venue. To someplace here on Orcas Island."

"Can you even do that?"

"Apparently. And honestly, that's part of why I've been so excited to get out here. Despite suggesting the change, Matt has very few ideas. I'd love to figure out somewhere we could rent fast and cheap."

Ian reached over for her hand. "We're here now. We'll find a place."

He let her hand go when he pulled into the restaurant in Rosario. Layla stepped out of the car and took a moment to appreciate the beauty of the cove: The docks stretched out over the blue-green water. Homes and cabins peeked through the sentinel evergreen trees. She wished they could perform *The Diary Project* here, but having helped Ian do a bit of research on the resort already, she knew Northwest didn't have the budget. Besides, as beautiful as it was, it wasn't quite right. It was perfectly curated, and *The Diary Project* needed a setting that was a little...wilder. Looser.

They walked into the restaurant hand in hand, and Ian asked to speak to the events planner, a warm and spunky Pakistani woman named Sara. She led Ian and Layla to the best table in the house, one with perfect views of the marina, where they talked guests, menu, dessert, and centerpieces. For a second, Layla let herself imagine they might have this conversation for themselves one day. But as soon as Layla began indulging in that fantasy—imagining Ian in a suit, herself in a vintage-inspired wedding dress—she became light-headed, her palms clammy. Instead of standing next to Ian, she saw herself standing next to Randall.

A heavy weight on her chest, Layla tried to shake the memory off, but she still felt caught; she again heard them both yelling, felt the scratchiness in her throat she used to experience just trying to get him to hear her. She felt the cold isolation, the angry silence that would stretch out for days in that apartment, the one that never felt like home.

She tried again to mentally bring herself out of LA and back to the island. Instead, she was in her mother's car and Rena's face was tearstained. Then Layla was in her childhood room, lying on her bed, crushed under the weight of debt collectors and an endless flood of shame.

Layla closed her eyes, breathed, and opened them again. She was here, in the restaurant. Sara and Ian hadn't noticed her slip—they were busy discussing the logistics of a dance floor.

Not for the first time, and definitely not for the last, Layla hated Randall for robbing her of so much. She hated herself even more for falling for him.

To remind herself of where she was, who she was with, she reached her arm across the back of Ian's chair and rested her cheek softly on his shoulder. *There.* Ian was sturdy. He was safe. The problem was, sign from the universe or not, she was also starting to hate herself more and more for what she was doing to this good man beside her. Once again, her chest tightened and ached. Everything was so horrifically complicated.

"I'll e-mail you some more possibilities," Sara said, and suddenly all three of them were standing. Layla had missed most of the meeting, lost in her toxic thoughts. Guilt slid through her. *Girlfriend of the Year over here.*

"Sounds good." Ian put his arm around Layla. "We'll go over everything and let you know what we want."

They said goodbye and left the restaurant. Being outside helped calm Layla down. She promised herself that when Ian got the e-mail from Sara, she'd be more attentive to the details.

"Your parents are going to love it," she said, trying to be more engaged. "What you're doing is incredibly sweet."

"I wish Matt saw it that way." Ian unlocked the car and they got in.

"What do you mean?" Layla asked, noting the way Ian gripped the steering wheel as he backed out.

"I mean I've asked him for help with the party and he basically ignores me."

"I'm sorry. You know, Matt told me—" She bit her lip and hesitated, wondering if she was about to betray a confidence. But Ian was her priority, and he was obviously hurting. "He told me about meeting your biological father. About Dennis."

"That's surprising, because he never told me."

"What do you mean?" *That can't be right.*

"All he said was that I shouldn't bother looking for him. He had nothing to offer us." Ian took a breath, his complexion pale. "And? So what did Matt tell you? About... about Dennis?"

"Pretty much the same thing," Layla said lightly, not sure how much she should say, frustrated that she'd been put in this position, that Matt had never told Ian. No, the irony of her frustration at this secret was not lost on her, and that only compounded her frustration. Still, she said, "It would probably help you both to talk about it again. Matt might have more to say now that there's some distance."

They drove in silence through the evergreens and she tried to quiet her nagging guilt.

"How do you do it?" Ian drummed the steering wheel with his fingers nervously. "I've only got one brother and I can't seem to make it work. You've got a family of—"

"Roughly nine dozen?" Layla said wryly.

"Exactly. And yet you manage to be close with all of them."

I ignore all the family texts because I find them overwhelming and alienating, she thought. *I slap a smile on my face at Sunday dinners. I resign myself to the fact that Bobby and Jude regularly meet up, and Rhiannon's and Cecelia's families go on spring-break trips together. But I can tell myself I'm happy they have each other. Because I don't feel like I belong with any of them and the one person I thought I belonged with, my mom, hasn't been the same since LA. In fact, I've made her so miserable, she's probably thinking about starting a new life with a new man.*

But what would Ian say if she admitted all that?

Instead, she said soothingly, "It'll come. With you and Matt."

Thinking about the boys who snuck into each other's rooms to eat raw ramen and worry about their mother, the teens who'd been camp counselors together, she hoped she was right.

"Wait!" Layla had an inspiration. "Can we turn around?"

"Everything okay?" Ian's brow furrowed. "Did you forget something?"

"No, but could we go check out that camp you and Matt worked at? Is that too far?"

"No, of course not. Sounds mysteriously important." Ian pulled off to the shoulder, waited until the road was clear, and made a U-turn. He took them past the restaurant again and down a winding road. Layla's excitement was building as they grew closer. She barely waited for Ian to put the car in park before she got out and started taking pictures of the clearing, the great firepit, the adorable surrounding yurts, the expansive sky, and the trees. She texted them to Matt and Manjit.

"What's going on?" Ian had to jog to catch up to her. "What did I miss?"

"This is it." Layla couldn't stop smiling. "I told you Matt wanted somewhere cool on Orcas to do the show, and *this is it*." She ran toward the tents. "We'll do a different scene in each yurt and have the audience members set up in chairs or on tree stumps. They'll feel like voyeurs, watching actual lives, and then—and *then*—we pull them in, figuratively speaking, when we perform an improvised scene from *their* lives."

This was perfect. This was *right*.

She'd almost forgotten Ian was there until she heard him say, "You really are a force, you know that? Even if Matt won't say it himself, I can tell how good it's been for him too."

He pulled her into a hug and she let his arms and his words envelop her.

CHAPTER TWENTY-TWO

"I SEE IT."

Within minutes of receiving Layla's photos, Matt had texted back to say that he hadn't been to that campground in years and he'd get on the ferry the next day. At first she'd taken that to mean that Matt wasn't into the idea. But once he arrived, she changed her mind. He just didn't show enthusiasm the same way she did.

It was Sunday afternoon. Layla, Ian, Jeannie, and Craig had all met Matt at the ferry together. Layla was filled with nervous energy on the car ride over to the campground, hoping everyone else would see what she did. But she didn't need the external validation. Not really. Deep down, she knew she'd nailed this.

"Yeah." Matt turned in a slow circle, taking it all in. "I can see it."

She wanted to high-five the trees and break into a victory dance. Matt took things in quietly. He internalized them, processed them. But even with that understated response, she knew he was as excited as she was about holding *The Diary Project* here. The camp's owners were excited too, seeing the possibility for free advertising. Layla stood with the Barnetts, her cheeks beginning to hurt from smiling.

"What about weather?" Matt asked, a line forming between his eyebrows.

"I thought about that. Northwest has a bunch of those big canopy tents we use for summer festivals. If we get rain, the show must go on and the audience can stand under those. If the storm gets too bad, we'll refund the tickets or add another date."

"Everyone can handle a little weather. And people around here know what they're getting into when they buy tickets to an outdoor performance," Jeannie said, patting Matt's shoulder. He nodded in agreement and their little crowd dispersed; Jeannie and Craig walked around remarking on the beauty of this place, reminiscing about their kids' time as camp counselors. Ian watched Layla proudly as she pulled Matt by the sleeve to show him the different yurts.

"So there isn't a specific order that people have to see the scenes in, right?" Matt asked, poking his head into an unoccupied yurt.

"Exactly. Maybe they can choose."

"Choose your own adventure." Matt's eyes were dancing. "Hey, we should have a place afterward where everyone can gather and talk about what they saw."

"Like, compare notes? And maybe have a drink?" Layla scanned the field. "Wait, no liquor license, and I don't have time to get one. Scratch the drinking."

"But wouldn't you want to do that after?" Matt asked. "Hang out around the fire and unpack everything?"

"Absolutely. Oh! Instead of a regular concession stand," Layla said, her heart racing as swiftly as her mind, "we could have—"

"S'mores," Matt finished.

"Yes! We'll have s'mores kits for purchase!"

"If you need someone to help out with the s'mores station, I volunteer," Craig said as he approached.

"Hire Craig and he'll eat all your inventory," Jeannie teased. "A play in the middle of the woods? This is going to be so fun. I'm going to invite all my friends from the school and everyone from my book clubs."

"We'll sell out," Matt said dryly. "Don't you belong to roughly a hundred and seven book clubs?"

"*Three*," Jeannie said, ruffling his hair. She turned her attention back to Layla. "You'll give me the details when you have them, won't you?"

"Yes, of course," she said. In truth, she still harbored concerns about whether Northwest End's regular patrons would be willing to make the trip. It was helpful to know Jeannie could rally her local troops for support, ensuring the show wouldn't be a total box-office failure.

Jeannie looked at Ian, who was chatting idly with the manager. "We'll take Matty back to the house. You and Ian join us when you're ready."

"Sounds good."

While Jeannie and Craig debated dinner options, Matt took a step toward Layla with some trepidation. She observed the way he shoved his hands in his pockets almost shyly. "Thanks for figuring this out."

"What do you mean?" Layla asked, reminding herself not to be a smart-ass.

"I mean," he said, giving her a knowing look, "the whole change-in-venue thing was a huge headache for you. You made that pretty clear."

She bit back a smile. "My poker face needs work?"

"Yeah. It was the face that tipped me off, not the yelling." He let out the smallest of laughs. "Anyway, this show is really special and I think this place is going to do it justice."

"So do I."

"Ready to head out?" Craig asked Matt, putting his arm around him. Matt nodded. Layla noted happily that things between them seemed warmer than they had her first weekend out.

"Unless..." Jeannie scanned Matt's face for an answer she didn't seem to receive. "Would you rather ride back with Ian and Layla? So you aren't stuck with the old folks?"

"I think I can handle a car ride with you old folks. As long as you turn down the John Denver." Matt linked his arm through his mother's.

They said their goodbyes; Jeannie sang "Annie's Song" to Matt as they strolled across the clearing toward Ian.

Standing amid the yurts and the trees, envisioning what was to come, Layla pushed herself to embrace it. Surely this was the sign she'd craved? Not only was Ian less of a workaholic, happier, and more *Ian* than he'd ever been, indulging this second chance had led her to *this*. This place, this chance. Had led both her *and* Matt, really.

And *this* had been missing in her life. For too long.

Not wanting to forget this moment, Layla retrieved her phone from her purse, held it up, and took a picture of herself for Instagram, nature providing the backdrop. She never took selfies, but she was feeling her career, her love life... herself, even. If ever there was a time for a selfie, this was it. And, hey, if someone saw her looking fabulous and figured she'd gotten her life together, that was only a bonus. She captioned the post *Seducing the muses / working on something exciting in this glampground*.

Across the clearing, Ian was talking to his parents and Matt. They were too far away for her to hear what they said, but she watched their body language, saw the way Ian was speaking, so animated, as he tried to get a reaction—to get *something*—from the brother he couldn't seem to crack. She felt a bubble of frustration. *Even here, Matt?* But then she shifted to watch Matt himself. Hands in the pockets of his jeans, a neutral expression on his face.

Ian reaching out.

Matt shutting down.

Eventually, Matt left with Craig and Jeannie, who gave Layla one more wave before disappearing through the trees to get to the parking lot.

Ian didn't come to her right away. He gave himself a moment, took another breath, and plastered a smile on his face as he walked back to her.

An uncomfortable feeling spread in Layla's chest, eclipsing the joy she'd been feeling mere minutes ago. She'd just witnessed Ian making an effort to be cheerful. *For her.*

For the first time, she wondered if he was really one hundred percent himself with her.

Because she knew she wasn't one hundred percent herself with him. How could she be when she was lying to him? The guilt she felt over her betrayal wasn't new. What *was* new was how she'd felt watching Ian and Matt interact, the building suspicion that asking Matt to keep her secret had added another wedge between Ian and his brother. Layla squeezed her eyes shut as a single, unexpected tear rolled out and down her cheek.

"What's the matter?"

She opened her eyes as Ian approached, looking at her with those caring blue eyes she loved. Ready to be whatever she needed. And she wasn't being anything *he* needed.

She wiped the tear away, pretending it was a rogue eyelash. Meeting his gaze, she felt wretched. It wasn't just Matt's countdown; it wasn't just lying to this entire family. It was there, in that trust in Ian's eyes. The trust she didn't deserve.

Inhale.

Exhale.

It was all on the tip of her tongue. The lie about their breakup, the truth about wanting to be with him forever. It was all there.

But.

If she unleashed these ghosts now, she might lose Ian forever. And worse, now she might lose everything else too.

"Layla?" Concern was etched in Ian's voice.

I'm lying to you. "I'm okay," she told him instead. There it was. Another cheerful Ian smile.

"We're both going to be okay," he said so quietly she wondered if she'd imagined it. He reached out his hand and she slipped hers into it.

It felt so right that she let herself believe him.

CHAPTER TWENTY-THREE

AS IT TURNED out, managing to skip the Sunday scaries did not make Monday any easier. Layla had been so focused on traveling back from Orcas Island with Ian that she'd forgotten to dread work (and, with the first of the month approaching, her pending credit card payment).

Now, fresh out of an admin meeting with Charlene and clutching the variety of half-eaten snacks she was hoarding like an anxious squirrel, she surveyed her desk. It was cluttered with inventory forms, phone messages, office-supply orders, and, from the marketing department, requests for volunteers to help with the last-minute push for *The Diary Project*.

"I just checked the food-truck app. Viet Tacos is down the street," Pearl said, flipping her hair out from under the collar of her wool coat.

"Glad to hear this day isn't completely cursed," Layla mumbled. She threw her snacks on top of her papers, grabbed her vintage red slicker, and pulled up her hood as they walked outside.

It was the type of precipitation Layla loved, a crisp and steady mist. Sure, it frizzed up her hair, but it also cleaned the world around her, giving downtown what felt like a fresh start. She felt marginally better already. Marginally.

"You seem down. Are you mad about the volunteers? Or about how many taco fiends got here before we did?" Pearl pointed to the long line for the food truck and they grudgingly queued up.

Layla shrugged, not knowing where to begin—or if she could even tell Pearl all the reasons she was in a funk. Pearl was great about not judging Layla, but Layla wasn't convinced she didn't deserve some judgment right now. She just didn't have the resiliency to take it.

"I'm sorry. I know how much it sucks to beg people to help out. But we really need a whole team if we're gonna get the word out this late," Pearl said.

"I'm not mad," Layla said. All the marketing department wanted was for her to do her job. It just turned out she really hated her job.

"Well, I don't know what's turned you into a grumpy old man, then, but let's focus our annoyance on the true enemy here." When Layla gave Pearl a look of confusion, she said, "The original playwright who couldn't come up with his own fucking ideas."

Was she still mad at him? If there had been no scandal, there would be no *Diary Project*. Still, for Pearl's benefit, Layla loudly declared, "May he get anal fleas."

A punk couple turned around and smiled appreciatively at the curse.

"May he get anal fleas," Pearl agreed and leaned forward to high-five the couple in that casual, friendly way she had. How did Pearl manage to move through the world with such ease? Layla sighed. Pearl shimmied a little closer to her as if intuiting her need not to feel so alone. The rain drifted into an even lighter mist as the sun tried to poke through the thick layer of clouds.

"Are things going better with Matt? Everyone at the theater seems really happy, and it's been a while since you've complained about him."

Layla had shared as many of her frustrations with Pearl as she could without feeling disloyal for grumbling about her rising star. But now she considered Pearl's question. Certainly, the instinct to strangle Matt with the strap of her purse had (mostly) subsided. At least until she remembered Matt had installed a red countdown clock above Ian's head. She considered telling Pearl about it all—she'd considered it a dozen times since blueberry vodka night—but she could already hear Pearl's response in her head: *So I know and Matt knows and Ian still doesn't know? This is getting really fucked up, pookie.*

Layla would tell Pearl everything as soon as she told Ian. Of course this whole thing was unsustainable—she'd sort out this whole mess soon enough. Just not today. Or tomorrow.

"Matt's doing well. I'm pretty surprised at how this is all shaping up, honestly," Layla said, cringing at her own casual use of the word *honestly*, seeing as she was a heap of lies in a (fabulous) trench coat.

"I always thought he was cute on the show, but a few years older and in person? *Wow.*" Pearl fanned herself with her hand as their turn at Viet Tacos' window finally arrived. Knowing Layla's favorite combo as well as she knew her own, Pearl leaned forward and placed the order for them both.

"You really think Matt's that good-looking?" Layla considered this. Or pretended to, because she didn't want to consider this. "I guess he is, in a Jon Snow–meets–Richard Linklater kind of way."

"You said it." Pearl tapped her credit card. "Lunch is on me, baby."

"What are you doing?" Layla held up her own card. "I can pay for my lunch."

"Yes, but now that I've bought you tacos, you'll be less mad when I point out that you love Richard Linklater movies."

They stepped aside to wait for their order. Layla felt heat rush to her cheeks despite the cool weather. She slipped off her hood and let the rain ruin her hair. "I love *some* Richard Linklater movies."

"Despite your weird obsession with Hollywood's dead leading men, you think Kit Harington is a handsome, if bewildered, devil." Pearl's stare grew more intense.

"Did I say that?" Layla didn't remember saying it, though it did sound like her. She was a sucker for bewildered.

"Ergo"—Pearl pointed a finger at Layla—"you think your fake boyfriend's brother is a hubba-hubba bombshell."

"Ohhh-kay." Layla swiped Pearl's finger away, irritation rising. "First of all, Ian is not my *fake* boyfriend. He's my real boyfriend—"

"That's debatable."

Even though Pearl's tone was teasing, it poked the fire in Layla's belly. "Second," Layla went on even though she knew she should drop the topic altogether, that continuing to entertain it was a very the-lady-doth-protest-too-much move, "your evidence is flimsy. I like watching Julie Delpy and Ethan Hawke, *ergo* I think Matt Barnett is hot?"

They walked back and reached the theater at the same time as one of the actors, who had obviously been eavesdropping. He said, "Matt Barnett *is* hot," with a wicked grin before pushing past them to enter.

"I don't know who that was," Pearl said, holding the door open, "but let it be known that Matt Barnett's hotness has been a topic of watercooler conversation."

"Well, please leave me out of that entirely. Thanks for lunch." Layla wasn't sure why she was so annoyed, but she turned around and stormed away, container of tacos in hand.

She didn't have a destination in mind; she knew only that she needed to leave the theater, leave Pearl, for a bit. She headed back outside and saw that the sun had successfully broken through the clouds.

Her phone buzzed. She didn't look at it. It buzzed again. Just in case it was Charlene or Manjit, Layla pulled it out for a glance. There were two messages.

The first was from Pearl: Sorry for taking things too far, followed by a sad-face emoji and the emoji that allegedly meant "hug" but that Pearl and Layla maintained meant "jazz hands." The emoji was a staple for them both.

The second text was from her mom. I'm in the neighborhood. Want me to bring you a coffee? And suddenly, Layla longed to spend some uncomplicated time with her mom. She hoped that was possible.

"Do you want something sweet or something strong?" her mom asked by way of hello when Layla called. She could hear the unmistakable sounds of a café in the background: baristas calling out orders, bursts of steam from the espresso machines, and smooth jazz. Layla knew where her mom was and crossed the street.

"Something sweet," Layla said. "You're at Beans, Beans, right? I'm one minute away."

"I just put my coat on a table by the window." Hearing the return of her mom's usual enthusiasm sent a torrent of conflicting emotions through Layla.

There had been a time when getting her mom to herself had been such a treat. So often Layla was either competing with her siblings for attention or getting into mischief for the wrong kind of attention. But Rena had always been good at giving each of her five kids one-on-one time. She'd take Bobby out for ice cream and let him practice his debate speeches. She'd get nosebleed tickets to football games for Jude. With Cecelia, she'd watch *Jeopardy!* and they'd gleefully yell out the answers together. Rhiannon got visits to museums.

As for Layla, she had always been her mom's shopping partner. Whether it was for clothes or groceries, they'd go up and down every aisle, talking animatedly. It'd been so easy. What had happened?

But Layla knew. She'd abandoned Rena when she ran away with Randall.

At first, she'd stayed with him for love. She'd impulsively gotten in his car and driven to LA with him because she, too, could see the gleaming chance of a new life.

Then she'd stayed out of stubbornness, determined to stand by her choice, to make the relationship work.

After his growing disdain wore her down, the shame kept her there. She couldn't admit to her family—or Pearl or the world—that she'd made such a colossal mistake.

Finally, one night she'd realized she was staying only because she was trapped. She didn't have money for bus fare and was too scared to hitchhike. She decided to call her mom, and she knew she had to do it before Randall came home or she'd never again have the nerve.

"I'm coming" was all her mom had said.

Rena must've driven all night because she arrived the next morning, looking exhausted and older than Layla had ever seen her. Though Layla was sure she herself had aged at least ten years over the past three months.

It was the end of November. Layla had already missed Thanksgiving with her family and would have missed Christmas if not for the rescue. The long drive back to Bellevue had been flecked with flash floods, crackly FM radio, and a silence so thick, Layla thought it might smother her. At one point, the storm shut down part of the highway. She and her mom were forced to stay overnight in a motel with a pool that was empty—except for rainwater—and mattresses that were thin and lumpy.

"Thank you for coming to get me," Layla had whispered into the darkness after they turned out the lights.

Her mom had simply said, "I just wish you hadn't waited so long."

It was a memory that was as comforting as it was painful, and ever since, Layla couldn't experience one emotion without the other when it came to Rena.

Beans, Beans was semi-busy, but by the time Layla pushed the door open, jingling the cute little bell at the top, Rena was already seated with two steaming drinks on the table. She stood to give Layla a hug. As soon as she smelled her mom's familiar combination of shampoo and soap, Layla felt like breaking down. Being both comforted and discomfited by her mom's company wasn't a new feeling, but with everything else going on right now, it was more potent. And for the first time in Layla's life, *she* wasn't the only problem here.

"How are you?" Layla asked politely as she sat down.

"Me? Fine. Good. Teaching's going well." Rena took a sip of her drink, not offering any more details.

"So what brings you to my neck of the woods?" Layla asked, opening her taco container. "I hope you don't mind that I brought my lunch."

"Of course not. And I wanted to see my youngest daughter. Is something wrong with that?" Was that wariness in Rena's tone? "With all these weekend trips you're taking to the San Juans, we've missed you." Before Layla could feel too guilty, Rena added, "Plus, my favorite music store in Bellevue just went under."

The store, Musicology, had been a staple in their neighborhood. It was where they bought recorders in elementary school, where Rena got all her piano music, where twelve-year-old

Layla had begged for and gotten a harmonica, just to see if she had the blues inside her (if she did, it didn't come out musically), and where teenage Layla had bought a tambourine after she decided she wanted to be known as "a tambourine kind of girl."

"Yeah, I believe you mentioned that," Layla said coolly. Maybe that part was true, but it sounded like a tidy little explanation for why Layla had seen her at the music shop the other day.

"Such a shame." Rena shook her head solemnly. "I'm in the market for a new store, so I'm scoping things out around here."

Rena didn't know about the *second* time she'd been spotted, by Pearl, with that same man. Layla took a big bite of taco.

"I've been trying that shop you saw me in before," Rena continued, sounding more and more like a liar, "but it doesn't have the selection I needed."

"Mmm," Layla said. She swallowed and added, "We both know that's not why you were at that music shop, so why don't you tell me what you're really doing with that sixty-something skater boy?"

Rena choked on her coffee. Layla's taco, which she was holding in midair, dripped onto the table. A barista glared across the room at them. *If you think this is a mess, you should see my life,* Layla thought, holding his gaze and letting it drip some more.

"The man you saw me with is Sameer." Rena put down her coffee and stared at her hands. "I know you've lived a very...*full* life, but you're too young yet to understand real regrets."

Layla dropped her taco and scoffed. "You think *I* don't understand regrets? My entire life up until a few weeks ago has been one giant flaming ball of regret."

Her mom's eyes softened. Guilt? Empathy? Layla countered her own surge of the same feelings with thoughts of her poor, sweet dad sitting at home. Completely unaware.

"So what are you going to do about all that regret, *Rena?*" Layla asked, noting her mother's flinch at her first name.

"I'm working on it," she replied, meeting Layla's eye. "I promise."

They sat there for a moment. Rena eventually reached across to take Layla's hand. "Now do you want to talk about whatever you're clearly going through?"

"Don't worry about it," Layla said, standing and grabbing her purse. She parroted back her mom's line: "I'm working on it."

After dealing with her mom and then a bunch of admin tasks she hated, Layla was relieved to get a message from Ian asking if she could come over that night and help out with an important part of the anniversary party. She was ready to stuff envelopes or make centerpieces or write an original love ballad if it meant she could distract herself from everything. But when she got there, Ian, who'd put himself in charge of the guest list, had locked himself in the bedroom to contact everyone by phone or direct message, to make sure the party stayed a surprise.

This left Layla and Matt in the living room tasked with putting together an Oscar-worthy slideshow. She worried Matt might be able to psychically sense that she'd been a participant in a conversation regarding his hotness that day, so she settled in on the opposite side of the room.

"You can't possibly see the albums from over there," he pointed out.

She moved closer, wondering when Ian would emerge.

"You sat beside me all through auditions for *The Diary Project* and we both survived. Layla, I'm sorry you have to hang out with me at work *and* here," Matt said, not sounding sorry at all, "but stop being weird."

He was right. She was being weird. She plopped down beside him.

"Well, now you're too close." He inched away from her.

"Make up your mind," she protested. When she saw the amusement on his face, she cracked and laughed. But only a little. "Congratulations, you ass, you broke the ice. Now can we focus on the slideshow?"

They ended up moving to the floor so they could spread out all the albums and loose photos. As they combed through them, Matt marked the ones he claimed had the most vivid memories attached to them: Jeannie in the hospital holding a newborn Ian; five-year-old Matt sticking out his lower lip at Jeannie as far as it would go because he didn't want to leave her side and go to kindergarten; Jeannie and the boys posing with Santa at a town festival.

"If we change the music cue here," Layla suggested, "then we can move on to the part where Craig and your mom start dating."

"What about this one?" Matt grabbed his phone out of his pocket and started playing "The More I See You" by Nat King Cole.

Chills speckled Layla's skin. "It's perfect."

They selected photos from early on in Jeannie and Craig's courtship right up to their wedding at the tiny courthouse and the day Craig officially adopted the boys. Seeing the arc of their journey, the devotion Craig had to his new family, made Layla emotional. She dabbed at the corners of her eyes, careful not to get any of the photos wet with her tears.

"Are you..." Matt ventured.

"Yes, I'm crying, shut up about it," she said, daring him to tease her. "Everything makes me cry, okay? Being sad, being angry, being happy, seeing these stupidly beautiful pictures of your family coming together...it all makes me cry."

"Huh." Matt sat back. He seemed to be considering something.

"What." She glared at him. "What do you have to say about my crying?"

He paused. "I just really like that about you."

Her insides froze, thawed, melted. For a moment she couldn't move. And then, thankfully, the bedroom door opened, and Ian loudly declared, "It's going to be a full house. So far, everyone's said yes!"

CHAPTER TWENTY-FOUR

"WHY HAVE WE never gone to Swing Queens?" was one of the first things Ian said Thursday night when they were both too tired to fight traffic and hang out in person. Instead, they'd pressed Play on the same episode of *The Great British Bake Off* (admittedly, Layla's pick) and let the soothing sounds of Bread Week act as background noise to their phone call.

"Why *haven't* we ever gone to Swing Queens?" Layla pretended to be as shocked as Ian was, though she knew why they hadn't: because the big-band dance club run by drag queens had opened only a few months ago. They had discussed going when Layla first heard about it from a college friend, but then they'd broken up.

It had been tricky, deducing what Ian remembered and what he didn't. Whenever she attempted to gently prod, he said there were still several weeks that were fuzzy. The lack of clarity loomed over Layla like a dark cloud.

"So are we going to go?" Ian said cheekily. "Or are we just going to keep asking ourselves why we haven't?"

Before, Ian would talk about making plans, express a desire to be spontaneous, but never commit. Now he was seemingly up for anything.

"Name the day," Layla dared him. "You know I have an entire wardrobe just perfect for this."

"Big band is at least half your aesthetic," Ian said, his voice getting far away and then close again as he presumably put her on speaker to look at his calendar. She flashed back to his company holiday party the year before, when every other woman had worn a little black dress, and she'd shown up in a buttercream tropical-print dress circa 1951. She'd paired it with a faux fur coat and a hat with a veil and felt like a million bucks. The overall response had been mild alarm paired with sartorial respect. She couldn't wait to go all out for Swing Queens.

"Let's go tomorrow," Ian said.

"Tomorrow?"

"Hey, do you think it's a good idea or a *great* idea to invite Matt and Jojo?"

Layla frowned. "Are they even dating? I thought they went out once and cut it short."

Ian paused. "Why would you think that? They've been out almost every night this week."

Why did Layla think that? Because Matt hadn't seemed that into Jojo that first night? Plus, she saw him at least five days a week at rehearsal, and, though they mostly discussed the show, he'd never so much as mentioned Jojo.

Which, fine—it was none of Layla's business. Nor was it relevant to their working relationship.

"Layla?" Ian said, interrupting her thoughts. "Should I invite Matt and Jojo?"

"Absolutely," she said and immediately regretted it.

So here she was on a Friday night, going all out with her checkerboard dress, lace socks, saddle shoes, and pin-curled hair. She could raise Glenn Miller from the grave with this look. And when Ian arrived, he did not disappoint. With his hair slicked back and a soft gray jacket paired with darker gray pants, he was at his most handsome.

He looked her up and down, then clutched his chest and stumbled back, cartoonishly indicating she was giving him a heart attack.

Gamely, she did a little twirl.

"Oh, wow. You really went for it," a voice said. Layla had somehow missed Jojo, who was standing right behind Ian. She was not so subtly giving Layla the once-over, a wind machine blowing her blond bob to highlight her glass-cutting cheekbones (or maybe it was just a small well-timed breeze).

"Thanks. You look great too," Layla replied, even though Jojo hadn't actually complimented her. But Jojo did look great. She was wearing a chic dress with an hourglass silhouette.

That's when Matt appeared in a 1940s-era light brown suit and fedora. He'd been talking to their rideshare driver.

There were guys who put on a fedora and looked like they were trying to get you to party in Fort Lauderdale. And then there were guys who put on a fedora and looked like they'd just stepped out of *Casablanca*. Matt was the guy who could convincingly say, "Of all the gin joints..."

Layla wanted to tell him she was impressed, ask him where he got the suit—and, more important, the hat—but just as she opened her mouth, he said, "We should get going," effectively cutting her off.

"Wait," Layla said. Matt raised his eyebrows, so she raised hers right back. "Can we at least commemorate this night on which you all look as fabulous as I do every day?" She held up her phone.

Ian laughed and gathered Matt and Jojo and Layla in for a picture; Layla took the photo and just happened to crop off part of Jojo's face.

They walked around the corner to where their ride was waiting. Despite the cool spring temperatures, the city felt warm. All around them, people were mingling, laughing, gathering to soak in the beginning of spring. Ian and Layla snuggled in the back seat of the minivan while Matt and Jojo took the middle bucket seats.

Ian seemed lighter than Layla had seen him in years; passing a park, he joked about the day he'd taken Layla to his tennis club and how every time she'd hit the ball, it'd gone straight up to the ceiling.

"Oh, you play?" Jojo said, turning to face them. "I was on my college tennis team."

"So was I," Ian said, brightening.

Matt, who'd skipped college to drive across the country, stayed conspicuously silent.

"Anyway, it's revenge time," Layla said, elbowing Ian in the ribs. "We both know you feel about as comfortable on a dance floor as I do on a tennis court."

"Hey," Ian said mock defensively. "I am a *stellar* slow dancer." Their bodies were as close as the seat belts allowed, molecules bouncing between them. She wondered if Matt would go home with Jojo, and this was the night Layla and Ian would finally consummate their second chance.

The club didn't look like much from the outside, just a brick building with a bouncer in front who was wearing an intricate Victor/Victoria costume and sporting biceps roughly the size of Layla's front door. She loved this place already.

They showed their IDs and entered the world of Swing Queens. A wrought-iron staircase led them to the belly of the club, where tables surrounded a dance floor packed with dozens of bodies under flashing multicolored lights. On the stage was a full orchestra, the conductor and each musician in it a gorgeous drag queen.

Layla wanted to tear up the lease agreement on her apartment and move directly in here.

"Are you in love?" Ian said into her ear, reading her thoughts.

"I could get pregnant from this energy," she shouted over the horns.

Ian insisted they all get a drink before braving the dance floor. They managed to find a table on the mezzanine with a great view. They sipped on bee's knees cocktails while Layla showed Ian a few basic moves. During a spin that landed her in Ian's arms, Layla saw Matt whisper in Jojo's ear.

"I think you've got the hang of it," Layla said to Ian and took her seat. Matt was still whispering. Layla drained the rest of her cocktail *and* Ian's cocktail, which stunned them both—she gave him a cheeky wink—then remembered she hadn't eaten much dinner. The alcohol hit her fast and potently. She saw Jojo throw her head back and laugh. She was *stupidly* hot.

Why fight it? "You're the hottest human I've ever seen in person," Layla told her.

"Thanks," Jojo said, obviously accustomed to this sort of compliment.

"She did some modeling in Europe," Matt said, turning to Jojo for confirmation. "In high school, right?"

"Matt and I bonded over what it's like to be in the spotlight," Jojo murmured, making full-on sex eyes at Matt.

The alcohol blurred the edges of Layla's world. "In high school I once saw a local news team filming a segment, so I ran in front of the camera and yelled, 'Hooray for Irving Berlin!' I was on the six o'clock *and* ten o'clock news that night."

"*What* did you yell?" Ian asked, puzzled.

"You yelled a Charlie Brown quote with your one shot at fame?" Matt said wryly, which made Layla laugh in embarrassment but also a little delight. The night that segment aired, she'd been pretty proud of herself.

"I modeled for only a year or so," Jojo said. "It probably felt like the length of that news segment."

All at once, Layla decided she might like Jojo after all.

With apologies, Ian slipped out to take a quick call, leaving the three of them to sit awkwardly, busying themselves by watching the dance floor fill and flow. Layla tried not to let Ian's sudden phone dependency worry her. Eventually Ian returned, looking pleased about something.

Well. She could be *much* more interesting than his phone.

"It's crowded enough, don't you think?" Layla purred into his ear, feeling excited and restless and needing to get into the center of the club's action immediately.

Ian wrinkled his nose and looked down at the dance floor.

Eventually, she convinced Ian that there were so many people, no one would be watching him, and they made their way into the middle of the jumping, jiving, and wailing bodies. He was self-conscious at first, but after a couple of songs, Ian seemed to forget to be Ian and let his body go. It was the first time Layla'd ever seen him dance. They'd had opportunities at work functions and weddings, but he'd always opted to mingle, pulling her into his arms only when the tempo was slow enough. Watching him let loose was *amazing*. Layla laughed until tears streamed down her cheeks as he mixed the simple rock step in with surprising TikTok dance moves and classics like the sprinkler, the robot, and one he called "groovy mime trapped in a box."

"Y'all are so sweaty, I can smell the cocktails seeping out from here," the conductor said after a particularly high-tempo song ended. "I'm Glenda Miller and welcome to Swing Queens. If you've been here before, welcome back. If this is your first time, hang on to those panties because we want you to shake your hips, shake your booties, shake your tits until local governments insist we stop serving."

Layla and Ian cheered along with the crowd.

"Now, all you gorgeous creatures, we're going to slow things down because we have a request." Glenda Miller leaned forward, practically eating the microphone. "We're honoring this request because it came from a six-foot-three drink of yowza, and I never say no to a man that tall."

Sure, there were plenty of guys over six feet in the room, but Layla found her eyes flicking to Ian. His expression was unreadable except for a little quirk of his lips.

"Whomstsoever gets to rub up on him during this song…" Glenda fanned herself. "I envy you. And now, 'Night and Day.'"

Suddenly, Layla knew there had been no phone call—Mr. Grand Gesture had snuck away to request her favorite version (Sinatra's) of her favorite song.

The unmistakable drawn-out strings of the intro began, and Layla slid into Ian's arms. They clasped their right hands and held each other tight with their left, bodies pressed together. She didn't care that she was sweating through her dress or that his collar was damp as well. She didn't care that they were surrounded by so many strangers, they could only rock back and forth in place. All she cared about was being right there, in that moment.

She noticed eventually that Ian was moving them out of the heart of the crowd. They passed Matt and Jojo, who looked very cozy indeed. She raised her eyebrows at Matt. He raised his back and mouthed, *Hooray for Irving Berlin*.

"What's so funny?" Ian murmured.

"Nothing. I'm just happy."

He twirled her in response.

"Where are we going?" she finally asked, her lower lip grazing his ear.

"I can't dip you in a crowd," he said.

She pressed her cheek against his so he could feel her muscles move as she smiled. "You're going to dip me, are you?"

"It's all part of my plan." Ian lifted her right arm, twirled her again, caught her, and, as promised, moved her into a dip so deep, a nearby table applauded. "Layla Rockford, will you move in with me?"

"*What?*" It came out as a screech as he righted her, bringing them both up straight. She pressed a hand to her heart, sure it was about to beat out of her chest. She was going to cry; she was going to pass out.

How many times had she dreamed about this moment? How many times had she fantasized about living with Ian? And she'd been begging the universe to give her a sign that Ian felt as she did, that their lives belonged together, destined to be lived side by side. *This* was her sign.

She tried to swallow, but her mouth was dry. This was what she wanted. So why did it feel so terrible now that it was happening?

"Will you?" he asked again, his face less confident, eyes searching hers. This hesitation was breaking his heart, which would surely shatter her own. She couldn't take it. But she also didn't know what to say.

"I..." She could barely bring herself to look at him. *I'd love nothing more, but there's one tiny thing you should know.* Or maybe *I don't think you'll even want me when you get a load of this...*

She opened her lips to do the right thing, to say, *Yes, but*...except the words wouldn't come. Instead, with mounting horror, she found herself slowly nodding.

The joy on Ian's face nearly ended her.

"Layla," he said, sweeping her into his arms. She buried her face in his neck, wanting to stay there forever in this moment so she didn't have to live out the rest of this tale that was surely cursed. *If I'm not honest, this will never happen,* she scolded herself, surprised to feel her face growing wet. Damn her overactive tear ducts.

Ian pulled away and saw how overwhelmed she was, so he led her back up to the mezzanine where it was a little quieter. A bottle of champagne had been conspicuously placed on their table.

As Ian poured them each a glass, Layla perched on her stool, dizzy but finally finding her voice. "So what are you thinking, timeline-wise?"

She felt like she was tumbling down a hill and couldn't stop.

"That's something I wanted to run by you. This is obviously a joint decision." He took a sip. "How long do you have left on your lease?"

Layla wrinkled her nose and tried to remember what time of year it was when she'd signed it. "Probably about three months?"

"That gives us plenty of time to figure things out. You could move into my place or we could sell my condo and find something together."

Three months. *More time.*

She knew it was wrong, but a tiny, happy, awful part of her relaxed a fraction. If he had three months in mind, maybe she could play along with her lie for these final weeks? Seeing how happy he looked—was he brushing away a tear of his own?—she just couldn't take this away now. Was it so wrong to live in this fantasy for a few more weeks? What harm would it do?

A lot of harm, the smarter part of her chimed in, adding, *You monster.* But Layla knew from experience that the champagne would silence that voice.

Besides, maybe three months was enough time to work things out between them. Maybe this would all be okay.

The image of a countdown clock flooded her mind. *Oh God, oh God.* She was on an express train to hell, and she deserved the seat.

No. This was fine. This was going to be *fine.* She had time to tell him the truth.

"What about Matt?" she asked, unable to banish that stupid yet valid countdown clock from her thoughts. "What does he think about all this?"

"I'm going—"

As if on cue, Matt appeared, his hand on Jojo's lower back.

"That was a cute surprise," Jojo said. "What's the significance of the song?"

"Layla loves it," Ian said simply, his eyes on Layla. She felt hot and cold and terrified that her courage to tell Ian the truth was waning.

"The Sinatra version is definitely the best," Matt agreed, but he seemed grim, his eyes darting from Ian to Layla.

Even Jojo sensed the change in her date's mood, because she whispered in Matt's ear, and they waved goodbye and disappeared into the crowd again.

"So? About that other roommate of yours?" Layla pressed, trying not to bite the inside of her cheek too hard.

"I haven't talked to Matt about this yet," Ian admitted. "I wanted to wait and hear what you think first."

I think I don't ever want to tell you we broke up, Layla thought, tears stinging her eyes. *I don't want the way you feel about me to change.*

Ian tipped her chin up with his knuckle to kiss her. "I hope those are happy tears, my sweet Layla. Because I'm happy too—and, hey, don't worry about Matt. I'm hoping to get in a better place with him before I tell him about our plan. I think three months is plenty of time to work out the details."

"And I think," she said impulsively, needing to get as far away from working-out-the-details and Matt as possible, "that if you take me home right now, you're going to get lucky."

Ian leaped off the stool so quickly, it toppled over behind him.

Since there was no guarantee they'd be alone at Ian's condo, Layla and Ian piled into a taxi and gave the driver her address.

At first, she snuggled into him in a very PG fashion as she tried to work through her muddled thoughts. But when Ian's hand went down her back and then lower, and lower still, her thoughts went out the window. Soon they were kissing, pawing at each other. His fingers traced the hem of her skirt, grazing her thigh and pebbling her skin. She reached her hand across to his chest and popped the buttons of his shirt. By the time they reached her apartment building, his shirt was open and she was trying not to pant; they bumped into nearly every door and wall in the lobby as they stopped to kiss along the way. In the now-quietly-functioning elevator, Layla nibbled on his neck, and he rubbed his strong hands slowly down her back.

They stumbled through her apartment, leaving a trail of clothes—his pants, her dress, a shoe here and there—though they managed to avoid a very pissed-off Deano. By the time they were at Layla's bed, they were both out of breath.

"Are you sure you're ready—" she began, but stopped herself. Ian was looking at her like she'd hung the moon *and* every star in the sky.

She rolled to her side as he lay down next to her, one hand tracing down her arm and her leg. The moment was so sweet, she thought she might cry. Or was she just feeling weirdly emotional? Sometimes feelings came first for Layla, and she had to examine them later, follow the stem to the seed.

She wanted Ian. She knew that. Her body was sending crystal-clear messages she did.

But.

Did she want him *this* way? She sighed, loving Ian's touch and hating how she'd gotten to this moment. Because even though Ian wanted her right here, right now, she didn't want any part of their intimacy to be laced with deception. For all of Layla's faults, she wasn't a sleaze who tricked people into sleeping with her.

In that instant, all of the crystal-clear messages her body had been sending stopped. Ian must've noticed the change in her, because his hand paused. "You okay?"

This was it. Her moment to come clean. To just blurt it out already: *I love you and I haven't been honest with you.* She told herself to say it. To open her stupid mouth and get it over with.

"Layla?" Ian asked gently. "We can stop. It's okay if you want to keep taking this slowly."

She nodded, even though in her heart all she wanted to do was keep going with this, with *them.* "I'm sorry," she said, her voice barely above a whisper.

I'll tell him after The Diary Project *opens.*

"Don't be sorry, sweetheart." He pushed the hair back from her eyes. If he was confused or disappointed, he was hiding it well. His mouth quirked at the side. "Be my big spoon?"

I'll tell him after his parents' party.

"Always."

I'll tell him.

They fell asleep like that, curled up on her bed with her holding on to him as best she could.

CHAPTER TWENTY-FIVE

LAYLA HAD A strange relationship with time. She'd been taught it was predictable, linear, measurable, and yet for her, it was anything but.

The two weeks between Ian ending things and the call from the hospital had been lethargic and cruel. Minutes, hours, days had stretched out as though in slow motion. Now Layla couldn't believe that was the same amount of time they had left to prepare *The Diary Project*. These final two weeks of rehearsals? They flew by in an adrenaline-charged fury.

She knew, too, these were her last few weeks before Matt's deadline. Approximately thirty-six thousand times a day, her mind ping-ponged between devising ways to tell Ian the truth and trying to come up with ethical reasons why she didn't have to (so far she had zero).

She distracted herself by working nearly nonstop. In those small pockets of time when she wasn't working, she was at home, too exhausted to cook or clean or, irritatingly, sleep. She whiled away the night by trying to get Deano on board with her fantasy of moving.

Right now, that was all it was. A fantasy. But Layla had

always known that Cary Grant and Deborah Kerr would find each other at the end of *An Affair to Remember*, and she had to believe somehow this was going to work out between her and Ian. Otherwise, what was this all for?

"Think of all the new things you can bat off surfaces!" she told Deano when neither of them could sleep. Deano raised his head, and she quickly said, "Actually, please don't. Ian's very particular about his belongings."

Meanwhile, she hoped Ian and Matt were figuring their stuff out. Once Matt realized Ian and Layla wanted to live together, would he return to his life of couch-and-state-hopping? Layla wondered. Maybe, now that he was securing a spot in the Seattle theater community, he would find a space of his own. Grow some roots.

The part of her that couldn't smother the image of the doomsday clock wanted Matt gone. She wanted to pack him up in a FedEx box with snacks and water, maybe some breathing holes, and ship him to Australia.

The part of her that had been working with him, getting to know him, wanted him to stay. The fact was, Matt had a unique way of looking at the world.

And then there was that part that considered him not just a work colleague and collaborator but a friend. That part of her would miss him.

One evening during rehearsal, he noted how jittery she was. In her defense, she'd already worked a full day in Northwest's office and spent time trying to find a DJ for the anniversary party, plus she hadn't slept the night before because Manjit had told her she was going to be in charge of preparing the actors for their improv, so she'd stayed up researching games that would help them warm up.

During a break, Matt disappeared. When he returned, he handed her a small bag.

"What's this?"

He shrugged and walked away. She looked into the bag and found Silly Putty. When she charged after him and asked why he'd bought her a toy, he simply said, "Trust me."

The rest of the rehearsal, whenever she felt nervous energy building, she took out the Silly Putty. Working it with her hands allowed her mind to settle and clear. From then on, she brought it every day. Still, somehow, dress rehearsal had snuck up on Layla. The night it arrived, unceremoniously, she agreed to ride in Manjit's car to the island. It would be everyone's first time running the show in the space. Manjit, a consummate professional, was cool and relaxed, an anchor for Layla, who felt like she could float away on her fears of the million and one things that could go wrong.

The drive to the ferry terminal was mostly filled with small talk. Once they were parked on the boat, they walked up, found two seats, and enjoyed the scenery of the San Juans.

"There's something I want to chat with you about," Manjit said, and Layla immediately began thinking of worst-case scenarios. Manjit laughed. "Don't look so scared, Layla, it's a *good* thing."

Remember, Layla. Good things can happen too, she heard her father say. Layla attempted to arrange her face in a less panicked expression, though she must've failed because Manjit laughed again.

"Look, I've been really impressed with you. When I first tasked you with saving the emerging-playwright show, I wasn't totally serious," Manjit confessed.

Layla had suspected as much. It seemed to be a bit of a throwaway, a rhetorical assignment: *You know a writer? Great. Take this terrible problem off my hands, even though you aren't qualified to.*

"That said," Manjit continued, "you really saved the show. You saved Northwest's reputation. Not only that, you've shown a real knack for producing and—and I think you have real potential as a director."

"Thank you." Layla couldn't remember the last time someone had praised her like this, and she felt a little choked up. She'd thrown her heart into this show, but in all of the chaos, she hadn't had time to question whether she was any good at it.

"I'd like to offer you the opportunity to coproduce one of our shows next year—and be my assistant director. As you know, our budget isn't huge, but we can pay you a bit of money for the job—in addition to your admin salary, of course."

Layla blinked, digesting, and Manjit kindly stepped away. She noticed a couple awkwardly trying to take a selfie on the deck and volunteered to take their picture for them.

The interruption gave Layla a moment to let the offer sink in. She thought about how much she'd loved working on *The Diary Project*. About how, even though her work had doubled, she felt energized by it. Well, energized by one of the jobs. Her day job was still slowly sucking away her soul like a dust buster low on batteries.

The idea settled inside her. Of course she was going to say yes.

When Manjit returned, she said with a wink, "I think I just convinced that selfie couple to come see our show."

Presale tickets were solid already, thanks to locals who were keen on an outdoor performance so close to home. Marketing had done a great job running a social media campaign that highlighted the beauty of Orcas Island, and she and Manjit saw posters for the show when they stopped in Orcas Village to get water and snacks for the cast and crew. Layla also suspected Jeannie had strong-armed every person she knew into buying a ticket.

Due to time and venue constraints, they had to combine dress and tech into one rehearsal, so it was likely to be a long night. Layla was anxious to get to the campground and see if she'd been right to push for it. Even mid-setup, the clearing, speckled with yurts, looked more enchanting than it ever had. She didn't want to jinx anything, but her scalp was tingling and she had goose bumps. Something spellbinding could happen here.

Her heart lurched as she caught sight of Matt lurking in the trees. To the untrained eye, he was being aloof. Too good to hang out with the cast and crew plebs. But she knew better now. Matt Barnett was *afraid*. Afraid he cared too much about this production, that he was going to sabotage it somehow. That he'd be forced to run away from this.

Immediately, she was flooded with guilt. Even if Matt was threatening to end things for her and Ian, he was doing it because he thought it was the right thing. He thought he was protecting his brother. Maybe he even thought he was protecting *Layla*. From who...Ian? Herself? *Oh God.*

The thoughts pulsed in her mind. She'd been so busy, so determined to pull everything off, she'd forgotten to step outside herself and see what was going on.

Matt cared about her.

She crossed the clearing, dodging actors stretching and doing vocal warmups, and joined him in the shadows. His body shifted, turning ever so slightly toward her. There was a quirk of his mouth, not quite a smile, but close enough. Matt loved to appear laid-back, always reclining in chairs and leaning against doorways, but she knew it was an act. And yet, in this tense moment, she could see him visibly...relax. Because of her? Matt was full of contradictions.

"Looks like we're about ready to start." Her voice was soft, despite her nerves, as she gestured to the action on the campground. What she really wanted to do was grab him by the collar of his plaid coat and cry, *There are a million elements that could cause this show to go sideways*, but that wasn't productive. So instead, she said, "Can you believe you created all this?"

"Well, I had some help." But before Layla could modestly accept some credit, he turned back to the camp and said, "That guy has been an inspiration." Matt pointed to a crew member, who promptly tripped over a tree root.

"That guy has really gotten us through the tough times," Layla agreed, noting that Matt might not boo people, but he had his own defense mechanisms.

"You nervous?" he asked, maybe just to make conversation, maybe because he could sense how tightly wound she was.

"No, I'm good," she lied. And then, because she couldn't stand putting one more lie out into the world no matter how inconsequential, she whispered, "What if this show is terrible?"

She'd said the same to Ian on the phone the night before, perched nervously on the edge of her bed, wiggling her toes as Deano pounced on them.

"There's no way the show will be terrible," Ian had assured her. "Haven't you been telling me all along how well it's going? Don't doubt yourself now."

"What if I've been wrong? What if we've created this weird show that no one will get?" She'd picked at her nail polish and then cursed herself for picking at the nail polish that she'd only just applied.

"Hey," Ian had said soothingly. "You've put so much time into this, and you've had the approval of Manjit at every step. You're not an amateur, Layla, you know what you're doing. You've been in theater for a decade."

She'd tried to let his words comfort her. But they weren't loud enough to muffle her fears.

When she asked Matt the same question, he didn't reassure her right away; he took his time to answer. His gaze moved over the campgrounds—the performers joking around, the crew members setting up lights, Manjit going over a checklist with the stage manager.

"If it's terrible," Matt finally said, "then it's terrible. People will still have something to talk about. And we'll have had another terrible adventure in this life, not unlike"—he pointed to the actors who were laughing together—"those people who are about to share some of their worst and most complicated memories with an audience."

"Yeah," she agreed and took a deep breath. Because Matt was right. Besides, she wasn't in this alone, and she let his confidence boost her own.

"Shall we?" he asked, his deep brown eyes full of anticipation and a little mischief, a shared secret.

They *did* share a secret. They were both people who'd fallen down the tree of life, bumping every branch along the way. And here they were, appreciating that even at the bottom, the trunk was solid.

"We shall," she replied with her own tone of tentative excitement.

They headed back to the clearing, pine needles and branches snapping under Layla's ankle boots. "I can't believe we did all this in such a short time. If tonight goes well, we should fly straight to Vegas because we are two lucky sons of bitches."

"No matter what happens tonight," Matt said, suddenly serious, "we consider this whole thing a success. Right?"

"Deal." Layla put out her hand, and he shook it. Her hand was freezing, so she took pleasure in the temporary warmth of his fingers.

"You wanna watch together?" Matt asked, and if she hadn't known better, she'd've thought he sounded apprehensive. She nodded and they chose a scene at random. The rehearsal began. Certainly, there were hiccups. Despite the simultaneous scenes happening in each yurt, the technical aspects were straightforward—a couple dozen lighting and sound cues per yurt. Once those were ironed out, it was time for the dress rehearsal to begin.

After performing the diary entries Matt had adapted, the actors would attempt the improv scenes for the first time. The crew had provided the scene suggestions, written on little slips of paper that the performers would draw from a bucket. Waiting as they drew, Layla reached into the pocket of her houndstooth coat and pulled out the Silly Putty. She saw Matt smile to himself.

Over the course of the evening, she and Matt moved from yurt to yurt. They laughed, they shouted when additional suggestions were requested during the improv, they congratulated the actors when beat after beat did—in fact—land.

But in the last yurt, during the improv section about a proposal gone wrong, the actor looked so much like Randall, it took her breath away. It was ridiculous. Stupid, really. The actor had just changed into jeans and a gray V-neck T-shirt. But something about how he wore them, about the part in his hair, about the way he skulked in that small space…Layla dug her nails into her palms as the actor growled, "So let's get married already." Not Randall's exact words, but not far off.

Layla couldn't inhale, couldn't focus. The lines sounded like they were coming through a tunnel from far away. She saw the failure of her relationship with Randall. She felt the imminent failure of her relationship with Ian. And it was all threatening to pull her down.

Her eyes darted around; she kept her smile plastered on as she searched for a place to hide, even briefly. All she needed was a few minutes. If she could take a few *fucking minutes* to have a breakdown, she could collect herself and continue the night.

"Should we head over?" Matt asked, appearing at her side. Somehow, the sketch had ended. He was gesturing to the bonfire, where the cast was gathering to receive their final notes from Manjit.

Layla nodded quickly. Too quickly. Maniacally, probably. *Shit.*
Matt put his hand on her arm. "Are you okay?"

She nodded again, even faster. There was a weight on her
chest and she couldn't get Randall out of her head and she knew,
she *knew*, that when it came to him, she couldn't escape this
feeling. She could never predict it, never tell what might ignite
it, but here she was—on fire.

"No, you're definitely not okay." Gently, tenderly, he guided
her back into the trees to a patch lit by the moon and out of the
way of prying eyes. "What's going on, Layla?"

It was the smallest thing, hearing him say her name. And that
small thing led to an avalanche.

"I was married." Her hands were shaking, so she shoved them
into the pockets of her houndstooth peacoat. She couldn't look
at Matt. When he didn't respond, she couldn't stop herself. "I
started dating Randall when I was twenty-five. We met through
mutual friends, and from the beginning, we were obsessed with
each other. I mean *obsessed*. In a way I'd never been before. He said
he hadn't either. He was charming, *so charming*. The type of guy
who seemed to know something the rest of the world didn't. Our
whole relationship felt like a secret no one else was privy to."

She hated that even now, after *everything*, she still missed the
feeling of being in Randall's orbit, feeling like the two of them
were connected on a different plane.

"We wanted to be with each other, near each other,
constantly—even when we were fighting." Layla squeezed her
eyes shut. "There was a lot of fighting."

There was a sharp shuffle of pine needles, and her eyes flew
open. Matt's posture had changed and a swirling ferocity had
gathered in his face, so she clarified. "Not physical, just stupid
arguments."

"Okay." His tone was soft, but the protectiveness of his gaze
remained.

"From the first night we met," Layla continued, "we joked about running away, about getting married. Because no matter how serious we were about each other, how committed we were, it was never enough. Our love, our passion, he kept saying it was too big. We needed to take it further."

Layla thought back to the times she'd brought Randall home with her. Thought of the guarded expression on Bill's face. Of the way her mom seemed to draw away from her. Of Jude telling her Randall was a dick and she could do better. Of Bobby mocking Randall for taking himself too seriously. Of her sisters refusing to talk to her, leaving her drowning in this relationship alone.

"My family didn't approve, his family didn't approve, and somehow this emboldened us. He was a screenwriter and wanted, more than anything, to move to LA." She shrugged. "We drove to Vegas first, got married, then went the rest of the way to LA. Randall was broke. He didn't get a job because he wanted to give his writing his full attention. I used my pathetic savings to get us a place to live. I took a job at a twenty-four-hour diner to keep us afloat. But it was never enough, because Randall had to go out to 'network' and 'be discovered.'"

The discomfort, the stress she'd felt standing at his side at parties, at restaurants, at the Chateau Marmont, for crying out loud, while he ordered expensive drinks and tried to pitch people who weren't interested was still visceral. They'd go home after racking up charges on her credit card and he'd be in such a foul mood, he'd ice her out.

"Anyway, the whole thing was a complete disaster. After a couple of months, I called my mom crying, and she drove through the night to come pick me up." The dust of her story settled between them. Even though the evening air was cold, she could feel the dampness of sweat at her hairline, down her back.

"What happened when you told him?" Matt asked, his tone unreadable.

Layla remembered every detail of that day as though she were living it now. The gray V-neck T-shirt Randall was wearing, stretched out where he'd pull on it when he felt blocked. The stained linoleum of their kitchen floor. The smells of their neighbors' cooking wafting through the vents. Feeling overwhelmed and depleted all at once and knowing she had to get out of there, that it was now or never.

"When I told him I wasn't paying for the apartment anymore, that I wanted a divorce, I expected him to yell. He and I were so good at fighting. Better at making up." She smiled sadly. "But he turned cold. Unresponsive. It was like he hated me so much, he could flip the switch to indifference without a second thought."

Layla hadn't told anyone that part of the story, ever. "I haven't told Ian about this, by the way." She lifted her chin, daring him to judge her.

He could've thrown that in her face, tossed out something cruel like *There are a lot of things you haven't told him.*

Matt *wasn't* cruel, and he simply said, "Why not?"

Any time she'd asked herself this question, she landed on the simplest answer. "It's not relevant to our relationship." But she knew that wasn't true. She was a coward. If Ian knew he wouldn't technically be her first husband, would he care? Would the way he saw her change? She couldn't bear it.

Logically, she knew how common divorce was. That there was no shame in saying, *This isn't working. This was a mistake.* But she was also sensitive, scared of being judged, embarrassed by her own foolish choices. That and all the years in her twenties she'd spent partying instead of planning her future...

No. Layla couldn't imagine telling Ian any of that.

Matt didn't respond, so she risked a glance at him and found

246 •   Annette Christie

his eyes glistening with tears. Not angry tears, not manipulative tears. Empathetic tears. *For* her. Because she'd suffered.

Without thinking, she threw her arms around him and squeezed him tightly. He was caught off guard, but only for a second. Then he wrapped his arms around her waist and held her—not just with his arms, but with all of himself. He was only a couple of inches taller than she was, and her face was in his neck, his face in hers. Something in her chest exploded. She held on as long as she dared, her own tears stilling as his breath calmed her down.

And then they broke apart. Layla couldn't *not* look at Matt. Couldn't *not* see that tears were still streaming down his cheeks, that he was trying to tell her something very important— beyond empathy and compassion. Something without words or description.

She closed her eyes. That seemed the safer option.

When she opened them again, she turned around and ran.

CHAPTER TWENTY-SIX

IT WASN'T UNTIL Layla reached the parking lot that she remembered she'd gotten a ride there with Manjit. She looked around frantically, praying someone else was leaving too. Finally, a semi-familiar crew member appeared, keys in hand.

"Can I get a ride to the ferry with you?" Layla was breathless, desperate. The guy nodded.

They might have spoken during the bumpy, winding, dark drive to the ferry, but Layla wouldn't have been able to say about what.

Once on the ferry, Layla got out of the truck and wandered off in search of a place to be alone. She found a seat and tried to regulate her breathing. *Almost home. Almost safe.*

But ferries moved so slowly. They forced you to stop, to observe. Whatever feelings had exploded in her chest when she'd hugged Matt turned to shame, shame that sank and burned inside her. That licked at her cheeks. She tried to smother the shame by telling herself she'd done nothing wrong.

But she had. The list of things she'd done wrong was lengthy, ever growing. And now *this*. Coming between two brothers. Forgetting her own boundaries.

She was so foolish. So predictable. If given the choice between a path that was smooth and one that was jagged with rocks, somehow she'd find a third path to take that was populated with rabid coyotes. Why couldn't she be more like Rhiannon and Cecelia? Hell, she'd even take being a little more like Jude. Even Bobby.

The ferry docked and she exited with the rest of the pedestrians, following them to the taxi stand. Waiting in line, she called the first number that came to mind. The one she'd always called when she'd been unsure or had made a mess of things.

"Layla?" Her mom's voice sounded groggy yet trepidatious. Layla missed the days when her mom would greet her with all the enthusiasm she had.

What was she doing? Why was she calling her mother? Her instincts were truly the worst.

"Layla?" Rena said again, more worried this time. Layla's temper flared. Sure, she was a screw-up, but how *dare* Rena worry when she herself was running around town with some overgrown Green Day enthusiast (probably) who, judging from their conversation in the music store, she had to beg to go out with her.

"You *don't* need to worry about me, I'm fine," Layla snapped. "Do you know who you should worry about? Yourself. Believe me, I know a thing or two about blowing your life up, and, sugar, that's where you're headed."

Then she hung up and got in a taxi. The cabbie glanced in the rearview mirror and asked where she was going.

"Home," she replied numbly.

"Where's that?" he asked, clearly annoyed.

As she was about to give him her address, she realized home was the last place she felt like being, the apartment where she was sure to drink cheap wine and spend too much money on faux-fur shrugs and pantyhose with the sexy seams down the back that even she could admit were impossible to keep straight. She needed distraction; she needed company. She needed someone who loved her no matter what.

She needed *Pearl*.

She'd been avoiding the loft since she'd gotten back together with Ian, knowing the crowd there didn't bring out her best side. But she missed being at her former home with her best friend. Before she could second-guess herself, Layla gave the driver Pearl's address.

Pearl lived in a historic building in Capitol Hill. The loft was decorated with tiny plants and twinkling Christmas lights, lights Layla herself had put up quite precariously, back when she wasn't afraid of anything, least of all falling off a ladder.

The plants? Those were relatively new.

Even though Pearl usually had at least three roommates at any given time, there were always additional friends and stragglers hanging about. There was a giant pine table in the middle of the living space that always held a variety of snacks (Layla jokingly referred to it as craft services) and usually some booze as well, since one of Pearl's friends designed merchandise for a local whiskey distillery. All were welcome, any time of day; that was something that Pearl and Layla had vowed when they'd first moved in. It was a motto that remained true to this day.

The building was a walk-up with virtually no security, but Layla texted Pearl to tell her she was popping by. The door was already ajar when she arrived. Even though it was around midnight, the space was alive. There was an ironic/sincere game of Uno going on in one corner, a couple fully making out on the sectional, and someone sitting on the kitchen counter tuning a banjo.

Layla stood in the doorway. This was either the best or the worst place she could be.

"Pookieeeee," Pearl said, throwing her arms around Layla.

She stage-whispered, "Devin is playing Uno over there. Isn't he cute? I want to kiss his forehead and face. I think I will once Uno ends."

"Wow," Layla said, squeezing her back, trying to banish the memory of the hug she'd shared with Matt from her mind. "You are riding that THC wave, aren't you?"

"The edibles that D-Chow brought are giving me a gratitude attitude," Pearl confirmed. "But I feel like you are not feeling as conducive to peace and joy as I am right now."

High-as-a-kite Pearl was making Layla feel marginally better. She took Pearl's outstretched hand. Pearl swung their clasped hands back and forth a little before leading Layla to the sectional and sitting them both down, Pearl's back to the couple.

"They're getting to know each other," Pearl whispered.

"And how," Layla replied. Now that she was here, she didn't know what she was expecting. She wanted to be distracted, but she wasn't sure that was possible. She blinked back tears.

"Hey. Pookie." Pearl sat up on her knees and took Layla's face between her hands. "You seem discombobulated. Tell me how I can help combobulate you."

Layla managed a small smile, though the quiver in her chin gave her away.

"Ohhhh nooooo," Pearl said, stringing the syllables out. "That's the I'm-sad-about-Ian face. I know that face well. I hung out with that face for two whole weeks—or at least, I tried to, but the face kept hanging out with the cat instead."

"I'm a mess," Layla said, tears spilling over and down her cheeks.

"You're a beautiful mess," Pearl corrected her, and Layla gave a self-deprecating laugh.

From the kitchen, the guy with the banjo started to play a song. It took Layla several choruses to recognize the eighties hit "Take On Me."

"Did you and Ian break up again?" Pearl said gently, starting to braid Layla's hair. It was odd but also, Layla thought, kind of nice.

"No, I just...I'm afraid..." Layla couldn't even begin to explain the Matt of it all. Finally she said, "I've screwed everything up again. I'm incapable of making good life decisions; I'm just walking idiotic chaos and destruction."

"Oh, pookie." Pearl pulled on the tiny braid she'd achieved, yanking Layla forward into her arms. "You are not a destructive idiot."

"But I am chaotic?" Layla asked pathetically, remembering the day she'd moved out of the loft to run away with Randall. Pearl had hugged her tightly and whispered, "Are you sure?" so quietly that Randall couldn't hear her and Layla could feasibly pretend she hadn't either. More than anything, she wished she could take back that silence, wished she had told her best friend, *No, I'm not sure, I'm never sure.*

"We-ell," Pearl singsonged as she helped Layla right herself on the couch. She laughed and gestured around the loft. The Uno game in the corner erupted in wails and cheers. "What's wrong with chaos? I love a little chaos. Chaos makes life interesting. It makes us change and grow and play Uno on the floor. Chaos is life. You are life, my pookie-doo friend with the fake boyfriend and the real heart."

Layla laughed through her tears and tried to imagine Ian here, sitting beside her. She pictured him rigid and uncomfortable. Then she thought back to him at Sunday dinner. To the way he'd arm-wrestled her niece and defended her to her siblings.

She summoned every bit of courage she had to think about Matt, but there, her mind shut down.

"Sometimes," Pearl said quietly, "I think you're extra-hard on yourself. You are the rigatoni trying to fit into the elbow-macaroni hole."

"I think you're mixing your metaphors, but I appreciate the sentiment." Layla reached out and squeezed Pearl's hand. And then she admitted, "I'm just so sick of being myself."

"What if you're actually sick of *not* being yourself?" Pearl squeezed Layla's hand back.

Layla paused and looked at her best friend. *Really* looked at her. Yes, Pearl was very high. And, yes, she also lived in an appalling open-concept space at the age of twenty-eight with a baker's dozen roommates. But Pearl was at peace with her life. She cared about her friends and family; she paid her bills on time. She fell in and out of love without resorting to drinking too much or lying to medical professionals.

Pearl had her shit together. Why didn't Layla?

"I think I forgot who I am," Layla said finally. The notion was as terrifying as it was freeing.

"I know who you are," Pearl assured her. "You are a delicious pasta and a smart cookie. Do you want to sleep in my room? I promise this will all look better in the morning."

Layla took Pearl's advice and walked up the rickety staircase to where Pearl's quasi-bedroom was cordoned off with bedsheets. She *wanted* things to be better in the morning. But Layla wasn't sure she knew how to look at the situation with new eyes, and she wasn't sure that if she did, she'd like any part of what she saw.

As she lay there, she thought of how she'd felt when Matt hugged her back.

CHAPTER TWENTY-SEVEN

IF LAYLA HAD gone to sleep then, who knows what the morning might have looked like. But she hadn't. She'd laid in Pearl's bed listening to the Uno game, to the banjo player, questioning all her choices until her life didn't feel like hers anymore. So she'd rolled back out of Pearl's bed, clomped back down the rickety staircase, made her way to the kitchen area, and sung along with the banjo player's eighties covers until her voice was hoarse and she was so tired she was on the brink of delirium. There might have been some whiskey involved too.

Then she went back upstairs. Now, twisted in Pearl's bed, with Pearl snoring and half flung over her, her clothes sticking to her thanks to several hours of perspiration, Layla was semi-hungover and yet, surprisingly, less despondent. Because Pearl was right—she *was* tired of not being herself. And if she wasn't ready to be honest with Ian just yet, at the very least, it was time to be inwardly honest about a few things.

Okay, so she'd had teeny-tiny feelings for Matt, but guess what—she'd just unloaded her trauma on him and he'd responded with compassion, so of course, in a moment of vulnerability, she'd hugged him too long. And connected with him on a deeper level. And then freaked out about it and run. But if Layla didn't make it a big deal, it didn't need to be a big deal.

And, yes, she needed to work things out with Ian, but she also had to get through opening night of *The Diary Project*. It was unrealistic to try to deal with both things at once, so Ian could wait.

There. She was shutting off the lights and calling the cops. This pity party was officially over.

Charlene, saint of a woman that she was, had given Layla the day off since she'd been working two jobs and it was opening night of *The Diary Project*. If Charlene was aware of the ways in which Layla had been dropping the ball in her office duties, she kindly hadn't let on.

So instead of thinking about work, Layla took full advantage of her day off. Before heading back to her neighborhood, she bought pastries from Pearl's favorite local bakery as a thank-you and left them on the loft's craft-services table with a note. She went home, cleaned her apartment from top to bottom, and did the laundry that had been piling up. She even sent a peppy text to the Rockford Peaches to invite them to opening night and graciously responded to their quick replies that they were all— somehow—busy. Orcas Island was inconvenient for a pack of parents; she got it.

She washed Deano's water bowl and even opened a can of his favorite treats. He'd been initially pissy with Layla for leaving him alone so much, but he warmed up and spent the duration of a *Sabrina* rewatch—the Audrey version, of course—purring on Layla's chest.

Finally, it was time to catch her ferry.

She put on her lucky dress, a mini mod cut paired with leggings to keep her warm and booties that allowed for walking in the woods. She even put on fake eyelashes. Regardless of what happened in the future, she couldn't wait to see a real audience react. It was like hundreds of lightning bugs were buzzing around inside her.

In order to get to the ferry on time, Layla picked Ian up from work. He kissed her hello and they pulled into traffic, getting comfortable while they inched along. Layla tried to feel normal, to act normal, as they chatted about their days, but Ian seemed agitated. She clung to her newfound calm, assuring herself he had just had a tough day at the office. Until he asked, "Did you tell Matt about us moving in together?"

Well, *that* was unexpected. Though she wasn't sure what she had been expecting. (Maybe *Did you give my brother a long hug and then run away last night?*) She answered him honestly. "No. Of course not."

He blew out a breath. "I didn't think so. I just..."

"Hey." She reached out a hand and squeezed his shoulder. "What's going on?"

"Last night he was particularly weird. Maybe it was because he ended things with Jojo? But it felt like something more."

"He ended things with Margot Ro—Jojo?" Layla's stomach flipped. So much for feeling normal. She nearly pulled over so she could dry-heave on the shoulder of the road.

"I don't know what else to try with him." Ian looked out the window, apparently too distracted to dwell on his hot neighbor.

Layla took a deep breath. "You know, it's opening night tonight. I bet he's just nervous."

Ian seemed to think for a moment. "You're probably right."

Traffic started moving and Layla navigated her way to the ferry terminal.

"It's just...I was calling him more often even before the accident," Ian said, almost to himself.

Layla bristled. The last time they'd discussed this topic, Ian had told Layla that he didn't talk to Matt; he got live-streamed texts from Craig while Jeannie talked to Matt. But Matt had told Layla that Ian had called him when he and Layla broke up.

Was Ian remembering?

"I thought, when I asked him to live with me, that it would be like when we were kids. We'd have our stupid inside jokes, we'd hang out more. Instead..." His voice cracked. Out of the corner of her eye she saw Ian shake his head. Although she was internally freaking out, her heart ached for him. "It goes beyond the stuff with Dennis, because I've tried to talk to him about that and he fully shuts down. It's like even being in the same room with me makes him angry or something. I think he genuinely just doesn't like me. Not just as a brother, but as a person."

"I'm so sorry," she said, because that was all she could think to say. When she'd first met Matt, she thought he was impossible to read. He was still a closed book, but she was getting better at peeking at the pages; she knew now that his shutting down was often about battling his own demons.

Matt seemed to take things as they were, to accept the world as it came. When he closed himself off, it was because, like Layla, he worried that he was on the verge of taking a wrecking ball to something good. If he refused to talk to Ian about meeting their biological dad, it was probably because Matt was still embarrassed and angry. Because Ian didn't make mistakes. Layla knew firsthand how hard it was to be honest with him.

But in what world could she tell Ian she understood his brother better than he did? Not this one, that was for damn sure. Besides, she was still worried that making Matt complicit in her lie was fueling their tension.

"He won't talk to me, he won't spend time with me," Ian went on. "I don't know what I'm doing wrong or how to make it better."

Under different circumstances, Layla would've encouraged Ian to broach all this with Matt. To be honest. But if Ian was brutally honest with Matt, Matt might just see an opening to be brutally honest back.

Layla felt sick.

Maybe it didn't matter. Maybe Ian's memories were return-ing and it was all horrifically moot? Ready to crack from the pressure of keeping this charade up, she almost hoped that was true. But she knew she couldn't deal with all that. Not on opening night.

"Things aren't always easy with my siblings either," she ad-mitted, realizing it was the first time she'd told him that. "I feel like they judge me for making different choices than they would, that they're harder on me than they need to be. I worry that they're always laughing at me behind my back, talking about all the flaky, stupid choices I make."

When Ian didn't respond, she realized she might have gone too far. She tried to laugh at herself. "I mean, siblings, right? I probably sound so paranoid."

"No, I don't think that at all," he assured her. "I'm just surprised to hear you say that. You're one of the most responsi-ble people I know. Why would they think you're flaky?"

One of the most responsible people I know. The comment sliced through her.

"Who knows," she lied. Then, gathering herself, she added, "We're hardest on the people in our family because we have the fullest picture of them. But that doesn't mean we always *know* them. Give Matt time. Give yourself time. I hope you two get back to what you had."

"Thanks, Layla," he said softly. "You're so good for me."

The newfound optimism she'd woken up with that morning was careening away from her. Through the lump in her throat she replied, "You're good for me too."

*   *   *

Opening night was sold out. As Manjit had expected, a lot of locals showed up, but there were also plenty of Northwest's loyal patrons who'd made the trek, as well as some of the business owners and employees from Northwest's neighborhood. The most surprising development was that the daughter of the owner of the campground happened to have a huge following on Instagram. She was a #VanLife enthusiast who posted about her adventures on the West Coast, and she'd caught part of the dress rehearsal and raved about it online. At least half the people at the sold-out show were there because of her.

It was thrilling and petrifying all at once, unveiling *The Diary Project* to such an enthusiastic and large crowd. Every time she heard an eruption of laughter or saw people dab tears from their eyes during the performance, every time she saw a new conversation starting up at the bonfire, Layla's heart grew three sizes. Three *hundred* sizes.

But every time a scene ended and she returned to reality, she also had to return to the reality of what she was doing to Ian. In one moment of hysteria, she envisioned writing down *I lied to my ex-boyfriend after he forgot we broke up and now we're supposed to move in together* on a piece of paper for the actors to use in their improvised scenes.

Layla was going to get emotional whiplash from the evening.

She took dozens of photos between scenes. Every time she tried to post one on Instagram, she couldn't think of a caption, couldn't find it in herself to tell everyone she was having the most incredible night of her life because she wasn't. Ian's misery on the car ride over had given the undercurrent of her deception new strength. And it was getting harder and harder to ignore the fact that once opening night was over, she'd have one less excuse to keep pretending.

In the end, she forwarded the best shots to Pearl and asked her to post them to the theater's social media accounts.

As she moved from yurt to yurt with Ian on her arm, roller-coastering between the high of this successful night and the low of being a garbage person, she couldn't help keeping an eye out for Matt. Would things be awkward when she eventually bumped into him? Would he mention her odd behavior the night before? But when their paths finally crossed, between scenes two and three, the awkwardness was, surprisingly, between him and Ian.

"Congratulations, Matty," Ian began with a hearty slap on his brother's back.

Matt only nodded in response. Layla wanted to elbow him, prompt him to say *Thank you* as though he were a child.

"You and Layla have really made something special," Ian tried again.

"She's pretty incredible," Matt said. And then he clarified. "This show's incredible. She took a lot of work, but she was worth it."

Layla looked at Matt. And then at Ian. And then back at Matt. Had he actually just referred to the show as *she?* Like it was a boat? Or was he covering up a slip of the tongue? Electricity shot down her arms, her legs. That hug. *That damn hug.* Layla banished it from her thoughts, held on a little tighter to Ian's arm, and heaved a sigh of relief as they made their way to the next yurt to watch another scene where she could escape from reality a little longer.

By the end of the night, Layla found herself wiping away tears—which she turned quickly away from Ian to hide, not sure where she'd even begin if he asked her what she was feeling. But in the midst of all her regrets and worry and confusion, she was surprised to find some of the tears actually came from being *proud* of herself. Because, her shitshow of a life aside, Layla knew Matt was right. The show was incredible.

*   *   *

Jeannie and Craig had insisted they all stay the night, rather than
taking the ferry back to Seattle, so, following the performance,
they returned to the Barnetts' cozy home, changed into pajamas,
and gathered around a fire Jeannie had started in the fireplace
while Craig made some of his famous hot chocolate. Having
Jeannie around seemed to soften the Barnett brothers; they were
on their best behavior and playing nice for once. It helped that
Matt was practically beaming over the success of the show.

Perhaps *beaming* was a stretch. But he wasn't scowling and
that wasn't nothing.

Craig asked Matt questions about his writing process, told him
which parts he liked best, a conversation Matt quickly engaged
in. Those two were definitely making progress. Meanwhile, Ian,
talking to his mother, gushed about how Layla had managed
to work two full-time jobs; Layla just smiled and focused on
adding more miniature marshmallows to her hot chocolate. She
appreciated the praise but didn't feel like she deserved to be
talked up by anyone right now, least of all Ian.

"You know what's missing?" Jeannie asked during a lull in
the conversation. "A good charcuterie board. It's time to send
someone to the store. Craig, get the bushing coins."

After Jeannie and Layla won the first rounds, Jeannie declared,
"You all have to go. Get out of here, boys."

Craig gamely agreed and practically dragged Ian and Matt
out. Jeannie and Layla remained curled up by the fire. It
was Layla's first time alone with Jeannie for more than a few
moments. The one-on-one time felt orchestrated, something
that flattered Layla as much as it concerned her, but there were
no signs of tension in Jeannie's demeanor, no indication that she
knew how complicated Layla's relationship with *both* her sons
had become.

"I'm so glad you're here," Jeannie said.

"I'm glad I'm here too." Layla gave Jeannie a warm smile and tried to keep the worry from her eyes.

"You've been really good for Matt." Jeannie seemed to throw the comment away and took a sip from her mug.

"Hopefully I've been good for Ian too," Layla quipped, but Jeannie gave her a look she hadn't seen before. Layla willed her heart to beat a little quieter.

Jeannie put her mug down. "You know how special Matt is, but he often seems a little lost. Like he's heading somewhere but then gets in his own way."

"He's really talented," Layla offered, still having no idea where this conversation was going. "Working with him has been...I'm just really happy about how everything turned out. I've loved this whole experience."

Jeannie nodded, her gaze traveling to the dwindling fire, embers popping sporadically. "Did my boys ever tell you about their biological father?"

Well, this was a surprising direction. "A bit."

"I thought he was it for me. I threw myself into that relationship with everything I had, and I got lost in it. I thought if I could be my most selfless with him, I could make it work. Instead, I was miserable."

Layla's thoughts drifted to Randall. To the all-encompassing nature of their relationship. She knew Matt didn't talk much to Ian but she wondered if he confided in his mother. Did Jeannie know about Layla's past? Was that what this conversation was about? She waited to feel the paranoia of Matt holding on to yet another one of her secrets, but when she thought of the way he'd cried with her, how he'd held her, she didn't believe Matt had said anything.

"I'm sorry you went through that," Layla said truthfully—and still a bit cautiously.

"I'm not." Jeannie turned toward Layla and away from the fire, her face serene. "That relationship gave me my boys—you know how easy they are to love. They've made my life infinitely more interesting; they've brought me unparalleled joy."

Not knowing what to say, Layla finished her hot chocolate. Randall hadn't given Layla a child to love. He'd left her with nothing—less than nothing.

"Do you know what else my first marriage gave me?" The words were light, syllables dancing, and yet Jeannie's eyes pleaded with Layla to pay attention. To listen.

"What?" It came out as a whisper.

"It gave me the path to Craig."

The declaration stayed between them, the weight of it filling the room. Layla bit her lip and wondered: Would she be where she was if she *hadn't* married Randall?

She'd never wanted to think of it that way before, never wanted to be grateful for any part Randall had played in her life. But the truth was, Layla knew she wouldn't be sitting here if it weren't for him—and knew she wouldn't want to be anywhere else.

"Sometimes our mistakes are what lead us to the right path," Jeannie said before picking up their empty mugs and taking them to the kitchen.

Layla watched the fire dance with light and heat. She didn't need to feel grateful to Randall. But she could acknowledge that the choices she'd made hadn't irrevocably fucked up her life.

As it turned out, sweet little Jeannie had wisdom for days. But now Layla's heart was racing ahead, pulling her in a direction that scared the hell out of her.

CHAPTER TWENTY-EIGHT

NOW THAT *The Diary Project* was up and running, Layla found herself opening and reopening Twitter and Instagram several times a day, trying to gauge audience reactions to the show. But then she would freak herself out—what if she saw something really scathing?—and shut everything down.

So anytime she was tempted to check but afraid of hurting her own feelings, she sent Pearl a message, asking her to look and "be gentle" with her honesty.

As they pulled into the parking lot of the restaurant, Layla's phone dinged. "More texts from Pearl?" Ian asked. He was driving her hatchback so she could catch up on her work e-mails.

"The show's getting a lot of good attention and Pearl wants to keep me in the loop." Layla wrinkled her nose. "Sorry for being on my phone this whole drive."

"It's okay," Ian assured her. "This is a big deal."

"It's not the only big deal tonight." She silenced her phone and put it in her purse, still glowing from the latest review for *The Diary Project*. It was from a major Seattle news outlet and said the show was "outrageously funny and surprisingly cathartic."

In fact, Ian had used the success of *The Diary Project* to lure his parents to their own anniversary party under the guise of wanting to celebrate Matt and Layla's accomplishment.

The plan was for Ian and Layla to get to the restaurant first and make sure everything was in place. They'd meet the guests and tell them where to gather and what the schedule for the vow renewal was. Matt was responsible for bringing his parents to the restaurant at six thirty.

"It looks beautiful," she gushed when Ian opened the front door. There was a clear aisle leading up to an arbor adorned with vines and flowers, where the ceremony would happen. It was the type of arbor Jeannie and Craig might have said their vows under if they'd had a different wedding so many years ago. Along the aisle were round tables with crisp white linens and peony centerpieces. Romantic music was coming through the speakers; it was loud enough to be heard, but quiet enough to encourage conversation.

This was the best part of organizing an event—seeing all the small choices, all the big choices, woven together to create something special.

It had finally arrived. Her last uncomplicated night to enjoy her relationship with Ian. Okay, perhaps *uncomplicated* wasn't accurate. But this was definitely her last night of living in this we-never-broke-up version of their relationship and she was determined to enjoy herself. She could deal with the confession and fallout tomorrow, but tonight? Tonight she was going to *live*, countdown clocks be damned.

"Thank you for letting me plan this with you," Layla said, putting her arms around Ian's waist for a hug.

"Are you kidding? I couldn't have pulled this off without you," Ian said, squeezing back. But she knew he could've. Because he was *Ian*.

Through the big bay windows overlooking the parking lot and marina, they saw several cars pull in. Ian winked at her. He looked so handsome in his dark blue suit. "You tell educators there's a party, and they show up."

"For the free food," Layla agreed.

"More likely the open bar," Ian corrected.

"Well, I'm game for both. Let's eat too much, get tipsy, and slow-dance tonight," Layla said.

He kissed her forehead. "Deal."

A crowd of educators and administrative staff from the school burst through the doors, already laughing and exchanging stories. Ian and Layla were greeting them when another group entered. In the sea of unfamiliar faces, Layla spotted two very familiar ones.

"You invited my parents?" Layla squealed, feeling the thoughtfulness Ian put into the gesture, the excitement of seeing people she loved in an unexpected place.

Which was followed by the thud of remembering the last several conversations she'd had with her mother. Very suddenly the evening became about slapping on a smile and pretending everything was fine.

But Ian was still beaming, so proud of himself for surprising her *and* his parents, all on the same night.

"I thought it was time for our parents to meet." Ian looked at her, searching her eyes. "Who knows. There might be another celebration in the future for us to plan."

Was he . . .

Was this . . .

A reference to another wedding? *Their* wedding?

Layla didn't have time to contemplate the idea because she was suddenly whisked into her parents' arms.

"Thank you so much for inviting us, Ian," Rena said, releasing Layla and giving him a hug. Layla avoided her mother's eyes. If she pretended she hadn't called and yelled at her mother, her mother would have to pretend the same. Besides, she couldn't think about her and Sameer right now. She needed to focus on the Barnetts.

"We can't wait to meet the happy couple," Bill added. The poor sweet man thought he was part of a happy couple too. Layla wanted to shake her mother, to scold and reprimand her, make her take back whatever she'd done.

"When did you invite them? How?" Layla asked Ian, changing the subject.

"I had Matt get their number from your phone, then distract you with the photo albums while I went in my room to call them."

"Sneaky." The thought of Matt swiping her phone and getting their number didn't feel like an invasion of privacy, for some reason.

Once all the guests arrived, Ian and Layla had them line up on both sides of the aisle leading to the arbor and instructed them to start humming "Here Comes the Bride" as soon as Jeannie and Craig were spotted. Layla was the lookout.

"We're sorry we weren't there for opening night last weekend," her mother said, coming to stand beside her at the window. "It was the same night as Bobby's fundraiser and we'd already—"

"It's okay. I know you have a lot of claims on your time."

"I think Rhiannon's going to try to make it this weekend. And Rachelle and Jude too." Rena smiled, though it didn't reach her eyes.

"I'll reach out and ask them if they need comp tickets," Layla promised.

It was thoughtful of her mother to mention the show. Still, Layla hated that this moment was so complicated. For most of her life, she and Rena had been able to communicate so easily. As a child, Layla would park herself in front of her mother, hold up a brush, hairspray, and a hundred bobby pins, and ask her to try out elaborate hairstyles because she knew that while she sat, her mother brushing and pinning, they would talk. About everything. From school gossip to dream vacations to ranking their favorite songs. But as Layla aged and her choices got bolder, as her relationship with her mom turned into a Gordian knot, their conversations rose to surface-level small talk. Layla longed for the days before Sameer, before Randall, before the tangles of adulthood, when this conversation would have been simply a conversation, not a suitcase full of subtext.

"Anyway, since we missed opening night, we went to the performance the next night," Rena said casually.

As angry as she was at her mother, Layla was also caught off guard. She turned toward her, away from the window. "You *did?*"

"Of course we did." Rena looked almost wounded. "We are so proud of you. It was a spectacular show. Your dad cried during one of the scenes."

Layla pressed her hands to her chest, thinking of her tender-hearted dad.

"You really created something so special," Rena continued. Layla could feel her mother trying to connect with her, but she couldn't set aside how angry Rena's false cheer was making her. *I'm supposed to be enjoying tonight like it's my last meal,* she wanted to tell her mother. *Stop complicating it.* She was searching for a more appropriate reply when Rena suddenly pointed to the parking lot. "Isn't that them? Matt *is* a handsome fellow, isn't he?"

Through the window, Layla saw Craig laughing at something Matt was saying and Jeannie swatting Matt on the shoulder. Matt shrugged and gestured to the restaurant. Apart from the night they'd gone to Swing Queens, Layla had never seen him dressed up. He wore a fitted black suit with a white shirt and a simple, skinny tie. He looked like someone in a gangster movie. Or a band that took itself too seriously.

Or at least, that was what Layla tried to tell herself. Because, truthfully, he looked devastatingly handsome.

Layla turned her thoughts away from Matt and herself away from her mother to yell, "They're here!"

The crowd immediately hushed and took their places. Layla smiled, thinking this was a little like directing a play. As the guests began humming "Here Comes the Bride," Ian, across the aisle, caught her eye. Layla could feel her mom, beside her, take in the moment too. Rena reached for Layla's hand, but Layla pretended to spot a piece of lint on her dress and moved her hand away to pick it off.

Across the aisle, Ian smiled as though to say, *This could be our future*. She returned his smile, because tomorrow didn't exist tonight.

She couldn't help herself; she imagined having a real wedding, a real marriage. One that made her feel safe, one that wiped clean every stain from her relationship with Randall. She pictured herself with Ian growing older, maybe having children...

And then gorgeous chaos erupted like fireworks as Jeannie and Craig entered, the surprise dawning on them slowly, beautifully. They burst into tears and laughter as they were drowned in hugs and wishes of congratulations and love, surrounded by the people that had become their community over the course of their lives together. The people that had become like family.

At the end of the aisle was the local Lutheran minister, an irreverent and yet deeply spiritual woman named Pastor Katie who quieted the room with a clearing of her throat.

"Are we..." Jeannie gasped, clutching Craig and wiping tears from her eyes.

"Katie, are you marrying us again?" Craig asked, his apple cheeks as red as Layla had ever seen them.

"If that's okay with you two," Pastor Katie said with a wink. Jeannie and Craig nodded vigorously while the guests erupted into spontaneous applause.

As the ceremony unfolded, Layla found herself fighting tears.

She was happy for them, but there was another feeling swirling inside her too quickly for her to catch and name.

"You may now seal this union with a kiss," Pastor Katie said in closing. Jeannie grabbed Craig by the lapels and laid one on him. The guests went wild. Layla turned to catch Ian's eye and caught Matt's instead. His mouth parted as though he wanted to say something, even though she wouldn't have been able to hear him over the din. Unable to take whatever was in his gaze, she looked away. All around her, the event morphed into a casual but upbeat reception.

But she couldn't avoid Matt all night. Not at his parents' party. If she wanted tonight to go smoothly, she needed to make sure he was on board for that.

"Are we all set up for the slideshow?" Layla asked, sucking it up and finally sidling up to him. Matt was watching the party unfold from the corner of the room. He nodded, not meeting her eye.

Stubbornly, she sat down in the chair next to him. If this night was awkward, it was his own damn fault. "This turned out perfectly. You guys did a great job."

"Pretty sure this was all Ian," Matt said crisply, still refusing to look at her.

Summoning her courage, she ventured, "Are you okay?"

He turned a steely gaze on her. "No, Layla. I'm not *okay*."

The response hadn't been loud, but the intensity shook her all the same. "Oh."

"Are *you*?" he asked her, still cold.

"Am I okay?" She looked around nervously, afraid he wasn't committing to giving her this last night of freedom, afraid he might cause a scene. She had to keep things light. "Yeah. I'm great. The party turned out really well and it's nice that my parents are—"

But she didn't get to finish her sentence because this time, Matt abandoned *her*.

CHAPTER TWENTY-NINE

LAYLA SHOT OUT of her chair like a rocket. *No.* Matt hadn't stolen the past few weeks of her life, the past few weeks of her *happiness,* just to abandon her like that. He wasn't going to get away this easily.

Because why did he get to be the one who ran away? The deal was that she got to make it *through* this night, damn it. And here he was, pouting, killing the party buzz, trying to bring tomorrow's problems into tonight.

She zeroed in on Matt's location and saw him heading for the door leading to the patio. She crept around the edge of the room and was right behind him.

"Why won't you talk to me?" The words burst from her just as she burst through the door. Despite the beaming heat lamps, she was shivering.

"I'm pretty sure you don't want to hear what I have to say."

She crossed her arms and stared him down. The pose radiated confidence. She felt none. "Try me."

Matt's own cool confidence cracked, and he raked his fingers through his beard. "I cannot believe you're still acting in this Lucille Ball–level charade."

"I'm not...I'm not *acting*," she stammered.

"Bull*shit*. You're standing in front of the conveyor belt shoving chocolates into your mouth and down your dress, and the fact that I know that's what you're doing makes me your Ethel Mertz."

"I didn't ask you to be my Ethel!" She didn't know at what point during his speech she'd moved toward him, but they were inches from each other.

"Yeah. I'm well aware of that." His tone, the wild look in his eyes, the way he kept pushing his hair back even though it wasn't falling in his face all announced *There's subtext here*, but Layla didn't want to see it or hear it.

Or feel it.

"You," she said, stabbing him in the chest with her finger, "told me my deadline was after the anniversary party. And here we are *at* the anniversary party, and you're yelling at me for not telling him yet? That wasn't what we discussed!"

"Yeah, well..." His face was so close to hers, she could've nipped his nose. "Things changed, didn't they?"

The hug. He had to be referencing the hug. And the incriminating way she ran from him afterward. The blood drained from her face. She wanted to turn around and run again. She hated herself so much in that moment, she thought she might asphyxiate from self-loathing.

Matt didn't move a muscle. Neither did Layla. They were close. *Too close.* But she couldn't seem to move. And then he did, and she felt him take the breath out of her as he pushed off from the pull of her and walked away. Layla staggered back a step, felt the wall behind her.

Suddenly he turned back. "When did you and Ian decide you were going to move in together?"

Oh. "Um...the night we went to Swing Queens, I guess?" With Matt farther away, it was easier to remember what her endgame was. *Who* her endgame was. And it was Ian. It was always Ian. She wasn't going to screw that up. It was still possible she could make this work if Matt didn't rush her.

"I know I have to tell him, Matt. I know. But look, things have been so different, I think there's a chance he's going to understand. I think he's going to see this was for the good of all of us, you know?" She was babbling, but she couldn't stop. Spoken out loud, her plan sounded unhinged; it had made so much more sense when Ian smiled at her. When he looked at her the way he had from across the aisle.

Matt's hands were in his pockets, a pose she now knew well. It was his nonchalant, too-cool-for-real-feelings pose. The one that didn't let anyone get too close, didn't let too much of him out. He could lazily banter with *Common People* fans if his hands were in his pockets. He could keep his brother's girlfriend at bay and call her a liar.

That's what she was. *A liar.* A fresh wave of self-loathing rose up as she swallowed down a sob. She couldn't pretend it was all okay. Not with Matt. Not with everything he knew about her.

"I'm sorry," she said at last. She hadn't intended to apologize, but now that it was out, she didn't regret it. She *was* sorry.

"What are you sorry for?" Matt's hands were out of his pockets and balled up so tightly, she could see his knuckles turning white. His face might have been a mask of indifference, but there was nothing indifferent about the rest of him.

"I'm sorry I've made you so upset," she said.

"Can you not see how completely batshit this is, Layla?" The mask of his face broke. His facade was crumbling. "How do you think this is all going to work?"

"How *what* is going to work?" she shot back.

"Being with him when the actual foundation of your relationship is a lie?"

"It's not," she insisted, to Matt, to herself. "What we have is real. And I almost told him already. A few times."

"You *almost* told him *a few times*. Wow. What a hero."

"Stop being so condescending! Listen, I'm telling him to-morrow," she said. And then she quietly added, "Even you have to admit there's a chance he's going to understand. What we have is *real*."

There was a pause as a huge burst of laughter from the party carried all the way to the patio. Layla had forgotten there was a celebration happening and that at this very moment, she should be on her best behavior, clinging to Ian's arm. Smiling. Joking. Charming the friends and family of the guy she intended to spend the rest of her life with.

"If what you have is so real," Matt said evenly, "why are you out here with me? Why doesn't Ian already know the truth?"

Behind her, a familiar voice asked, "The truth about what?" and the world around Layla shattered—a mallet taken to a mirror.

She turned to see Ian on the patio, propping the door open with his hand, looking confused.

CHAPTER THIRTY

HOW COULD SHE be so stupid? Again and again, Layla acted without thinking. Followed her impulses, which were clearly himbos. Tonight she'd followed them away from the party where she was meant to be and onto the patio, and for what? To beg for attention from Matt? Someone who was hell-bent on undermining her?

She wanted to take the I HEART DIRTY BOYS WITH NO MONEY shirt her siblings had given her all those years ago and set fire to it.

Because all she really needed was standing before her in his blue suit. A guy who threw parties for people he loved, who helped Layla be her best self. The one who could stop her from sliding into old patterns and breaking her parents' hearts again. The one who could stop her *own* heart from breaking.

This wasn't how this was supposed to happen. She was going to tell him—she *was*—but not now and not by fucking accident.

"What am I missing?" Ian asked, agitated. "What's going on out here?"

"There was a problem with the slideshow," Layla blurted out, her improv skills finally showing up when she needed them to.

Matt kicked a nearby chair. "For fuck's sake, Layla."

Misinterpreting Matt's reaction, Ian went to Layla, put his hands on her arms, and rubbed them up and down soothingly. "Hey, no problem. If there's an issue with the slideshow, I can help you fix it."

I don't know if you can fix this, but I really want you to, she thought.

"I can stall until you sort it out," Ian continued. "I know how much effort you and Matty put into it, so do what you need to do. I'm sure it'll be worth the wait."

"Thanks," Layla said meekly, unwilling to meet Ian's eye. Or Matt's.

Satisfied, Ian turned to go back into the party.

"You coward," Matt said to Layla.

Layla flinched, her eyes still on Ian. Matt's accusation was spoken so quietly, it took Ian a moment to register it. "What did you say to her?" Ian was not a yeller—his anger came from deep in his belly, taking his voice down a full octave.

"Ian, wait—" she tried, but neither Barnett brother was listening to her.

Undeterred, Matt stuck his hands back in his pockets. "I said she's a *coward*."

"That's pretty rich, considering the source." Ian didn't go to Matt directly, but he began to circle him, worryingly like a coyote stalking its prey, Layla thought. Oh Lord, they were going to fight at Jeannie's second attempt at a perfect wedding and ruin everything.

"What have I ever done that was so cowardly?" Matt said. "Was it when I didn't just fall in line and follow you to college? Was it when I went after Dennis to find out the truth?"

"What does that have to do with anything?" Ian rubbed at his face, bewildered. When he removed his hands, his eyes were rimmed red.

"I don't know, but I swear it's your subtext every time you talk to me," Matt shot back.

"Subtext?" Ian shook his head. "Don't throw your theater jargon at me, I'm not in the mood. I'm here trying to do something for our parents, for our family, and once again you're sandbagging me. Once again, I'm stuck being the golden boy who has to make up for the brother who keeps devastating Mom—not to mention the stepfather you've never appreciated. I keep waiting for you to learn from your mistakes, and yet here we are. The same place we've been since you were in high school."

"You know nothing about me and *nothing* about my relationship with Craig." Matt's chin wavered so subtly, Layla was sure Ian had missed it, because he didn't let up.

"I know that it killed him when you went chasing after Dennis."

"Well, that wasn't exactly a teddy-bear picnic for me either, so..." Matt's chin trembled one more time. He looked up at the sky, arranging his face in a scowl.

Layla thought she might cry. She wanted to hug him, but the last time she'd done that had been an unmitigated disaster—and she needed to protect Ian.

"Ian, now's not the time," she said, trying to stop the snowball already careening down the hill. "Why don't we go back in and—"

"Layla's right," Ian said to his brother. "Let's talk about this later, put a pin in it or whatever. Tonight's supposed to be about Mom and Craig."

Hands still in his pockets, Matt pursed his lips until they went white. He relaxed them and said, "Don't you want to know *why* I called Layla a coward?"

A gust of wind blew through the patio and Layla shivered again. Ian's posture changed. He was clearly no longer interested in putting a pin in anything.

"Coming from you? I'm assuming it's some bullshit reason." Ian actually cracked his knuckles. Ian *never* cracked his knuckles.

Her stomach dropped. Oh no. Were these two really going to fight? Neither one of them were fighters. The first time Layla had laid eyes on Ian, he was breaking *up* a fight, for crying out loud. And Matt wasn't some macho toxic alpha. He was stubborn as all get-out, but he had a gooey center. Of that she was certain.

"What is your problem with me, man?" Matt asked. It wasn't an attack, even though the phrase was often used as such. It was a sincere question. Matt's hands were out of his pockets now; he was no longer able to project James Dean. Layla could see him as the younger sibling—frustrated. Misunderstood. It was a role she knew well. "When are you ever going to trust me?"

"Trust you?" Ian scratched the back of his head, seemingly in the midst of some internal fight with himself. "Do you want to bring up what you said to me when I gave you rent money after the *Common People* fiasco? After I let the Dennis thing go—"

Matt scoffed. "*Fiasco?* Okay, Grandpa. It wasn't a *fiasco*, it was...a convoluted situation. And come on, you've obviously never let the Dennis thing go."

"I bailed you out and you said, 'Thanks, now lose my number.'"

Matt gritted his teeth. "I only said that because you told me I didn't deserve all these second chances you and Mom and Craig were giving me. Why did you even ask me to leave California and come here if you can't stand having me around?"

"I *can* stand you," Ian shot back. "I just want you to grow up and, I don't know, *evolve.*"

"And I keep waiting for you to accept me as a person instead of treating me like some fucking obligation."

Their mom's Spidey senses must have been tingling, because

Jeannie popped her head outside. Matt and Ian immediately shut up.

"This party is just so lovely, boys," Jeannie gushed. "And Layla, of course. Ian told me how much you helped. Thank you for putting this together."

With the door ajar, the music from the DJ Layla had hired swelled toward the patio. Layla, Ian, and Matt plastered on convincing smiles. But Jeannie wasn't just a parent, she was a former teacher, and she frowned. "Everything okay out here?"

"Just getting the last surprise ready," Layla chirped as if she weren't on the verge of tears. She heard Matt let out a dis-believing puff of breath.

Jeannie told them she looked forward to it and went in, closing the door behind her. Silence ensued.

"Now is not the time for us to rehash all this, Matty," Ian said quietly.

"I agree, *buddy*, we've got more important things to discuss."

Layla's body went so cold, she thought she might perish then and there.

"Are you going to tell him why I called you a coward?" Matt looked at Layla. "I'm tired of being the villain in Ian's story, so are *you* going to tell him the truth or what?"

All at once, cold was replaced with fiery hot and her eyes flashed with anger. They'd had a *deal*, and he was drop-kicking the deal into the ocean just because he couldn't communicate with his own fucking brother. Through gritted teeth she asked, "While the party's still going?"

Ian stepped forward, his face growing pale. "Tell me the truth about what?"

"The slideshow's fine," Layla admitted. But that was all she was admitting to. Because she was so close—*so painfully close* to getting what she wanted. She squeezed her eyes closed and could see the look Ian had given her while the guests were humming "Here Comes the Bride."

"Layla..."

Ian sounded as though he were ready to come to her, to hold her, and her eyes flew open just as Matt blurted out, "I can't take this anymore!" He put his hands in his hair as if he were trying to keep his head on. "You broke up with her, Ian! Why? I don't know—because you're an idiot, I guess. But you two definitely broke up, and then you had the accident, which somehow made you forget that you were an idiot. So Layla swooped in, took advantage of your little lapse in memory, and has been acting like you two are together even though you aren't! You haven't been for months now!"

Layla swayed, dizzy, unable to comprehend what Matt had just done. How everything she'd been holding on to so tightly was slipping through her fists like water. Wind chapped her cheeks and blew her dress against her legs. *Ian knows. After all this time, after everything, he just... knows.*

Her eyes were fixed on her feet. She needed to sit down and put her head between her knees before she passed out, but she also couldn't move. The world shifted in and out of focus as the seconds following Matt's confession stretched and compacted until time didn't seem real anymore.

Even though they were outside, even though the air was the pure, expansive stuff you could only breathe near the ocean, all the oxygen had been sucked from that patio. Out of the corner of her eye, she saw Ian's head drop. He put his hands on his hips. Then he rubbed at his face. Then he put his hands back on his hips and raised his chin slowly, so slowly. *"I know."*

Layla could barely speak. "You *know?*"

He rubbed his eyes, threw his head back, and inhaled a great big breath. She watched his lungs fill. She watched them deflate.

"Of course I know, Layla. I had a concussion, not a lobotomy."

"But…" Her mind was already flying through every inter-action, every conversation they'd had since she'd picked him up at the hospital. "When? When did you know? Were you faking the whole time?"

Ian took her hands in his and sat down on a patio chair. His fingers felt strange to her, rubbery. Maybe this was a dream? But his movements encouraged her to sit in a chair opposite him, and that felt solid enough.

"No, I wasn't faking the whole time. I really was confused at the hospital. I was definitely in shock. When they called you and you came to pick me up, I was so relieved to see you, so glad not to be alone anymore. Something seemed off, but I chalked it up to the concussion. It wasn't until we got back to my condo—"

"To the parking spot," Layla said, the realization dawning.

"Yeah," Ian admitted. "Then. But it felt so good to be around you, I asked you to come up anyway. You fit back into my life perfectly—I fit back into yours too. The breakup was a mistake, Layla. And suddenly that mistake didn't seem to matter any-more. It was erased. We got to start over without starting over at all. How could I fight that? I know you felt that too."

"I did," she said, her face cold from the wind, her mind a mess.

"I was so much happier with you. I didn't say anything be-cause I didn't want to risk complicating things, risk losing what we had a second time," Ian finally said. Overwhelmed, Layla felt her eyes fill with tears. He squeezed her hands, and she felt every cell of his skin on her own.

Matt kicked a chair, startling them both.

"Congratulations," he spat, breaking the spell between her and Ian. "You two deserve each other."

He walked directly between them, forcing their hands to let go, and went back into the party. Through the window, Layla saw him retrieving the laptop needed for the slideshow.

"We should probably go in too," she said after a long silence, feeling numb, not knowing what else to do.

She rose from the chair as Ian reached again for her hand. She slipped her fingers between his and watched the way they weaved together. All this time she'd been afraid of what would happen if the truth came out. All this time she'd been torturing herself for indulging in this second chance. But it turned out they were more alike than she'd thought.

"Layla." A million emotions fought a battle on Ian's face. "You look so sad. Are you angry with me for lying?"

Her head shook back and forth, slowly, the sides of her mouth rising as she fell into the arms of the only good man she could see forever with. "How can I be angry when I've been lying too?"

They held each other for seconds, hours, a lifetime, then went back to the party together. They began chatting with guests as if nothing had happened. They stayed side by side as they went through the motions of the evening. Layla gave a convincing performance, if she did say so herself. But she couldn't say that her heart was in it. Because her eyes kept searching the crowd for Matt. All she saw was the troubled gaze of her own mother looking at her. And Jeannie with a very similar expression on her face.

She tried to process what had just happened. *It was a sign.* It had to be. Further proof she was on the path she was meant to take. It was true—she and Ian were meant to be.

So why did she still feel like she was letting everyone down?

CHAPTER THIRTY-ONE

THE REST OF the evening passed through Layla like mist. At the end of the night, she hugged and shook hands, returned many iterations of "It was so nice to meet you too," smiled and blushed through a few sly variations on "This could be you and Ian in a few years." But none of it felt real. None of it felt substantial.

The only thing that felt real was her need to get away. To take all these heavy, jumbled thoughts and feelings and process them somewhere quiet. Somewhere she could be alone.

"Maybe you should get a ride back with Matt?" she asked Ian, grateful they had taken her car to the island for once. "You can't leave things between you two that way. You need to try to fix this."

He nodded, because what she was saying was absolutely true. What he didn't know was that she was also saying it because, selfishly, she needed space.

"You aren't staying tonight?" The plan had been to go back to Jeannie and Craig's house again.

"I'm exhausted," she replied truthfully. "And I've been abandoning Deano too often lately. I'll call you in the morning."

Before he could try to talk her out of leaving, she stood on her tiptoes, kissed his cheek, and left. She didn't even remember to say goodbye to her own parents. She vaguely remembered glancing at her phone and seeing a text from Pearl, something about how every performance of *The Diary Project* had officially sold out and that members of some Seattle theater-award panel had requested tickets for closing night. It was something else to celebrate, but she couldn't think clearly enough to do it.

By driving far too quickly, Layla made it just in time to squeak onto the ferry. She got out of the car and went up to the deck, even though it was too cold to be out there and the wind felt as though it were slapping her cheeks. Her hair blew around her face, twisted into knots. Her heart squeezed, twisted into knots. Despite Layla being free from her lie, her self-loathing was back with a vengeance.

Leaning against the railing, staring out at the sea and the sky, both so dark you couldn't tell where one ended and the other began, Layla attempted to unravel everything tangled inside of her.

Ian had known all along. She should be thrilled; she should've danced on the tables at his parents' anniversary party. Instead, she wondered why, if he had known all along, he hadn't mentioned it. Why hadn't he called her on it? And why had she let herself lie for so long? Why couldn't they just be honest with each other?

And she still didn't understand why he'd broken up with her in the first place, so how could she be sure they weren't just following a new path to the same heartbreak?

If they weren't being real with each other, how real was their relationship? It was like they were each playing a role so they could get to the happily-ever-after part.

But this didn't feel very happy.

She squeezed her eyes shut as tears leaked out and streamed down her cheeks, only to be immediately swept away and dried by the persistent wind.

If she was being honest with herself, brutally honest, yes, she loved being with Ian. But it had taken effort. All along, she'd thought being with Ian was bringing out the best in her when in fact, it was like Pearl had said: she was tired of *not* being herself.

But in those sparkly moments, the times over the past several weeks she'd stopped making an effort and just let herself *be*...there'd been peace in that.

Before she could stop her next thought, she admitted that she didn't have to try to be perfect or completely together, that she could let herself just *be*, when she was with Matt.

The admission made her knees buckle and she leaned on the railing for support, her dress blowing wildly in the night.

When she argued with him, it wasn't like arguing with Randall; he wasn't self-righteous, he wasn't putting her down, making her feel less than. When Matt pushed her buttons, it was because he was encouraging her to open up and be real with him. Every time he challenged her, she woke up, stopped trying to be perfect, and started being the truest, most creative and alive version of herself. She knew damn well she did the same thing for him.

You are not alone in this world, Layla. But that means you have to do better. For all of us. The words her mother had said on the ride home from LA came back to her.

I am alone. And I don't know how to do better, she silently responded.

She rested her face on her arms and sank into despair. If she couldn't get her shit together by now, when she was quickly approaching her twenty-ninth birthday, it would never happen. She could pretend to want what, deep down, wasn't right for her—something that required her to put on an act—or she could allow herself to want what she shouldn't.

But she didn't want to keep hurting the people she loved.

"Layla?"

The wind carried her name, and she knew the voice that had spoken it. Layla turned around and ran into her mother's open arms.

CHAPTER THIRTY-TWO

"WHAT ARE YOU doing here?" she sobbed into her mother's shoulder, definitely ruining what appeared to be a new dress. Even the way Layla broke down was destructive.

"I knew something was wrong at the party." Her mother stroked her hair soothingly and let her cry. "When I saw you leaving alone, I told your dad we had to go after you."

Layla raised her head. "Dad's here?"

"He's reading in the car." Rena gave her a sad smile and put her arm around her. "I'd rather have you to myself for a bit anyway. But let's go inside, it's freezing out here."

The ferry was quiet, and they were able to find seats that offered some privacy. Layla began the arduous and painful task of detangling her hair with her fingers.

"You want to tell me what's going on?" Rena ventured.

Layla stopped finger-combing her hair, her eyes filling with tears again. "I mean, it's nothing new. I'm a screw-up. I self-sabotage. I make the wrong choices." *I think you know a thing or two about that*, Layla wanted to add, wondering unkindly if all her worst tendencies came from this woman. The woman who'd raised her on black-and-white movies where people sang about the beautiful pain of love and spent most of the story missing each other.

"Is this about Ian?" Rena asked, brushing the hair out of Layla's eyes just as she'd done when Layla was little.

"I don't think Ian's the one," Layla whispered, not knowing that was what was going to come out. As soon as she said it, the truth of her own words burned her from the inside. "I know you want him to be—I want him to be—but I can't see how we can make things work. He's kind and he's smart and he's *good*, but..."

"That doesn't mean you're good together," Rena finished.

Layla nodded. "I'm sorry to disappoint you," she said, waiting for her mother to sigh or get sad.

"Honey, I'm the one who owes you an apology."

It wasn't the reaction Layla was expecting and she looked up, eyes still filled with tears. "Why?"

"Because *I've* been screwing up." Rena leaned back and took a deep breath. Her eyes were filled with tears too.

Layla held her breath, waiting for her mother to tell her about her affair with Sameer.

Instead, she said: "You were such a precocious child and then you were a bit of a reckless teen."

Layla thought back to the many times her mother had cupped Layla's face in her hands and said, *What am I going to do with you?*

"Your impulsivity continued and, yes, you made some decisions that had consequences."

"Which you bailed me out from," Layla said.

"No." And then Rena *did* cup Layla's face in her hands. The familiar gesture both soothed her and ushered in a deep melancholy, because after nearly three decades on this earth, Layla still needed this.

"Yes, you did, Mom. You and Dad. If you hadn't let me move back so I could pay the lawyers and pay down my debt—"

"*Layla*," Rena interrupted. "You are *allowed* to make mistakes. For crying out loud, how else are you supposed to figure out what the hell you want out of life? I'm apologizing to you because once you moved back home, you deliberately curbed that impulsive, reckless *Layla* side of you. Your light dimmed. You became quieter, and up until this play, you stopped doing anything creative. I'm sorry we gave you the impression that this was how you were supposed to be. All we ever wanted was for you to be *you*."

"Ian was so good for me," Layla insisted. "He gave me a reason to get my life together. He *fixed* me."

"Oh, Layla," Rena said, her eyes searching Layla's. "You were never broken."

"Even if I'm not broken, I *am* an idiot," Layla said miserably. She contemplated telling her mom about her lie and about Ian's forgotten-not-forgotten memory of the breakup and how complicated everything was, but she was too exhausted and the ferry ride not nearly long enough.

"We're all idiots," Rena said softly. "Thankfully, we're lovable idiots. And I love you the way you are. So does your dad. And your four siblings, if you'd text them back once in a while."

"Do you know how many texts they send?" Layla deadpanned with a sniffle. "They're worse than teenagers."

Rena chuckled, and then they sat there, Rena rubbing Layla's back, while the conversation and what it all meant gathered and came to rest. Layla had been sure she was making her parents happier by settling down. It had never occurred to her that they saw her unhappiness. That they missed the daughter who felt before she thought.

"I know I'm the mom," Rena added, "but you've always inspired me."

"What do you mean?"

"Up until recently, you've always been so unabashedly *you*.

Like you didn't care what the rest of the world thought as long as you were chasing your own bliss, your own dreams." Rena shrugged, a shy smile crawling across her face. "You remember that picture you and your brothers and sisters found? Of Heaven Under the El?"

Layla nodded. "Your band, yeah."

"Well..." Rena looked embarrassed. "Do you remember when you ran into me at that music store?"

Layla's heart thudded as she nodded again.

"The guy who owns that store, the one I was talking to, that's Sameer. The old drummer."

"The douche-canoe?" She tried to reconcile the image in the photo with the man she'd seen her mother with.

Rena grinned. "The very same."

"You really are like Fleetwood Mac," Layla mumbled.

"What are you talking about?" To her credit, Rena sounded genuinely confused.

"I know you've been sneaking around with him," Layla said. "That's why I yelled at you on the phone the other night."

"Ah. So *that's* what that phone call was about." Rena nodded, understanding appearing on her face. "I figured you were drunk-dialing me again."

"What—I don't drunk-dial you," Layla insisted, unsure if this was true.

"Anyway, I wasn't *sneaking around*," Rena said.

"You were acting strange when I saw you with him," Layla said. "And then Pearl saw you with him near the theater, and when I called, you lied about where you were."

"Because I was embarrassed that I was trying to get my band back together. At my age," Rena said a bit too loudly. A handful of passengers looked their way and she covered her face with her hands as Layla burst out laughing.

"Now who's the idiot?" Rena said into her hands.

"What? No, Mom, I'm not laughing about your band," Layla insisted, taking her mom's hands down so she could look at her. "I think that's *amazing*. I'm laughing because I'm relieved. I thought you were—that you and Sameer—"

She couldn't say the words, now that she saw how wrong her conclusions had been. Realization dawned on Rena's face. "Are you kidding? Honey, no. *No.* In fact, Sameer came over for dinner this week with his husband, who happens to be Damon, our bassist."

"The douche-canoes got *married?*" This was too good.

"Now that they're both on board, we just have to convince Juliette."

Layla threw her arms around her mother, relief coursing through her. "You are the single coolest person I know."

"Back at ya," Rena said into Layla's hair. They hugged for a moment, then Rena released her and continued. "At first, I contacted Sameer just for old times' sake. It'd been so long since we'd caught up and that photograph made me so sad. So nostalgic. It was like the missing piece in my life was suddenly ready to be put back in. I casually mentioned a little Heaven Under the El reunion, but Sameer wouldn't have it. When the band broke up, there'd been all these petty arguments, things he didn't want to relive. I was going to let it go, but then I thought, *If my daughter can put on a play, I can definitely get this band back together.*" A pause. "You and I aren't so different, you know."

Layla smiled at her brave, kooky mother. "I'll take that compliment."

The ferry sounded its horn. They were nearing Seattle. As the city harbor came into view, Layla felt her fears beginning to close in on her again. Rena must've noticed the change because she said, "As for Ian, he is a very nice young man. We love him. But I think I was trying as hard as you were to see you two together long term. I thought he made you happy, but it's always been clear you two were never quite on the same page."

"I have something terrible to confess about all that," Layla said, wondering if she should fling herself overboard rather than admit the truth.

"Let's hear it."

"I think I like his brother," Layla mumbled, throwing her head back onto her arms in shame and embarrassment.

Rena laughed.

"It's not funny," Layla insisted. But her mother's laugh was infectious, and soon she found herself laughing too.

"It's a little funny." Rena nudged Layla with her elbow. "And I can see why you'd like him."

"You can?" Now that she'd said it out loud, Layla was desperate to talk about it.

"Absolutely. He's interesting. A real still-waters-run-deep kind of guy. But you can also see..." Rena seemed to consider her words carefully. "He has a really good heart. It was evident in the care he took in writing that play, and it was evident tonight in the way he interacted with his parents, with their friends...even with you."

Layla scoffed. "What are you talking about? He and I spent half the night arguing out on the patio."

"Yeah, I peeked out the window and caught that. So did Jeannie," Rena said with a smirk. "But did you see the way he looked at you when you argued? He was clearly fighting for something."

For me? Layla thought back to the hug, to the way his arms had held her, the way he'd cried with her. She thought back to the way they bickered until they finished each other's sentences. To the way he accepted her exactly as she came and how she wanted to do the same for him.

If she added up all the tiny details of their interactions, right back to their first encounter when he'd pushed her because he was trying so hard to learn who she really was...she saw a glimmer of hope. Hadn't Jeannie told her that mistakes can still lead to good places?

Huh.

What she wanted—what she *needed*—wasn't what she'd been chasing this whole time, and yet it was still where she'd ended up. Sure it'd taken a pep talk from Pearl, insight from Jeannie, and honesty from her mom, but the universe seemed to understand Layla needed a few signs and a few messengers to really get it. Nice of the universe to understand she was a remedial student.

She squinted out the window at the stars, at the big bright moon, and felt tiny. Minuscule. But not like she didn't matter.

CHAPTER THIRTY-THREE

THERE WERE THE nerves that descended when you were debating doing something risky. They buzzed and ricocheted; they clouded your thoughts and made you question even the most trivial of choices. And then there were the nerves that came on the precipice of a big life change, one that was as exciting as it was scary. When you decided it was worth betting on yourself and seeing how far you might go. Most people referred to the feeling as butterflies, but in this moment, Layla was sure the creatures she was feeling were more substantial than that. She was pretty sure she had eagles.

For a while now, she'd been focusing on the chances she'd taken that ended badly. She'd forgotten that the best things in her life had also come when she'd done something risky.

And today was all about risks.

Manjit and Charlene were waiting for her in Manjit's office. She knocked on the open door with one hand, her other hand holding her lunch.

"Come in," Charlene said encouragingly. She was sitting on the couch opposite Manjit's desk. There was a chair designated for Layla and she took it. "You must be so excited about all the buzz this show has gotten."

"I know we are," Manjit said with a smile.

"Absolutely," Layla agreed.

"I filled Charlene in on what we discussed about next season." Manjit stopped to take a bite of her wrap, holding up a finger to indicate she'd continue in a minute. Once she swallowed, she said, "Have you been able to give it any thought?"

This was it. The moment when Layla could turn back. But those eagles in her stomach didn't want her to. And neither did she.

"I have." Layla put her lunch on Manjit's desk. She was so nervous her hands were shaking and she didn't want to send shredded chicken and black beans flying out of her leftover enchiladas. "I am deeply grateful that you took this chance on me. And Matt, really."

"He's so talented," Manjit gushed.

"We've even discussed offering him a playwright-in-residence position once he has a few more shows under his belt," Charlene added.

"Oh, wow. I bet he'd love that." Talking about Matt felt like conjuring up his ghost. Layla wished he were really there now. That she could see him and speak to him. That he could witness what she was about to say. She had a feeling he'd be as proud of her as she was of herself.

For the hundredth time she thought about reaching out, even just a pathetic little *Hi, how are you?* But there were a few things she wanted to take care of first.

"We've been discussing next year's season, if you want a sneak peek?" Manjit opened her desk drawer and fished out some scripts. "Here you—"

"Actually," Layla said, interrupting her. "I really appreciate your offer, but I don't think I'll be able to take you up on it."

Manjit and Charlene exchanged a look.

"I think it's time for me to move on. I've absolutely loved working here. It's been such a pleasure and I've learned a lot from both of you. I just…"

"You want to see what else is out there," Manjit said, and it wasn't a question.

"I do," Layla agreed. She shifted in her seat. "I'm considering asking Matt if he wants to tour *The Diary Project.*"

It was the first time she'd said it out loud and she found herself holding her breath while waiting for a response. She didn't have to wait long, because Manjit yelled, *"Yes!"* and Charlene yelled, *"Do it!"*

Layla felt like laughing—with relief, with surprise.

"This show is begging for a tour," Charlene said.

"Will you take the ensemble with you?" Manjit asked.

"I was thinking of assembling a collective in each stop." Ever since the ferry ride with her mom, Layla had stayed up late working out the details.

"I love that idea. That'll mean it's a brand-new script, a new show every time. Totally in tune with whatever city you're in. Amazing," Manjit said. Charlene nodded in agreement.

There was a lump in Layla's throat when she said, "I can't thank you enough for hiring me two years ago."

"Well, you've got our full support in this next stage." Charlene stood up, opening her arms for a hug. "The theater's a small world. Our paths will cross again."

Manjit came around her desk and Layla joined them. For the past two years, she'd been trying to balance being true to herself with making safe choices. Now she was going all in on big swings.

And she still had one more to take.

*   *   *

She texted Ian to ask if she could bring him lunch at work. He immediately agreed and suggested they go up to the roof. It was partly cloudy, but the sun was high and warm. The roof was decorated with brightly colored patio furniture and plants. They sat near a glass railing where they had a view of downtown. The lunch crowd gathered and clumped before crossing streets, everyone in a rush, everyone headed to clear destinations. Layla tore her gaze away from the street and back to Ian, who was already eating the sandwich she'd brought him. Since she'd eaten with her bosses, she told him she was there to keep him company. And talk.

"How are things with you and Matt?" she asked.

He put down the sandwich. "I don't know. We...we hashed some things out after the party. He admitted he's been pushing me and Craig away, I admitted I've been trying to turn him into something he's not. We both have work to do."

"That couldn't have been easy. I'm proud of you. Both of you. And I really think you'll get there," Layla said lightly, hoping it was true for all their sakes. Regardless of what she was about to do, she cared about them. All of them. "You're talking through it and that's probably the hardest part."

"Yeah. It feels like we're finally on the same page." Ian smiled sheepishly. "I guess we just had to really yell at each other before we could move on. You know, get it all out."

Layla nodded, truly glad but also a little sad. She'd let herself get in their way for so long.

But she wasn't here to feel regretful.

"Everything okay?" Ian asked. He was guarded with her, his body pulled away from hers, his eyes searching. It was a fair reaction. They'd barely spoken since his parents' anniversary party.

The sounds of traffic filled the silence between them. "I was married," Layla said. "Briefly. Before I met you." The words whooshed out of her like a gust of wind pushing through an open door. It wasn't what she'd planned to say; she hadn't intended to tell him at all, not now, not when it didn't matter anymore. But it was time for her to stop being ashamed. Layla had owed Ian honesty from the very beginning of their relationship. She was finally going to pay up.

"*Married?* I…why didn't you tell me?" There wasn't any judgment in his response, only surprise and curiosity.

"I was afraid of what you'd think, afraid it would change how you felt about me," she said. And then: "But I want to tell you now."

So she told him about falling in love with Randall, about pulling away from everything she knew and loved and coming back feeling shattered. And then she told him about building herself back up and how it led to meeting him.

"You are such an important person in my life, Ian. I will forever be grateful for the way you loved me."

"I still do," he said. There was a wistfulness in his voice, and he rubbed at his eyes. His strong, broad shoulders fell. "I'm an ass and I lied to you."

She gave him a crooked smile. Bless Ian for being *Ian*. For trying to take responsibility even now. But he didn't need to do that for her anymore. "In fairness, I lied to you first."

"No. You didn't." He pulled his palms away from his eyes, which were now red. "When I broke up with you, it wasn't just because we couldn't seem to make time for each other."

Now it was Layla's turn to be surprised. "It wasn't?"

"There was a woman at work, in a department near mine. We started flirting in the hallway, innocent stuff. Then we'd bump into each other at the cafeteria. God, it was like high school, only instead of classes and peers, we'd talk about work and clients—and a bit about our backgrounds. One night, we were both here late and ended up in the elevator. Alone."

Layla's stomach dropped. Even though she'd come here to end things, she hadn't been expecting this.

"We kissed. Just once—and I felt so guilty that instead of telling you, I broke up with you."

What am I doing? Suddenly the words she'd heard him say after he ended things carried a different tune. She shut her eyes and tried to replay every beat of their relationship.

But too much had happened. And it didn't matter. Not all of it, anyway.

Some of it sure did. Like...

"Did you start seeing this person? Should she have picked you up from the hospital instead of me?" Layla asked.

Ian shook his head. "We went on two dates. She wasn't...I don't know. She made me miss you. You're so fun and different and weird in the best way possible. When you and I were in the car outside my condo the day of the accident, and I remembered we'd broken up...it felt so good to be with you again, I let myself have a do-over with you."

The Layla of a few weeks ago would've been mortified, inconsolable. The Layla of today was able to hold the betrayal she felt alongside an understanding that Ian wasn't the perfect person she'd always thought.

"Wow, are we a couple of fuckups," Layla said wryly.

He smiled sadly. "I'm so sorry, Layla. It was a shitty thing to do, and I spent so much time kicking myself for doing it. That's why I was thinking of you that day, when I got in the accident. I was trying to figure out how to make things right between us. And then...fate stepped in."

"Fate is a hit-and-run driver?" Layla asked, but not unkindly.

He let out one short laugh. "I don't know. I really thought this was going to work between us, but it just..."

"Well," Layla said, saving him from having to say out loud what they both knew—that if they had to lie to make their relationship work, it wasn't much of a relationship. She adjusted her hands in her lap, feeling fidgety and calm all at once. "I'm sorry too. I was never fully honest with you. I kept wanting you to fix me, but it turns out I was never really broken."

The silence between them was heavy.

"It's over, isn't it," he eventually said.

She nodded. They caught each other's eyes, both glassy with tears.

"Well, you can't say we didn't try," he said softly.

"More than once." She smiled at him.

"I don't regret it." He took her hand and squeezed it. "You will forever be one of my favorite people. We just aren't meant to be together like this."

"I know people say this all the time, but I actually mean it: I want you in my life, Ian. I adore you and I want to be friends." It was the one cliché she owed him because it was the truth.

"I'd like that too." He sighed and smiled, the corners of his eyes crinkling, though he still looked sad. "I have a feeling we could wind up in each other's lives anyway."

"What do you mean?" Layla's heart sped up.

"With everything that happened between us, didn't you find it strange how upset Matty was?"

"I…" This was too weird. She wasn't ready to tell her new ex that she had feelings for his brother.

Even though he'd just admitted he'd cheated on her.

"It's none of my business," Ian said, releasing her hand. "I mean, it's sort of my business. Just…give me some time? But I do care about you both and I want you to be happy."

Unable to speak, she just nodded. And then: "Even if it's awkward as hell?"

He laughed. "It's going to be awkward as hell."

CHAPTER THIRTY-FOUR

LAYLA HADN'T BEEN to *The Diary Project* since opening night. It seemed fitting for her to attend the encore performance to see how it had evolved. Even though she was trying not to let regrets weigh her down any longer, she knew that if she got a second chance with this show, she was going to properly enjoy it.

Thankfully, between social media posts and word of mouth, it was back by startlingly popular demand. Manjit and Charlene had suggested the encore performance when they'd processed the buzz, hoping to gain a whole host of new Northwest End patrons. The owner of the campground, who'd seen bookings for the yurts skyrocket, was more than happy to offer the setting for free.

Meanwhile, in the two weeks following her second—and final—breakup with Ian, Layla had gone through and read the reviews properly. As it turned out, there was a way to avoid assholes on the internet and focus on connecting with fans who had really lovely things to say. She and Pearl had spent hours at the loft talking about its potential for awards, about its future. She'd pulled her favorite quotes from reviews and social media and sent them along to Matt, who never responded. Just in case he was ever curious about her, she peppered her personal accounts with little updates about her day that she thought he might appreciate; photos of Silly Putty in her hands, a video of Deano batting a series of bobby pins off her desk one by one, and a couple of selfies where she looked almost as hot as Jojo if she did say so herself. She was surprised how easy it was to share her life when she wasn't trying to stage everything from the start.

When she couldn't resist looking at his accounts, she found herself scrolling through his photos from the show. She saw one picture she didn't even realize he'd taken. It was from the night of the dress rehearsal, before she'd hugged him. The camera was fixed on one scene, but there she was at the edge, her head turned back toward Matt, her eyes full of delight, of excitement. Of love.

Shit.

She really was in love with him.

Desperate, she scrolled through the rest of his photos, stopping on one of his face. He was petting a black Lab, presumably one of the dogs he'd trained in California. She was flooded with a longing to see him, surprised by its ferocity. She missed arguing with him; she missed the way he challenged her, the way he accepted her. She missed pushing his buttons and she missed how alive she felt when he pushed hers.

She missed the fireworks she could admit she'd felt in his arms. There was no guarantee he'd come to the island for closing night, but her heart told her to have hope. He'd want to see this through.

All the elements were the same, but tonight's performance had a different energy. She could feel the buzz the show had generated coming from the audience. She watched the crowd scope out the sets and discuss which one they wanted to watch first. She heard people chat about how they'd come to see it multiple times already and that they couldn't wait to see how tonight's performance would be different. Manjit stood at the fire and called for everyone's attention. The audience obediently gathered around.

"I've been the artistic director of Northwest End Theater for twelve years. We're known for taking chances. Some pay off, some…not so much." The audience laughed. "Tonight, I am pleased to present an encore performance of *The Diary Project*. A show that was conceived under difficult circumstances but one that has flourished and grown—even over its run. Every show has the capacity to change and evolve, depending on who's watching it—it's one of the things I love about live theater. But that is particularly true of this show. And Northwest End is grateful for and inspired by the ways our audiences have affected, have *embraced*, this experimental slice of honesty. Before I let you settle in to enjoy what I've found to be a powerful theater experience, I would like to say some words of thanks."

She listed the board members, the main crew members, Charlene. When she got to Layla she said, "Layla Rockford has been with us for about two years and over that time, we've learned she's capable of pretty much anything. She is a force to be reckoned with and we cannot wait to see what she does next."

What I do next. She blew Manjit and Charlene kisses as the audience applauded.

"Finally," Manjit said as the audience quieted down, "we would like to thank this year's emerging playwright, Matthew Barnett. Some of you may recognize him from the television show *Common People*, a credit of which he should be very proud. But I also know he has so much more in him. We're grateful for his time and talent, his stubbornness, and his willingness to compromise—though it took some time to develop that bit."

The audience laughed again. Layla scanned the crowd, looking for signs of Matt. Her hands were shaking, her heart in her throat. When she finally found him, hands in his pockets, nearly cloaked in the forest itself, her whole body—her whole being—stilled. *Him*, her heart hummed. *It's him.*

Layla didn't hear the rest of Manjit's speech, only watched as Matt waved good-naturedly to the crowd. She refused to take her eyes off him for fear of losing him again. When the show began, quietly, stealthily, she floated from crowd to crowd, trying to make her way closer to Matt. He managed to stay away from her, deliberately or not, during the whole show.

And then something unexpected happened. Once the show was over and the company received an extended ovation, Manjit got up again. "Please feel free to stay for the after-party. We've got s'mores, we've got hot chocolate, and we've got some surprise entertainment. May I present Seattle's own...Heaven Under the El."

Layla's head whipped around. Her mother, Juliette on lead guitar, Sameer on a bongo, and Damon on another guitar started playing a lovely version of "In My Life" by the Beatles. Layla had heard her mom sing thousands of times, but she'd never heard her quite like this. And then she caught sight of her dad singing along, enraptured by his wife. She wanted to say hello but decided it was best to wait.

As she listened to the familiar song performed in a whole new way, she wondered who'd planned all this.

And then a small movement caught her eye, and she turned her head just in time to see Matt disappear into the trees.

She moved to catch him but lost him in the shadows. Frustrated, she whirled around, only to find him right behind her.

"What are you doing?" she demanded.

"Finding a private place to talk to you," Matt said, eyebrow cocked. "Jeez."

As quickly as it flared, her anger dissipated. It was time to offer him the only thing he'd ever seemed to want from her: pure, unfiltered honesty.

"Good. This seems like a great place to tell you I've missed you, you ass. Why haven't you responded to any of my texts? It's been *weeks*." This was definitely not the speech she'd planned, but it worked. Matt immediately softened, a small chuckle escaping his lips. Her eyes snagged on those lips. Now she could finally appreciate the fullness of the bottom one, imagine what it might be like to catch it between her teeth.

"Even in this dim lighting, I can see how you're looking at me," he warned.

"I broke up with Ian," she blurted out, wanting him to know she wasn't engaging in any more shenanigans. That she was here to be genuine.

"A while ago," Matt confirmed. "We *do* live together, Layla. He told me."

"*So?*" she demanded.

"So?" he replied innocently. He was such a smart-ass. She wanted to toss him into the nearest body of water. She wanted to kiss him so badly, her lips ached.

"So do you have any thoughts on that?" she lobbed back just as innocently.

"I do, actually." He paused and she held her breath, desperate to hear what he might say. "I'm relieved. You two were a terrible match. I'm thinking of setting him up with the neighbor. I believe you once referred to her as a sexy praying mantis?"

Excitement rippled through Layla, crackling like lightning. And then everything inside her went still as his eyes softened and he said, "I've missed you."

She might have nodded, she might have whimpered ever so slightly and embarrassingly. Still, she managed to get out the words "I've missed you too."

The energy between them changed and it took everything in her not to leap into his arms right there and then. But they had some things to discuss first.

"I have some thoughts on you and me," she said, raising her eyebrows, inviting him to play.

"Oh?"

Suddenly nervous again, she pretended to examine her nails, even though it was too dark to properly see them. "I want you to take *The Diary Project* on tour. With me. I've worked out all the details."

"You have, huh?" Matt's hands were fully in his pockets, and he was giving away nothing. Well, to the average person he was giving away nothing. But Layla could read him by now. There was the faintest quirk in the side of his beautiful mouth. The tiniest of twinkles in his brown eyes. If she watched his chest closely, the rise and fall was quick. And he'd already admitted that he missed her.

He was into this idea. He was into *her*.

Emboldened, she continued. "I have some suggestions for cities we could stop in, but I'm open to your opinion. I figure, before we leave, we put out posts on various actor and crew websites, and in each location, we find a cool venue. You can write the show, I can direct it—we'll produce it together. If we get tired of touring, we can come back here. I know Manjit and Charlene will give us work."

"You seem to have our future all mapped out." *Our future*. A single future. One they'd share. The thought made her want to leap into his arms. It made her want to stand still here, in this forest, forever.

Even though he'd been the one to say it, even though there was the tiniest of wavers in Matt's voice, she wasn't one hundred percent confident of his feelings. Not yet. She needed a sign—from him, not from the hard-to-read universe.

"But what about Deano? Something tells me he's not one for a life on the road," Matt said.

"Deano and my dad have a weird bond. Deano will happily live with him when we're touring and with us when we're not."

Matt nodded, his Adam's apple bouncing ever so slightly. She waited for him to react to the part where she'd made them roommates, but he seemed to just accept it. *Well, well.* She resisted the urge to do an embarrassing victory dance.

But it was time to take the biggest risk of all.

"I'm in love with you, you know," she said. "I figure this time I'm going to start things out with radical honesty. So. Here goes. You're one of the smartest people I've ever met—one of the most interesting. You drive me completely bonkers, but I think that's a good thing. I love to argue with you. I'm going to love it even more if we get to the point where making up afterward includes making out."

Matt choked, apparently on nothing. Layla bit back a smile and went on.

"You're incredibly sexy. We should talk about that. Explore it a little or"—she shrugged—"a lot. Whatever you're comfortable with."

Matt's mouth opened and nothing came out. He shut it. Her words were making him bashful, a side she hadn't seen before, and it was giving her *life*.

"We could have the best, most exciting life together. And when it's boring, it actually won't be boring because it's you and me. It's us."

There it was. Her heart on a platter for Matt to take or throw away.

She started to say, *What do you think*, but she got out only the "What d—" part before Matt's fingers were in her hair, his mouth so close to hers she could feel the warmth of his breath on her lips.

"Can I ki—"

This time she finished his sentence in a much more satisfying way than she'd finished any sentence. Ever. She put her hands on his waist and pulled him as close as she could, and their lips crashed together like waves finally reaching the shore.

After a second, after a lifetime—Layla didn't know; time was meaningless—he pulled away.

"Nooooo…" she said in a tiny voice. He threw his head back with glee. It was the first time she'd ever heard Matt full-on belly-laugh.

"I'm sorry I'm not kissing you anymore," he said, looking at her in a way that made her whole body feel like it could spontaneously combust.

"Then stop *not* kissing me and get back to kissing me," she pleaded.

"We have some business to discuss first." He put a finger to her lips. She let out a blissful hum that made him grin. Skin-to-skin contact. It would mollify her. For now.

"First of all, I will absolutely get a say in what cities we go to," he began. She started to groan but he cut her off. "Second, I will also get a say in casting."

"The playwright never gets a say in casting."

"I think I've already proven that wrong." He leaned in and kissed the freckles across her nose. *Bribery!*

"What else do we have to cover before we can get back to kissing?" She pulled at his shirt playfully, rubbing her nose softly against his.

"I'm in love with you too," he whispered.

Wrapped in Matt, kissing him like he was her past, present, and future, all she could do was *feel.* Eventually, they grudgingly pulled apart, but he held on to her, and they stared at each other.

"Now that you've launched yourself at me," Matt teased, "any second thoughts?"

"About *you?*" Layla batted her eyelashes and pretended to think.

"About all of it." Matt took his hand off her waist and used a curved finger to caress her cheek so tenderly, she thought she might cry. "Are you ready to drive and talk and live and write and rehearse and argue and make up with me over and over again, all over the country?"

A feeling of peace, of contentment, settled over Layla as she looked at him. The first guy she'd ever let see the best and worst parts of her, and the one she loved with her whole heart. "I can't think of anything I want more."

His forehead touched hers. They were so close and not close enough.

"Me neither," he agreed. He kissed her again and again. "Now let's get out of here."

Layla took him by the hand, relishing the warmth of it, the way their fingers intertwined. They stayed that way, hands clasped, staring at each other, for a delicious moment. And then Matt's eyes glimmered, Layla grinned at him, and they ran.

ACKNOWLEDGMENTS

Though this book is most definitely a work of fiction, Layla and I do have a few things in common. We were both theater majors, for example, and there's some overlap when it comes to our taste in music. More important, we are both lucky enough to have found creative jobs that we love and to work with people who inspire us.

I am deeply grateful to my editor, Helen O'Hare. Our brainstorming sessions brought this book to life, and your feedback continues to make me a better writer. Thank you so much for your patience, for trusting me to get this story right.

Little, Brown has been such a dream publisher. Thank you to Bruce Nichols, Judy Clain, Terry Adams, Craig Young, Ashley Marudas, Katharine Myers, Liv Ryan, Mariah Dwyer, Jayne Yaffe Kemp, and the rest of the wonderful people on your teams. Many thanks to Tracy Roe, my thorough and delightful copyeditor, and to cover designer extraordinaire Kirin Diemont.

I remain a little bit in love with the team at Alloy Entertainment, specifically Viana Siniscalchi, Joelle Hobeika, and Josh Bank. I will be forever thankful to you for helping me find the right story for Layla, Ian, and Matt. Whenever you three are near, magic happens.

Jess Dallow, my agent and so much more, I am deeply grateful for you—for your endlessly helpful notes, for fielding my melt-downs disguised as check-in e-mails, and for your continued guidance.

The writing community is made up of some of my all-time favorite people and my life is richer because they are in it. Thank you, critique partners and friends, for making me laugh, for inspiring me with your talent. Much love to Jenny Howe, Sonia Hartl, Kelsey Rodkey, Andrea Contos, Auriane Desombre, Susan Lee, Rachel Lynn Solomon, Roselle Lim, Milo Mowery, JR Yates, Suzanne Park, Jen DeLuca, Elizabeth Davis, and Erin E. Adams.

I never intended to write about theater, but it's always been a substantial part of my life, and I am truly hashtag-blessed to have friends who've been like family to me at the Utah State Theater Department and in the Calgary and Edmonton theater communities. I wish I were doing ridiculous vocal warmups with you all right now (and please note I am spelling it *theatre* in my heart).

I'm very appreciative of the support I receive from family and friends, in particular my parents, Ray and Sally, whose enthusiasm and encouragement have made this roller-coaster journey even better. Thank you for passing along your love of reading to me; thank you for being so excited about my career that you've called bookstores across the country just to see if they carry my book (which was as endearing as it was embarrassing).

My kids are a source of endless joy. G and A, I super-duper love you. Thank you for cheering me on; thank you for being two of the coolest and sweetest humans I will ever know.

The reason I'm drawn to writing about romance is that I get to live my own love story. MLC, my hottt husband, we've gone from elementary-school acquaintances to partners for life. That's some kind of relationship glow-up. I love you now and always.

ABOUT THE AUTHOR

Annette Christie is the author of *The Rehearsals*. She has a BFA in theater and a history of very odd jobs. The back of her head is featured prominently in the film *Mean Girls*. She currently resides in Phoenix, Arizona, with her husband and two children.

ALSO BY ANNETTE CHRISTIE
THE REHEARSALS

"A sweet, delightful romance."   —Lisa Greissinger, *People*

"An enchanting and compelling look at life's what-ifs. Christie writes with honesty, heart, and a great deal of charm."
          — Helen Hoang, *USA Today* bestselling author of *The Kiss Quotient* and *The Bride Test*

"Irresistible...Annette Christie has written a fun, yet thought-provoking, rom-com."   —Elin Hilderbrand in *Marie Claire*

"Terrific fun from beginning to end!"   —Sarah Haywood, author of the *New York Times* bestseller and Reese Witherspoon X Hello Sunshine Book Club pick *The Cactus*

AVAILABLE IN PAPERBACK WHEREVER BOOKS ARE SOLD

Back Bay Books